# The Assassin

## An American Life

# The
# Assassin

## An American Life

### Robert Mayer

**Combustoica**
a prose imprint of About Comics
Camarillo, California

# Other books by Robert Mayer

### Fiction

*Superfolks*
*The Execution*
*Midge and Decker*
*The Grace of Shortstops*
*Sweet Salt*
*The Search*
*I, JFK*
*The Origin of Sorrow* *
*The Ferret's Tale* *
*Danse Macabre* *
*Confessions of a Rain God* *
*Eyes* *
*1741* *

### Non-Fiction

*The Dreams of Ada*
*Notes of a Baseball Dreamer*
   (First published as *Baseball*
   *and Men's Lives*)
*Monkey Brain: A Writing Life* *

* Available in print and e-book from Combustoica. Look for them where you got this book, or at www.Combustoica.com.

Paperback edition ISBN-13: 978-1-949996-11-1
Continuous printing starting September, 2019.

Published by About Comics, Camarillo, California.

Questions? Email *questions@aboutcomics.com*

# Part One

That day began like any ordinary day, Eliezer's mother handing him and Rachel lunch boxes with their names written on them in black ink, already packed with cheese sandwiches and a fresh apple each, the boy, who was 10 years old, leading his little sister, who was 8, out the front door and onto the dirt road and slightly uphill for a kilometer to the one-story wooden schoolhouse painted the color of rust.
That day ended for them like no other.

That day when they opened the front door, Rachel pushing her way in first to hug their mother around the waist, drink the milk that already would be waiting for them in canning jars on the blue kitchen table, they did not see Merele or the milk, the house was silent as a wind-free night. The children put empty lunch boxes on the table and looked at one another with raised eye-brows and empty shrugs. This had never happened before. Then banging started that day as if someone was hammering on wood, loud but also muted in a sickly, tortured way. The children cocked their heads to the right in perfect unison, like comic actors rehearsing for the stage. The hammering seemed to be coming from the bedroom their parents shared, a room they had been taught never to enter without knocking. They hurried toward it, eight steps for the boy, ten steps for the girl, and stopped. The thick wooden door was closed, which was unusual during the day. From inside the room they could hear knocking continuing, louder now. Painful.

Mama, may we come in? the girl asked. Papa, are you in there? the boy said. The banging continued, offered no response. The children were becoming frightened. We have to go in there, see what's happening, the boy said. I'm scared, his sister answered. I'll go in by myself, you stay here until I come get you, don't move you hear me. He saw tears forming in her eyes, kissed her cheek, pulled on the large wooden knob. The door was heavy. He leaned back, pulled harder, using both hands until the door slowly swung open. He stepped inside. The banging was louder still. No lamp was lit, the black shade on the window beside the lumpy double bed had been pulled all the way down, it was difficult for him to see.

Fearful, he stepped closer. It was Papa. Something odd was happening, something bad. Papa was raising his face off the pillow, slamming it back down, producing a clunking sound. The feather pillow would not make that sickening sound. What was on the bed?

The boy moved closer. The feather pillow was on the floor. Papa? No answer. Just the raised head and then the slamming down of the face and forehead and nose into the clunk. Like a strange new torture device being demonstrated at the provincial fair. Papa was not wearing his shirt. His eyes were closed, his face pressed into the pillow that was not a pillow. Papa? His head raised, slammed down again. Clunk. The boy knelt beside the bed to see what was making the noise as Papa slammed his face down. He recoiled, not understanding. Mama's heavy iron skillet was on the bed where the pillow should have been. Tears came. Why was Papa doing that, he was hurting himself. The boy grabbed the feather pillow from the floor. When Papa's head came up the boy tried to shove the pillow between Papa's face and the skillet. Papa saying nothing, his face and nose dripping blood, he shoved the pillow away and banged his face into the skillet again, as if he were under a spell. The boy grabbed one shoulder and with his other hand managed to twist the skillet off the bed. When Papa's face hit only the sheet and the mattress he stopped banging his head. He lay quietly, breathing heavily, hairs on his hairy back hanging with drops of sweat. Papa? Papa? Slowly the man turned his head, faced the boy, opened his eyes. His face running blood from a gash in his forehead, from his nose. Rachel, fearful of waiting alone outside the door came running in. When she was close enough to see in the dim light from around the shade Papa's bloody face, she screamed. She threw herself at her big brother. The boy held her close and let her cry.

Something was on the floor beside the bed. A crumpled piece of paper. He picked it up, there was writing on it but the room was too dark for him to read. He shoved it into his pocket. Papa lay still, saying nothing, oblivious to the blood dripping now into his ear. Outside the feather-pillow shop in the small Austrian village of Linz, just four kilometers from Wien, Papa was known as Jacob the Magician; on Sunday afternoons in the town square with his worn Bowler hat over his yarmulka he would make people laugh and ooh and aahh and laugh again at his jokes. He made them happy. Why would he do something terrible like this?

Mama would know. She always knew things. Mama when she came home would tell them what this was about. Outside the rear door in a narrow rectangular yard a pony called Feathers was munching the grass of spring. The boy lifted his sister onto the pony's back and led them together around the yard until her sniffling abated, stopped. He rubbed the pony's wet black nose. His sister did the same, and laughed as the creature sneezed and snorted. She petted his neck. Next morning at first light he lifted his short pants off the wooden trunk at the end of his bed to retrieve the crumpled paper he had shoved into his pocket the day before. It wasn't there.

Her name was Merele. This he remembers. He does not know how she died. There was no long illness that he recalls, no sipping tea with honey while huddled under thin gray blankets, wearing a torn pink nightgown that had not been changed for days, too courageous to whimper at the pain that was eating her stomach. In a dark room smelling of camphor and alcohol, a mustached doctor with dark hair combed straight back arriving each day carrying his black bag to examine her and do nothing. There was nothing like that he can remember. One day she was there, the next day she was gone. As in one of his father's magic tricks.

## A WEDDING

The boy cried for his mother for days. His sister never stopped, not really. She kept asking him where their mother was. Fairy tales, little Rachel loved fairy tales, so to calm her, to distract her, he made one up about their mother. He had heard, he said, that she had been hanging wash in the yard when two golden eagles came along. They grabbed her and flew away with her. Why did they do that? Rachel asked. Because they were going to teach her to fly. Did she want to go with them? No, she wanted to stay here with her children. But they flew off with her anyway. Why didn't she call the police? Rachel asked. Because the eagles were the police. Will she ever come back? the little girl wanted to know. The boy said he was not sure, but maybe. Maybe when she learned how to fly. The boy was astonished when the fairly tale he had made up helped himself to cope. Instead of an emptiness where his mother had been, an emptiness that made his stomach hurt, he could visualize her up in the clouds, testing her wings. The girl stopped crying, but every morning when she jumped out of bed she ran to the window and raised the shade and looked up to see if Mama was on her way home.

The boy wondered if he should tell the story to his grim father. He did not. Grown-ups did not believe in fairy tales.

The small temple was overcrowded with men in black yarmulkas and their finest clothing, which was not very fine. The boy's father Jacob whose beard was short stood in front of the altar in a repaired black suit, a small thread the tailor had missed dangling from his right sleeve. Beside him stood the boy and his sister in faded but freshly washed clothes. The girl pulled at the thread but instead of breaking off it cut her finger and became longer. Her fingers burned so she let it go. This was shabbas so you could not use scissors. The cantor began to sing in Yiddish in a voice that when he was young had not been hoarse, the bride walked slowly down the narrow aisle in a new white dress and new white shoes, which though she did not know it she would not wear again except while washing the kitchen floor in New York. It was not long after the boy's mother disappeared that his father was marrying Cecile. Jacob made and sold feather pillows and Cecile worked with him in the two-story wooden building they called the barn, where from screaming birds feathers were plucked each day with which Jacob stuffed the bedding. When the pretty bride with curling blond hair moved into their house, in addition to overseeing the children and doing the cooking and the cleaning and the laundry she inherited the plucking as well. She was 19 years old.

Standing in front of their small house a year after the marriage the family hugged, tears flowing from the children. Jacob Maisel had told them he was sailing to America, he had just enough money for one passage, he'd said; they must need feather pillows in America, too; as soon as he could earn enough money he would send for them.

## WELL UPHOLSTERED

Young Cecile Maisel was described by the men in the town as "well-upholstered." The boy understood what they meant. But now he remembers her mostly as she was soon after they came to America, where she was called *Bubbie* at his father's insistence, a Yiddish word for grandmother, to make clear to all that she was not their real mother. Their real mother was Merele who had disappeared and must never be mentioned. Cecile's blond hair had been gone then, her artificial baldness covered by a brown wig held in place by a hair net that matched the wrinkled dark stockings she wore, the broken house slippers that cried out to the boy, *I am still young;* the Cecile who had sprightly eyes and cherry-colored lips cherry-colored not with wax bought in a store but with the juice of fresh cherries. She who was well-upholstered seemed to have disappeared as suddenly as his first mother had, as soon as they reached America. Like magic.

Except for certain sweaty evenings later that he would relive with pleasure and with guilt.

## NEW YORK, ELLIS ISLAND, 1934

This is the style here, Jacob Maisel told the boy and his sister.
I won't dress like that when I get older, Rachel warned Mr. Maisel.
Wait, you'll see, Mr. Maisel replied, any married Jewish woman who does not dress like that will be a whore in the streets.
Very well then, I'll be a whore in the streets, Rachel said. The boy was happy to see spirited Rachel standing up to their father. She did not yet know of whores in the streets.

## THE ARRIVAL OF EXIT

How I got my name was on Ellis Island, a big arrival hall. Huge doors and windows, a vast central room with a vaulted ceiling. Thousands of men and women and girls and boys like Rachel and me lined up in maybe six different rows, most of us carrying battered suitcases or cardboard boxes tied with string, wearing two coats many of us, Rachel a ribbon in her hair and me a wool newsboy cap. Carrying papers we had been given in Austria, more papers from Holland where we boarded the ship, stamped with government stamps in vermillion, Mama Cecile herding us like a mother goose, everybody sweating, the place stinking like a butcher shop, babies crying, pressing our hips together because we needed bathrooms and there were long lines, people vomiting from delayed seasickness.

*I doubt my brain will be sliced like Dr. Einstein's into slide-sized slivers and deposited under microscopes,* he thinks. *Much against Albert's wishes. The Person of the Century, Time Magazine had named him. Imagine. And I had known the man, sort of, had broken bread with him.*

## WHITEBREAD

The last day on the ship, anchored in New York Harbor, the Statue of Liberty rising like a teasing queen out of the morning mist. I looked about for Rachel, she was leaning on the rail, trying to see the future, but a young man in a pea coat was getting in her way, trying to talk to her. I could tell she was not interested, wanted to be alone with her thoughts. Hey, Whitebread! I said as I moved toward them, leave her alone! Not sure why I called him Whitebread except that he had two layers of light-colored hair that was truly white. You talking to me? Mind your own business. This is my business, that's my sister. I'm just talking to her he said, placing his hand on the elbow of her burgundy coat, this is America, we have freedom of speech now. I'll show you America I said and moved closer. He dropped Rachel's elbow and jumped into a boxer's stance, one fist beside his face, the other in front of his belly. He looked as if he knew what he was doing. I didn't come to America to fight I said. No? He pulled his arm back as if to smash me. I didn't wait but shot my right arm straight at his chin. I was taller than he and my arms were longer and when he ducked I missed his chin but his nose crashed into my fist, a glare-blinded bird crashing into a window. He staggered toward the rail, blood pouring from his nose like Uncle Joshua's *vin rouge,* spilling over his clothes. Rachel grabbed my arm, why did you hit him? Because he was bothering you. I can take care of myself, Eliezer, you have to learn that. Every person on this boat has just escaped the Nazis, she said, you don't have to fight each other. That's true I said but even in America we'll have to show we're tough. Now let's get out of here and led her and Cecile below decks before Whitebread could stand and come after us. I don't know if he looked for us right away, there were thousands crowded on the second deck chattering excitedly that our long journey was almost over. He did not find me until three weeks later.

Rachel was at the head of her line with Mama Cecile and I was at the head of the next line when we were waved over. They seemed to go through quickly and be sent down a hall to the left where a doctor would have to sign a form that said they were healthy enough to enter the United States of America. Don't ask me what year that was — 1934, I think — but the scene is like a stereoptic in front of me — or inside of me — black and white slides with sepia overtones. All of us immigrants are sepia.

## WHATEVER YOU SAY

I go up to a man sitting behind a wooden desk and give him my papers. Maisel, he says. Yes, sir. You are 14 years old. Yes, sir. You are tall for your age, by the time you are 20 you might be 6 feet 4. Yes, sir.

(In fact I quit growing at 6-2, which was tall for a Jewish kid back then, way taller than Papa.)

Born in Wien, Austria?

Linz.

What is Linz? I never heard of Linz.

It's near Wien.

We'll put down. Wien, Vienna. Everyone knows Vienna. Now what is your first name, Eliezer? It seems wrong, here there are seven letters where you signed your name and ten letters where the Wien clerk wrote it. So which is it? Eliezerski? Never mind, this will be a problem all your life in America, registering in school, getting married, joining the Army. What you need is a simple American name, is that alright with you?

Whatever you say, Mr. Clerk.

The clerk looked around the crowded hall, trying from his squeaking seat to peer over the heads of the awed but noisy throng, stretching his neck one way then the other. Over there, you see that yellow door over there? Yes, sir. Can you read what it says? No sir, I have little English. It says Entrance. No, that is not the one I mean, the one next to it, that says Exit. Entrance seems a bit feminine to me — it hints of En-Trance, like a ladies' toilet water. But EXIT— that is a good strong name, with a solid E and a T and even an X. I doubt there is a woman anywhere named EXIT. But you, a tall, slim young man — for a Jew you have an angular face, nicely set eyes — you can create EXIT in your own image, as they say. Some day you will thank me.

The man does not mention my slightly large ears, perhaps because Celine has let my dark brown hair grow over them; ears which in every

mirror are trying like birds to flee my angular face Celine tells me this
is a silly obsession, I am a handsome young man (never mind ears that
light up in my mind when I blush around girls.) Or my sturdy chin,
she says, which with my dark eyes make a handsome package. Years
later, during the war, when I am in uniform, my face would sometimes
be compared with the actor Montgomery Clift. Or was it Maximillian
Schell? He was in that movie, what was it called? *Judgment at
Nuremberg*. I saw it on a date near Columbia with a college girl. Men
were not allowed in the girls' dormitory but she sneaked me in. Was
sweet and well-upholstered and cried a lot after the film, which made
for nicely moist sensations. At this late date Hippocampus won't give
me her name, just naked images. Good enough. Mostly, however, once
I had to wear the eye patch people said I looked not like an actor but
like Moshe Dayan, whose face, oddly, was round. I became a military
hero by association.

Take this paper with you — don't forget your box — and off you go
to the doctor, through that door over there marked . . . Entrance.

## WASHINGTON, 2020

"I think they're ready to start," Priscilla said.

On the low lectern in front of him half a dozen microphones sat like
crows on a wire. More than a dozen reporters and photographers and
video technicians sat on the redwood chairs. He himself sat beneath
a large leafy maple. On a table beside him was a sweating glass of iced
tea laced with honey.

"I guess we should begin," he said to them. "Welcome to Dunsinane.
Some of you may have been here before, but not most. We don't make
much news these days." He glanced at a stenographer's pad hidden on
a shelf inside the lectern. Peered through strong rimless rectangular
glasses — Benjamin Franklin style. "Mrs. Duckworth, let's begin with
you."

A squat elderly woman wearing a flowered dress too young for her
age and a leftover Easter bonnet does not rise from her seat. "Thank
you, Mr. Ambassador. Now that you are nearing one hundred years
of age, how does it feel?" A softball. "To quote my late friend Bernard
Baruch, when asked the same question at a similar occasion, he
replied: "It feels wonderful, given the alternative." Easy chuckles.

The Post has sent a sportswriter. That Lipsyte fellow. Ingenuity
lives. "Sir, you began your career as a prize-fighter. Is it true you were
taught by the great Benny Leonard?"

"Yes, that is true. I was very lucky. Mr. Leonard taught very well. Unfortunately, I did not learn very well."

Smiles.

"What was your record as a fighter, sir?"

"You bring up days long ago. As an amateur I was 12 and 0."

"And as a professional?"

"As an amateur I was 12 and 0."

More chuckles. A good group.

"What was your complete record?"

"As an amateur I was twelve and 0."

Priscilla seated next to him whispered something. "By the way, this is Priscilla, my secretary. She worries about my hearing despite these hearing aids. It's all right dear, I heard the question just fine. I merely chose not to answer. But I suppose I should. As a professional boxer I lost only one bout."

"Really! Out of how many bouts?"

"One."

The laughter was worth the fib.

"By the time I was lifted off the canvas I was applying to law school. I was lucky again, Columbia sent my records to Harvard but not to Ring Magazine."

At Columbia there had been no boxing team. But the fencing squad was one of the best in the nation. One day he climbed to the top of the gym at Morningside Heights to watch them practicing. White uniforms hanging from the walls, oval face masks made of wire, in one corner fencing equipment, thin swords, for lack of a better word, resting in what appeared to be an umbrella stand. He did not know the names of the different weapons — epee, and so forth — he had never been here before but he felt welcome as the fencers nodded to him before returning to their bouts. Someone slid onto the bleacher board beside him. Rachel.

*What are you doing here? I have calisthenics next period but Barnard has no gymnasium so we work out next door. Crossing the campus I saw you hurrying this way so I increased my pace. What are you doing here? Just wanted to see what it's like. Someone shushed them as the bouts began. Liquid grace. Balletic form. A foil streaking forth like his feared right cross. That was him out there, always had been, not a bloody boxer but a fencer like these guys, tall and thin with angular faces, slightly pointed noses. Rachel squeezing his wrist whispered, You could do that, whispering apparently being permitted after points had been scored. She could see it, only Rachel, no one else, no one else ever had. The invisible fencer in him.*

The reporters were liking him. A haughty young well-upholstered who had not done her homework asked which Presidents he had advised.

"Everyone from Roosevelt to Truman to Johnson to Obama, with the exception of a few Republicans like Nixon, who had his Kissinger. The bastard."

The Ambassador sipped his tea, listened to a whisper from Priscilla.

"Did I really say bastard? He was a cur, is what he was, Harvard men should not call each other bastards. Even if they are."

"Why do you say Dr. Kissinger was a cur, professor?"

"From his own words. You may know only his most famous quotation: 'The illegal we do immediately. The unconstitutional takes a little longer.' Somehow I never found that funny. Especially when juxtaposed with his basic worldview, which was that innocent people do not matter, the little people do not matter, it's godly to kill thousands, of civilians in the perceived pursuit of our national interest.

"We did that in Guatemala, in Vietnam, in Cambodia, all with Kissinger's approval, even his cheerleading. Some have called him a murderer. Since he is still alive, I think — sometimes it's hard to remember — I will not say I agree. But also I will not say I disagree."

"Ambassador, when President Obama visited Hiroshima a few years back, the first sitting President to do so, it reignited the old argument of whether we should have dropped the bomb to end the war. I assume Dr. Kissinger would have approved. How about you, sir?"

"I thought you all were here for some homey feature about the old man dribbling spit into his ice cream. But I'll ramble about my views on the bomb if you think anybody still cares.

"Late in the war I was a military attaché at Los Alamos Ranch. I was at Trinity Site when they tested Fat Boy — or was it Little Man? Bombs grow up faster than kids these days. Not to mention missiles. Especially in North Korea. I wonder sometimes if that is how the world is going to end. Nuclear kaboom with rice. So do others, of course.

"Anyway — life is full of surprises — at Trinity Site I witnessed the first mushroom cloud since the creation.

"We were miles from the blast, wearing dark goggles. Dr. Oppenheimer scrawled something on a sheet of paper, clipped it to some diagrams, shoved it into a leather folder, had a Major attach the folder to my wrist with handcuffs. A waiting Jeep sped me hellbent through the dusty desert for a hundred miles, to a tiny rail stop called Lamy — we could still see that big dark cloud behind us — where I caught a train for Washington. A day later a cab took me to the White House. I'm sure I was not the first to bring east the news that the bomb worked. They didn't trust cross-country phone lines or the telegraph back then, any number of Japanese spies might be tuned in, but they surely must have sent a coded message somehow. Was it The Eagle Has Landed? Something like that.

"The leather envelope was still shackled to my wrist when I reached the Oval Office, where a Three-Star General unlocked the cuffs. What the contents were I have no idea. It might have been sensitive material, or I might have been just a decoy, there might have been a Colonel on the train dressed as a tourist, carrying the real McCoy. Or they might have sent it on a two-seater plane hip-hopping across the country. I think it was only a few days later that the military brass met with the new President to discuss how best to use the bomb. I was on my way back to the ranch by then, carrying sealed notes from President Truman to Oppie and General Groves. Nobody needed or wanted my opinion on what to do with the bomb. I have often thanked the Lord for that.

"I think I have meandered a bit. You do that at my age. Not a serious condition, just embarrassing. Or perhaps I was a professor for too long. As for your specific question, if I still remember it, we can't go back in time and second-guess. There was a terrible war on. The President was new to his job. All the Generals, or most of them, told him we should drop the bomb on a Japanese city right away to end the war, perhaps save a million American casualties that would result from an invasion of Japan. Mr. Truman in his haberdasher gray suit was in no position to disagree. My own preference, like that of many of the scientists', including Oppie, including Einstein, would have been to invite the Emperor's top generals to an aircraft carrier, point them toward an uninhabited atoll down wind, drop the bomb, let them see the entire atoll disintegrate into a cloud in seconds and the ocean begin to boil. Tell them that unless they surrendered at once, without conditions, the next bomb would incinerate Tokyo. I suspect they would have surrendered quickly."

"What would that have changed, sir?"

"Aside from several hundred thousand civilians not being killed or maimed? We would occupy a much higher spot in the world's moral history."

Another of the well-endowed: "Ambassador, you have spent almost all of your long life in politics. Who in history is your favorite politician?"

"Disraeli. Without a doubt, Benjamin Disraeli."

"Why is that?"

"Why is that? Let me ask you a question, young lady. What is your favorite ice cream? Chocolate? Strawberry? You say maple walnut? Why is that? Do you get my point? Some affinities I don't think we can explain. Not to any useful purpose. They just are. Love perhaps being the most important. If Disraeli and I had lived in the same century we might have been brothers. That is the closest I can come."

Just one more question, Priscilla, ever watchful of my strength, warned them. A young blond woman. "To bring us up to date, sir, you were our first Ambassador to Israel, you were Einstein Professor of ethics at Georgetown for years, at times a visiting lecturer at Princeton, you graduated from Columbia with a double major —"

"— International Relations and Biology, I could not decide —"

"—you've written several books. Now you're officially retired, yet you're still known as an Adviser to Presidents. Has the current President sought your advice?"

Ambassador Maisel nodded with weary eyes. He had been expecting that question all afternoon.

"There are two reasons I cannot answer that. If I said yes, you would be all over me, asking what, where, when. I would not tell you, but you would make a headline of it anyway. If I answered no, I might lose my nice government pension to a nastier question: 'what is the old man good for anyway?'

"Now I have a question for you. Do you think my face is too angular? A fellow at Ellis Island thought so."

Uncertain expressions. Perhaps they had not heard him right.

"But before we march inside for lemonade and Margaret's home-made ice cream, I need to give you your reading assignment. A marvelous book by the Nobel Prize winner José Saramago. It's called *Death With Interruptions*. Sounds grim, but is quite a funny book. You should have no problem finishing it in a week, even if you have homework in math and English. Our attitudes towards Death are more important."

The reporters and photographers were looking at one another, puzzlement squinting their faces. Priscilla was uncertain what to do.

"Your specific assignment," the professor continued, sipping his tea "is to choose one sentence from that book that you like or find especially meaningful, and be prepared to discuss its implications."

He turned on his side, rested his head on the pillowed back of his wicker chair, was asleep, snoring lightly, almost immediately. Priscilla, horrified, stepped to the front of the buzzing group.

"Ladies and gentleman, please! Ambassador Maisel, as you know, is elderly. That is why you are here today. A fact not widely known is that he suffers from Parkinson's Disease. What just occurred happens often to the elderly and ill, especially when they are tired: their attention wanders, they may forget where they are."

She wanted to keep them there; the longer they were away from their offices the sooner the Ambassador's lapse would fade into unimportance.

"I can give you some biological information," she said, "having once been a P.A. The place in our brains where memories are stored is called the hippocampus. It's in two halves, two parts that curve around the brain like a small horse-shoe. Everything we do or see or say is a potential memory. In what you could call electronic form they all go into the hippocampus. But there is a limited amount of storage space there. So things of no importance — give them a D grade — such as what you had for dinner last night, are sent packing. But if at dinner you saw your spouse or lover with some handsome stud, the triple A alarm goes off. Deep into the hippocampus the memory gets shoved, and there it remains, no matter how painful it is, no matter how much you want to be rid of it.

"Parkinson's is not fatal. But it is also incurable. It can affect memory as well as balance.

"There is a lot of traffic going in and out of the brain. Think of an old railroad terminal. The rails have grown rusty with age. There also are loose wires blowing through the terminal, and if one of them lands on a rail, one memory can get crossed with something else. You just saw the effect. This is not rocket science, but it is science nonetheless. I'm sure you can find a better explanation with your smartphones.

"Why am I explaining this? Because some of you have the Ambassador's unfortunate digression on tape. I implore you not to use it on the air, or post it on YouTube or Facebook or any other of the so-called marvels of the information age. I cannot stop you, of course, freedom of the press and all that, but exposing Ambassador Maisel to ridicule for the crime of growing old and ill would be rude in the extreme. I dare say it might harm your own careers more than it would harm his.

"You are all still invited for refreshments in the dining room. Just follow the stone path where it veers to the left. And please don't let any squirrels accompany you into the house, once inside they are difficult to corner."

They gathered their cameras and handbags and moved silently toward the rock path. Priscilla found her chair and sat and turned away from them. And closed her eyes against tears.


*Rachel sleeping with her head near the ice cream painted a picture of her asleep in her bed at home with its threadbare quilt of chocolate and vanilla; and screaming. Throwing off the quilt and wrapping herself into a ball in her green pajamas and screaming again and fighting a terrible nightmare. Mama! Mama don't. Me jumping from my bed across the small room and leaping into hers and cuddling the small smelly ball of her into my body, it's okay Rachel it's okay it's just a dream Holding her as she drifted back to sleep, slipping back to my own bed and her screaming again and me waking her again, just a nightmare baby girl that's all it was. Papa not hearing her screams or coming to rescue her because he had drunk half a bottle of whisky before he could fall asleep. How many terrible weeks or months he did that before tapering off on the schnapps I cannot remember. How many weeks of nightmare dreams little Rachel suffered through I also cannot remember. She crawled into my bed to finish her sleep more times than I can remember. Nor could I count my own nightmare dreams of what had been done to Mama, which I suspected were worse than hers. Too awful for even hippocampus to store them. Then I saw the truth of it. Papa the magician entertaining people in the town square. Two tall men approaching Mama, who was smiling from under an oak tree nearby as people laughed. It was his seven hat trick, which always made them laugh the most, no other magician in the region did more than five. He had invented it himself, was proud of it, Mama was proud of him for inventing it between stuffing pillows. When Papa saw the two tall men approaching Mama, taking hold of her arms, he ran straight at them to see what they wanted. One of them pulled a pistol from his pocket and pointed it in Papa's face and waved it, he should mind his own business and go back to his wooden platform on the green and finish his tricks. The other tall man pulled a pistol from his belt and pressed the barrel against Mama's ear and they led her away from the crowd to a wooden cart with a mule attached that stood docilely across the road. The crowd watching where they were taking her but doing nothing to stop them.*

## WASHINGTON, 2020

"I was not sleeping, Ben. Just remembering."

"Whatever you say, sir. Do you want me to lay out another suit, maybe a dark blue? Or are casual clothes enough for coffee?"

"Just casual, slacks and a pullover shirt. For croquet."

"Does the President play?"

"If not I will teach her. I hear she does little to take her mind off the country's troubles. Crossword puzzles are not enough, she has to truly relax sometimes, they all do. The first thing I told Ike during Korea was to play more golf. He listened. After blasting the ball up the fairway a few times every day he did not need to bury the Chinese, he could accept a cease fire, as I suggested. The cease fire has held for sixty years. But with the new Dear Leader flaunting his nukes in Julia's face, anything can happen. Croquet, Ben, croquet."

"This is fun," the President said. "I'm enjoying it."

Following his suggestion she had kicked off her heels, was playing in her stockinged feet.

"I can't believe you were not exposed to it at the Seven Sisters."

He could never recall which one she had attended.

"Our required sport was field hockey," she said. "Much more strenuous than this."

"Were you good at it?"

"Not really. They had to keep me on the team or I wouldn't graduate. So they made me back-up goalie. That's rather like being Vice President."

"That's wonderful, Julia. I must quote you to the V.P."

"For that I shall place my ball beside yours, as you showed me, and smash you to Rock Creek Park."

"That would not be ladylike, Madam President."

"All the more reason to do it."

An eager chipmunk was watching from the grass a few feet away. She inched her ball beside his, swung, hard. "Ow" she yelled as instead of slamming her mallet into her ball she slammed it into her ankle. Hopped two steps in pain, scaring off the critter, fell on her butt in the grass. "Damn!" she said, rubbing her foot, "this is dangerous. I'm glad I didn't bring the White House photographer today."

"A shame you didn't. Would have made an endearing shot: 'Splendor in the Grass.'"

"For the Republicans."

"I'm sorry. Perhaps we've played enough for the first time. Let's start back."

He leaned on his wooden cane, the one with "1973 Kentucky Derby — Joshua's Pleasure" engraved on it; the year on the curved handle almost illegible from handling. Three canes stood in the umbrella stand beside the door, this one, the one that said "1973 Preakness Stakes — Joshua's Pleasure." The third said only "Joshua's Pleasure." No race or year; he did not use that one often. "Ben can find the ball later. I want to ask you a question. When was the last time you thought about Beloved Leader?"

Madam President hiked up the trousers of her pantsuit, brushed off bits of grass. She was wearing pale green today. He had no idea how many suits she had, perhaps hundreds. If that were published it would hang another so-called scandal on her sullied name, like Imelda's shoes. At least she had never dabbled in extra men, so far as he knew. If any photos of such existed they would have surfaced by now.

"I don't know, I certainly did not give him a thought while we were playing."

"Good! Point taken? There's plenty of room to set up a croquet court on the White House lawn. You could play with the girls. Even with Tom."

"My ex-linebacker? I think he would be embarrassed to play croquet."

"Challenge him to a match. And beat him. You'll have to practice, though. Here, do you mind if we sit on the veranda for a bit? I need to catch my breath. Would you like another sherry before you go?"

"I'd better not, though I would love to."

"No harm if you did. You take Nixon, he did all his relaxing with alcohol. And the girls on Bebe's yacht, of course."

"Are you teasing me? You can't do that, I'm the President."

"I have heard that bruited about."

"You're in a good mood, Ambassador, I'm happy to be sharing it with you. I have one question, then I'm due back at the White House. You're such a whiz at croquet, did you play much sports when you were young?"

"Not really. I did box a bit. It's odd, that subject came up with the reporters today. I did not tell them the entire truth, though."

The President stood, smoothed a wrinkle in her pants. "Do we ever?"

## NEW YORK, 1938

The posters still are there, imprinted on his retina. Hand-written on butcher paper: Friday night fights, Bobby Cohen vs. Exit Maisel, three rounds, Prince Street Gym. Exit Maisel vs. Jack Lowry, three rounds, Prince Street Gym. With some colored pencil added: K-O Exit Maisel vs. Boomer Bloom, five rounds, Prince Street Gym. Undefeated Exit Maisel vs. Louie Kowalski, six rounds, Prince Street Gym. Others. And then in full color, larger, printed in a shop: Professional Boxing, Friday Night, St. Nicholas Arena. Unbeaten Exit Maisel vs. Slugging Buster Diaz.

He paused while blasting the heavy bag, waves of muscle in his upper arms built while training for months in the gym, causing the reluctant bag to swing slightly. His manager/trainer watched. You know Friday is my last fight. Yeah, yeah, Whitebread said, you told me a hundred times. And I'll tell you for the hundredth time, you're out of your mind. You know how much Benny Leonard made in the ring? I know, a million dollars — and lost it all on Black Friday.

And took some time off and came out of retirement and made another million. He's set for life.

I'm going to Harvard Law. I wasn't put on earth to hurt people.

Who you been talking to, some rabbi? You really think lawyers help people? Open your eyes. And you ain't hurting people — maybe just the guy in the ring with you. You're entertaining people. In these hard times that's a blessing.

I've had long discussions with my sister. She agrees with me.

The Virgin Rachel. I thought she might be behind this. Well, I can't fight her. So I took you at your word. At least we can make some money out of this. It's all set. The bookies have made you an 8 to1 favorite.

Why? Diaz is a pro.

He's also a Spic. And you're undefeated. Twelve knockouts in 12 fights, all inside three rounds. Diaz is tough, but he's lost three fights out of ten. A glass chin is the word from the Bronx.

At 8 to1 we won't make a dime. Which is fine with me, I've already got my tuition.

We'll make a bundle if we bet on the other kid.

What? Exit looked hard into his eyes. You think I'm gonna lose? He slammed his right into the heavy bag, which seemed to groan, a left uppercut, the right again. Paused. You didn't answer me. You think I'm gonna lose? This was something new.

Whitebread's voice was lower. I know you're gonna lose.

What are you talking about?

Slicer told me.

Who the hell is Slicer?

You ever hear of Lucky Luciano?

Of course.

He's God in the city. Slicer is one of his enforcers. When Slicer tells me you're gonna lose, I tell you you're gonna lose, and when I tell you you're gonna lose, you're gonna lose. Fahrsteist?

I don't believe what I'm hearing. You're telling me to take a dive?

It's your last fight, you say. Your record won't matter anymore. You know what this is, pulling a paper from his pants pocket. This is a receipt for five grand. On Buster Diaz. In your name. After the fight it will turn into 40 grand, like magic. You could go to Harvard and Yale, and also Princeton if you want.

Just for losing the fight.

Just for losing the fight. I got ten grand on him myself. The whole neighborhood will be on it. Your father could start that new business he wants.

Whitebread?

What?

Go fuck yourself.

That's brave, jerk. Tell that to Slicer. Tell that to Luciano. See how brave you are. You win this fight, see how many fingers you got the next day. How many balls.

Exit grabbed a towel from a railing. I won't talk about this anymore, I'm goin' home.

Good, go home, think about it. Get your too-smart head straight.

He was half way down to the street when he realized he had forgotten his gym bag with his clothes in it, his shoes, his books. This was not possible, he told himself, just a nightmare, Whitebread had been his best and perhaps only true friend besides Rachel since they landed in America together five years before; he would never do such a thing. But the stale sweat that saturated the stairwell and the sticky sweat in his workout trunks and the aching behind his knees as he trod back up the stairs told him he was not dreaming.

## WASHINGTON, 2020

Carefully he crossed the gravel drive that curled uphill for fifty yards, ducked his head only an inch or two to pass under the arch of grape vines that denoted the entrance to the poppy field. Similar vines covered the top, sides and back of the wrought iron pergola to provide shade for those who wanted to sit and gaze at the flowers, as he often did, the bench strewn with pillows for the comfort of boney rears. He eased onto one, set his Stoli and his cane beside him on a small matching iron table, one of two placed there by Hallie years ago to hold drinks and her pistachios; examined the green grapes, not yet ripe, ranging in size from green peas to immies, one of his favorite English words.

Hallie. She had conceived of the poppy field even before they bought the Birnham place at the suggestion of JFK. The level field was one reason. He would have liked to play there with his children or grandchildren but they had neither. In front of the pergola she had planted a square perhaps 80 by 80 feet of the brightest of the reds, in memory of all those on either side who had died in either war. Beyond the reds the eye was carried off by vistas of white Oriental poppies, pink, yellow, orange, purple, even blue. Many early guests at Dunsinane believed poppies came only in red. Not so. Some thought they only were made of paper and sold with twists of green wire for a veterans' charity. Not so.

Hallie.

## New York, 1936

The big man who was carrying the two boxes and the valise easily as if they contained nothing but feathers came up beside them and set his burden on the asphalt. Jacob thanked him, said to the children, *Kinder*, do you remember who this is? Rachel shook her head shyly. Her big brother squinted into the lowering sun that was glaring off the bay and asked, Is that Uncle Joshua? Attaboy, the big man said and rubbed Eliezer's head. Good boy, son, you were only four years old when Joshua left for America to make his fortune, it's nice that you remember him. He motioned Cecile forward, Cecile this is my younger brother Joshua. Joshua, meet my wife. Cecile lowered her head, Joshua shook her hand, said, Such a pretty bride. Cecile blushed and pulled off her hat and veil, I forgot I was wearing that she said. I did not mean to embarrass you Joshua said, it looks very nice. But she did not put it back on her head, she held it in her hand.

"Guess what," the boy said. "They gave me a new name."

"Why?" his father asked.

"They said mine was too long for America."

"That's meshuganah."

"What's the new name," Uncle Joshua asked.

"Exit."

"Exit?"

"Exit?"

"Exit?"

"Why Exit?"

"The man said it's a good American name."

"I never heard of it," his father said.

"That's what he wrote on your papers?" Joshua asked.

The boy nodded, starting to feel awkward about the name. Joshua noticed this, said, "That's good. It's important to fit in here. Family, we all should get used to this right away. So from now on this is Exit." He shook the boy's hand.

Rachel bit her lip, asked, "Will he need another bris?"

Exit's ears flared, he pushed his palm into his sister's face. Gently. She began to laugh. Kissed his palm before he pulled it away. He made a fist as if to punch her. Jokingly.

A stout woman wearing a gray apron over her house dress, a dark red blotch covering the side of her nose and part of her cheek, emerged from the kitchen. Her face reminded the boy of Whitebread's bloody nose after he'd slugged him on the ship the day before. He hoped no one had hit this woman that hard; he could not imagine punching a woman. Ursuline tells me supper is ready if you're hungry, Joshua said. I know I'm hungry.

We call it six, Joshua said, the bathroom doesn't count. Why not, that's a very important room. Yes, it is, to tell you the truth, I've been in the business for six years and I still don't know why the bathroom doesn't count.

Tochter, Jacob said, tossing his bowler on one of two beds in a large bedroom, pulling a black yarmulke from his vest pocket and fitting it onto his thinning hair, when you walked here with Uncle Joshua did you happen to notice signs in front of a lot of the buildings, large white signs with black writing? I did. What did the signs say? They said John Maze something something. John Maze Construction Company, her father said. Do you know who John Maze is? She shook her head, her dark brown hair cut short swishing across her neck. John Maze is your uncle Joshua.

How can that be? Eliezer — now Exit — who had been listening quietly to the conversation, too overcome by these new surroundings to speak, now asked. They changed your name too on that island?

No, Joshua said, I know they do that sometimes, but mine I changed myself after I was here a few months. Why did you do that? the boy asked. I just thought it sounded more American, that it would help my business. You mean it sounded less Jewish? Rachel said. You're 12 years old, aren't you the smart one. They grow up smart in Europe nowadays, Celine said. If they grow up at all. The brothers looked at her with an expression that was hard to read.

A stout woman wearing a gray apron over her house dress, a dark red blotch covering the side of her nose and part of her cheek, emerged from the kitchen. Her face reminded the boy of Whitebread's bloody nose after he'd slugged him on the ship the day before. He hoped no one had hit this woman that hard; he could not imagine punching a woman. Ursuline tells me supper is ready if you're hungry, Joshua said. I know I'm hungry.

They took turns washing their hands in the bathroom that didn't count, then sat around a large table in the dining room made of dark wood, with silverware and napkins and small glasses set at five places, two candles burning in brass candlesticks, a bottle of rare schnapps in the center. When Ursuline left the room Rachel whispered, isn't she hungry too? The help eats in the kitchen, her father said. I asked her to prepare just big salads, with fresh fruit on the side, Joshua said, I know you don't get those things on ocean crossings. And challah of course. The plates piled high with fresh fruit seemed ablaze with color when Ursuline reappeared carrying two of them and set them in front of the men, then went back for three more. They ate in silence, savoring the juice of the fresh fruit on their tongues. The boy broke the silence by asking, Uncle Joshua — is it all right to still call you Joshua? Of course, at home I am still Joshua Maisel. Only at work am I John Maze. You can do the same thing. The boy looked at his father. The other kids called me Smelly Ellie. I got so mad I wanted to punch them.

Why didn't you? Rachel asked.

I was afraid I'd get thrown out of school.

So you like your new name better? Joshua asked, what is it again, Exit?

The boy nodded.

Well, that is unusual, but is that all right with you, Jacob, if he goes from now at home too by Exit? Jacob, his mouth wrapped around several strawberries, nodded. Exit Maisel grinned like a newborn. Joshua filled his glass and Jacob's from the bottle of schnapps and lifted his in a toast, To Exit Maisel he said. But you had another question I think. Yes sir. In gymnasium we were learning about economics, May

I ask you about economics? Of course, learning is the most important thing in life. Some people think it ends when school ends, but the fact is you can keep learning all your life. You should.

Rachel, too full to eat more fruit, set her fork beside her plate. My girlfriends say the most important thing in life is love, she said.

They do, do they? Celine raised her eyes from her plate, glanced quickly at her husband, lowered her eyelids again. No one noticed.

You are growing up quickly. You love your brother, Exit, and your Mama and Papa, of course.

And my Uncle Joshua.

Well, that is sweet. But for other kinds of love, you need to wait until you are older. Much older. Celine will talk to you about that some day. Now back to economics. Exit?

## Washington, 2020

A buzzer buzzes not far from his wicker chair. Will you get that, Margaret? She does. Calling is Priscilla, the Ambassador's personal secretary. Margaret presses a button to connect the speakerphone. "Yes, Priscilla, he's awake, you can tell him now."

"Ambassador, this is Priscilla. I have a message for you from the White House. The President will not be able to come to luncheon today. She said, and I quote: 'Glorious Leader Pong is taking too much of my time.' She said she will try to visit for coffee and talk in mid-afternoon if that is alright. She added, 'I am floating out to sea on a gallon of pink *insam cha*.' Whatever that is."

"Julia knows what insam cha is. As do I. I got sick on it myself one time in Seoul for Mr. Truman. Tell her mid-afternoon will be fine."

"Yes, sir, I did."

## New York, 1935

Leaning back in the sticky wicker, resting his eyes. Clouds over the city are lowering, threatening rain, as the boy walks home from Extra English class. The pickles in the barrels outside the deli on the corner spike his nostrils. He tries to ignore them, continues walking. On the brown stone steps in front of the tenement he spots trouble sitting, waiting, hair seeming to flash a warning. Whitebread. How does he know where he lives? You for revenge come? I don't want revenge, I want to talk. I never see you in school, Stark. Wilbur Stark, is that correct? Don't need to go to school after 17, Maisel, are not you 17?

Fifteen. You're tall for your age. And it's not Wilbur, it's Whitebread. The boy laughs, I made that up.

I always hated Wilbur, it's too soft; when I joined the club I switched to Whitebread.

What club is that? The Prince Street Boxing Club, that's what I want to talk to you about, let's go get a pickle. Can't. I got money, I'm buying. The boy shrugs, sets his school books on the stoop, they walk towards the corner. The pickles are sour, juicy, squirt on their chins. They laugh.

What's this boxing club to do with me? I don't box, don't want to box. I think you should. Why? Because you got promise. Who says I got promise? You see this bend in my nose? That says you got promise.

The crisp pickles squirt again, they laugh again, wipe their chins with the backs of their cuffs. You want another one? They're five cents each, the boy says, when did you become rich? I work afternoons at the gym, sweep up, stack towels. The boy nods, they each pick another from the barrel of extra sour.

So how come you're not working now? I am, I'm here on business. Recruiting new club members is business. Knobby Levine, he's the trainer, allows it. You ever hear of Benny Leonard? No, who's he? You never heard of Bennie Leonard? He was only the lightweight champion of the world for seven years. Grew up in the neighborhood, his Mom and Pop live around the corner. Learned his every move in the Prince Street gym. Listen, you don't got this late English class tomorrow, am I right? Who told you that?

Rachel.

Of course Rachel.

Thunder breaks across the tenements like a warning, followed by lightning. The boy grabs his school books, they step inside the dark wooden doors, the boy choking on his last nubbin of pickle, waits for the sour to pass. She's only 12, you bastard! Hey, don't throw a fit, you got nothing to worry about, she's smart, she's nice to talk to, that's all; I got me a babe who's 20, a Catholic girl, comes to the fights Friday nights. Likes her whiskey.

So who is it cares if I don't have late English tomorrow? We do, me and Knobby. Come to the club right after school. I can't join, don't have money. Did you hear me mention money? Just be there, he only comes to work with prospects on Wednesdays. Who are you talking about? Benny, of course. The Champ.

You told him I was a prospect? I told Knobby, he told Benny. And they believed you? I showed them my nose.

## NEW YORK, 1936

To start at the beginning, Joshua said, when I came to America six years ago I had some money I made in Austria, buying and selling real estate. That's land. I did not know if Austrian money would be accepted by the banks here so I changed it all into gold. Everyone accepts gold. What I found here was the country going *meshuganah* to buy stock in new companies with bright futures. They would go to banks and if they wanted to buy a hundred shares of some company, let's say the Adolph Ford company, they would give the bank ten dollars and the bank would lend them the other ninety and give them a paper certificate saying it was worth 100 shares of Ford Motor stock. In other words, the bank was lending them 90 dollars, which everyone figured they would pay back as the stock kept climbing. After all, who could not believe in the future of the Model-A. But I did not like the idea of giving a bank my gold in exchange for a piece of paper. So I did not do it. When the stock market crashed — meaning the stocks in companies became worth less and less — nobody really knows why that happened — the banks called in their loans, as it is described. Few people had money to pay back their loans, so the banks took back their stock, and many people became paupers.

I heard some men jumped out of windows and killed themselves when that happened, Exit said.

I'm afraid some did. I saw one or two falling bodies myself. My good friend Izzie was one.

Jacob Maisel pointed at his young wife Cecile across the table, then at Rachel; the girl had fallen sleep, her ice cream melting in the bowl in front of her. Cecile nodded, said I'll put her to bed when we all go, I don't want her to wake during the night and not know where she is. I'm tired myself, we all must be from the crossing, perhaps we should say good night soon.

Yes, we'll do that Jacob said, adjusting his yarmulka, just let Joshua finish his story.

Thank you, Jacob. Where was I? Yes, when the banks could not get their loans back some of them closed. Then people who had their savings in banks panicked, they were afraid if their banks closed they would lose their money. So they lined up at the banks — a run on the banks it was called — to take their money out. But the banks had invested their money in the markets, too, and had little with which to pay back the depositors. More and more banks closed all across the country, gloom settled over the land, suddenly no one had faith in the future, people stopped investing, companies stopped building housing because people had no money with which to pay rent, this left hundreds of thousands of construction workers without jobs, which made everything worse. The current figure is that 25 percent of all workers have lost their jobs.

Exit shook his head, dabbled with his spoon at his ice cream.

To speed up my story, I figured that things could not get much worse, the big companies now were actually worth much more than their flattened stocks indicated. So I began to buy some. Just a few. Mostly I figured people would always need places to live, and immigrants were still arriving from Europe. I knew something about real estate from Vienna, now I saw on all sides half-built tenements that had been abandoned when the crash occurred, others left in disrepair because the landlords had no money to keep them up, many acres of flat land in perfect locations to build new tenements. So I started to do that. I hired hundreds of construction workers to fix up the older buildings and to start new ones. That required plumbers and electricians and plasterers and woodworkers. Soon it was thousands I hired. This put money on their tables so they could rent the very apartments they were building.

This was John Maze doing the building? Exit asked.

Yes it was. Soon others copied me. I offered your father to be a partner in the business, to share the money I was making, but he is not a practical man, your father, he is a dreamer, which is fine, we need dreamers very much.

A partner, Jacob spluttered, that is not what you offered, you offered a one quarter share. Yes, that is correct, but if I had offered a half share, or even an equal share, would it have made a difference? It would not, because you did not want to support your family on the shoulders of your little brother. I understand that, it is admirable in a way, but if I may say so, stupid in a practical way. So you held on to the feather pillow business until even you realized it was dead and would not come back. You said once you have a new idea, do you want to tell us?

Cecile motioned to the sleeping child, Jacob nodded, put up his hand, just one more minute. And told of his idea.

Picture frames.

Picture frames? The unspoken reaction circled the table in the disbelieving eyes of the adults.

There is going to be a war, Jacob said, adjusting his yarmulke again. Everyone knows that. These America Firsters led by Colonel Lindbergh who is a friend of Mister Hitler wants to keep us out of it.

But Hitler has made his intentions clear. He plans to invade Austria, Poland, the Balkan states, France, probably attack England with rockets and pApples. We cannot stand for this, or we might be next. So there will be a war.

Papa, what does that have to do with picture frames?

I'll tell you what. When we start shipping hundreds of thousands, even millions of our boys across the sea to fight the Nazis, what are their parents going to want most? I'll tell you what. Picture frames. Photo studios will spring up to take pictures of the boys in their army or navy uniforms before they go off to fight. They will look very handsome. Or people will buy cheap cameras from the Kodak company and take the pictures themselves. They will be proud of these keepsake images. But when the boys go off to war, what will their parents and brothers and sisters and maybe grandparents do with these pictures? They will not want to stick them on the side of the ice box with tape, that would feel cheap, would feel like an insult to their fighting men, would soon get torn and drop to the kitchen floor. So they will take from what little money they have and buy a nice professional frame, hand-made, burgundy velvet perhaps with a gold-plated inner frame to hold the photograph. With an attached flap behind it so it can stand proudly and unshakable on the dining room table, or a living room end table, or hang on a wall if they prefer. Every day they will look at their boy in uniform standing so proudly, looking so brave, and it will make them feel like real Americans; they will try not to think of the deadly shells that might be falling on his barracks or the torpedoes that might be snaking under the ocean toward his ship.

Joshua Maisel was nodding with perhaps slight approval. Exit asked, What will you call these frames?

Picture frames, what else?

The name of the company, I mean.

I haven't thought much about that, there is time. Maisel Frames, I suppose.

Exit with his spoon tried to scoop up a bit of his melted ice cream, without much success. Still toying with the spoon he asked shyly, What if you changed the spelling? What if you called it Mazel Frames.

His father looked at Joshua, then at Exit. You know what Mazel means? Of course, good luck. Mazel Tov is good luck, without the Tov Mazel is just luck. He was getting a bit excited now. But there is nothing wrong with just luck, is there? I see what you are saying, my boy. Joshua, is this boy a genius? I told you he was a genius. Blushing, Exit suddenly was bursting with talk. Some of those boys who go to war will come back proud and healthy, but many will come back wounded, and some won't come back at all. It will be God who determines these things, not Mazel Frames. We will never suggest that they will, not in any of our advertising. Listen to him, Our Advertising! Jacob says. And parents and grandparents will know that, of course. But if they decide that a little bit of luck from a Mazel picture frame might win God to their side, who will it hurt?

John Maze, nee Joshua Maisel, said to his brother, just one practical question, which I know you hate. War will come, but it might not come for a year, or two, or three. God will decide that, too. Or Roosevelt, Exit said. So, how will you support your lovely family until that time? What I was thinking, Jacob said, was to offer you a quarter of the business if you let us stay in this apartment for free until I can start paying for it. Jacob, I already told you all of you can stay here as long as you want, it's convenient with my place just four blocks away. But I see that is a burden on your manhood or something. I'll tell you what, I will think over your proposal. You said 25 percent of Mazel Frames, correct? He leaned back in his chair, quickly leaned forward again. Make it 26 percent and we have a deal. He stuck out his long arm and shook his surprised brother's hand and reached for the bottle of schnapps and refilled his glass and Jacob's. To Mazel Frames! he said and the two brothers drank. Cecile, eyes unwilling to stay open a moment longer, head nodding onto her well-upholstered chest, smiled through sleep that would not be denied

*Yom Kippur* night, my first professional fight. Papa was napping in the afternoon on a break from *schul* and Bubbie called me into the kitchen and told me to sit at the table covered with yellow oil cloth and set in front of me a bowl of chicken soup with carrots and onions and slices of dark meat in it and a chunk of *chalah* beside. I can't eat I'm fasting I told her but she said you're fighting tonight you can't fight on an empty stomach; if you wait until dark you'll be too full to fight. I hadn't realized she kept such close tabs on my boxing, she had never come to a fight.

Outside it was a deaf person's night. Pure silence. Two inches of snow in the streets muffled the sound of passing cars but this being Yom Kipper night and also the start of Shabbus there were hardly any cars. I was lucky, a man coming home from Uptown got out of a taxi and I climbed into it, shaking snow off my rubbers and rode it to St. Nicholas Arena. Inside was as quiet as outside, the arena still empty, fight-goers perhaps waiting for darkness or for the falling snow to stop.

A small light burned outside the door of the dressing room. I opened
it and there stood Whiteread, I should have a expected that, arranging
bottles on a shelf. Without a word I took off my coat and hung it and
my shirt and undershirt and changed into my boxing trunks, white silk
with turquoise blue M's running down both sides, designed and sewn
by Rachel of course, and without a word sat on a bench. Whitebread
without a word approached holding tape and taped my hands. It was
way too early to put on my gloves but he slipped them on anyway and
tied them tight at my wrists. My robe, green, was hanging on a nail.
I slipped into it, began doing light warm-up jabs. Neither off us had
anything to say but we couldn't keep still. I had the strange thought
that the third man in the ring this night would be God.

I must have dozed on and off in the dressing room because the next
hour or two comes back to me staccato, jumpy as an early movie film.
What I next see clearly is the door to the dressing room standing open,
crowd noises swarming in as if the arena has filled or partially filled,
me following Whitebread down the aisle between sections of cheering,
waving fans, Lower East Side boys, down to the ring, a three-legged
stool waiting in the corner, a referee in a black and white striped shirt
toweling his face as if he had just reffed the previous bout. Ducking
through the ropes onto the ring I saw the far side of St. Nick's well-
occupied by fans of my opponent as if chunks or parts of the Bronx
had ridden the subway down in the snow — maybe it had stopped
falling by then — to urge him on, then he was there himself across
the ring, stocky and muscled Buster Diaz or whatever they called him
loosening his shoulders, not looking at me, getting read to deck me. I
did not know if he was in on the so-called fix or not. I didn't care. I did
a few bends to loosen my knees. My eyes roaming over the home boys
saw not only Rachel in a seat in the fourth row but someone beside her
who looked a lot like my father. In the dim light I could not be certain,
the ref was calling us to the center of the spotlighted ring, he spoke his
ref's words and we touched gloves lightly and then came the bell. The
stools disappeared from the corners. Whitebread and I still had not
spoken a word.

The first two rounds I don't remember. I'm sure we must have
danced around, feeling each other out, throwing some light jabs not
intended to hurt. Not yet. Me sitting on my stool after the second,
Whitebread toweling off my shoulders, my face, my head, finally
speaking the first words he had spoken to me that day, leaning close,
almost whispering, You know what you gotta do, go out there and
make us some dough. Was he crazy, speaking those words aloud, what

if someone overheard, but then I calmed, this was my first pro fight, my manager saying go out and make us some dough would sound normal enough. That fell away but the other part rankled, You know what you gotta do.

No one tells me anymore what I gotta do, I do what I want to do. That rang and rang in my head like a bell. Don't tell me what I gotta do. I could take a dive if I wanted and I would fool the whole arena, writers and everyone, Exit had an off night they would write, he took Diaz for granted they would write. There's only two people in the whole arena I couldn't fool. One was myself. The other was Rachel. After getting beat I would shower and dress and meet her in the lobby and she would turn to look at me but her bright and lively eyes would be slow and warm and slightly wet, like the eyes of a puppy. She knew. And she knew I knew she knew. But she would not mention it, not then, not ever. Papa would be standing beside her looking sad and shaking my hand because I had lost but he did not know the truth of it, never would. Just her. Suddenly a Spanish torpedo was coming at me, Buster Diaz in a full-on charge across the ring, the bell for the third had rung and deaf in my thoughts I had not heard it, he had every right to do what he was doing even hit me while I sat on the stool if he wanted. I heard him and stood and felt his charge through the corner of my eyes and twisted and took his wicked blast of a right on my shoulder. I shook him off and stood in a bit of a daze as he stumbled into the ropes from his momentum. He bounced off and was ready to fight again but by then my instinct was automatic. He tried to get inside my longer arms. He may have been expecting a wild right roundhouse, I do not know, but instead his chin connected with a straight right cross that had all my strength behind it, the same punch that had broken Whitebread's nose on the boat and KO'd twelve guys in a row. He went down like the rest of them and lay flat and motionless while the ref shoved me to a neutral corner and began his count. At eight the guy stirred just like Whitebread had told me to do and tried to stand and the ref stopped his count. But the guy's knees were kosher jello — well, maybe not kosher — and he couldn't stand and went down again. The ref started his count from One as my home boys booed and yelled but at his ten the fight was over. He held up my arm to signal the winner half the place was yelling EXIT! EXIT! EXIT! but on the other side the contingent from the Bronx was sitting quietly, maybe sullenly. When I went to my corner head held high like Joshua's Pleasure would years later in the Winner's Circle in the rain the stool was there but not my robe and where the hell was Whitebread? I looked around and didn't

see him anywhere. The outer doors were being opened on all sides
as chatting people sloughed off hesitantly into the snow. Without a
rubdown or a robe I was feeling chilled. Where the hell was that son
of a bitch? An arm was grabbing my green robe from outside the ring
and Rachel climbed over the low rope and ducked under the high as
smoothly as if she were dancing ballet. She held out the robe and I slid
my arms into the sleeves and tied it. The remaining Bronx guys did
not look menacing any more. After I kissed her cheek and she kissed
mine I pulled her toward the dressing room. My father was waving at
me and I waved back and Rachel pointed to the nearest exit door and
yelled something and he put his Bowler on his balding head over his
yarmulke and nodded, he knew he was to wait for us there. Is Bubbie
here I asked. Rachel turned an odd look on me, why do you ask that,
she has never come to a fight. I know but neither has Papa, I thought
he might bring her with him since he was coming alone. He was not
coming alone he was coming with me. It's amazing I said, Yom Kippur
night, to be here on time he would have had to leave schul early, break
his fast early, ride in the taxi on Shabbos. Amazing! You know what he
said to me as the cab arrived at the gate, Rachel said, he took my hand
in his and squeezed my fingers lightly and said, God will forgive me for
this; and if he doesn't, I shall deal with it later. But why, why this of all
nights? Maybe because thinking about it he accepted that you his only
son was in some deep part a fighter and he never would know that part
of you unless he came, you had said ten times this would be your last
fight, maybe he heard that as an invitation. Or a warning. And maybe
it was.

The door to the dressing room was open, I could hear the hi-jinx of
some of the home boys gathered in there as they always did after a
winning fight, which of course is all there had been. But Whitebread
was not among them. When Rachel opening the big leather buttons
on her coat followed me in the raucous laughter suddenly paled as if a
priest had appeared. Someone had brought a case of beer and the boys
were well into it, someone pulled a can for me and tossed it over with
a new church key. The same fellow asked Rachel. She hesitated, looked
at me, I shrugged. She reached into the box, pulled out a beer and the
guy popped it. When she held it high and drained some of the golden
liquid into her mouth the room erupted in cheers. Beer in cans was a
new fad back then.

    The hi-jinks continued until a scowling visage appeared in the
doorway. Whitebread, black shirt buttoned at his wrists, black

trousers, face ruddy beneath his shocks of white hair, ruddy it seemed from a drink or more likely two in that short time, not beer, he must have a flask with him. He stumbled into the dressing room, looked about. Out, he said, and the others obeyed. When Rachel lingered near me his tone was softer, You too, he said. She told me she would wait with Papa. I nodded as she quietly closed the door behind her.

So, Whitebread said, looking right at me, what the hell was that all about?

What are you talking about?

You know damn well. You were supposed to take a dive.

That's what you wanted. I never said I would.

So how come I lost a ton of money?

You bet before you asked me. That's not my fault.

You think Lucky Luciano won't be able to find you in Harvard Yard? You think next week or the week after or in a month Slicer won't step from behind a tree and slash you to pieces.

Cut the bull, Whitebread. Lucky Luciano owns four casinos in the city and gets a 10 per cent cut from all the others. He owns maybe a dozen brothels. He says he doesn't deal in drugs, Puritan that he is, but who knows? Until prohibition ended he delivered every bottle of whiskey that sold in every speakeasy in New York, got the booze on Long Island beaches from boats brought in by Joe Kennedy. He's worth millions, they say. Why the hell would he get involved in a rinky-dink fight at St. Nick's? He wouldn't. You were trying to scare me into throwing the fight and it was all crap. If you were desperate for cash and told me, maybe I would have considered it. Probably I would not have done it anyway, but scaring me? You should know by now that I don't scare easily.

Yeah, I was too much of a nice guy, Whitebread said, I held back on tossing in what would have made it work.

What Is that?

Rachel.

I stood up from the bench.

I was gonna tell you that if you double-crossed them they would go after your sister with long knives.

I threw down my gloves and grabbed him by the shoulders. Fury was routing blood to my head. If you had brought Rachel into this I told him, I would have punched you from here to Broadway, and kicked your balls into the river.

I felt his thighs closing. His neck was dripping sweat. He was afraid I would knee him right then.

I didn't mention her, did I?

That maybe saved your skin. This was a pro fight, I get paid, you can keep all the money for the dough you lost. Now get the hell out of here while I shower, I don't want to talk about this no more. Not ever.

With his back against the wall he slid towards the door and left. My one true friend. We didn't speak again for a year.

## HARVARD, 1941

Wave after wave of Japanese planes came roaring in in a sneak attack. Ship after ship of the American fleet sank to the bottom of the sea, carrying thousands of our boys to watery deaths. You know all that. A Day of Infamy, FDR famously called it. December 7, 1941.

No American of sentient age will forget that day. The Japanese became Japs. Roosevelt declared war on them and Hitler's Nazis, with Mussolini's Wops tossed in like garlic. Hibernating factories began to roar to rebuild the Navy. The Depression ended. American boys from Maine to California lined up to enlist.

I was not one of them.

Don't get me wrong, I wanted to, it just did not work out that way. I was in my first year at Harvard — law school being only two years back then — this was a Sunday morning, those of us who had stayed out late on Saturday night dates, maybe a dozen, were eating a late breakfast in the cafeteria, when the news came over a radio. Someone turned it louder. At first we were stunned into silence, listening for more details. Then like one person we swallowed the rest of our cornflakes, swigged coffee, hurried from the building, started jogging almost in unison, as if we had been rehearsing this moment for years, jogging to Harvard Yard, which we had decided with a single unified brain would be the most likely place to enlist.

Everyone wanted to be first, I think, in their memories if not in fact, but a group of undergraduates had beaten us there. An Army Major and a Navy Ensign standing near a card table in the sun already were giving instructions. Enlistment centers across the country will be overtaxed today and tomorrow and in the coming days and weeks and maybe months, including those here in Boston, they said. Here is what you need to do. Leave a signed note with the college registrar. Gather your things. And go home. Home to wherever home is for you. Spend a few days with your families and your friends, whom you may not be seeing for a while. Within a few days a recruitment office should be operating in your town, or in the nearest city of any size. You will be given orders on where and when to report for Basic Training.

Banter buzzed under the trees, more students arrived and the two officers began their speeches again. I felt a tapping on my shoulder. It was Professor Lawrence Price, my favorite among the law school faculty, whose most crowded class was Ethics and the Law. Professor, are you here to enlist? I asked. I'm afraid I'm too old for that — at least for now. Fact is I came here to find you, Maisel. To convince you not to enlist.

He led me to a bench in the shade. That's crazy, sir, of course I'm enlisting. Well Maisel, I feel you should think twice. At least listen to what I have to say. My mind was jarred into pinball places. Was my favorite professor a Nazi spy? He did not look Japanese.

Where was I? You're number one in your class, Maisel, the Professor said, and when you graduate in 18 months you'll probably be number one in the school. Enlist now and you will leave Basic Training as a Private First Class. That means you will be shipped to Europe as fodder for Nazi cannons. That sounds awful, I know, but it's true, it will be true until our military can refine plans for a counter-offensive. Which will take a while. I know you are antsy to go fight, believe it or not at 52 I am antsy as you. But listen to me. Graduate first and enlist then. The war will still be going on, I assure you. From Basic Training apply for Officer Candidate School. With your record you will surely be accepted. You'll emerge as a Second Lieutenant. From there you can lead men into battle if that is your desire. But you'll have other options. The Army will need our best brains to win the war, no matter what their professions. Lawyers will not be last on the list. I know it's absurd to plan two years ahead, especially in wartime, but give yourself breathing room, see how the future unfolds. That is all I am suggesting.

How did you come up with this argument for me, sir, in what, two hours?

I was thinking what I would do if I were 20 years younger.

We sat in silence. Professor Price squeezed my knee and walked off. I watched dozens of my classmates whooping and hollering about their coming enlistments as if they were cheering for the maroon and gold. Harvard Yard is a dozen acres of grass and trees, that day December-naked trees; as I walked by myself back to my dorm shuffling through fallen leaves I did not have the spirit to kick them. The triumph of reason over emotion can be a lonely victory.

The next 18 months are mostly devoid of memories. Real estate law and tort law were scant competition for the battle scenes from Europe and the South Pacific that we watched in the weekly newsreels or read of in the daily papers. Most classes were half empty and most of us were bored. To engage my mind I spent most of May and June writing a paper on some small part of America's defenses, and turned it in for extra credit. After 50 years I have no memory of the specifics, but you could say that paper changed my life. Professor Price, impressed by my idea, whatever it was, sent it without my knowledge to the White House. Of all the mail that arrives each day at 1600 Pennsylvania Avenue only about two per cent back then actually reached the desk of the President; my paper was one of them. FDR read it through, then buzzed for his secretary. He told her to contact Harvard Law School and get a message to a senior named Exit Maisel, who, the message said, was invited to stop by the Oval Office in Washington at 2 PM the day after I received my degree. That was just a week away. My head fogged with nervous sweat until I decided the invitation was a joke, what would the President of the United States want with me? By showing me the White House telegram he had received in confirmation, Professor Price convinced me the outrageous invitation was real.

## WASHINGTON, 1943

Despite his grim visage in the newsreels, FDR turned out to be an affable man with a ready smile that often filtered into a Puckish twist. This despite the wheelchair to which polio had confined him, despite two wars raging of which he was despite his useless legs the intellectual epicenter. I arrived at the White House ten minutes early and was ushered to the Oval Office ten minutes late by FDR's personal secretary, Grace something. She pulled open the glass door and I just stood there, unable to move, as if some ancient god had willed me into a statue, as motionless as the President. Until a hand on my lower back edged me forward. I stumbled several steps and was entranced again. Pigs. There were pigs covering the President's huge wooden desk. Not real pigs but carved pigs, enamel pigs, brass pigs, whatever.

Mr. Maisel I believe.

His rotund voice summoned me to the real world. The pigs still were there.

Have a seat Mr. Maisel, congratulations on achieving your law degree.

Thank you, Mr. President.

And thank you for writing this. He held up my war paper. It is thoughtful, well-conceived. I've sent a copy to the War Department to see if they have any use for it.

Thank you, Mr. President.

It made me want to meet you, that is why you are here. I'd like to ask you a few questions, if you don't mind.

Yes, sir. No sir.

Sweat breaking out under my collar.

Mr. Maisel — Exit, that is your first name?

Yes sir, I can explain.

No need, it must be an Ellis Island fabrication, I meet lots of those. Have you thought of changing it?

Not really. I boxed under that name, was pretty lucky, so I decided to stay with it.

A boxer, glad to hear it. That must keep you in pretty good shape. I wanted to tell him I did not box any more but he kept on talking. Now that you have your law degree, Mr. Maisel — Exit — what are your plans?

To go home and kiss my family and enlist.

I thought that might be your answer. You could put up a shingle on Canal Street and let the money role in, but the desire for combat seemed threaded through your prose,unmentioned. So Basic Training will be the first answer. And then what?

Sir?

After Basic, have you thought of applying to Officer Candidate School?

It has been suggested to me.

But you would rather ship out to Europe or the Pacific as a private and take your chances. As opposed to going as an officer.

Well, I haven't really thought about it that much. The delay in getting into combat concerns me.

OCS is 17 weeks, Maisel. I'm sorry to say the war will still be going on when you become a second lieutenant.

Yes, sir.

About combat, Basic will get you started, but I'm told OCS puts you through the wringer physically and mentally as much as two years at the front. Many candidates drop out. Think about it, it's your decision, you still have free will, you haven't enlisted yet. Roosevelt grinned that room-eating smile of his. If you apply and have trouble getting in, which I doubt, let me know, I could make a phone call. Thank you, sir.

At the end of the course, when you're getting your lieutenant's bars, an order will be waiting for you. It will direct you to report within one week to 1600 Pennsylvania Avenue. The school's commander — it may still be Omar Bradley, who invented the program — will not object, the order will be signed by the Commander-in-Chief. Any questions? Yes sir, what will I be doing here? Good question. I have a bug in my ear, Maisel. It hasn't hatched yet — do bugs hatch? — but I'm sure it will before you get here. Then we will both know.

The President removed a cigarette from a white marble box, inserted it into his famous long cigarette holder, lighted up, leaned back in his brocade-covered chair. Exit, if I may, when you first entered the office I believe I saw you look askance at my collection of pigs, is that true? I was just surprised, sir, I might have expected donkeys perhaps. As you can see I do have some donkeys, even a few elephants. But the pigs are a secret. Everyone knows my chief hobby is stamp collecting, I've been photographed inserting a special new stamp into the album many times. I don't recall how the pigs began, or even why it was pigs, but after I bought my first one at a folk market near Warm Springs about five years ago, my friends who saw it began a competition: on their travels, who could bring me as a gift the most distinguished pig. These are just a sample, there are more up in the living quarters, still more at Hyde Park. I have to ask you not to mention them to anyone, though, they are a carefully guarded secret. Why is that, sir? Because in your own Lower East Side it might not go over well. Our neighbors are your biggest supporters, Mr. President, Many of them love you. That's always nice to hear, but would they love me as much with a side of bacon? There are Lower East Sides in every city. I'd rather not find out.

May I ask you, sir, about something else on the desk, that picture frame over there; may I look closer at it? Of course, but please don't leave fingerprints on the glass, Eleanor gives me hell for that. I leaned forward and reached for the frame. It was burgundy colored velvet with gold accents, about 12 inches square with separate photos of Roosevelt's four sons in it, all smiling broadly in their military uniforms. Ah, that is my favorite gift, the President said. The back flap that held it upright could be folded over the front to make a carrying case. I looked inside the flap near the bottom and found a small cut-out, in which were scratched two tiny letters. JM.

Mr. President, my father made this frame! JM it says, for Jacob Maisel. Really? Let me see. Which I did. He smiled looking at the pictures of his handsome sons, murmuring: James — Elliott — Franklin

— John — pressed a buzzer in his desk. Grace he said do you recall the picture frame with all the boys in it, I believe it arrived only a few months ago. One moment sir, his secretary said, then was back on the line. Yes sir, it came in January from New York City. From Mazel Frames. Of course! Do your notes show if I sent an appropriate thank you? Yes sir, a handwritten note; you even asked them to make another just like it, which you plan to give to Eleanor. Thank you Grace, and said to me, how could I forget that, Mazel Frames, what a wonderful idea, your father is not only a fine craftsman but a clever merchandiser, what parents could resist surrounding their boys in the service with a bit of extra luck? Do you speak Yiddish, Mr. President? Oh, just a word here and there, but everyone knows Mazel Tov. He handed the frame to me and I returned it to its place.

This is quite a coincidence, sir. In what way, he asked, stubbing his cigaret in a large glass ashtray. Well, my father sent you this frame, which I did not know, being away at school, and then out of the blue you invite me to the Oval Office, and the frame is here. Isn't that a coincidence?

Well, take it a few steps back. You chose not to enlist the day after Pearl Harbor, as some of your classmates did, but to continue with law school. Had you not done that you would not have written this paper. If you had not, your professor could not have sent it to me. Had he not, I would not have invited you here, you would have not seen your father's frame. So, where does the coincidence begin, how many separate coincidences should we count? I have a theory that coincidence is life's determinant. We accept or endure 101 of them, then we die. I call it Coincidence 101, a terrible name, it sounds like a remedial course at the Vatican, but I have not thought of a better one. Is that like a religion, sir? That's what I am working out. In times of extreme stress it takes my mind off the casualties of war.

You mean when we reach 98 or 99 coincidences in our lives, we will know that death is approaching?

It's not that simple. Because in life we don't know what to count as a single coincidence, or three, or five or whatever, as with you and the picture frame. Not until we reach 101 can we look back and see them strung out behind us like festive cans rattling on a Just-Married car.

How did you arrive at 101, sir?

A good question. There is already a cult that disagrees with that number. The Half-Lifers, they're called, they believe in only 51 coincidences. Many an angry debate has left the matter unsettled. It's like with Jesus and John-the-Baptist. Some ancient texts say Jesus had a brother, even a twin, that John was that brother; its followers argue that since John baptized Jesus, he was the more powerful brother, it is John we should be worshipping. Jesus has of course won the game thus far, but some believe worship of John is gaining on him.

Religion is strange, I offered, weakly.

But the arguments are fun. Pilpul, I believe your rabbis call them. Certainly more useful than brooding about our expected losses come D-Day.

D-Day?

That I cannot talk about. Have a good trip home, Exit, give my personal thanks to your father, let me know of your progress. Excuse me if I don't walk you to the door.

## WASHINGTON, 2012

For decades now the Universal Brain of the Known World has been this thing called Wikipedia. Like a stopped clock it is right at least twice a day. Unfair joke, but I have discovered it to be wrong, or only half right, when it writes about poppy fields. Wikipedia says poppy fields are presided over like conquered fiefdoms by hundreds or even thousands of bees, which land in the poppies late in the afternoon, scratch about until their legs are covered with pollen, which they carry off to fertilize other fields, perhaps in Flanders for all I know. But when I sit with Hallie and enjoy our field I see no bees — alright, perhaps my one-eyed vision no longer is clear enough, but definitely I see butterflies, hundreds of butterflies of every color and mix of colors, mostly Monarchs I think, dancing a few feet above the poppies, perhaps providing distraction for bee enemies — do bees have enemies? — as the alleged bees do their alleged work. Wikipedia in its sometime ignorance does not even mention butterflies in poppy fields, which I take as a personal affront. Especially since as I have mentioned it was Hallie who planted the poppies with her own hands and invited the butterflies to live on our property. I know of course as she sits beside me and holds my hand that she is long gone, but we watch and enjoy and discuss the butterflies some afternoons or evenings as if there were no threaded cloth of not-life hanging between us. She knows as I do the function of the butterflies, which Wikipedia apparently does not. Once the bees if they even exist have buzzed off to the wilderness the butterflies flutter lower and in the setting sun dance just above the fat round blossoms, whose protective petals fold over them, fuzzy, like blankets Mama made. Snug and relaxed the butterflies inhale not pollen but memories. Or electrons of memories. These at dawn they deposit into my waiting hippocampus. How this transfer is executed remains one of the unsolved mysteries in the science of memory, despite Dr. Brian White's patient attempts to solve it. He even flirted with asking Dr. Einstein at Princeton for any thoughts he might have. But Einstein's views were aimed more at the stars.

## WASHINGTON, 1944

The pigs still paraded across the President's desk, the four-photo frame still peered proudly above them when Second Lieutenant Exit Maisel fresh out of OCS reported as ordered to the White House. In the Oval Office he saluted the President, who returned his salute quickly with a fleeting flick of his hand, without standing, and motioned Exit to a chair. You're looking fit, Lieutenant, the President said, but what happened to your eye? When I was in uniform I realized from the looks on their faces that people assumed I had tragically been shot squarely and heroically in the eye during some epic battle whose tale would be told and retold tearfully until the end of time. Written by some godlike Homer.

In truth, it had not been like that. The last day at OCS was track and field day, for relaxation. The last event was the high hurdles. Racing down the track, I heaved myself upward. But someone had left a small rock on the dark earth near the last hurdle. As I leaped. my foot landed on the rock, my body twisted, I caromed smack into the wood. My right eye drove at full speed into the corner of the hurdle. It hurt like hell, Sir.

I can imagine. How long will you have to wear that patch?

Forever, Sir.

What! Doesn't Bradley have doctors out there, wherever the hell that camp is.

Yes, Sir. I thought the eye doctor, Captain Reed, was very good. She said the eyeball was hanging on my cheek by a thread.

She?

She had only two choices, she said. To stuff the whole eye back into the socket and sew my eyelid closed to keep it there. Which risked an infection some day. Or to remove the damaged eye and put in a glass one. Either could be covered with a patch. With the first option I might feel handicapped, she said. With the second, the patch, I could play pirate with the young ladies. Her words Mr. President. Either way that eye will no longer function, she said.

Did Bradley say an honorable discharge was in order?

No, Sir. Since I was already assigned to the White House he said he would leave that up to you. Sir.

Damn. I know how eager you are for combat, Lieutenant. But I can't send you into battle with one good eye. Not fair to anyone. On the other hand, we're going to need every able man and able brain we can enlist. I'm going to keep you in the Army, but you'll be limited to non-combat roles. Hell, I'm going to win this war without legs. You certainly can help me with one eye. Do you agree?

Yes, Sir, Mr. President.

Good. A week's home leave is standard after OCS. Be back here in six days and we'll settle you in.

Thank you, Sir.

Despite your eye — on the very last day! — I gather you enjoyed the program, given that you were named tops in the class. Enjoyed is not the word I would choose, Mr. President, excuse the language but it was a bitch. So I have heard, Mr. Roosevelt said, directly from General Bradley; if it were not a bitch, he told me, it would be of little use in winning the war. Do you agree with that assessment?

I'm in no position to say, Sir. Well, who would be in a better position to judge, Lieutenant, than a fellow who won the ten mile scramble over spiky hill and muddy dale dragging a dangling eye and an almost fractured leg. Do you have spies everywhere, Mr. President? That's the essence of my job, Captain.

Excuse me Sir, the silver on my shoulders is bars, not stars.

Until now, Exit. But while you were away that bug in my ear finally hatched. What it told me was that when you leave this office today you will be a Captain.

I don't understand, Sir.

I'm the Commander-in-Chief. I can do that. Now don't get excited, you will not be happy with the assignment I'll be giving you.

Not possible, Mr. President.

Hear me out, Maisel. I will not be sending you to lead a division into combat along the Rhine or anywhere else. I suspect that is what you expected before the accident.

Well, yes, Sir.

That would not be my decision to make in any case. Some field major's or such. You see, I am right, you are not happy. But listen to what you already know. The task on the battlefield is with tanks and artillery and rifles to take an enemy town or hold an enemy hill. The job of the President is to climb over the blood and guts of others until we win the war. I want you here in the White House helping me do that. Does that sound awful?

No Sir, of course not, whatever you say, Sir.

Exactly. That comes with this desk. By the way, did you thank your father for this beautiful frame?

Yes sir, he was most honored.

Good. Now to get on with this. It deals with the unfortunately true cliché that most generals want to fight the last war. Only natural. I'm afraid I have witnessed much of that in our own War Councils. So, how do we change that logical tendency? The bug in my ear, after much itching and scratching, told me the way to do that was to seek the advice of younger officers. But they would have little experience, I told the bug. No matter, the bug replied, they will have clearer, unfettered minds, fresh ideas, a new way of looking at the problems of the battlefield. Lieutenant, I do not know if this is true. But between us I hope to find out. For that purpose I am appointing you my military attaché. As such you will accompany me to all meetings of the War Council. The top brass would look askance at a second lieutenant sitting in, but if I bump you up two ranks to Captain they will not object. That is your rank as of now.

But Sir. . .

I remind you I am the Commander-in-Chief. Do you have a problem with that?

No, Sir.

Thank you, Sir.

The President waved Captain Maisel to the door.

In the outer office Grace, a sturdy blond woman, called him over. I have something for you, Captain. She was controlling a smile. In this envelope is a copy of your promotion papers. The original is already on file at the War Department. Yes ma'am. In this box are silver stars, I assume you know what to do with them. Yes, ma'am. Would you like me to put them on for you? That's not necessary. Well, I think it is, like a small celebration. She stood from behind her desk in her military brown blouse and skirt and came around and unpinned my brass second lieutenant's bars and slipped them into my pocket. She affixed the gleaming stars to my epaulettes. Too bad we don't have music she said, something to make the day memorable. I suppose this will have to do. She extended up on her toes and kissed my cheek.

One day while on leave Exit stood looking out the window at the familiar street; nothing had changed since they moved in. But across the street this day he saw Whitebread standing, leaning against the wall, wearing a sweat shirt, cradling a basketball. He lived with his family a few blocks away on Henry Street, was this a concession of some kind? Exit pulled on a light jacket, went outside, sat on the tenement steps, not looking at Whitebread or calling out to him. For a time Whitebread looked the other way. Then nonchalantly be began bouncing the ball, bounced it as he crossed the street, carried it onto the sidewalk a few feet from Exit. You feel like a pickle? The first words expressed between them in more than a year.

Did he feel like a pickle? Maybe later, after we shoot some hoops.

Whitebread cradling the ball sat on the tenement stoop beside him. Neither had anything to say. Finally Whitebread spoke, trying to sound casual. I hear Rachel is getting married. That's nice.

His voice did not sound as if he thought it was nice.

Saturday night. He just finished Basic with the Navy. He ships out Sunday to go kill Hirohito.

That's nice, Whitebread repeated. His voice sounded weak, uncertain. You think it's a good idea they get married before he ships out? Not wait till he comes back?

Why should they do that?

You know. In case . . .

Whitebread, in love there's no in case.

That sounds like a song title.

It does. Maybe I'll write it.

Decision time, Exit thought, more of this bullshit or should we be honest friends again? He turned slightly. Listen, I know you like her. She likes you, too, or she wouldn't have hung out on Henry Street so much. But there's liking and there's liking.

Yeah, tell me about it. Who's the guy?

Name is Steven Gold. She met him at Columbia. A champion fencer.

A fencer? La di da. Sounds kind of effete.

You think Rachel would fall for someone effete?

Whitebread scraped his sneaker along the cement. She's really in love, huh? I wonder what makes that happen.

God, I guess.

You still believe in God, after what they say is happening in Germany, in Poland?

I don't know. Who the fuck knows?

Yeah, who the fuck knows? What does your father say when he comes home from schul?

What the rabbis always say. Mysterious Ways.

Yeah, mysterious ways. Them Ways got a whole lot to explain these days. A whole lot of ovens. A whole lot of smokestacks. A whole lot of smoke in the sky, from what I hear.

Whitebread bounced the ball as they walked the two blocks to the schoolyard. Exit bounced a different memory, the night months ago when Rachel told him she had become engaged. He's a good looking guy Exit had said. How do you know? We met him the same time, in the Columbia gym, don't you remember? Rachel nodded, threaded her long fingers along the spread on his bed where they were sitting. Something wrong? She continued to toy with the spread, studying it as if Athena the goddess of weaving still was working on it. Exit, in my entire life I've told you only one lie, that's not too bad, is it? Not even a real lie, just a sort of misrepresentation.

He waited.

That time in the gym. I wasn't really there by accident, or following you. I came to watch Steve practice. We'd been dating for a month already.

Her fingers moved from the spread to smooth her green and black Scotch plaid skirt, which framed her waist like a poppy in bloom, beneath a light blue sweater. I don't know why I didn't tell you then. I guess I was afraid you wouldn't like him. Or would think I was too young. You always thought I was too young.

As they reached the schoolyard he breathed deeply. He had not been a player in an unconscious twisted girlish psyche after all. Thank God.

## Washington, 1945

FDR was dead, and the nation cried. He was in his unthinkable fourth term. Had he lived they would have elected him again, again, they would have elected him King if he had wanted. Like Washington, he would have turned them down.

After all these years it seems as if he died the day after he made me a Captain. But that was not so, I attended at least two War Council meetings, though what was talked about is long gone. His doctors noticed he had been looking wan and weak; they ordered him to rest. He went by train to his favorite retreat, in Warm Springs Georgia. One day he complained of a severe headache. Then he collapsed. He died of

a cerebral hemorrhage. He was 63 years old. To much of the nation he
had seemed immortal. Zeus does not die, neither would FDR.

A train brought his casket to Washington, the tracks lined with
hundreds of thousands of folks paying tribute as it chugged by. The
funeral was small, in the East Room of the White House, which holds
only 200 people, so only his family and friends and Eleanor's family
and friends and leaders in the Senate and the House and on the Court,
and the top military brass, were invited. I was not, but stood outside
the door as the people filed in, many with tears in their eyes, though
not Eleanor, who was being stoic as always. Their four sons were away
at war. Missy LeHand, his long time assistant, had died of a stroke
in 1944. As the chief usher was closing the door after the last of the
guests, I slipped in. Glancing at my Captain's dress uniform he did not
stop me. I stood at the rear and listened to encomiums and prayers.
The words are lost to me and most likely to history. His body did
not lie in state but was shipped to the family manor in Hyde Park for
burial. What is not lost to me is the overweening experience of being
one of the pallbearers of FDR. Even though I was not.

It is a dream, my helping to carry his coffin. But it is a recurring
dream, evincing itself once a year at least, in full color and multiple
senses, the leaves on the trees turning within the dream from green to
maple red, the country road smelling of asphalt and horse droppings
and apple pies being baked in his honor in nearby cottages, distant
dogs barking, bronze statues standing on either side of the gate to
the estate, or just outside it, one of Missy LeHand, FDR's aide for
more than 20 years, the other of Eleanor's secretary Lucy Mercer, his
mistress from an earlier time who had returned to his side at Warm
Springs in the days before he died, more statues along the path to the
family cemetery, his Uncle Theodore, Presidents Wilson, Lincoln,
Washington, Mr. Churchill, Benjamin Disraeli, sometimes Dr. Einstein,
sometimes Oppenheimer. How these had been selected, by FDR
himself or by Eleanor or by my own hippocampus I cannot say, they
were visible only in my dream.

Years later I visited Hyde Park with Hallie and we took one of the
public tours. In a re-creation of his Oval Office the picture frame
my father had made for him, including the photos of his sons in
uniform, stood on his desk right where it had been during his life. Mrs.
Roosevelt left her own private office to greet us, which did not surprise
me much; Rachel was by then her chief assistant. We winked, subtly,
but maintained decorum until Mrs. Roosevelt left; then, like thirsty
birds, we flew together and hugged, after a moment Hallie joining

in. My wife and my sister loved one another, which was the joy of my middle years, Rachel even lending us her twins at times.

But I did not get it right. I did not convey, as I meant to do, the essence of what it had been like to carry FDR's casket. Things visible beside the road did not matter, what mattered, what signified, was mostly internal, mostly invisible. A feeling of exaltation that coursed through my body, my uplifted arms, as if it had replaced my platelets. The weightlessness of his casket, though he was not a small man, weightlessness as demonstrated later by the astronauts in space, except this was not reflective of the absence of gravity — my shoulders, my legs, still felt their earthly pull; only the casket floated. Soft music was playing, by musicians never seen, as if, like Hamlet, flights of angels were singing him to his rest. We walked up a gentle incline, though the road beneath us was level, until the casket itself sprung wings, delicate, white, and carried their weightless burden to the clouds. We could not speak, could only read, four words floating high above us in scentless white smoke: This Was a Man.

I always woke then.

## WASHINGTON, 2017

Cold lobster salad. Along with curled raw carrots, Italian breadsticks, iced tea. Ambassador Maisel was pleased, he knew Madam President's favorite lunch in her private dining room was green chile enchiladas, with the chile gruesomely hot. But she knew his stomach at times was unreasonable and she had bowed to that. Tough as she could be in foreign policy, her relations with individuals were warm and considerate.

"I've been reading about the Presidents," Madame President said, spreading her white cloth napkin, embossed WH, on her lap. "'The top-ranked three, according to most historians, are of course Washington and Lincoln, in whichever order, and FDR. But after that there's no consensus. Popular opinion would appear to favor Jefferson or Teddy Roosevelt, with Republicans pushing Ronald Reagan."

Swallowing a sip of tea, the Ambassador choked slightly.

"Is that an editorial comment?"

"That purple pantsuit you're wearing is my favorite color on you."

"Good. I'm glad that's settled." She bit the end off a breadstick. "As I told you on the phone, I'm deep into a biography of Truman. He might be my candidate for number four. That's who I want to learn more about, stuff that's not in the history books."

"Well, you've come to the right place."

"That's what I figured," the President said. Both dug into their lobster salads. "Hmm, good," they murmured together, mouths still partly full. They nodded, grinned. "Are you paying your chef enough?"

"I certainly hope so. I would hate to lose him to Trumpf Tower."

Exit smiled. He loved these last-minute invitations, even if there was no crisis at hand. They made him feel younger, as if he were still in the game. Especially if the weather was nice.

"You were with Truman his entire eight years. Or almost eight years."

"In one capacity or another."

He chewed on a carrot stick. "May I begin at the beginning?"

"Of course. My sister took the kids to the zoo. My afternoon is free. So far."

He wondered if they might have time for a game of croquet — he had noticed a new court on the back lawn — but he soon was caught up in April of 1945.

"The history books tell us Harry Truman was calm, mild, considerate, not the least bit self-important. All of which is true, all of which are rare traits in a politician, as you know. In a novel he might blend in with the wallpaper. But two things made him different. History, which stretched him to the heights, and something known to very few: his temper. He rarely displayed it in public, but he could cut loose with the sting of a scorpion."

"Really! 'The little haberdasher from Missouri.' He never even went to college, I read. That surprised me."

"In his case it was no loss. He had quiet convictions simmering inside, mostly for the betterment of the common man. But about his temper — it exploded within minutes after I met him."

"How awful!"

"Luckily, it was not directed at me. As soon as he was sworn in, his new chief of staff wanted my desk spot for an aide, so they moved me to a small office four doors down, not much bigger than a cubby hole, I had to duck my head to enter. No matter. I did not get to meet the new President for almost two weeks. He had more important things on his plate of course. Then around quitting time one day he summoned me, introduced himself. He seemed at once calm and somehow strained. 'Please close the door and sit,' he said. 'Captain,' he said. 'I am going to use you as a sounding board. I hope you do not mind.'

"Whatever you say, sir."

"He told me he was usually a calm fellow, with a mellow Missouri temperament, I think those were his words. 'I don't know if I am up to this job,' he said, 'but Fate has chosen me to be up to it. And so I will. But I will need the help of everyone around me.'

"'Yes, sir.' That's when I began to wonder what I had done wrong.

"'I am talking about my generals,' he said. He did not name them. 'Captain Maisel, I have been President of the United States for 11 days. Eleven days, Captain. Yet just two hours ago I was informed by the generals that for two years, in secret, our top scientists have been working out West somewhere to create a bomb so powerful it will immediately end the war with Japan. And that they expect it to be ready for testing in July. As Vice President I knew nothing of this. Perhaps that was FDR's decision, I do not know why. But now I am the President. Their Commander-in-Chief. And it took them 11 days to inform me.'

"His chest was rifling in deep breaths. 'Eleven' — if you will excuse the expression, Madame, '11 effing days before they let me know. That was insubordination! I cannot tolerate behavior like that. I ought to have stripped them of their stars immediately. But I did not do that, that would be no way to begin my relationship with the Army.'

"'No, sir,' I said.

"'Because I did not fire them, you are bearing the brunt of my anger. It had to go somewhere. I am sorry about that, Captain.'

"He was stalking about the office, still furious, trying to calm himself. 'If I can't trust my generals, who can I trust? Anyone? FDR appears to have trusted you, Captain, inviting you to sit in on War Council meetings. Let me ask you directly: Will I receive from you the same loyalty that President Roosevelt did?'

"'Absolutely, Mr. President.'

"He picked up some papers from his desk, glanced at them, tossed them.

"'Good. I shall take you at your word. I have an assignment for you.' The assignment was staggering. He wanted me to go out to Los Alamos and be his eyes and ears there. He wanted reports he could trust on the progress of this project, or the lack of progress. He didn't want to be consumed by doubts. 'Perhaps I am being paranoid,' he said, 'which is not in my nature. But those 11 days of unexplained silence have given me good reason.'

"He stopped pacing and took several deep breaths. 'By morning you will have top security clearance, to wander at large through the Manhattan Project, as they are calling it. As my military aide, you will attach yourself to Dr. Oppenheimer, who heads the scientific side of things. And report to me in coded messages. According to the generals, on the success of this project depends the lives of perhaps a million of your fellow servicemen. Keep that in mind at all times.'

"'I will, Mr. President.'

"It's curious. I kept calling him that in order to buck up his courage. Me, Exit Maisel from the Lower East Side of New York. Later I realized it was not courage he needed, he had plenty of that. Just momentary reassurance, perhaps."

A light knock on the door. A White House waiter entered, carrying a tray of chocolates, which he set on the table between them before topping off their tea and taking their plates.

"That was quite a diatribe I just spewed on you, Julia. I hope it was not too much."

"No, it was fascinating."

"One other important thing. How modest Truman was. He never cared about getting credit, as long as things got done. The best example being the Marshall Plan, the most humanitarian project ever undertaken by the U.S. government. You know the basics. Most of western Europe had been reduced to rubble during the war. General Marshall thought it would be in our own interests, as well as a great deed, for us to help them rebuild — which of course is not the normal action of conquerors. Truman loved the idea, told the General to develop such a program. It went on for years, at a cost of untold billions, and was a brilliant success. Another President might have put his name to it, but not Truman. It never became the Truman Plan, though he had authorized it. It was the Marshall Plan, from beginning to end. And will be down through history."

"Do you think he approved the plan out of guilt for using the A-bomb?"

"I don't think so, Julia. I really don't think he felt guilt about that. He believed it had to be done, he did it, and put it out of his mind. But he did have a practical motive for the Marshall Plan beyond making the U.S. a saint."

"If we did not rebuild Europe the Communists would move in."

"Exactly."

Both of them sampled the chocolates and washed them down with tea.

"How do I remember Truman's exact words, or nearly so? I have discovered through the years that there are certain moments, scenes in life that sear your soul, that remain embedded in your brain like scar tissue. For better or worse. For me his explosion, letting his hair down in front of me, was one of them. There are several more, but I'll save those for another day. If you are interested."

"Absolutely," the President said, neatly folding her WH napkin.

*Impish hippocampus can be iconic. (A word in fashion these days to the point of irony.) Take the atomic bomb. When memory asserts itself I see not Oppie and the scores of other scientists hard at work creating it at windy Los Alamos. Not the long curving drive down to Trinity Site, where they will test the bomb — Fat Man or Little Boy, I forget which was first — being hauled across the desert on a truck. Not the thin steel tower on which it was to be mounted along with the invisible hope that it would not explode prematurely — a hope of the men installing it, who could be vaporized by a short circuit or a loose bolt but also the ignorant hope of an entire country unaware of its existence. Nor was my image that of the brightest explosion known to man, which we witnessed, wearing dark glasses, from eight miles away. Not even the devastation served upon Hiroshima, on Nagasaki. No, the droll hippo each time sends to my brain only the clichéd image of the mushroom cloud, which has stamped itself like an American trademark, like* ARM & HAMMER, *upon the war; on what some fear will be the future. It has become iconic, this atomic mushroom. Much more widely known than the words alongside it, the words of one of its creators, who when the explosion and the mushroom cloud blotted out the sky for miles in every direction, said: "Now we're sons of bitches."*

*Much as it tries, the hippocampus is not very good at comedy.*

## NEW YORK, 1943

*If not you, it will be someone else.*

It was not the lobster salad that kept him awake, as at first he believed; it was those eight words, lit up in his hippocampus as if in blue neon.

If not you it will be someone else.

He had come home the summer between his two years at Harvard Law. He'd heard that Whitebread was working at Gristede's, the biggest supermarket in the neighborhood, and he walked over to see him. Whitebread was not there, he was "out with the wagon." A moment later he heard the hooves of a slow-moving horse on the cobblestones; a horse and wooden wagon with large wooden wheels came to a stop in the alley beside the store. Whitebread jumped off. They shook hands. Exit asked what was going on.

"I tried to enlist," Whitebread said. "The doc said I had a heart murmur. There was nothing to worry about he said, there was nothing they could do about it, but it disqualified me from joining the Army. So I took a job here. The whole neighborhood shops here. But I knew from my mother that it was not convenient. At first she would come and buy her fresh vegetables for the week, but the bags were too heavy to carry seven blocks and her back started hurting. She had to cut her list, shop twice a week, or three times. I figured many of the customers must be doing this, so I took an idea to Mister Grjstede. Why not get a horse and a wagon, pile the wagon with crates of oranges and apples, cauliflower and broccoli, carrots, onions, peaches, cherries, whatever. Bring the store to the customers. He liked the idea, agreed to try it as an experiment. I think he rented the wagon and the horse at first. He assigned me to be the driver."

Whitebread began removing empty, fresh-smelling crates from the wagon as he talked, replacing them with crates full of vegetables.

"Well, turns out I'm a genius. The Einstein of Cauliflower. As I drove the wagon slowly through the streets, stopping every few minutes, the ladies began pouring out of the tenements. By the second day they were lining up. They didn't have to pack their bags too heavy, because I would be back tomorrow, and the day after. Every day but Saturday. Mr. Gristede gave me a nice raise, bought two more wagons and horses and hired two more guys, to cover the whole Lower East Side. His profits doubled, then tripled, I heard. C'mon, ride with me, I have to go out again, Friday is my busiest day."

When Whitebread climbed up behind the horse, a dappled gray swayback, Exit circled to the other side and vaulted up beside him. With the light tap of a whip Whitebread moved the horse and wagon into the street. "I can't believe this," Exit said. "My best buddy: the Icarus of Broccoli. Do you like it?"

"What I like best is the horses. Brushing them down, watering them, tying on feed bags. I even talk to them."

"Do they listen?"

"Depends if I have new jokes."

With the wagon stopped in front of tenements on both sides of the street Whitebread jumped down to help the customers bag the produce they wanted, write up their bills with a pencil stub on a small yellow pad, wish them a good Shabbos, move on to the next customer, the next tenement, the next street.

A blanket of gray clouds had moved in over the city. "What happens when it rains? Exit asked. "I get wet," Whitebread said.

"Perhaps you should invent the raincoat, or the umbrella."

"I think Einstein already did that."

Exit realized the street looked familiar; they were in front of his own building. Women came hurrying out to the wagon. He thought Bubbie might be among them, but didn't see her.

"This is my stop," I said, and hopped off the wagon.

"Shoot some hoops tomorrow?" Whitebread asked across the wagon bed. "It's my one day off." Exit said, "I'll come by around noon. Good luck with the job." He petted the ivy flank of the horse. "I've got a better idea, though. Run this nag at Aqueduct."

Whitebread grinned. Exit leaped onto the stoop and into the tenement and unlocked the door to the apartment. His father as he did every Friday would wash up at the frame shop and walk directly to shul. Rachel had said she'd be spending the night with a friend. He heard the bathroom door open and knew it was Bubbie. Except it was not Bubbie. His mouth hanging open, he gaped at the barefoot young woman pulling the belt of a yellow bathrobe tight around her wet body, tugging at her blond curls. It was Celine. He had not seen her looking so beautiful for years, not since they arrived in America.

"What's the matter, don't you recognize me?" she asked.

He was too stunned to speak, to move. She approached him, took his hand in hers, kissed him lightly on the cheek. "You look as if you miss your Bubbie," she said.

"No, I . . . it's just that . . ."

"I'm so young?"

"You're so . . . beautiful."

She smiled slightly. "I was waiting for you. We need to talk." Still holding his hand she led him down the hallway to his room. She sat on his bed, patted the place beside her. He sat like an obedient child, his mind running he knew not where. She took his hand again, rubbed his knuckles. He felt his manhood stirring. He touched her wig. "When did you get this?" he asked.

"The wig? A long time ago. Right after my hair was shorn. I put it on sometimes when no one is home."

"And do what?"

"Put on nylon stockings instead of brown cotton ones. Look in the mirror. To see if I am still alive."

'Then what?'

"Usually I wash the floor."

He bit his lip, felt his heart rate speeding. She carried his hand inside the top of her robe, pressed it to her breast. He gasped.

"Celine, we can't . . ." He did not remove his hand.

She placed a finger on his lips, leaned forward, kissed him lightly, then harder. He tried to hold back his feelings. It was difficult. He broke away.

"Celine, this is not right. You're my . . ."

"What? Your Bubbie? Your grandmother? You know I'm not your grandmother. Not your mother, either." She was trying to slow her breathing. She put her fingers on his lips when he started to speak. "Listen to me," she said. "Just listen to me. I'm very grateful to Jacob. I always will be. For marrying me after your mother . . . disappeared. For bringing us all to America two goose-steps ahead of Hitler. I will stay with him always for that. But when we married I did not know about Bubbie. Not until we arrived here. Would I have come if I knew? I suppose. What was my other choice? Still, it was a shock. But your father is the man of the house, I owe him, so Bubbie came to life, and Celine mostly died. It's silliness. It's all about stupid tradition, what the neighbors would think. He's stubborn that way. But the obvious thing is he is not happy with Bubbie, Mazel Frames is his only joy now. Where he spends all his time. Celine could have made him happy."

Sweat broke out on her forehead, tears clouded her eyes. "You go back to Harvard in six weeks, am I right?"

"And after that into the Army."

"See, that's perfect." Now tears hung on her cheeks. "There will be no time for us to fall in love." She touched his face, kissed his lips again. Her tongue found its way into his mouth. At first he resisted, then he sucked on it, hard, before pulling away.

"I can't, Celine. I'm too conflicted."

"About your father? He will never know. Look at it this way. If not you, it will be someone else."

The words etched themselves into his chest as with a blade. If not you it will be someone else. "I am twenty-seven years old," she said. "I must have a life."

Her face pressed into his shoulder. He felt her fingers roaming his belly, inside his shorts. Ferociously kissing her hair — her wig — he no longer felt conflicted. Or so he told himself.

## GERMANY, 1947

3,970.

That's how many B-29s had been produced by Boeing under contract with the U.S. Air Force. The total cost exceeded by well over a billion dollars the entire expenditure on the Manhattan Project. Each Superfortress, as they had been nicknamed, cost several million dollars. They were the only planes in the world large enough and heavy enough to carry an atomic bomb. What should be done with these bombers after the war? You did not melt them down into bobby pins.

After President Truman ordered the dropping of Little Boy on Hiroshima, of Fat Man on Nagaski, after the Japanese surrendered, ending the war, after the jubilation of tens of millions Americans celebrating across the country — the boys would be coming home! — that was one of the questions taken up by the War Council: What to do with all those B-29s.

Several hundred had been lost during the war. Scores would be kept in combat readiness, some at bases in the U.S., others at bases in England, France, smaller allied nations. As a deterrent against whom? Japan's military, under the surrender treaty, no longer existed. Germany was in ruins, as was most of Europe.

"Our friends the Russians," the President allowed. "They had hoped to occupy all of Germany when the war ended, turn it into a Soviet state. We did not permit that, as you know. Since then they have not been acting very friendly in diplomatic talks. But that's only a possible concern down the road. Devastated by hardships, by their loss of sons and fathers and brothers in fighting off the Nazis, the Russian people are as sick of war as all of us. And the whole world knows that only we have the bomb. But let's get back to the B-29s."

General Archer, with the Air Force, presented the plan they were working on. "Moth balls. Storage. That's all we can logically do until they are made obsolete by future technology. Some of which is already on the drawing boards. This will take up ground space, but we have plenty of it out there in the west, in the deserts of New Mexico and Arizona. We propose storing the B-29's at the lowest cost possible, by covering parts of the desert with cheap asphalt, with simple runways."

"You'll need electricity from generators hundreds of miles away," Navy Admiral Birch said. "Poles, wiring, transmitters. That's a lot of manpower, not to mention the costs."

"We're planning to keep it simple," General Archer said. "A few generators for runway lights, if nighttime takeoffs are needed. Which is not anticipated. Remember, this is just for storage."

Listening to all this, Captain Exit Maisel, sitting beside the President, taking notes, felt antsy. He had never spoken at a War

Council meeting, under FDR's instructions. He had assumed the same rule applied under President Truman. But now he felt he could not hold back.

"May I say something, Mr. President?"

The President's eyebrows rose for just a moment. "Of course, Captain." The others looked at Exit with apparent amusement or with knitted brows.

"With all due respect, gentlemen, isn't that asking for another Pearl Harbor?"

A buzz of comments, most of it soto voce, circled the large table. To Maisel it sounded derisive.

"How so?" the President asked.

"Granted, as you said earlier, Sir, we are speaking now of a hypothetical enemy.
But if this enemy wanted to launch a surprise attack, as the Japanese did in 1941, its spy planes would photograph the essence of our Air Force nestled together on the ground like sitting ducks. A few squadrons of fighter-bombers could take them out in an hour. Maybe less. With no fighters nearby to take them down.

"That's nonsense," General Archer responded.

"So was Pearl Harbor," Maisel said. "Until it happened. In half an hour our Navy was gone."

"Not all of our Navy," Admiral Birch put in.

"Most of it," Exit said.

"You're speaking like an eye-witness, Captain," the Admiral said. "I was there. May I ask where you were on that terrible day?"

Exit reddened. He took off his cap, wiped his now sweaty forehead with his sleeve, replaced the cap. Trying not to sound sheepish, he told them, "I was in law school." Which was greeted by a round of hearty laughter. Except for the President. He cut the laughter short by saying, "I shall take this discussion under advisement. What's next on the agenda?"

When the meeting broke up the President nodded Exit toward the Oval Office and closed the door. "Don't mind the others," he said, taking his seat behind his desk. It was not as big as Roosevelt's had been. With no room for pigs. Or frames, for that matter. "They've all been through a long, grueling war. They don't want a young whippersnapper telling them their business. They all could use an extended vacation. You saw what the war did to FDR."

"Whippersnapper?"

"Not a New York word? Just a joke. I'm glad you spoke your mind, Captain. But I do have a question. Given your valid objection to the plan on the table, what would you suggest instead?"

"It's very simple, Sir. It's much the same plan. Just scatter these temporary storage fields around the country. Not only in the southwest, but in the south, the west, the northwest, even the midwest. Enough so that no surprise attack could be successful. Near existing active bases when possible."

"Wouldn't that cost more than the Air Force plan?"

"A bit, I suppose. But not more than the cost of two or three B-29s, I suspect."

The President nodded, pressed his fingers together like a church steeple. "I will have them look into it," he said. "Thank you for your input. I have to read some cables now. Just two more little things. Bess has asked me to invite you upstairs for dinner some night. Would tomorrow evening work for you?"

"I would be honored, Sir."

"Good. The other thing is, the next time you have to explain that you were in law school, you should say 'Harvard Law.' You might get to complete your thought that way."

Grinning, Exit left the Oval Office and walked down the hall wanting to kick his heels together. Not a very New York idea, he thought; and at 26 he was much too old for that.

When FDR took him on as military attaché he had rented a small garden apartment within walking distance. He retained the apartment under President Truman. On occasional train trips to Prince Street to visit his father and Whitebread and Rachel and Steven Gold, who had moved uptown with their twin babies, and Uncle Joshua, he greeted Bubbie/Celine with a kiss, an impassioned kiss if they happened to be alone. But nothing more than that. His father had never learned of his summer of happiness tinged, for Exit, with guilt; he intended to keep it that way. Jacob and Bubbie were still together in at least superficial contentment, his father perhaps married to prospering Mazel Frames. He never asked Celine if after he returned to school that summer there had been or still was someone else; perhaps a long line of someone else's. He did not want to know.

## A NEW ASSIGNMENT

President Truman summoned him to the Oval Office. The President was leaning forward in his chair as he tend to do unconsciously in times of crisis. "I see by your file you speak fluent German, is that still current?"

"Yes, sir."

"Any other languages?"

"Just a bit of Yiddish from childhood."

"That's fine, it's the German that's important."

"Sir?"

"After two years of peace, trouble is brewing in Germany. I can feel it in my bones. Also see it in the intelligence reports."

"Sir?"

"As the war wound down the Red Army was liberating concentration camps in Poland and the eastern part of Germany — aside from the unspeakable things their troops were doing to defenseless German women, many of whom had been made widows by the war. Uncle Joe Stalin hoped to occupy all of post-war Germany, as he did Poland, Austria and the like. We said no. As you know, Germany was partitioned into four zones. Berlin, the capitol, was also partitioned that way — but Berlin was situated deep in the Russian zone. Stalin was irritated from the beginning by being forced to have bits of the West functioning within East Germany. It was an itch he always wanted to scratch; maybe it kept him up at night. We have reason to believe from intercepted cables that he is planning some action soon. This concerns you, Captain — this is off the record — because Ambassador Clifford is not well. His doctors have urged him to resign and get away from the pressure. So far he has chosen not to do so. He's a good man, I don't want to call him home against his will. But if Stalin makes trouble I want someone there to ease Clifford's burden. That will be you, Captain. I'd like you to keep a second uniform and a suitcase of necessaries in your office, so you can leave on a moment's notice should that become necessary."

"Will do, Mr. President."

I did not have long to wait. Intelligence on Soviet troop and equipment movements suggested they planned to blockade all roads, canals and railways leading to West Berlin, blocking deliveries of coal, food, paper, everything. This was probably about two weeks away, but could happen at any time.

"General LeMay says he could blast through any blockade with no trouble," the President told me. "But what if the Russians respond with real force? I don't think Stalin wants to start World War III, with us having the bomb. But giving LeMay his head could lead to that. So

I vetoed his plan. But we still need to supply Berlin for at least a few weeks, somehow, until Stalin backs off."

The President had hung his suit jacket over the back of his chair and was working in shirt-sleeves. This was unusual for him.

"Could it be done by air, Sir? With all those B-29s sitting in mothballs?"

"Good thinking, Captain. This time I'm a step ahead of you. I've already talked with the Air Force. It seems B-29s are extremely heavy in order to carry the A-bomb, and loaded with so much gunnery that there is not much room in them for supplies. We have a new troop transport rolling off the assembly lines, the C-54, which they think would work. We've shipped several to England already. This morning I've ordered a speed-up of production on the C-54 and increased the original contract. But the first thing we need to do is figure out how many tons of what supplies we'd have to fly into Berlin each day, each week. General William Tunner, who supervised the airlift over the Hump to China during the war, is on his way to Templehof to oversee the delivery set-up. The Embassy says they've got a Warrant Officer who's a whiz at statistics; he should be making calculations as we speak. I'd like you to get there quickly to help Ambassador Clifford. Could you leave this evening?"

"Ready to go at any time, Sir. Might I make one suggestion?"

"Shoot."

"You might want to send a few B-29s to England anyway — in case of war."

"Or perhaps to discourage war. I just might do that, Captain." He pushed up the cuff of his left sleeve and looked at his watch. "There's a plane leaving Andrews for France at 8:30 tonight. They'll adjust their flight plan to drop you in Berlin before circling back to Paris."

Adrenaline rushing, I stood and threw him a crisp salute. His answering reply seemed weary — and the project had not nearly begun. "Be safe, Exit Maisel," he said. As if sending an only son and his eye patch into battle.

## GERMANY, 1948

*Bellevuestraße. Bremer Weg. Eberstraße. Behrenstraße.* The street names in Berlin were not exactly the same but in sound took him back to his childhood in Vienna, mostly pleasant days, learning so much in the schools — learning new things always made him happy — explaining them to Rachel who absorbed his every word, dinners

with her and their parents, watching Jacob perfect new magic tricks while Merele practiced ballet leaps — she had taken a class once — until his mother disappeared and his father began banging his head on the iron skillet for no reason ever explained — that remembrance he pushed to the back of his mind as the Jeep pulled up at *Pariser Platz 2*, site of the American Embassy. The building was massive, three stories high but immense in length, at least as long as a football field, perhaps two, windows visible in every office on every floor, a long, curving park across the street smelling of new grass; it must have rained that morning. Exchanging salutes with the private who was driving he leaped out of the jeep, holding his suitcase in one hand and his fresh uniform in the other, bounced up the wide marble stairs of the main entrance, stepped through the open glass double doors and paused inside, looking around. A WAC with short red hair, seated behind a glass partition, asked if he needed help.
"Captain Maisel reporting for duty."

He hesitated but at first did not salute, he was in unfamiliar territory, had never encountered a WAC before. But when she saluted him he saw a Corporal's two stripes near her shoulder, set down his valise, returned her salute crisply.

"Welcome aboard, Captain. We've been expecting you. I hope you had a good flight."

"Thank you, Corporal, I caught some good sleep. Can someone direct me to Ambassador Clifford's office? I would like to check in with him."

"I'm sorry Sir, the Ambassador is not feeling well and did not come in today. Your office is on the second floor, beside his." She pressed a button on her desk, and a stocky private appeared from around a corner. "Please accompany Captain Maisel to 2C," the WAC said.

The private took his valise, led him around another corner and up a flight of stairs. Across from the top of the stairs were closed double doors with frosted glass windows. One door said in black paint: Ambassador. The other door said: The Honorable Charles C. Clifford. The private led him down the hall to a single door with a clear glass window.

"Maintenance planned to have your name on the door before you arrived, Sir. But I believe there was confusion about the spelling. They're repairing something out on the property now, but if you leave the correct spelling with Jane — she's the corporal near the door — I'm sure they could get it done in the morning."

"That's fine. And I'm not 'Honorable.'"

"Sir?"

"I don't want my door to say 'Honorable.'"

"I'm sure it can say whatever you want, Captain."

They exchanged salutes and the private left. Exit wondered if he indeed deserved that term. Or ever would.

He assayed the room. Large mahogany desk with a brass cup containing pens, sharpened pencils; two telephones — one black, one white — and a note pad. Off to the left a matching mahogany table with six chairs. To the right a matching file cabinet. In front of the tall window a low cabinet of blond oak, with wide drawers for holding blueprints or maps, it appeared. The map cabinet stood at a slight angle to the wall, as if it had been brought in hurriedly. He moved to straighten it, saw scrawled on the top in red crayon the words "Exit Loves Jane." He stopped, closed his eyes, rubbed them. He must be more tired than he thought. When he opened his eyes the words were gone.

A brisk knuckle-knock on the open door. Another WAC standing there. He could see no stripes of rank. Auburn hair barely touching her shoulders — the maximum length permitted WACS — with slight flecks of gray in it, though she appeared no older than he. No make-up visible. This lady did not seem to need it.

"Come in. I'm Captain Maisel."

She stepped into the office, saluted. "Warrant Officer j.g. Rosen, Sir."

During the flight over he had perused an Army manual. One thing It said was that WAC Warrant Officers were to be addressed as Miss. Odd. He returned her salute.

"Is there something I can do for you, Miss Rosen?"

She moved closer. Standard uniform: tailored olive jacket to the waist, khaki blouse, tie, skirt below the knee. Barely visible worry lines on her forehead. "I suppose you're used to being addressed as Miss."

"Yes, Sir."

"Why do you suppose that is?"

"I don't know, Captain. I suppose the Generals could not think of anything more virginal."

Spunky. "There was a war on when you women were admitted. The Generals, as you call them, may have had more pressing things on their minds."

The WAC blushed slightly, accepted his mild rebuke in silence.

"So, how may I assist you? I've just arrived from the States, I'm not sure I will be of much help."

"Sir, yesterday I was assigned to a new project. Top Secret."

"Yes, I'm aware of that."

So this is the Embassy's statistics whiz. Warrant Officer j.g. Rosen.

"To begin work I need aerial photographs of all of West Berlin. Clear and up to date. Sharp enough that I can determine which structures are lived-in homes and which are rubble." She removed a folder from under her arm. He had not noticed it. "I went directly to Research. These were the best they had." From the folder she took three black and white photographs and spread them on the table. The Captain bent over them. "They are rather blurred," he said.

"And three years old. Taken right after the war. That won't do for this project. The Germans are notorious for keeping accurate records, but that disappeared toward the end of the war. The Marshall Plan is slowly rebuilding the city, but it can't recreate records that don't exist. I have to start from scratch."

"It may be the Germans did not want an accurate count of soldiers they lost in combat. There were millions."

"Or the number of citizens that died in Allied bombings. Or people they murdered in the camps. Also millions."

"If I catch where you are going, these pictures certainly won't do." An unexpected scent brushed his nostrils. "If am not being too personal . . . Miss . . . Rosen, is that lavender I smell?"

She did not seem offended. "Honeysuckle. My favorite flowers are poppies, but they don't have a scent."

"That's like an infantry without tanks. What happened to their scent?"

"Did you ever hear how an artist knows a painting is finished? When she adds the stroke that ruins it."

The Captain smiled in appreciation.

"Poppies are so beautiful they don't need perfume," Miss Rosen said. "At least, that's what I believe."

Some women are like that, the Captain thought, but did not say it.

"Are you an artist?"

"I wish. Only on my fingernails. But since I use clear polish, I'm not really appreciated."

His brain, uninstructed, filed away her offbeat humor. And ordered him to get on with business.

"The pictures you need. When do you need them?"

"Yesterday."

"How come I knew you were going to say that? I'll see what I can do."

She was swallowing a frown as she gathered up the photos, saluted, turned to go.

"Miss Rosen, I was not dismissing you. Please sit while I make a phone call."

She shrugged, pulled out one of the chairs from the table.

"I hope I am not disturbing you too much, Captain."

Before he sat he looked directly at her. Small wrinkles beside her eyes. "Miss Rosen, listen carefully. This project that we — mostly you — will be working on, is urgent. As if we were at war again. I want you to think of it that way. Nothing has a stronger claim on your time. Or mine. Any day. Any night."

"Yes, Sir."

"Fine. Now please sit while I make my call."

He looked at the two phones, guessed that he wanted the white one, which had no rotary dial. He eased his eye patch into a more comfortable spot. When he lifted the receiver a voice said. "This is Debbie at the switchboard. How shall I place your call?"

"This is Captain Maisel, Debbie . . .?"

"Sergeant Stubbins if you prefer, Captain."

"Debbie is fine. I need the White House. The Oval Office."

"Yes, Sir." Crisper than before. "Please hang up. I will ring you when I have your party on the line. It should not take long."

"She's going to ring my party." The Warrant Officer nodded, returned his satisfied smile. Her eyes were blue-gray. "This is worse than chatting with the President in person," he said. "I wonder why."

The phone rang. He grabbed the receiver. "Captain, the Oval Office is not answering. I have a Sergeant Peters on the night line. Hold on."

After several clicks he heard breathing. It may have been his own.

"Is that you, Pete?"

"Yes, Captain."

"Has the President gone home early? He rarely does."

"No, Sir. He's working in his office, a sandwich and coffee on his desk. With the door closed. Not answering the phone."

"Good. Sergeant, I have to get him a message. Tell him he needs to authorize a reconnaissance flight over West Berlin at once. For aerial photography. Got that?"

"Yes, Captain. I'll give him the message first thing in the morning."

"No, Petey. Now. He needs to get this started immediately. Jog down the hall and get his attention, I don't care what he's working on. Kick the door down if you have to . . . Yes, I'll pay for it."

He was grinning as he hung up the receiver. Yet discovered his forehead and the skin below his patch and his underarms were wet.

The WAC seemed to be fighting a smile. With moist lips. "Captain, if I'm not being too personal now, did you keep me in here to impress me?"

He took several deep breaths. A shameless charmer. Wiped his forehead with his handkerchief. "No, Miss Rosen, of course not. But I impressed the hell out of myself."

"I'm sorry, Captain, I spoke out of turn. I should not have asked that. I apologize."

"As a general rule I encourage people to speak their minds. Presidents Roosevelt and Truman taught me that." Flushed with the appetite of rank, he felt a devilish mood overtake him. "So, Miss Rosen, is that what you were thinking?"

She pulled her own small handkerchief, pale brown, Army issue, from the pocket of her neatly ironed skirt. Apparently felt trapped, could think of no appropriate reply. Could not deny it, would not admit it.

"Never mind, I withdraw the question," Captain Maisel said. "Better still, I'll take a rain check on the answer. But tell me something else. I don't even know your full name."

"My birth certificate, wherever it now molders, says 'Hallie Rosenwald.'"

"Rose forest. Lovely. Was it butchered on Ellis Island, as mine and so many others were?"

"No, Captain, not Ellis Island."

Her handkerchief was twisting slowly, perhaps unconsciously. She watched it turn in her hands as if it were a somnolent snake. It seemed to take an effort for her to look at him.

"Not Ellis Island," she said. "Auschwitz."

"Oh, shit!" He took a deep breath. "I'm sorry." Another deep breath. "I'm glad you survived, that you were one of the lucky ones."

"No, Captain." Her blue-gray eyes seemed far away, then fierce. "I survived. I was one of the unlucky ones."

He swallowed mucus that was gorging into his throat. She was too . . . too what? Too open, too . . . lovely to have experienced that. He needed to change the subject.

"If I may, how did you become a WAC, if you are a German citizen?"

She composed herself, crossed her legs at her slim ankles. "Do you want the boring life of Hallie Rosenwald in one paragraph? Born near Hamburg. Loved learning. Was teaching graduate mathematics and statistics at Gottingen for several years when Nazism swept Austria along with the Germans. The Special Police raided the university, removed all Jews from the faculty. It was hard to find any job permitted to Jews. Then the Germans solved that problem by rounding us up. A year's holiday . . . more like eighteen months . . . in Auschwitz. When the Russians liberated the camp the American Red Cross took us in, gave us clothing, helped us regain our health. I had no family left, no place to go. I came to the Embassy to apply for a visa to America. They said I needed a passport or a birth certificate. Thanks to the Nazis I had neither."

She was speaking evenly, as if this were someone else's life.

"So how . . .?"

"Ambassador Clifford heard of my case, kindly listened to my story. With the war over many of the WACs who had enlisted for two years were going home to their families. The Embassy was understaffed, the Ambassador said. Would I enlist in the WACs to help out, in return for citizenship? Was that legal? I asked him. Any number of senators he called could make it legal, he said. With a private bill, something like that. So here I am."

Mouth dry. What to say after that?

"And highly regarded. I was told in Washington the other day that the Embassy had on it's staff a statistical wizard. I guess that's you. I assumed it was a man."

"Most people would."

"Where did you learn English?"

"When I knew I would become a citizen I wanted to learn. I studied at night school for two years. As you can hear, I never quite conquered my accent."

To the Captain her accent was slight and charming. An aural aphrodisiac. He did not say that. He stood, glanced at his watch, looked out the window, where the early summer sun was settling into the park. Turning, he asked, "Miss Rosen, do you have the correct local time? My watch and my body clock are both on the fritz. Oops, I did not mean to say that."

She was smiling. "I hope not." She pushed up her right cuff and told him it was 1:30 in the afternoon. Thursday afternoon.

"No wonder I'm hungry."

"There's a cafeteria in the basement. It's not bad."

"But not the way I'd like to start my stay here. Is there a good German restaurant nearby?"

"There are several."

"Have you had lunch yet?"

She seemed to hesitate before replying. "Not really. A doughnut. With the Ambassador ill I did not want to miss your arrival. To request the photos right away."

"Would you do me the honor, then, of having lunch with me? Lunch and conversation?"

She seemed to blush slightly. "If we leave the building together the gossip will start immediately."

"I don't mind gossip. Washington lives on it. But that's selfish of me, would it be a problem for you?"

"No. I don't care much what people think. I have memories. But I won't talk about the camps. That's what most people want to hear."

"Of course not. And we can't discuss the project in a restaurant. But I'm sure we can hit on a pleasant subject."

"How about the weather?" the Warrant Officer said. "I'm pretty good on the weather."

"My favorite topic," Exit said. "Will we talk Fahrenheit or Celsius?"

"That's your call, Captain. I'm ambidextrous."

They walked in separate silences, in separate worlds, three blocks to the Restaurant Gesundheit, his mind aswirl with mythic images. Athena in khakis, or Diana. One of the three fates in contemporary war dress. Sashaying into a cover of *Time* magazine depicting "A Modern Woman at War." As they left the embassy, her hat pert on her auburn hair, he had noted those ankles nicely turned in her stockings, in her brown Army-issue low heels; her waist slim, thin hands, unpolished fingernails closely clipped, the better for typing he assumed; of barely tanned flesh emerging from her cuffs. A bosom beneath her gold-buttoned jacket neither large nor small. There might be a dozen WACS like her in the Embassy. So what was her allure, at once subtle and overwhelming? She appeared to be a bit younger than he, perhaps 27 or 28 — how could you tell, what did it matter? They merely were walking to lunch, why was his chest thumping? Despite their differences in rank bantering with her was like fencing. But that was absurd, you do not fall in love from lightly accented conversation. Or do you? He must not shellack surviving Auschwitz with a false glow.

## WASHINGTON, 1987

*Ambidextrous.* From that first day the word had become code for them, eliciting secret smiles, a touching of hands, perhaps a hint of evening sport. After Hallie's death it had become bittersweet for Exit, like Eliot's April, mixing memory and desire. Only Exit Maisel of all humanity saw the statue this night raise its head, heard him whinny with pleasure before settling back to chomping.

"How you doing, old buddy?" the Ambassador asked. "The grass to your liking tonight?"

A bronze bench sat in the opening of the U-shape of trees. Leaning on his cane, Exit touched the sitting surface; it was not as cold as it often was; the sunwarmth of the day still adhered. Comfortable in his robe, Exit winked at the stallion, closed his eyes, soon was hurled by his hippocampus back to the rainy first Saturday in May of 1973, Joshua's Pleasure, undefeated as a two-year-old, winner of the Breeder's Cup Futurity, winner of the Woodward, talk in racing circles that he could become the first Triple Crown champion in 37 years, the first since the great Citation, Joshua's Pleasure pounding down the muddy track, damp mane flying behind him, even at the 16th pole with second choice Navigator II who was driving along the rail. The two horses even until Pleasure's rider Hector Gomez waved the whip in front of his eyes and JP switched to a higher gear and leaped ahead of the tiring gray and finished five lengths in front. Hallie beside him in her pale blue rain coat crying with joy and encircling Exit with her arms and kissing him firmly on the cheek, Rachel next to him doing the same with husband Steven Gold, the four of them closing into a laughing four-way hug. A blanket of roses was settled onto the horse, the jockey waved his whip at Exit, they all made their way through the crowd to the Winner's Circle. Exit's only regret was that Uncle Joshua, who had bred the horse, had not lived to enjoy this day.

Whitebread Stark, assistant trainer of McClatchy Farms' Navigator II, still sporting his crooked nose like a badge of courage, handed the reigns of his gray to a stablehand and moved to the edge of the crowded circle and hugged Exit and hugged Rachel, which led to a three-way hug. "Good race," Exit said as they shook hands. "We'll getcha next time," Whitebread said.

## Race Tracks, 1967

How did Whitebread get into racing? Exit's memory was failing him.
How did he and Rachel become owners of a race horse? That too was
blurred for a moment, then it came back. During LBJ's term Joshua
had suffered a heart attack that had done permanent damage; his
doctors told him he might live just a few more months. Joshua decided
the fortune he had designated in his will he would rather distribute
while he was alive, face to face with his family. A meeting was held
at the midtown office of his attorneys, Bradley, Bradley and Bradley.
Seated in a circle in deep leather armchairs they had listened to
Uncle Josh give away his vast holdings. A large donation to the Jewish
National Fund, another to the American Red Cross, then Joshua
turned to the family. Snuggled permanently in Exit's hippocampus
were his words and living bequests: "To my brother Jacob Maisel
I happily give the sum of two hundred thousand dollars, plus my
quarter share of Mazel Frames, which under the circumstances he
cannot refuse." Joshua looked at Jacob, who, smiling ruefully, nodded.
"To Jacob's wife Celine Maisel I give in her own name the sum of fifty
thousand dollars." Bubbie's hands in white gloves rose to her cheeks;
she blushed; or what was to Celine blushing. "To my nephew Exit
Maisel and my niece Rachel Maisel Gold I hereby and happily present
all of my stock market holdings, to be divided equally between them
by my attorney, Lemuel Fink. These include thousands of shares of
the Radio Corporation of America, General Motors, the Columbia
Broadcasting System, General Electric and others." Joshua, wearing
gray pants and a casual shirt over his rotund belly, set aside the paper
he'd been reading from, found the eyes of first Rachel, then Exit. "Most
of these stocks have done very nicely by me since I began purchasing
them in the 1930s," he said, less formally. "I hope they will continue to
profit both of you, and your families. I see no reason why they should
not.
"One more thing," he said, not looking at his notes, "one that is very
dear to me. As some of you may know, and some of you may not, one
of my fondest joys as I grew wealthy was to leave business behind
several days each week and spend time at a race track — Aqueduct,
Belmont, elsewhere, watching the beautiful Thoroughbreds run,
sipping wine with my colleagues. One day a friend suggested that
since I love the horses so much, why not start a breeding farm of my
own? I thought about that for a time, but the minute it was suggested
my heart — it was in better shape then — leapt at the idea. I did some
reading, talked with men in the business, decided to go ahead with it.

Four years ago, as you may know, I incorporated Joshua Stables, with headquarters and acreage in nearby Elmont, Long Island. When I die I expect to be laid to rest at the Jewish cemetery in Elmont — from which I might still hear the cheers from Belmont Park — so it seemed like the perfect place. I hired experienced management, instructed them to recruit the best trainers available and buy the most promising prospects at the yearling sales. Thus far we have had only modest victories, but I am assured that with our improving stock big things will not be long in coming."

Joshua wiped his face with a large white handkerchief. "I seem to have rambled on, as I always do when I become excited about the future. To get to the point, as of this morning I have signed Joshua Stables over jointly to Exit and Rachel. My one request is that they serve as co-owners for as long as they are able, and keep it running as long as possible. Who would have thought that as part of my legacy this immigrant from Wien would leave his name on a horse-racing stable, which one day will produce champions here in America. That is a joy to me."

## A WINNER

His uncle's prophecy did not take long to fulfill itself. A promising three-year-old named Joshua's Pleasure won the Kentucky Derby going away. Hugs all around, kisses, thank-yous, the shaking of hands, adjournment for dinner to a fancy restaurant. Hippocampus had stored it all, for which Exit was grateful.

It had also stored the Preakness two weeks later. Eyes closed Exit watched the replay in full color on his retina. This time Joshua's Pleasure was trailing second choice Navigator II by a length. Exit remembered Hallie's fingernails pressing fiercely into his palm as the horses blew by; Joshua's Pleasure had never lost a race. But as if given renewed strength by the equine gods he began to gain on the leader, a foot or two with every straining stride. He was half a length behind, a quarter length behind, they drove toward the finish side by side, stride for stride. It was a photo but Exit knew. He knew JP had gotten his nose down in front. The photo proved his eyesight was good. More hugs, breathless kisses, as if the owners had run the race themselves. The second leg! The entire nation would be talking about JP tonight, tomorrow.

The blanket of flowers was Black-eyed Susans, the signature of Pimlico. Whitebread handed the reigns of a blowing Navigator to a stablehand and approached the Winner's Circle. Shaking his head he shook hands with Exit, with Rachel. "One more try," he muttered. "See you in three weeks." Exit feigned disbelief. "You're gonna try to beat JP out of the Triple Crown? The whole country will be rooting for us." Whitebread smiled grimly. "What are you implying?" he asked. "You want my horse to take a dive?" Exit was not sure if the words were coincidental or darkly remembered.

In Exit's hippocampus there was neither tape nor film nor memory of the 1973 Belmont Stakes. Joshua's Pleasure, Triple Crown hopeful, had not run in the Belmont Stakes.

They ran together into the rising sun down the slope to the wilting cherry trees. Stopped. Gasped. The Ambassador was lying on the ground. "Shit!" Priscilla said. "Fuck!" Margaret said. They thought the old man was dead.

But he was merely sleeping in the grass, his head beside the head of the nibbling bronze.


## The Shopping List

I do not believe in free will. Scientists have demonstrated that we react to a stimulus — make a decision — instinctively, nearly half a second before our reason tells us why. Two examples: Baseball players say they decide whether to swing at a pitch as the ball nears the plate. But studies have shown that they actually begin their swing as soon as the ball leaves the pitcher's hand. Second: When we are driving and a child runs into the road, we hit the brakes. Nearly half a second passes before reason tells us why. Apparently, then, I began carefully to kneel to the floor in front of my desk in the bedroom before I knew why I was doing so. But by the time my knees touched the carpet I knew. I pulled open the bottom drawer and removed an old cigar box. With difficulty I pulled myself off the floor and plopped onto the bed. The dry rubber band holding the box closed broke when I pulled it off. Inside the box something glittered. I lifted it out. Hallie's wedding band. I held it on my palm, looked at it in the streaky sunny silence. A thousand memories must have flashed through my brain in half a second. But the ring was not what I was seeking just then. I set it carefully back and pulled out a folded sheet of paper; it had yellowed with time but the list in Hallie's script still was visible, graceful as ever. She had called this her shopping list. It was her final estimate of how many tons of each product would have to be airlifted into West Berlin every day to keep the city adequately supplied:

*Flour and wheat — 646 tons*
*Cereal — 125 tons*
*Fat — 64 tons*
*Meat and fish —109 tons*
*Dehydrated potatoes — 180 tons*
*Sugar — 180 tons*
*Coffee — 11 tons*
*Powdered milk — 19 tons*
*Whole milk for children — 5 tons*
*Fresh yeast for baking — 3 tons*
*Dehydrated vegetables — 144 tons*
*Salt — 38 tons*
*Cheese — 10 tons*
*This total equals 1534 tons needed daily*
*Plus coal and fuel (mostly for industry)— 3475 tons daily*
*Total daily tonnage needed — 5009*

*Army estimates: a C-47 can carry 35 tons*
*Flights required: 1,000 per day*
*Not possible.*

*Army request:*
*More C-54 Skymasters: Can carry 3 times more cargo than C-47s*
*Result: 52 new Skymasters ordered for Berlin.*

There were no computers in those days, the only way to count things was to count them. Hallie bent over the new aerial photographs with a magnifier, sharp pencils, a ruler, a protractor, scratch pads, noting the number of working homes she could discern among the war's remaining rubble, estimating the average of each type of home in the different parts of the city. WACS she recruited from Research joined her in knocking on doors, asking how many adults and children dwelled in each house, compiling another average; asking the same residents to estimate how much of each product they used each week; dividing by seven. Amid the war-time rubble still surrounding them, Hallie had noticed, people still blushed when asked about toilet paper.

Russian tanks were lined up beside all roads leading to West Berlin, beside all railroad tracks, beside all canals. When I asked Major General William Tunner, who was in charge of the airlift, why the air corridors remained unthreatened, he said it had been written into the treaty signed at the Potsdam Conference that they must remain open at all times. So the obvious question was, why hadn't the sanctity of the ground routes been written in as well? He answered, "Somebody goofed." Clearly meaning state department diplomats. Then he back-tracked some. "The Soviet Union was our ally during the war. They had just agreed, however reluctantly, to the partitioning of Berlin in the same way Germany had been partitioned. No one expected a problem. We were too trusting." Then he muttered, "Somebody fucked up."

Though we worked in the same building, once the photos arrived I did not see her or speak to her for days. She was too busy. Eager as I was to spend time with her I did not want to disturb her. Saturday, though she claimed she was too tired, I convinced her to have dinner with me —"You have to eat to keep the body pumping" — but I promised to have her home early. Our flats, as the Europeans call them, were about a mile apart. I took her to a nearby Italian place I had discovered. We set a limit of one glass of Pino Noir each. What we talked about I no longer recall, some of it may indeed have been about the weather, which was about to become a serious concern in our lives. The Soviets were expected to close the roads within a few days, the airlift would have to start, clear sunny skies would maximize the number of daily flights possible; heavy rain, fog or thunderstorms would slow things down.

"You seem upset," I said over sausage ravioli. "I hope it is not because of me."

The restaurant was dark, we were sitting at a white-clothed corner table for two lit by a single candle.

"Just nervous."

Which, I thought in my innocence, such a pretty WAC with a come-hither-but-not-yet freckle at the tip of her nose should not be.

"I sent the general my estimates this morning. I haven't heard back, beyond a curt acknowledgement of receipt."

"Hallie, what could they say? They don't know anything. You're the expert, at least until they put the blockade into motion, see how close you came to the actual need. That will take a week of flights at least, probably two."

She gnawed on a breadstick. "The wait will be agonizing. There is so much at stake."

"I know. But suppose you were off by a ton or two, in either direction. They can easily make the adjustment."

"What if I was off by fifty?"

Looking down at her ravioli, Hallie took my hand in hers, looked at me. Her hair was pulled back in a bun, a homey style I had not seen on her before. When I said I liked it, she said she had not had time to wash her hair today.

"Captain," she said, "you have a nice, calming effect on me. I need that right now."

I wanted to say she had the opposite effect on me, but I did not.

## THE FIRST TIME

The first time with someone special you always remember. It is engraved so deeply into the hippocampus that it remains accessible even at my age, when other memories good and bad have been lost. Why evolution has decreed this to be so would be a lively subject for discussion. In any case, the first time with Hallie, well remembered, was a tortured day.

The airlift had been going on for two weeks, early reports indicated it was an initial success. C-54s laden with supplies were taking off from Rheim-Mein Air Base in West Germany every four minutes and landing at Templehof 37 minutes later. The Berliners were rejoicing. The question was how long the Allies — the British were doing an equal share, the French a bit — how long we could keep this going. Each good report I showed to Hallie, who was not being kept in the loop. She was a team player, she never complained, but I could sense she felt abandoned. Then I had a welcome insight. Thus far the airlift was in her mind only, a mess of hard work and statistics; perhaps seeing in three dimensions the tons of foodstuffs being delivered daily thanks in part to her, which was keeping more than two million people alive, would be good for her ego, her sense of self-worth, even her soul. So on a Sunday when we were not needed at the Embassy, without an explanation to her I signed out a Jeep and took her on a drive to Templehof.

The airport was a scene of controlled frenzy: empty C-54s taking off for their return flight to the West, parked planes being unloaded of their tons of supplies by ground crews at high speed, every half minute a huge silver-winged bird laden with tons of new supplies landing on the tarmac like a mother robin returning to the nest to feed her chicks; the three-man flight crew jumping down from behind the cockpit, a ground crew instantly beginning to wheel the tonnage from the rear of the plane to delivery trucks on standby fifty yards away, the trucks when full being driven off toward the city. I braked the Jeep to a stop just off the tarmac. We watched in silent awe. But I could sense Warrant Officer j.g. Rosen, seated beside me, beginning to fill with pride, with her old sense of self-reliance. Proof of meaning had returned to her world.

As if dropped from a puffy cloud in the blue sky a Jeep pulled up beside us, a private driving, General Tunner beside him. Hallie and I saluted the General, who returned it at once.

"Captain Maisel, good to see you. Out sight-seeing on a sunny Sunday? Have you been here since we started?"

He climbed out of his Jeep, so we followed.

"No, sir, this is my first time. I've been reading the reports, of course. In person it is amazing. I saw where you are aiming for 1,500 flights a day, 4,500 tons of produce a day. That is staggering."

"Thanks to President Truman, and to you."

"Sir, if I may correct you, I've had little to do with the operation beyond the initial planning. Let me introduce Warrant Officer j.g. Rosen. Miss Rosen is the brains behind much of this."

I could feel Hallie blushing beside me.

"Rosen. Rosen. Why is that name familiar?"

"Miss Rosen compiled the tonnage estimates, Sir."

"Warrant Officer Rosen! Of course! Miss Rosen, let me shake your hand. You did an impossible job brilliantly. I don't think you were off by more than a ton or two in any category."

"Thank you, Sir."

"General, if I may," I asked, so Hallie could avoid further attention, which was embarrassing her, "the first guesses were that the airlift would have to sustain for three weeks, until the Soviets got bored with the blockade. Does it still appear to be short-term?"

"No way in hell, is my opinion. Uncle Joe Stalin does not get bored easily. He wants us the hell out of West Berlin. He won't get bored until we retreat — or until he finally is convinced that we can run the airlift forever. Which I am prepared to do, if necessary."

"I thought that might be the case. Thank you for your candor, General."

He started to turn away, then turned back. "Captain Maisel, Warrant Officer Rosen, I wonder if with your fresh eyes you could try to solve another problem for me. But that's silly, never mind, it's just logistics. Look around as much as you like, enjoy your Sunday."

"Now you've intrigued me — us — General. What is the problem? Fresh eyes, as you say."

"Well, I don't want to bother you, but you are under my command. So here's the problem. It takes a fully loaded C-54 40 minutes from take-off to landing. The flight crews take a break in the canteen — for coffee or a quick meal — you can see it, it's about 500 yards from here. The ground crews the first weeks were taking 15 minutes to off-load the planes."

We turned to watch them at work.

"I got them to speed it up. It now takes 12 minutes. I think they can get down to ten. Five minutes off every round trip would let me squeeze in seven more flights a day. But that's not happening. The problem is that the planes stand empty, ready to take off when the flight crews return from the canteen. But that takes time. I won't take canteen privileges away, these pilots are doing a bitch of a job under stress. They're entitled to their coffee and a snack before heading back. But it's adding maybe fifteen minutes to each round trip. Reduce that and I could get more planes into the flow. Which I'm determined to do. But I've been observing here for two days and for the life of me can't figure out an acceptable way. I have to get back now. You two think about it."

We saluted but Hallie seemed off in another world as she watched the crew unloading. I nudged her elbow and she came to and saluted the General but as he rode off she riveted her eyes again on the nearest plane while another squealed in for a landing at the far end of the tarmac.

"Are you alright?"

She nodded absently but her face had drained white.

"Hallie, what is it?"

"Look at the off-loading crew. The big man with the slight limp. He's not in uniform."

I looked. The fellow she meant was enormous. He was wearing denim overalls, work boots, a plaid flannel shirt. "Maybe they couldn't find a uniform big enough. He's sure working hard, seems to move twice as fast as the others despite his size — and they're all working top speed."

"I think I know him."

"You think?"

"I'm pretty sure."

"From where?"

She whirled to face me, her back to the plane. "Captain, take me home, please."

We hurried toward the Jeep. "Oh, no," I said. "He wasn't a guard at Auschwitz!"

"No."

But she was trembling.

"I'll be back in a second," I said, leaping out of the Jeep. "I'll get some answers."

"Don't talk to him!"

"Not from him," I said.

Aware as I walked to the plane that my revolver was in the Jeep.

A Sergeant was supervising the hurried but calm unloading. I took him off to the side and asked questions abut the man not in uniform. After I started the engine I told Hallie what the Sergeant had said.

"The man is not in the Army. That's why no uniform. He's a local German citizen who appreciates what the airlift is doing to save West Berlin. He's out of work, so he volunteered to help. He's strong as an ox. This freed up a soldier for other duty. That's it."

"Does he have a name?" Hallie asked me.

I pulled a pad from my pocket. "Klaus Huffner."

"No. His real name is Moses Levkoff."

Cautiously I found the highway and headed home.

"Are you sure?"

"Almost. You don't forget a man that big. I can prove it tomorrow."

"How?"

"Come back and I'll get him to roll up his sleeve."

"You're saying he's Jewish? What does that prove? Why were you so frightened? You're still white."

"Exi" — she had started calling me that several weeks before, our own term of endearment. But only when we were alone. Only when the mood was right. It had a loving sound, I liked it when she called me that. "Exi" — she touched my thigh — "I need time to think. Let me just think the rest of the way home."

"Just one question. Are you hungry? We could get an early dinner on the way."

"I'm too nauseous to eat. Wine is what I need. I've got some at home. Let's go there and drink, and I'll tell you about Moses Levkoff."

"Roger," I said, or some such foolishness, and barely swung around a slow-moving black VW on the highway, lost as I was in awful imaginings.

Her tenement complex had a parking lot behind it. In her apartment she hung her Army-issue tan jacket in a closet, let down her unwashed hair, I tossed my cap, jacket and tie onto a chair in the living room and parsed the kitchen. A bottle of Pinot Noir stood on the counter, a Riesling lay on its side in the refrigerator.

"Red or white?" I asked as she joined me, taking my hand. Hers was cold as a dead lizard.

"It's your choice, Captain," she said.

"I remember. You're ambidextrous."

She grinned. I pressed her hand to my lips to warm it, encircled her with my arms. A slight tremble wrinkled her body. I poured two glasses of red, we moved to the living room. She sat on a beige sofa. I slid onto an upright chair and moved it closer to her.

"Are you sure you're prepared to hear about the Monster of Auschwitz?"

"Only if you want to talk about it."

It was the first time we drank wine without clinking classes and saying *l'chaim*.

## THE MONSTER

"One morning," she said, "we were all taken to Barracks 1. That was the first of a dozen male barracks, near the front of the camp. It was filled with skeletal men lying on their bunks, you've seen the pictures. The enfeebled women from Barracks 2 were made to walk there and line up inside. Those of us in the infirmary were also walked there. We were not starving as much as the others; Mengele wanted us healthy enough for his experiments. But they wanted everyone to see what was going to happen."

Hallie finished off her glass of wine, as if to oil her speech reflex. I refilled her goblet. She kicked off her shoes, folded her legs under her on the sofa.

"When we were all in there — the skeletons of Barracks 1, the emaciated women from 2, us from the infirmary — four SS men marched in carrying rifles. Between them was a tall beast of a man who limped slightly. They began by introducing him. 'This is your fellow Jew, Moses Levkoff,' the chief SS man said. 'He knows how you Jews should be treated. You in the bunks, all of you, stand on your legs.' Those who could stand did so. Some of their boney knees crumpled and they fell. 'Okay, Jew, show them what you will be doing every morning they are alive. I should have added that he used to be a prize fighter.' Levkoff walked to the right-hand bunk. He was wearing the camp's striped trousers, boxing gloves, but no shoes or shirt. His chest was huge and hairy. He stood eye to eye with the first standing skeleton, reached his right arm back and slammed his fist into the man's pelvic region, which was nothing but bones. The man cried out and buckled over onto the ground, tried to protect himself from further blows with his emaciated bones. A woman screamed — 'That's

my husband!' — and fainted. An SS man approached with a pail of
water, dumped it on her head to revive her, and yanked her upright;
she must watch the rest. The man moved down the line of inmates,
punched each one the same way, moved on to the next. A few of the
men managed to double over and cry out but remain standing; most
collapsed like marionettes whose strings had been cut. Women kept
screaming as they recognized husbands, brothers, fathers. All of us
were sobbing. When the giant had punched every man in Barracks 1,
the SS leader announced that Moses would return the next morning at
dawn to repeat his exercise. And every morning after that. Something
for them to look forward to as they tried to sleep, he said. For now
he had to move on to Barracks 3. They led us women away and as
we walked to our assigned cribs we heard screams emerge from the
starving men of Barracks 3 and the women from number 4 who were
being made to watch. Some of us women began praying in Hebrew or
Yiddish for death — or for their loved ones to die."

Tears were pouring unchecked down Hallie's cheeks as she
remembered. I poured her more wine and moved to the sofa beside
her and put my arm around her shoulder.

"That's enough," I said. But she needed to add one more thing. "That
continued every morning for days, weeks, months, until the Red Army
neared — raping hundreds of innocent German women along the way,
it turned out — and the Nazis fled and the camp was liberated by the
Russians to the American Red Cross. 'Find Levkoff,' some of us were
saying, whispering, but we did not find him."

She sipped more wine, wiped her tears with the backs of her hands,
looked hard at me. "Until today."

I took her hand in mine. It had warmed in the flames of her wrath. I
noticed for the first time the lone piece of art in her living room. It was
turned back to front, was barely visible by candlelight. "What is that?"
I asked.

"It's a reproduction of *The Scream*, by Munch. When I moved in
here I bought it, as a reminder that I should never forget. But after a
few months I realized I was tormenting myself. I didn't need Munch
to help me remember. So I made a feeble decision, and turned it to the
wall. It was too symbolic to throw away. This way I could turn it back
again if I ever wanted to. So far I haven't wanted to."

This led her to another memory. "One time in his operating room
Dr. Mengele was holding his scalpel near me, about to slice into my
abdomen — without anesthesia — and he asked me if I believed in
God. At that moment I was sure he was insane. 'In your lovely hotel,

Doctor,' I told him, 'how could I not believe in God? God is lethal gas.' I don't recall if he nodded or laughed. Only my scream as he plunged in the blade."

She was beyond tears now. She seemed unable to stop talking. As if she were opening for me a window into her soul.

"What I needed to think about on the way home," she said "was what to do about Levkoff. If I turn him in he'll be condemned to death as a collaborator. I never have killed anyone. It would feel like premeditated murder. It would burden me for the rest of my life. But if I ignore the past, if I don't turn him in, I'll be a traitor to all those he pummeled, some of whom died from it. A traitor to their wives, their sisters, their daughters. A traitor to everyone who was ever in the camps, those who drifted out the chimneys as smoke and those who survived. Is that who I really am? I asked myself why did he do it? Was he insane, did he hate his fellow Jews and take pleasure in torturing us? Had the SS told him he would be killed if he did not do what they wanted? In other words, was he inflicting such pain to save his own life? If so then he deserves to be hanged. But what if he had refused them? Once, twice, three times. What if he had told them to go ahead and kill him, he would not harm his fellow prisoners? If so, and the SS killed him, he would be a revered hero in the camps. But they did not kill him. So perhaps they had taken him into their torture room and showed him the machines that would be used on him if he did not do as they said: the vise-like iron lungs from the Middle Ages, the body stretchers that could pull him limb from living limb, the long knives with which they would hack off his arms, his legs, his penis, the serrated saws that could do the same, the painful poisons that would burn up his insides without killing him. What if threatened with all that he had fainted? Or not fainted but been unable to stand, unable to bear the thought. He was only human. Most of us could not face all that and still refuse them. He used to be a boxer, he had punched men for a living, what would be the big deal? Who would not have rationalized thus in his shoes? What if that was the case? Does he truly deserve to die for it?"

I did not know what to say. I gazed at the invisible *Scream* and said nothing.

We sat in silence for a time. It was clear she would not be able to eat or sleep until this was resolved. "You once told me you felt calmer, more relaxed, around me. Is that still true?"

"Of course."

"Listen to me, Hallie. You have to try to put this out of your mind, at least for awhile. The past won't go away — but it is past. The future, no one can predict. You need to close your eyes and try to relax and focus only on the here and now. The good things. If you want I'll stay here tonight and keep you company."

We were holding hands. "I would like that very much."

I leaned toward her and kissed her lightly on the lips. Then with more pressure.

When I awoke at dawn I was naked in her bed. Our clothing was strewn around the floor. She was asleep with her head on my chest. I thought: I have no idea what decision she should make. I thought I'd only thought it, but it seemed I had vocalized it. With her face in my chest she replied, sotto voce: "There is no right choice. Both choices are wrong."

She wanted to go back to Templehof to look at Levkoff's wrist. While she showered and dressed I drove to my place, showered, put on my fresh uniform, called the Ambassador and told him we had more work to do out there. It was not a lie. "What have you decided to do?" I asked her as we drove out. "I'm still not sure," she said. "I want to stand in front of him and look him in the eye. His eyes will tell me what to do."

I did not know what she expected to find in his eyes but that was not something to ask about, not rationally, not emotionally.

But Moses Levkoff was not there. Not with his usual crew and not with any other crew as we circled the seven or eight planes being unloaded. I pulled up near the Sergeant heading his usual crew. We exchanged salutes.

"What brings you back, Captain?"

"That big civilian fellow. Is he not working today?"

"He didn't show up."

"Does that happen often?"

"This is the first time."

"Any idea why?"

"Nope. He volunteered to work, so I put him to work. He showed for a few weeks, until today. If he shows tomorrow I'll put him back to work. A good man, hard worker. If I never see him again, which is possible, no big deal, an Army man takes his place. Life goes on. The airlift goes on."

"A fellow that big would not be hard to track down."

"For what? He volunteers, he leaves. As we say back home, Captain, it's a free country. Even if it is Germany."

By the time we reached the Embassy Hallie had decided not to pursue the matter. More concerned about her sanity than the perfidy of Moses Levkoff, I felt relieved by her decision.

## MEETING SARTRE

With the war over for three years, Berlin was attempting to regain its place alongside Paris as a capital of European culture. Helping with the airlift and other duties of the Embassy, we in the Army were not in the cultural loop. Rebuilt art museums were setting attendance records, concerts and plays were being performed in venues large and small, discussions of a new philosophy, called Existentialism, was all the rage in the late-night cafes. Hallie kept abreast of these cultural developments in the newspapers and magazines; I preferred spending my spare time reading the spate of war novels that had appeared at war's end, perhaps needing to inhale vicariously the smoke and sounds and cries of the wounded and the dying and the silence of the dead, which I had been spared in life. I recall one night seeing on Hallie's pillow a novel by one of the pioneers of Existentialism, a Frenchman named John-Paul Sartre, which was the rage of the young back then. If you have no such commitment to a cause or an idea I suppose you are not truly young.

The book was called *Nausea*.

"Not a very appetizing title," I recall saying. Which remark she ignored. The book, Hallie told me, dealt with whether God placed us on Earth as we were meant to be, or whether we arrived here with total freedom to create by our actions who we would become. That's not a very good summary of Existentialism, she said, but I share my pillow with a hippocampus that's at least as old as me.

Why, I wondered at the time, was this new way of thinking called a philosophy instead of a religion? I had lost any belief in a benevolent God the day my mother disappeared. Any such belief Hallie may have carried had been leached from her body and her soul in Auschwitz. Perhaps the same had happened to Sartre and his lady friend Simone de Beauvoir, a like-minded writer, during the Nazi occupation of France. Perhaps Existentialism was at its core a search for a new God.

Hallie was thinking deeply about this, much more than I was, when one day she got very excited. In her hand was a newspaper story about a new play by Sartre, which would be performed the following week right there in Berlin. She was reading the paper after dinner while sprawled on her bed; she rose to her knees, her skirt hiking high across her thighs. "Exi, I have to see this!" she said. Followed by "Oh, shit!"

"What's wrong?"

"A new play by Sartre. I want to see it. But it's already sold out."

I put a bookmark in *The Naked and the Dead* and sat beside her on the bed and read over her shoulder. The play was titled *Huis Clos.*

"What's it mean in English?" I asked.

"No Exit."

## Dialogue

Captain Maisel did not enjoy the play; his scattered French could not keep up with the dialogue. But seeing how engrossed Hallie was made his innards happy. At play's end the audience stood *en masse* and applauded and cheered and refused to stop until the author mounted to the stage. Sartre said words of thanks, then departed with his lady through a side door. A throng, including Exit and Hallie, followed them to a café across a narrow street, filled every table, ordered steins of beer, still buzzing about what they had seen. Exit was rewarded with a kiss on the cheek for obtaining the tickets.

As advertised, while the playgoers drank from steins of beer Sartre climbed to a small stage to answer questions, in German, about Existentialism. His comments disappeared quickly from Exit's hippocampus, but he could sense Hallie beside him growing tense, beginning to perspire on her forehead, then forcing herself to stand and speak.

"Mr. Sartre," she began, in English, "as a recent student of Existentialism, I have a dilemma I hope you can help me with it." She told in a few sentences how the other day she had spotted a Nazi collaborator who had been a Jewish prisoner at Auschwitz. "As I understand it, a basic premise of your philosophy is that we are all born free, and are free in life to forge our own personalities, with freely chosen decisions. In this case, I have the freedom to inform on Mr. Aleph, which presumably would lead to a trial, perhaps with myself as a witness, and most likely end with his execution. I have that free choice — but it does not feel right to me. Perhaps because I know that I myself am not perfect enough to judge another human being. Who among us is? My other free choice is more passive — to ignore seeing Aleph and let Fate take its course without my interfering. That choice has a certain appeal, but in my understanding it would make me a failure as an Existentialist, because I did not use my freedom to fight for justice. Could you enlighten me on this dilemma?"

She remained standing, waiting for Sartre's response.

"Sometimes we have to step back and look at an earlier time." The playwright-novelist-philosopher shaded his eyes with his hands. "In this dim light, Miss, it appears that you are wearing a uniform of the United States Army. Am I correct?"

"Yes, Sir."

"Well, there you are. Outside of concentration camps, prisons and perhaps the Catholic church, nothing enforces passivity more than the military. In any Army you are told when to eat, when to sleep, when to practice shooting, when to march across a field and shoot other people. The so-called enemy. And you are bound to obey, or you may be shot yourself. Not women as much as men, but that day will come. This is not freedom but enforced passivity, the abnegation of freedom. Which has no place in Existentialism. The moment you joined the Army, your personal radar, as it were, was set on passivity. Which is why you do not want to inform on the collaborator."

"With all due respect, Sir," Hallie replied, "I see it differently. The US Army, along with the British, freely fought at great cost in lives to free the citizens of your native France from occupation by the Nazis. Thereby restoring to them the personal freedom you cherish. We did the same to free those Italians who were not Fascists, Germans who opposed the Nazis, as well as Austrians, the Dutch, the Danes. We fought with our own free will to restore personal freedom to people in every occupied country. I was proud we were doing so. I was not passive in this endeavor, I was active, I was using my freedom to fight for the freedom of others. But I could not do it alone. Even now, as you are aware, along with the British we are airlifting into this city the food and clothing and fuel that keeps the city alive. US C-54 planes stuffed with tons of supplies are landing at Templehof every 21 seconds, day and night — supplies that include the beer we are now enjoying. I am part of that. I do not see that as passive."

Hallie sat, trembling slightly. Exit could hear her heart throbbing. He took her hand in his. A man near the rear of the café began to applaud, stood and continued applauding. Others joined in. Before long the entire patronage of the café was giving Hallie a standing ovation. She was blushing acutely, wanted, Exit knew, to crawl under the table. A pretty server with blond pigtails and ample breasts in a white peasant blouse with red trim placed a large pitcher of beer on their table. "From the management," she said, smiling. The cheering continued until Exit nudged her elbow and Hallie stood for a moment and waved to the crowd, who began to settle down amid shouts of Hurrah!

At the podium Sartre must have wondered how Existentialism had evolved so unexpectedly into patriotism. "Well, I suppose I will have to rethink my opinion of the military," he said. "But for now, on this note let us return to our beer — our airlifted beer."

He stepped down to return to his friends, but paused as he threaded his way to shake hands with Hallie, who stood to meet him. The cheering began again. "Jean-Paul Sartre," he shouted over the noise as their fingers touched. "Warrant Officer j.g. Rosen," she shouted back.

## Existentialism

As best he can remember, it was three weeks after their evening of Sartre that Exit asked Hallie to marry him. As they dined on wine and *Wiener schnitzel* in the Bauhaus Restaurant, drank more wine at her apartment, he was not the least bit anxious. They loved one another. There was no way she would say no.

But she did.

"No? How can you say no?"

He still can feel in his old age the pain of being kicked in the stomach.

She took his hand, squeezed it. "I've been dreading this moment for weeks. I love you. There is nothing I would rather do than marry you. But I won't. I can't."

His voice lacked strength when he spoke. Like a mouse hiding in a corner. "Well, which is it? Can't or won't? I'm confused."

"I've had a recurring daydream for weeks. Sometimes here at home, sometimes at the Embassy, with you not a hundred yards away. In the dream, the fantasy, you are on a large green lawn, playing with two children, a girl and a boy, about ten years old, perhaps twins. You are rough-housing, tossing a football or a baseball, all of you laughing for the pure freedom of it. I am standing off to the side, smiling as I watch. When the daydream ends and I return to reality I twist my head to the side to fight off tears. Most often I am not successful and I cry."

"But why? I still don't understand."

"Because that is how I picture your future happiness."

"So? I love that picture."

"Listen!" she said, sounding annoyed with him. "I can't have children. Thanks to the good doctor Mengele, I will not have children, ever. Does that make it clearer?"

He let go of her hand, shook his head, ran all his fingers through his hair. Silent tears slipped down her cheeks. He blew breath into his fist in consternation, again, again, stood, sipped wine, walked around the living room, looked out the window as if to see the children she had seen. It was dark, no one was playing outside. He sat on the sofa beside her. He wondered if in her daydream Mengele had been the father of her twins. He did not ask. He did not want to know.

She was wearing a bright turquoise dress, a white blouse, a beaded choker, small earrings. No rings. As if she were waiting for one. He took her hand, rubbed her fingers. Stood and paced. Looked out the window again, seeking words in the darkness. Returned to her side.

"Hallie, did I say anything about children? I just want us to spend our lives together. That's how I picture my future happiness."

"You say that now. But after two or three years, when most couples would have children, you'll watch fathers proudly showing off their precious little girls, or playing football with their boys. You'll long for that, why shouldn't you? Why should you be deprived of fatherhood, you'll wonder. A chance to perpetuate your genes. And you'll start to hate me. Maybe not consciously at first, but it will be there in the back of your brain. And the hatred will metastasize. I could not stand for you to hate me. That's why I can't marry you. Why I won't marry you."

He took both her hands in his. "Hallie, that's crazy. Is that what Existentialism teaches — to live life in fear of the future? I've been doing some reading myself. To me Existentialism means to live an active life now, in the moment. The future will be whatever it will be. We can't know that now, or worry about it. Actually, there is one thing I do know now. I could never hate you. Never." He touched her cheek. "Not for anything you might do. Certainly not for what that bastard Mengele did."

"Do you mean that? How can you be sure?"

"Of course I mean that."

She snuggled into him, lay her face on his chest. Exit realized he was breathing.

"I know that's the truth now, Exi. But my news must be a shock to you. Young sexy broad like me being barren." She blushed as she said it. "Perhaps I should have told you on our first date, whenever that was. But who could foresee love between the mighty Captain and the little Warrant Officer?" She sat up straight, pushed hair off her forehead.

"I have an idea," she said. "Starting tomorrow let's not see each other. No dinners, no talking on the phone. For a month. To give you time to think it through, discover what you really feel. Then you can ask me again — if you still want to."

Exit shook his head. "Now it's my turn to say no. A month is too long. We'll compromise. A week. We'll have no contact until next Saturday. Then Sunday we'll get married."

Hallie punched his knee.

"In the meantime I'll find us a rabbi," he said.

In some vague year for some unremembered reason they had exchanged IQ scores from their youths. Exit's was 159. Hallie's was 163. Some men would have felt threatened by this. Exit felt proud to have married up.


## A Plan

"Pretty girls."

Exit stirred in the bed.

"With trucks."

He turned to look at her, to see if she was speaking to him or talking in her sleep, which she sometimes did. In her sleep she also occasionally screamed. Her eyes were half open, as if she had just awakened but wasn't sure.

"Pretty girls with trucks. What the hell does that mean?"

Naked, she snuggled against him under the blanket, seeking warmth. And yawned a morning yawn. "I think I know how to solve the General's turn-around time. I was afraid to face him in person, I was afraid he might think my idea was stupid, so I wired him while you were gone. How was Paris, by the way?"

"Boring." He did not mention Allen Dulles. "Tell me about your idea."

So she did. "They would need two large trucks — they have plenty at Tempelhof — and outfit them with generators. One would power refrigerators to store cold food. The other for electric stoves to heat warm food. The canteen chefs would learn to cook in the trucks. Station the trucks near where the flight crews jump off onto the tarmac. Put a few picnic tables nearby, with umbrellas to protect against the rain or the sun. Instead of walking 500 yards to the canteen and 500 back after their meals, they eat right there. It's simple.

"Why would the flight crews want to do that?

"Because I've saved the best part. Round up the prettiest girls in Berlin. That waitress who brought us beer at the Sartré talk gave me the idea. There are hundreds of girls around as pretty as that. Mostly blondes with ample bosoms. Hire a bunch of them to be waitresses at the truck tables"

"'What will this do?' the general cabled back.

"I asked him, did you ever see a soldier who would rather walk a thousand yards than spend 15 minutes flirting with a gorgeous girl?

"The general conceded that he had not. That's why the plan will work, I told him. The flight crews will order food or coffee at the trucks and hang out out with the girls, making them laugh, or blush. Nothing will go wrong — no awkward advances, for instance — because both the men and the girls will know that the airmen have to be back on their empty plane and heading West within twelve minutes.

"'I must admit this is something I would never have thought of,' the general wired. 'But I'm going to give it a try.'"

"That's great. When do you expect to hear from him?"

"Actually, I received a wire yesterday. I was saving it for today so you could get some sleep. It's here under my pillow if you want to see it."

She reached behind her and pulled out a folded piece of yellow paper and gave it to me. I raised the Venetian blind for morning light. The wire had been sent from Templehof:

TO: WARRANT OFFICER J.G. HALLIE ROSEN, U. S. EMBASSY W. BERLIN.

FROM: GENERAL TUNNER.

DEAR MISS ROSEN: PLAN IN EFFECT THREE DAYS. RESULTS AMAZING. FLIGHT CREWS ALL SMILES GETTING OFF PLANES FLIRTING GETTING BACK ON KNOWING THEY WILL SEE WAITRESSES AGAIN IN AN HOUR AND A HALF. MOST IMPORTANT PLAN CUTS TURNAROUND AVERAGE OF THIRTEEN MINUTES. ALLOWS DOZEN OR MORE EXTRA FLIGHTS PER DAY. THATS TONS OF SUPPLIES. HOPE YOUR NEW HUSBAND APPRECIATES HOW CLEVER YOU ARE. TUNNER.

"He does, he does," her new husband says. Drops the fluttering telegram beside the bed. Pulls sheet, blanket off her. They celebrate how clever she is. Twice.

## A Summons

Hallie was breathless, as if she'd been running down the hall, as she burst into my office without knocking.

"What did I do?" she asked. "I'm terrified."

I was shuffling through paperwork at my desk. "What do you mean? About what?"

"I've been ordered to Washington. To meet with the President."

"Oh, that."

"What do you mean, 'Oh that!' I'm scared."

"Hallie, Hallie, calm down. Everybody loves you. Admires you. I was just given the same order."

"You were? Why? You think somebody like McCarthy or Roy Cohn accused us of being Communists? Just because I was liberated by the Russians?"

I stood and went to her and put my arm around her shoulder. She was shaking like a newborn puppy.

"Miss Rosen, I know President Truman. He's a good guy. We have nothing to fear from him."

"Then what does he want?"

"I have no idea. For a private audience — if that's what this is — he must have questions to ask."

"About how I became a citizen? I'm always concerned about that."

"If there were questions about that it would never get to the President. Not even to the State Department. Immigration and Naturalization would handle it. Probably right here in Europe."

Her trembling eased. "Then what else?"

I wanted to kiss her, to comfort her, but we had promised never to act romantic in the Embassy.

"Did it ever occur to you that this might be something good?"

"Well . . . no."

"I have an idea. We owe ourselves a honeymoon. Whatever the President wants, afterward I'll show you New York. More important, you can meet my family. They would love that. I would love that."

She broke our rule by kissing my chest through my shirt. Then she was gone, a different person than the one who had busted in a few minutes before.


## Washington, 1947

No pigs. There were no pigs on the President's desk. But this was not that President. This was not that desk. This was not that time. This was the time the President summoned us from Berlin to talk about something. As we were led into the Oval Office we did not know what. He greeted us cordially, I introduced him to Hallie.

"It looks as if living in Berlin agrees with you, Captain Maisel," he said, which I took as a compliment to my wife.

"It does, Mr. President."

"I have a note here to compliment you on your work with the Airlift, Captain, which does not surprise me. I do not know the specifics, but I do know General Tunner. That is high praise."

"In truth, Sir, the important work was done by Miss Rosen. But I accept the compliment for both of us."

Mr. Truman leaned back in his chair for a moment, stretched his shoulders as if to ease muscles. But perhaps I am projecting, Hallie and I were more than tense. It was an effort for us to breathe deeply, slowly.

"I imagine you are wondering why I summoned you here. I shall get directly to the point. Are you aware of the situation in Palestine?"

"As much as the newspapers report, Sir."

"Well, I'll give you some background. I'm sure you know that for two thousand years there has been on and off warfare between the Arabs and the Jews. Both sides laying claim to the same territory. In recent years the United Nations has tried to create peace in the area, which has been under British control for some time. But the British mandate will end in a few months."

"May 14th," Hallie interjected. "At midnight."

"Good, Mrs. Maisel, I see you are up on things."

"With all due respect, Mr. President," she said, crossing her legs, smoothing her skirt, "it is Miss Rosen. Warrant Officer j.g. Hallie Rosen."

The President's gaze appeared to dart a bit lower, as if he were checking our hands for rings. We both were wearing them.

"I see. I thought . . . Well, no matter. Back to Palestine. For a year there have been discussions at the UN as to what should happen after the British leave. Some parties suggest the only way to keep the peace is to create a joint territory administered by the UN itself. Others say that would be only a temporary solution, avoiding the underlying question: that this is the time to face the issue squarely. Personally, I subscribe to the latter view. That belief prevailed, and last summer the UN decided the land should be divided — one part for an Arab state, the other for a Jewish state. Of that I suspect you are aware."

"Yes, Sir," we said in unison.

"You also know that the Jewish leaders accepted this idea at once. A trickle of European Jews who had survived the war and moved to Palestine seeking a a place of safety became a flood as thousands, tens of thousands, of emigrants sought a Jewish homeland."

"Yes, Sir."

"But the leaders of the surrounding Arab states rejected this plan of partition. They do not want a Jewish state anywhere near their borders. Anywhere at all. You can guess what this set the stage for."

"Another war," I said.

"Exactly. Now, how does this affect the two of you? I must say that everything we talk about from here on is strictly confidential. It should not be repeated outside this room, whatever you decide."

"Decide, Sir?" Hallie said.

"We have it on good authority that the Jewish leader, David Ben-Gurion, plans to declare a Jewish state precisely at midnight on May 14. That would be 6 p.m. Washington time. Intelligence reports indicate that the four surrounding Arab nations are already massing troops and tanks at the projected borders. War is a certainty."

The President paused, sipped from a glass of water on his desk. My own mouth was desert-dry.

"It is my inclination," Mr. Truman continued, "for the United States to recognize this new Jewish state — they haven't chosen a name yet — as soon as it is created. I want the prestige of the U.S. to lead the way in welcoming it into the pantheon of nations. I must concede that there is disagreement, even bitterness, about this within the administration. Secretary of State Marshall, who has more prestige across the country than even the President, is firmly against it. He wants me to wait at least several months, until the Jewish state is up and functioning. Without doing so, he told me from your very chair, 'would be like buying a pig in a poke.'"

A pig on the desk after all.

"I've been warned by some that General Marshall might resign if I stick to my plan. That would cost me re-election at the very least. No matter. I know my intention is the correct one, for moral reasons if nothing else. After the Holocaust the Jews certainly deserve a homeland — one that can be celebrated. There is also a constitutional issue to reinforce. In our democracy the State Department carries out foreign policy — but the President determines it. When the time comes I don't think General Marshall will oppose me publicly. He is too much of a patriot."

The President paused for a moment. Hallie and I glanced at one another. She wrinkled her brow. We still had no idea why we were being told all this.

The President looked at his watch. "I seem to have babbled for too long. And still not cut the cake. So. Why you are here, Captain Maisel, is that once we recognize the Jewish state, I will need an ambassador there. To keep me appraised of what is going on. I would like you to be that ambassador."

"I . . . I don't know what to say, Mr. President. I am honored by the offer. But I don't know why you would choose me. You have so many professional diplomats."

"To choose from? Yes, I do. But the best of them have had dealings in the Middle East at one time or another. They have made friends, but also enemies. I view this situation as a chance for a *tabula rasa*. A clean slate. About which neither side will have preconceptions. That can be you, Captain. You have fulfilled all of your assignments with excellence." He lifted a yellow folder from the desk, a blue one beneath it. "I have complete faith that you would do so again."

"Well, thank you, Sir."

"But before you give me an answer, I have to warn you that there are a number of down sides to my offer. First, you would have to resign your commission. We can't have a military man as an Ambassador. If you have planned on a career in the military, that would be out the window. Technically, you would be an employee of the State Department. Miss Rosen, as the Ambassador's wife you would not be employed by the government. But you would have to resign from the Army as well. Secondly, you of course would have to move from Berlin, with all of its civilized advantages, to Tel Aviv. A small, growing city but one surrounded as far as the eye can see by ancient desert on one side and ocean on the other. I have never been there, but I gather it lacks many of the modern amenities. Most important, you very likely would be moving into a war zone. By dawn's early light, instead of birds you may well hear artillery shells bursting."

"You paint a grim picture, Mr. President," Hallie said.

"I believe in telling the truth, Mrs. Maisel. Miss Rosen. I don't expect an answer right way. Talk it over, think it over. Get back to me in two days with your decision."

"Mr. President, is it alright if we go to the cafeteria for a cup of coffee?"

"Not if you plan to discuss this, Captain. Use my private dining room. I'll send up coffee and apple pie."

"Very symbolic, Sir."

"More important, quite delicious. From a recipe created by Bess."

Saluting the Commander-in-Chief, we left the Oval Office and walked toward the stairs. Before reaching the dining room we both knew without saying a word that soon we'd be living in the desert.

## SIDE TRIP

My true image of how hippocampus works: it has nothing to do with hippos or rhinos or campuses. Inside hippocampus is a pond of clear water. A small man — an elf, perhaps, in a green cap and green tights — is seated on a granite rock. On his lap is a yellow pad attached to a clip board. As events in my life transpire, the elf scrawls notes in a secret shorthand at a rapid pace. If what is happening the elf regards as important, such as a conversation in the Oval Office, he (or she, or it — it is hard to tell with elves) secures the notes to a small, glowing stone and drops the stone deep into the hippocampus pond, where it may remain forever, hauled to the surface of consciousness only when hippocampus desires. What the elf perceives (sometimes wrongly) as less dramatic events also are noted, but with fewer details; if the elf is bored they attach to stones that do not glow. The sights and sounds of such memories gradually deteriorate, then disappear completely. The hippo pond has limited storage space.

My elf apparently was not very interested in our visit to New York. It is a soggy blur in my memory. I would have thought elves were more sentimental than that. But you can imagine it for yourselves. Embracing my father in the apartment on the Lower East Side, hugging Bubbie/Celine, kissing her cheek, introducing them to Hallie, handshakes, smiles, welcome to the family, happy that someone has settled Exit down. It's Sunday so sister Rachel, her husband Dr. Steven Gold and two shy twin tykes come as well, hugs and kisses, especially warm as Rachel hugs Hallie, binding her to the family; they are about the same age, like each other at once. Uncle Joshua motors over from his nearby apartment, more hugs, Joshua will take them all to dinner at a kosher restaurant to celebrate, chatter chatter chatter, that is all hippocampus recalls. I visit Whitebread the next day, he has stopped delivering vegetables, his love of horses has earned him an apprentice job as second assistant trainer at a racing stable at Belmont Park. Go Whitebread go! We manage to shoot a few hoops, no game, just fooling around.

## THE DECISION

"Is your wife not with you?" the President asked.

"No, Mr. President. I hope that is not a problem."

"She is not ill, I trust."

"No, Sir. We went to New York for the weekend so my wife could meet my family. Enjoyed a wonderful reception. Hallie and my sister, Rachel, hit it off instantly. In fact, Rachel came down with us last night so she could show Hallie the sights of Washington while they got acquainted. No disrespect was intended, Mr. President."

"I assume not. I also assume — correct me if I am wrong — that your appearance here in person means that you are going to accept my offer to become Ambassador to the Jews."

"Yes, Sir. Hallie and I have agreed to move to Tel Aviv as soon as you require."

President Truman, nodding, stood from behind his pigless desk, walked around it and as I rose he shook my hand. "Congratulations, Captain," he said. "I would say Ambassador, but I prefer to wait until you have a country."

"Thank you, Sir. Should I begin preparations at once, such as resigning from the Army?"

"Yes. But I have another thing to tell you. If Miss Rosen were here I would tell you anyway, I assume she can be trusted, but in a way her absence is a blessing. We'll start the Ambassadorial appointment moving at the State Department, need to know basis. Leaving blank the name of the country, which apparently still has not been decided. The outlook is for immediate war, as we discussed last week. You and your wife are two brave and patriotic individuals, for which I thank both of you, for myself and for the country. You I knew about, of course. While Miss Rosen's file easily passed muster, I did not get to read it personally until the weekend. Her background will be extra helpful."

"How so, Sir?"

"Before and during the war, thousands of Jews fleeing Hitler settled in Palestine, as I am sure you know, hoping that some day it might become a Jewish homeland. Land of their fathers, and so forth. When the concentration camps were liberated at war's end, thousands of the survivors found passage there. According to our intelligence reports, there is no more respected person in Palestine than a survivor of Auschwitz."

"I don't understand how that relates to the Ambassadorship, Mr. President."

"You don't? When we reveal that your wife is a camp survivor, all the more moral authority will rebound to the embassy. That will be quite useful, I believe."

"Reveal? Why would you reveal Hallie's personal history? To whom?"

"Whenever we announce a new ambassador, the press office puts out a brief biography. And that of his wife. As a convenience for the host government and the local newspapers. Saves you from answering a lot of questions."

I felt warm in my uniform. Before realizing it I was sweating all over — my forehead, neck, under my arms, between my legs. Angry blood began coursing through my veins. I could barely sit still. Ran my wrist against my damp forehead. I should not then have said what I said, but I did.

"With respect, Sir, I think that is shameful. You always seemed more sensitive than that."

Truman glared at me. His gray eyes turned to coal. The overhead light glinted off droplets of sweat on his forehead.

"Is that so, Maisel?" He spoke in a voice of steel, leaning forward. "Don't get too cocky. I'm still your Commander-in-Chief." He seemed to be holding back his words with his teeth. "Tell me — slowly — what I have done that you find so shameless." I noticed that his fists had clenched.

"Sir. You spoke of announcing to the world that Hallie is a survivor of Auschwitz."

"That is nothing to be ashamed of, Captain. It is looked on as heroic, I would think."

I spoke briskly. "It is also private. Something that no man or woman alive has the right to make public other than Hallie herself. Would you also reveal to the world that she was a prisoner in Mengele's laboratory? That she has scars across her abdomen from his experimental incisions — made without anesthetic? That because of this she cannot bear children? That at least once a week she wakes from a nightmare covered in sweat, her voice hoarse from screaming — unless I have stifled her screams to wake her, in which case she sometimes dreams she is being drowned? Will all that, too, be in the public domain?"

I took a deep breath, not certain if I had breathed at all during my outburst. In the Rose Garden beyond the window two pigeons were peering, looking puzzled, as if wondering why I was almost yelling at the President. Truman, too, was breathing heavily. Slowly his body unclenched. With what seemed like difficulty he stood, stunned, stepped behind his chair, looked out the window, his hands clasped tightly behind his back. His shoulders in his gray suit were rising and falling slowly as if he were still taking long, deep breaths. I don't recall how long he stood that way, five minutes at least, perhaps ten. All I knew was that I just had talked myself out of an Ambassadorship. When he returned to his chair he seemed calmer but his face still was red. My fury had one more torpedo to fire. I could not help myself.

"Mr. President, I must make myself clear. If the press office insists on invading Hallie's privacy, you can get yourself another boy."

I slipped my hat back onto my head.

"Meaning?"

"Meaning I shall turn down the position and see what private life has to offer."

The President waved his right hand through the air. A silver cuff link came loose and clattered noisily onto the desk. I could not tell if his awkward wave was an expression of disgust or conciliation. He reached for the link and with effort reinserted it into his cuff. The pause permitted a bit of sanity to return to my brain.

"Mr. President," I said, "I apologize if I spoke out of turn."

"Don't, Captain. Don't apologize. If anyone should apologize it is me. I was way off base. I should not have needed you to set me straight. But I am glad you did. There is a phrase I have always liked: Speaking Truth to Power. There are too many Yes-men around here, afraid to hurt the boss's feelings, fearful of my reaction. I'm glad you learned to speak up when you felt the need. Somewhere along the way you encountered a good teacher."

"If I may, Sir, that was you."

The President ran his hand through his thinning, graying hair. Squeezed his cuff link to make sure it was stable. "I will take that as truth, not flattery. Never forget it, especially in my company."

"No, Sir. Yes, Sir."

"As for your wife, her privacy is her own, as it should be. I'll make sure of that. She is such a strong, attractive young WAC, one would never think . . ."

He caught himself before compounding his error.

"Which brings me to a side job I'm giving you. A bit of intelligence work. It will be our secret."

"Spying?"

"I don't think of it as spying when it deals with our own people. The OSS was a disaster — Pearl Harbor and all that. I'm replacing it with

what we are calling the Central Intelligence Agency. I expect it to be
a lot better at providing me with timely information. The blueprint is
being drawn up by Allen Dulles. He will be the Director, there is no
way I can avoid that. But Dulles does not speak truth to power. He
does not speak truth to anyone. Including me, I have to assume. So you
will be my liaison with the CIA. Dulles thinks I'm a fool, and he won't
like you, either. But being based overseas you won't be a threat to him.
The occasional pouch from Tel Aviv won't attract attention. Nor will
your turning up at an occasional meeting."

I did not know what to say. I said nothing.


## NUREMBERG

*Magician.* The word bolted him forward in his seat like an electric
probe, drilled into his broken tooth like a dentist's bit. *A street
magician in Linz.* It had to have been his father!

They were in Nuremberg, a reasonable drive from Berlin, where the
second round of trials had begun. They had time to kill before moving
on to Tel Aviv. Exit was curious to watch a trial, perhaps because
of his legal training, but was surprised Hallie wanted to accompany
him. "It might bring back your nightmares," he said. "They come back
most nights anyway," she said, "do you think I'm asleep when I'm
whimpering?"

The city had a more pleasant atmosphere than they expected:
architecture from the Middle Ages, narrow streets, picturesque
churches. An odd place to have been chosen for the trials. Except that
the Nazis had won an early following here; in a broad open field some
of their largest rallies had been addressed by Hitler long before he was
Hitler. And its large courthouse had not been bombed during the war.

The major Nazi criminals had been tried the previous year — those
who had not, like *Der Fuehrer*, killed themselves. Most had been
convicted and hanged, but three years after the war, some were still
unaccounted for, if they were still alive: Eichmann, Mengele. West
German and American Nazi hunters were scouring the earth for them,
following every lead. The current bunch were less well-known, but
there were more than enough witnesses to send them to the gallows
for war crimes.

"Before we adjourned yesterday," the chief of the three-judge
panel said to the witness, "you told us of specific physical actions you
witnessed by the defendant. There will be no need to describe those
again."

The woman, whose face was heavy and mottled, gazed without visible expression at the defendant, a thin man in black garb seated on a straight-backed wooden chair in a glass-enclosed booth that surely was bullet-proof. The trials were being conducted by judges and lawyers from three different countries — France, Great Britain and the United States — which made them both unusual and controversial. Simultaneous translations were available to the public in four languages. In the courtroom where Exit and Hallie sat, a French soldier in a beret stood smartly outside the defendant's booth, a rifle strapped over his shoulder. The chief judge was British.

"Continue where you left off yesterday, Mrs. Lang," the judge said, putting on rimless eyeglasses, glancing at a sheet of paper. "It was a lovely afternoon in 1933, you told the court. In the village of Linz, townspeople and perhaps visitors were gathered at a small park where a street magician was performing under a large oak tree. He was well known to the villagers," you said, "they were smiling and laughing at the tricks he was performing with stuffed rabbits, small dogs, other objects, which he often did after closing his pillow shop for the day. Now, please resume from there."

Exit found himself squeezing Hallie's hand much harder than at first he realized, while trying to look stoic. "My parents!" he whispered, and thought: Why the fuck did we walk into this trial? FDR was right. Coincidence rules our lives.

"The magician was Jacob," the witness said. "His wife was Merele. She was my best friend, a good woman. Always looked nice, too. We used to go to the butcher shop together. She was standing near me under a tall tree, watching her husband perform. People were laughing, cheering. Maybe a dozen people. We heard a rumbling behind us. We turned and saw a truck pull up. When it stopped, six policemen jumped off. The back of the truck was open, the door rolled to the top."

"Go on."

"The magician stopped in the middle of a trick. The police moved among us. We were mostly women and children. They seemed to be looking us over. The defendant came over and looked at me and Merele. We were frightened. He put his hand on Merele's arm. He had a gun in a black holster on his belt. I could see Merele shaking. She was shy, she didn't saying anything. I was bolder. 'What do you want with us?' I asked.

"'Nothing with you . . . fatty,' he said to me."

The witness began to sob. "That's what he called me. He didn't need to say that. A little boy laughed. His mother clamped her hand over his mouth. . .The defendant began to pull Merele away from us. We watched, helpless. Her hat blew off. He led her toward the truck, where the other soldiers were standing. They all had guns in their holsters. Some were nodding approval at the leader's choice. Her husband Jacob took maybe three steps toward them. One soldier snapped open his holster and leveled his gun at Jacob. The poor man had to stop. Two of his little dogs yipped around him. 'What do you want from us?' I cried. 'We haven't done anything wrong.' The soldier holding the gun on Jacob lowered the angle. He pulled the trigger and shot one of the dogs. A little white hairless thing. The bullet ripped him into the air, spurting blood. Children began to cry, hid behind their mothers' skirts. Two soldiers hoisted Merele onto the back of the truck. She began to cry out for help. 'What do you want from her?' I shouted. 'Be quiet, fat broad,' the leader said. 'Unless you too want to pull a train.'

"I gasped. As did several other women. The magician ran toward the truck. He was not a tall man. A soldier grabbed his beard and twisted him to the grass. And kicked him in the face with his hard black boot. Jacob lay there, bleeding. The defendant waved his arm and all the soldiers climbed into the truck. Except one, who climbed behind the wheel.

"The leader said to us, 'Why are you no longer laughing? We are making the magician's wife disappear!' And the truck rolled away, Merele screaming as the soldiers knelt around her."

The witness was sobbing. She seemed unable to continue.

"Just one more question," the chief judge said. "Did you ever see Merele Maisel again?"

She shook her head.

"Please speak up."

"No. No one in Linz ever saw her again."

"As far as you know."

"As far as I know."

The judge dismissed the witness. The bailiff called another. I wanted to leave but was riveted. The defendant's glass box had become a blur of spurting blood. Hallie yanked me up and pulled me from the courtroom down a hallway into the stinking air.

Of all the on-going trials why had we walked into this one? In FDR's religion of coincidence, that day was Yom Kippur. After 14 years I finally had said yizkor for my mother.

## ISRAEL

My first written notes as Ambassador, preserved all these years under glass on my desk: "At precisely midnight on the 14th of May, 1948, David Ben-Gurion proclaimed the existence of the new State of Israel. Eleven minutes later, President Truman welcomed Israel into the community of nations. The U.S. was the first country to do so, which was what Truman wanted. Just hours later, the first bomb in the Israeli War for Independence fell on Tel Aviv."

Two fluffs of white hair, later to become world-famous, flanked Mr. Ben-Gurion's bald pate when I went to his office to present my credentials. Short, stocky, dressed in a wrinkled brown suit, he did not have the appearance of a soldier, yet a military aura draped him nonetheless; round-faced, his cheeks deep-set with wrinkles, he had fought for this day in bloody skirmishes all his life. He welcomed me warmly, said he had already called President Truman to thank him for his prompt recognition of the State of Israel. He asked if the accommodations for myself and Hallie at our new embassy were satisfactory. Quite so, I told him.

Months earlier, when it became clear that a Jewish homeland was in the offing, our State Department had purchased property on which to build an embassy. It was in Tel Aviv, a flat city facing beaches on the Mediteranean, not ideal for a secure location in the event of attack. But at the rear of the city stood a series of hardened sand dunes. The embassy was built flush up against these dunes, offering protection from the rear. A two-story building was fronted with hard woods, thick glass and steel in case of attack. When I described this to the Prime Minister, he said yes, he had walked by many times during its construction and had a good feeling every time. It told him American guards would be arriving soon. I did not mention the automatic machine guns that had been hidden throughout the structure, facing in every direction except the dunes. But the Prime Minister was aware of those.

"When you start from scratch," he said, "you must keep track from scratch."

He asked about Hallie. "She's worn little but her Army uniform for two years," I told him. "She wanted to walk down Rothschild Boulevard to see what civilian clothing might be in style for an Ambassador's wife."

"Normal protocol would require a reception to introduce a new Ambassador to all the others," Ben-Gurion said. "But since as yet there are no others, that would have been a lonely gathering. I could have invited our Cabinet and their wives to meet you, but as you know, as of today there is a war on, so creating such an inviting target did not seem like a good idea. Speaking of your wife, I am anxious to meet her. Word is that she is very bright in her own right, and plucky enough to have survived Auschwitz."

I jolted forward in my seat as if hit by a cattle prod. "How do you know that, Sir?"

"Thousands of our citizens are survivors of the camps. It is not a sign of shame but of heroism."

"That was not my question. How do you know?" I was trying to keep my anger under control.

"The one good thing to come out of the Diaspora," the Prime Minister said, "is that I daresay we have the largest intelligence operation in the world. Many still waiting to be trained, of course. One of them may have been with your wife at Auschwitz. Or recognized her photo when your appointment was announced. We share information. There could be a hundred ways we know. Why does it upset you so that I am privy to this?"

I sank back into my seat, letting my sweat cool.

"Hero or not, Hallie's private life is her own. President Truman wanted it to be included in that first press release. I told him if he did that, he could find himself another Ambassador. He gave me his word it would not be publicized until Hallie chose to do so herself. So when you came out with that . . ."

"You thought the President had broken his word."

"It would have been out of character. I know him fairly well. But . . ."

"I can assure you, Ambassador, the information did not come from Mr. Truman. Or from anyone in the United States. Not that there is anything wrong with it of course. On the contrary. But I will further assure you that it will be deleted from our files this very day, and will never be published by the State of Israel. I concede I am confused as to why this fact should be confidential. Thousands of our refugees are in that position. But you have my word."

"I thank you for that, Prime Minister."

The low table set between us was constructed of sandblasted raw wood. Perched on the wood was a large brass tray that had seen the better or the worst of at least three wars, attested to a by series of lumpen bullet dents. Ben-Gurion made no effort to explain. Instead he rang a small bell that sat on the table. Moments later a woman named Shona entered the room carrying a silver tray and set on the rickety table two tea cups already filled, spoons, napkins, a plate of warm apple ruggaleh. "Help yourself," the Prime Minister said, and did so himself as Shona left. "Mmm" was all I could say.

"We seem to have taken an unexpected detour by way of Germany," Ben-Gurion noted. "I'm glad we got that straightened out before a misunderstanding occurred." He spoke fluent English flavored with an accent from somewhere in Europe. "But there is something else I would like to discuss with you, if you won't mind an old fox giving a new hen a lesson in diplomacy."

"Old foxes are the best teachers," I replied. The Prime Minister nodded and fed his ample belly another piece of cake.

"Here is the deal, as you Americans say. As you know, our Arab neighbors on four sides declared war on us the moment we formally created the State of Israel. That has been their worst fear for 150 going on two thousand years. They believe we do not belong in this part of the world. In fact, rather like our friend the unlamented Hitler, they do not believe we Jews belong in any part of the world. You Americans, the British and the Russians set the Nazis straight on that. This time we Jews plan to set the record straight ourselves."

"Do you have enough men and armaments to fight four enemies at once?"

"Ah, that is the point to which I am getting, Ambassador. How would you like to send President Truman our best intelligence estimates of our varied strengths. In a secure pouch of course. That would be a nice surprise for him as your first communique, don't you think?"

"He would . . . why would you . . . ?"

"Here comes the diplomacy part. As you have seen, the land here is mostly desert. Israel, Egypt, Trans-Jordan, Syria, Lebanon. There is no place to hide even a part of an Army. I suspect your War Department possesses the latest in aerial photography, from which they have estimated the relative strength of the opposing forces. We've spotted their planes overhead many times."

"If that is the case, why would the President need what I send him?"

"Think, Mr. Ambassador. You do not know for certain that he already has this information. This is the latest Israeli Intelligence — where did you get it after only a few days in our country? I think that would earn you several feathers in the President's cap, don't you?"

"To be honest, Sir, I don't think much about feathers."

"That is now. Wait until you get older. In the end every man thinks about feathers."

My tea was cold. I poured another cup, took another ruggellah.

"If I may, Mr. Ben-Gurion, where does your interest fall in this . . .
transaction?"

"Good, good. For every quid there must be a quo. That is the
difference between war and diplomacy."

"And your quid is?"

"I imagine you are aware of the background. For years now, to
reduce the size of any war out here, your country has embargoed
shipments of war materials to any of the states in the region. Including
Palestine. That is us — now the State of Israel. The material you will be
sending him suggests the extreme odds we will be up against without
American arms. By recognizing us so quickly, he has shown to the
world his dedication to our survival. But he has not yet announced
a lifting of the embargo. Without American arms his allegiance may
mean little."

I looked over the intelligence reports he had spread before me:

"Without more arms, how do you expect to defeat four armies
simultaneously?"

"I'll let you in on a secret, Ambassador. Our secret is the Bible.
Let me tell you something." He orates a bit, then reads from a worn,
cracked black leather book, the page already marked.

"The Jewish faith is not only monotheism," he begins. "Intrinsic
to it is the national and territorial motif, which led to the profound
spiritual allegiance of the Jews to their ancient land, even while they
lived in exile. This motif finds expression in all the books of the Bible.
It appears in the first monotheistic revelation, in the first meeting of
Abraham, the father of the Jews, with God. It is not important whether
the story is a true record of an historic event or not. What is important
is that this is what Jews believe. We read in Genesis: 'Now the Lord
said unto Abram: Get thee out of they father's house into a land which
I will show thee, and I will make thee a great nation.' This is the first
statement of the national and territorial theme. Our prophets tell us
that the time is now. Indeed, if it is not now, after the Shoah it may
never be. We believe this from on High. This belief is our own Atomic
Bomb."

I nodded. "With, perhaps, a few gadgets added as persuaders, I
imagine. But military men would say that is a slim reed to rely on in a
brutal world. What is it you expect me to do, Mr. Ben-Gurion? I am
merely an Ambassador. I do not make policy for the President."

"Or course not. I am not expecting you to do so. But I need
information about when he plans to lift the embargo. Then we can
plan ahead. I don't want to ask him myself, that would be nudging

him too much. But a simple query from his new Ambassador — who might or might not share the information with me — seems within the bounds."

"A quid for the intelligence quo."

"Exactly."

We chatted a bit longer, like two old friends.

"Is there a shop nearby," I asked him, "where I might acquire a gun?"

"What kind of gun? A rifle? I'm afraid the military . . ."

"Just a handgun, Sir. I'm an Army man, and in a war zone I like to be able to defend myself if necessary. With any luck the front will never be closer than 30 miles from here. But when I have to travel for the government, leave my wife home alone, I would feel more comfortable."

"Of course. L'Chaim Gun Shoppe. Two streets down. Tell him Ben-Gurion sent you. You'll get a deal."

The fellow's name was David Kaplan. He was thin, bald, perhaps too old for the service. He showed me an array of merchandise, lethal and pretty. I told him I wanted something light in the hand but powerful enough to stop an intruder up close.

"The oncoming war has diminished my stock," he said, his voice raspy, as if he were still battling something from the last war. Gas, perhaps. But he picked out several that felt good and appeared deadly enough; the maker I don't remember, it may have been German. I told him Ben-Gurion had sent me; he offered a nice price. I remembered what I had been thinking about leaving Hallie alone. I bought two.

The diplomat pouch took four days to get to the White House and back. I envisioned it as a carrier pigeon of ancient days, bringing word to King David of peace or war. The President thanked me for the information without specifying what that was. Then Truman added, "As for your second question, NO." I was shocked. How could he endorse the existence of the State of Israel and then stand by and watch it be defeated, for lack of armaments, in perhaps a matter of days, by four surrounding states. It made no sense. The United Nations would become a laughingstock. After debating whether I should show his response to Ben-Gurion, I decided I must. The feisty Prime Minister seemed disappointed but not surprised. "It's politics," he said. "Mr. Truman has a difficult reelection campaign coming up. He needs the Jewish vote, and Jewish donations. But he also does not want to turn the entire Arab world against him."

I said nothing. Naively, I wanted to think President Truman was above politics.

The first bomb over Tel Aviv, that first day, missed by half a mile. The Egyptians are in a hurry, Ben-Gurion said. I used his phone to call our Embassy. Hallie was back from shopping, trying on her new clothes in the bomb-proof basement. I hurried to her, two polished pistols in a paper bag.

The Syrians, Egyptians, Lebanese, Trans-Jordanians all crossed their borders into Israel that very first day. Israeli intelligence gave their own country, despite its dearth of weapons, a fifty per cent chance of surviving the war. David Ben-Gurion expressed no doubts.

## THE DOCTOR

Mengele

Why does he come to mind now?

Because the Prime Minister had mentioned Auschwitz.

The Satanic doctor had escaped into the forests a week before the Russians liberated the camp. Three years later it was not known if he were dead or alive. Mossad and the CIA were searching for him all over the globe. If they were to find him alive, Hallie might be wanted as a witness. Voluntary, of course. To help hang him from the highest gallows at Nuremberg.

Mengele. He was never at the front of our minds. But he was always at the back of our minds.

Not much to report from the Embassy those first days. Hand grenades and machine guns triumphed over paperwork. Sand blowing off the windows. The Israelis doing well in major encounters but in isolated, ill-defended kibutzes were being massacred. At one kibbutz, 104 were killed in one attack alone, including 21 women. Their blood clogging my arteries day after day until I am finding it hard to breathe the salty air.

"The President will never approve," Hallie says. "You're his Ambassador, not a buck private. And for another country yet!"

"Then I won't ask him."

"You'll just take a dead man's rifle and wander down to Jerusalem and kill some Arabs?"

"They are killing us."

"They are not killing us. We are Americans."

"We are also Jews. Were you an American in the camps?"

"Exi, Exi, I know how you feel."

"Do you? I enlisted to fight. When in basic they taught me to fight it felt good. Ship over there and kill the Hun bastards. So I thought.

But greater minds sent me to OTC. To learn to kill even better. To lead battalions into battle. I dreamed of that day. They were good dreams, terrible as that sounds. So then what? I'm prepared to go fight for my country when Truman sends me to Los Alamos. To be a messenger boy. That was a hell of a bomb they tested. Our bomb. But not my bomb. And now? Holed up in this nice bomb-proof Embassy while our fellow Jews are bleeding rivers to create a homeland for our people. Battling four nations at once who would like to do to us what the Nazis did. I can't sit and watch any more. So no, I won't ask the President for permission. I'll ask Ben-Gurion. No, I'll tell Ben-Gurion. He knows he needs every man he can get."

"And the Embassy office?"

"You'll be the Embassy office. Signing my name to whatever is necessary."

"Wonderful. And what if you get hurt?"

"I won't get hurt."

"Or killed?"

"I won't get killed. God won't let me get killed."

"You've been talking to Him lately behind my back? You don't even believe in Him."

"We've been working on our relationship."

## COMRADES

*Shalom* he says to me though he does not know who I am. *Shalom* I say to him though I do not know who he is. We are not wearing uniforms just ordinary farmer's clothing, wool plaid shirts and dungarees and boots. The Israelis don't have enough uniforms for everyone nor do they have enough guns for everyone, maybe one of us in three carries a rifle so we march along weaponless, maybe a machine gun here and there taken from the stiff hands of dead Arabs. And hats, white cotton hats against the soaking sun of the desert or red bandanas wrapped around our foreheads against the blowing, needle-sharp sand; this is how we plan to conquer Jerusalem. No one asked my name, no one asks anybody's name, names do not matter in the blazing desert, find yourself a dead man's gun and a pith helmet if you can and join us on the road, join the march. You hear that whine, that is a small plane approaching, dive into the sand and cover your head with your arms and lie still and pray, even if you have never prayed before. The odds are not bad, the Arab probably has never flown a plane before. In village after village we leave bodies. Some are theirs and some are ours. The main thing is to never leave a gun.

"I know you. American, right? You're the Ambassador's brother," the man says. "I seen your picture in the papers. Or a magazine. With the eye patch. As if Dayan has his own brigade."

I don't reply as sand spits up around us.

"No? I get it. You're the Ambassador himself! But that's impossible. What the hell would you be doing out here?"

Still I don't reply.

"I suppose you need to kill these bastards. Just like the rest of us. Don't worry, I'll keep your secret. Where were you two years ago, in '45, '46?"

"Still in school." I was not about to tell him I was working for the President. I didn't know who he was.

"I slipped back into Germany then," he says. "Joined DIN. Men came from all over. Hunting Nazis who tried to disappear when the war ended. Some confessed, some denied it. We must have killed a thousand of them. Shooting, hanging."

"Without trials?"

"I never heard of trials at Treblinka."

"Did you feel guilt?"

"Some of us did, some didn't. Some of the time, all of the time. The 14th of May, the blue and white flags. The State of Israel. That's when guilt disappeared. We hadn't killed in vain. Now the bastards want to kick us out again. That ain't gonna happen."

Syrians, Egyptians, Saudies, Jordanians, most in uniforms, some not, but they bleed as much as do we. Uniforms of all colors drifting down from the skies like flags. White birds from the beaches of Tel Aviv taking flight into the desert. Lizards skewered on sticks, are lizards kosher? At defenseless kibbutzim Arabs with machine guns decimate defenseless Israelis. Firing from the rear I blow away Egyptian machine gunners. One man surviving hits me in the abdomen, near the spine. My partner without uniform commandeers a jeep and races through the desert to the nearest field clinic. The bullet is too near my spine to operate, the surgeon says. For days I lay there recovering. Thinking of Hallie, of my one-way covenant with God: not to die out here.

The rumor creeps into a weekly Israeli newspaper, circles the world in minor items from China to Peru. He is a diplomat, an Ambassador. How an Ambassador, name unknown, from a nation name unknown, helped defend a country village. Few believe the story, bored correspondents half drunk sometimes make things up.

He turns slowly in his bed, with his fingers touches gently the flesh beside his spine. His fingers find something near his abdomen. Scar tissue. In the shape of a bullet. Never will he tell the tale except to Hallie. But upon returning from a hospital to the Embassy finds in his bedroom a bouquet of flowers. The signature is David Ben-Gurion. Another bouquet for his wife. How many times he has had this dream he cannot say. But always when he awakens the scar tissue remains in his flesh.

## THE STRANGER

Jerusalem nights. Lovely Hallie, too, has an unexpected story. The Israelis won their War for Independence in nine months, the Egyptians, the Syrians, the Jordanians, the Libyans all believing at the outset that the Jews could not fight. All being disillusioned quickly. Each Arab nation knew they would destroy the Jews the next time, but meanwhile recognition of the new state poured in from every continent. The main boulevard in Tel Aviv became lined with embassies; the city grew quickly, it became the commercial, financial and political center of the small country. The Capital, in spirit and faith, would remain Jerusalem, with its ancient shrines of three major faiths, the birthplace of Jesus, the Temple on the Mount, the Dome of the Rock; new hotels built to house pilgrims who came from every part of the world while intermittently, like bloody rain, battles erupted over which nation or sect would control the divided city for the next few months. In these new hotels, where the architects tried to include replicas of ancient ruins or ancient Holy Places, guests could sip champagne to honor whichever country had newly bestowed recognition on Israel, while on the distant hills behind the city automatic weapons would periodically light up the night, no one sure of who was shooting at whom, the only certainty being that this was a city that was not yet complete in its rising and falling, nor ever would be.

On two consecutive Saturday nights, Hallie told me, while I was away in Washington for an operational conference — I think I first met Allen Dulles at one of them, the bastard — Hallie attended welcome parties in Jerusalem, as was her responsibility while I was away. At the first one a natty gentleman seemed to be keeping his eyes on her wherever she went. Feeling elegant in a bright new dress, with an

Embassy bodyguard in the car holding a loaded rifle across his knees, she thought little of the man while a limousine caromed over the sandy highway on the main route back to Tel Aviv. A week later, another party, a different dress, the same man was there, being much more obvious in his attentions to her.

When the extreme heat and humidity forced her to slip through French glass doors out into a private garden she lit a cigarette and leaned on a fresh-smelling wooden fence and looked out at the hills, where on this night at a least the skirmishing had stopped, at least for a time.

"May I borrow one of those?" the man asked. She had not noticed his presence. He was wearing a tuxedo on this night.

"I'm sorry, I don't smoke," Hallie replied, blowing light fumes away from his face.

"I see. Perhaps I am mistaken, and that is a Mannlicher between your fingers. Do you shoot?"

"Only when I have to."

"Are you good at it?"

"Only when I have to be."

"Just like your husband."

She hesitated, wondering who he was and how he could know about that. The diamond on her ring finger seemed to sparkle too much in the setting sun. She reached into her small beaded purse. "I really don't smoke," she said. "I bring just two cigarettes to every party. The first is for when I need to escape the boredom for some air. The second is to look stylish when I'm taking my leave. Since you appear to be a gentleman, you may have this second one."

"That's very generous, but I could not do that. Ony a cad would leave a lady without her getaway smoke. Unless I look at it another way, and surmise that you are in no hurry to get away."

"Surmise what you like," she said, "as long as you don't surmise the wrong thing."

"Oh, I would never do that, Miss Rosen. It is Miss Rosen, is it not? The wife of the American Ambassador?"

"You seem very well informed, Mr. . . ."

"Lev. Gerald Lev. That is part of my job."

"And what job is that, if I may ask?"

"Being informed."

"Is it difficult?"

"Sometimes more than others."

"Does it pay well?"

"Sometimes more than others."

"Take the damned cigarette, please. I fear I have run out of foolery. But first tell me your real name."

"Why should I do that? That is not a real cigarette."

"Sorry. Lucky Strike was all they had at the PX. They were out of Gauloises."

"Ah, bad luck. Maybe next time."

"You seem certain there will be a next time."

"Next time we shall discuss business. No more foolishness. Which I am the first to admit is a shame." He took a matchbook from his pocket, laid it on the table in front of her. "May I take you to dinner . . .?"

"My husband will be home . . ."

"On Friday, I believe. I was going to suggest tomorrow. Or Tuesday."

She fingered the book of matches. In small ink letters it was marked 8 p.m.

"It's not far from Rothschild," he said. "In Tel Aviv. Across from where you purchased that lovely red dress last week."

She began to get nervous. But even more curious.

"Do you have a telephone, Mr. Lev?"

"I'm afraid it's not that kind of business."

He fired up his Lucky Strike and left the small garden through a wrought-iron side entrance she had not noticed earlier. The Embassy limousine, the driver and her armed guard were waiting a block away.

She was wearing only a white slip as she sprawled on the bed reading a well-worn early Sartre. Showered after the long sweaty flight from Washington, I pulled my robe closed and told her to finish her story. "I assume you went to dinner with him," I said.

"I was so curious. Wouldn't you?"

"He didn't ask me."

"Oh, oh. Cranky. It was perfectly safe, he knew the guard was right outside the door."

"Not very romantic."

"Actually, it was kind of odd. He was waiting for me in a small room in the back of the restaurant. Just three small tables, the other two were empty. A candle was burning — but he was reading the local newspaper, by candlelight. And he was wearing combat boots. He politely pulled out a chair for me, ordered wine, we made small talk. Then he got down to business. He had seen my file, he said. Very impressive."

"Which file is that," I asked.

"My Army file. He wanted to hire me."

"Wait a minute. You'd better start from the beginning."

He sipped some wine. "Good idea," she said, and told me a story I never expected.

She set the Sartre aside, pulled her slip more ladylike over her thighs. I sat beside her on the bed.

"He was with Mossad," she said. "The Israeli Intelligence Service."

"Of course."

"They were always looking for well-placed eyes and ears, he said. The Embassy parties in Jerusalem and Tel Aviv are hotbeds for gossip. And spying. Since we get invited to so many parties, I would be well-placed to do something useful. Note any talk that sounds interesting, and pass it along to him. As the Ambassador's wife must be sociable, I would not be noticed for hanging around.

"I asked him how I would know what kind of gossip he would find useful. We would talk about that if I were interested, he said.

"I was flabbergasted, and I let him know it. 'How can you make such a request?' I asked him. 'I'm an American citizen, despite my lingering accent. You know that, if you've really seen my file. And grateful to be one. And you want me to spy against my own country?'

"'Whoa, calm down,' he said. 'It's not like that. We are close allies, as you know. You were the first country to recognize our statehood. That helped us a lot in the beginning. You wouldn't be spying on Americans, just tuning in to everyone else. I don't think we Israelis and you Americans are keeping secrets from one another. You've even begun selling us weapons, which is well known, much to the Arabs' chagrin. We'd just want to pick up on where they are getting theirs, that sort of thing.'

"I took a long sip of wine — it was red, not bad — and relaxed in my chair. We ordered appetizers for dinner. My brain was spinning like a helicopter blade. His offer felt like double-dealing on the American flag. But if I could be useful to our side as well as to the Israelis — well, who could it hurt? I think I felt like you did when you were so frustrated at not having seen combat, that you had to put on gardening clothes and go out and kill some Arabs."

"Nobody is asking women to fight," I said.

"I know, but that doesn't mean we don't want to. Besides, this would not be fighting."

"Just spying. You know what Arabs do to spies they catch?"

"I did begin thinking of that."

"Well, that's good. So you turned him down, I assume. Your new pal Gerald Lev."

"I wondered what you would think. Or if I even would tell you. That's what began to bother me most. We tell each other everything."

"Well, Miss Hallie Rosen, in my view you made the right decision."

"Not without some regrets," she said.

"Regrets. In life there will always be regrets." I rubbed her bare knee. "Your Mr. Lev is tall, am I correct? Lean face, almost horse-like, though not unattractive. Cracked his knuckles a bit too often. Maybe drank too much. Should you run into him again, his real name is James Jesus Angleton. At OTC he finished second to me in points. Mostly we called him Jesus. He is not with Mossad."

"Exit Maisel, how do you know any of that?"

"Sweet Miss Rosen." I resumed rubbing her knee. "Like your mysterious Mr. Lev, my job also is to be informed."

A pause. An uncertain look on her freshly scrubbed face. She goes to her dresser, slips on a pair of pajama bottoms, returns to the bed. I am not sure if this is because she is tired, or because I am tired, or if she is making a statement. Usually she makes her statements out loud. She pulls the top sheet over her. Is she cold?

"What about Part Two?" I ask.

"What is Part Two?"

"In such approaches there is always a Part Two."

"I don't understand."

"Ah, I get it. He pledged you not to mention Part Two to anyone. Including me."

"If you are correct, then I have nothing more to say, do I?"

## STATECRAFT

"Hallie, Hallie, don't be angry. Let *me* tell *you* about Part Two. The first part ended when he finally became convinced that you were not willing to work for Mossad. Surprisingly, he did not seem disappointed. In fact, he seemed almost glad, which he told you. 'The truth is, Miss Rosen,' or something like that, he would have said, 'I do not work for Mossad. This is strictly between us. I am with U.S. Intelligence. This whole episode has been a test. A test of your loyalty. Of whether you are committed 100 per cent to the United States. This may sound silly, or may not, but in view of your German birth, the Director insisted on it. He often does.'

"Am I right so far?"

Hallie said nothing, just stared at me.

"Everything I told you is true, he would have said. 'You get nothing but excellent reports. Your courage is . . . exemplary. Your work on the Airlift was outstanding. And we believe your position as First Lady here at the Embassy could lead to interesting information. The only difference is that you would be working for us, not Mossad. Which I hope would put your conscience at ease. Are you at least tempted by that?'"

"I was tempted. The WACS had been fine, I felt I had been doing something useful. Especially the Airlift. Seeing Palestine — Israel — has been fascinating: the camels, the donkeys, the sea, the sound of the minarets; even, if you can believe it, the gunfire in the hills. But I did not survive just to prettify a handsome Ambassador's arm."

"Which you do very well, by the way."

"I'm serious."

"I know."

"I told Lev I would give him an answer this week. I have just one question for you. Whichever I decide — and I may not be able to tell you — do you think it would come between us?"

I took her fingers in mine, played with them. So soft. Not kibbutz fingers.

"Sweetie," I said, "the Great Wall of China could not come between us."

"Are you sure?"

"When I was talking before, about Part Two, I went too far. Perhaps I was tired from the flight. Perhaps I wanted to show off to you."

'You never need to do that."

"But I did. So now you know a secret of mine — it's not all that new, by the way — which I will never again discuss. Has that secret come between us? Hardly."

"You swear mine won't?"

"Don't tell me what you decide. But take these pajamas off" — I pulled at them — "and let's see right now if there's any hint of a problem."

She did.

There was no problem.

## A Time to Kill

From Washington I had taken a train to New York to visit the family. Ate Sunday dinner with Papa, his beard grown long, a mix of gray and black, with Uncle Joshua, Bubbie-Celine, Dr. Steven Gold. Rachel was out of town with her boss, Mrs. Roosevelt. Dr. Gold had let the twins go out for a pizza pie and a movie. Oddly, it seemed as if no one in the family wanted to look at the others. Something was going on.
Papa looked pale, his hands were shaking, his napkin fell to the floor. As I leaned over to retrieve it for him hippocampus did something strange. It poured into my mind like blotted poison words on the crumpled paper I had found on the floor that day years before when Rachel and I had found him lying face down on the bed, pounding his head on the iron frying pan, drawing blood; a significant scar still was visible above his left eye. As I touched the napkin it metamorphosed into the crumpled paper I had found beside the bed that day. Their bedroom had been too dark to read what it said, but now I could.
It was a letter from Uncle Joshua in America, written weeks earlier. It said word had reached New York that Hitler was moving quickly against the Jews of Europe. Joshua had made plenty of money, he wrote, and he wanted to send Papa steamship passage for Papa, Merele and us children to come to America. We should leave as quickly as possible, before the storming Nazi dogs begin to bark and bite. Write him a safe address to which he should send the money, Joshua had written, and it would be on its way.

When I returned the napkin to Papa it was just an ordinary napkin stained with a fingerprint of chicken soup, but my neck was bathed in sweat. What had just happened? Why had hippocampus illuminated that note to me now? What did it mean? I remembered Joshua saying to Papa our first night in America, at this very table, that Papa was stubborn, that he always felt it would be shameful to take help from his younger brother, even to start Maisel Frames. Which was silly, Joshua had said, everyone who could was borrowing money from family or friends for important matters.

At first I saw no connection between the thoughts. Just the images from when I was 10 years old and Rachel was 8, Papa slamming his head into the iron pan, again and again, bleeding, Rachel running into the darkened room, seeing Papa, screaming, hurling herself onto my lap, crying. Then the meaning fell into focus like falling stars in a magnetic sky. Papa had not taken up his younger brother's offer to bring us to New York much sooner; that stubbornness Joshua had spoken of, the silly shame Papa had felt at the thought

of accepting such help. So a month had passed, and we were still in
Wien. Now Mama had not come home, would not; Papa must have
seen something terrible and knew she would not. It was his fault, his
stubbornness. He was punishing himself by slamming his head against
the skillet. He had never told Rachel or me we could have left Europe
earlier. He has been living alone with his guilt all these years — his
knowledge and his brother's knowledge. My beloved father. My God-
fearing father. The Magician. It would me many decades later, long
after my Parkinson's had been diagnosed and I had been started on
Carbidopa-Levodopa, before I realized that the words on the napkin
under the table might have been the premature start of it.

I wanted to retch. Worse. My head was disintegrating. I wanted
to scream, but could only croak. I needed to break something. Blood
swirled through my veins like rough water in an angry stream. Whose
blood? I wanted to smash bare knuckles into walls. I wanted to kill.

A weapon! The roasted chicken in the middle of the table lounged
in a pool of gravy on a silver platter, a butcher knife beside it, the blade
submerged in the gravy, the wooden handle dry on the platter's edge.
Leaning forward I reached for it. Lifted it to my chest, studied the
edge. Heart pounding nervously like the first day in Basic. Blade long
and smooth, sharp as a bayonet. "Are you going to carve?" Bubbie-
Celine asked. "Usually Joshua carves."

Carve who? Carve what? Thighs tight as drumsticks I stood, turned
my back to them, edged to the window. Twilight over the park. Kids
in the park running about, playing war. Knife blade dripping on the
rug. Papa's back to me, unmoving. Maroon cardigan sweater the color
of dried blood. I stepped toward him. A scream from Celine. "What
is he doing?" Joshua asked. Steven Gold leaps from his seat, gripping
his table knife. Jabs it at me. "That's not an epee!" I yell, leap around it.
He feints at my chest, lunges to the right, nicks my arm with the tip, a
stinging, perhaps blood. Hamlet, dead by poison. Murderer! Pushing
against Papa's chair, that murderer not moving, sitting still amid the
violence at his back, I raise the butcher knife, pause — insanity on
hold — then plunge the point powerfully. Deep into the breast of the
chicken. Brittle bones crack. Gravy splatters white cloth. Celine bites
her fist. Papa still not moving, as if this is a stage play for which he has
studied long; he knows the plot; these are his instructions from God
the Director. All of us frozen as in a tableaux of naked beauty on the
Reeperbahn.

## Hippocampus

Should I jab the knife again? At someone else? Not knowing how I got there I slump in my chair, sung there perhaps by flights of butterflies. Voices spill through the room like bees: What was that all about? Are you alright? Is he crazy? Are you sick? Does the Army tolerate that? He's not in the Army anymore. You've got a fever— Celine's soft hand on my forehead — you'll sleep here tonight, rest, too much stress. No can do, train to Washington at 8, flight through Rome to Tel Aviv in the morning. Back to Hallie. Every voice but Papa's. Glad the twins are not here. Lean my throbbing head on the tablecloth. To sleep, perhaps.

Later I realized that my Parkinson's, which about a million Americans live with, probably would not have been present at the time of the napkin under the table. It was not diagnosed until my 70s, which is far more common. Could it be that hippocampus, deciphering for me the writing on the napkin, was improvising? Is it capable of such? If so, why? How would Evolution explain what purpose a false memory serves?

Or perhaps it was not a false memory. Perhaps the hippocampus is smarter than we give it credit for. The terrible words I had read on the napkin under the table could not of course have been on the napkin under the table. Perhaps I had read them before, long ago, in the letter Uncle Joshua had written to Papa about going to America. Which I had found crumpled on the floor near their bed and stuck in the pocket of my pants. My recollection until now is that when I wanted to read it in the morning it was gone. I have always assumed that Papa had taken it back while I slept so I could not read it. But perhaps that is not what happened. Perhaps I had found the crumpled paper back then and read it that morning and the alert hippocampus had intervened. Had realized that at 10 years old I would not be able to accept or comprehend what it meant: that Papa out of stupid pride had unknowingly been responsible for Mama's disappearance. Her probably terrible death. What if knowing this my hippocampus had immediately blocked the memory of what I had read, had stuffed it deep into a pocket of my brain, so far down that I could not retrieve it, because to do so would have destroyed me. Driven my young brain into an abyss. And there the memory of Uncle Joshua's words of early rescue had lay, hidden and unknown; there to stay until hippocampus for whatever reason decided that now I could cope with it. The truth will out, people say, and this was hippo deciding it was time.

I stabbed a cooked chicken, Sunday night dinner, instead of killing Papa. Did hippo see that in advance and therefore act now? I am not a scientist, I cannot say. I have never heard such foreknowledge attributed to memory cells. But who can assert with confidence that Evolution ended with Darwin? Why should that have been? Who is to say that even as we sleep it is not expanding like a magician its bag of tricks?

From that day forth I did not hate my father. Not consciously. But from that day forth a small part of my brain was angry. Always. Wanting to lash out at something or someone. Pressured, as if a small vise had been planted therein like a computer chip and I could not shake it loose. Control it most of the time, yes. But enjoy existence to the absolute fullest, one hundred per cent, nothing held back? Hardly ever.

I tried to cover this disturbing agony with humor. Some of the time it worked.

Perhaps everyone goes through life thus crippled. Hides behind hollow laughter. Or drink. Or opiates. Is that how so-called God planned it? Or did He make a mistake during creation. Perhaps God's Father killed *His* Mother — and He still cannot accept the truth.


## BELMONT PARK

The sound is of bacon sizzling. The smell is of horse manure. You might be surprised at how nicely they go together. I wanted to share a meal with Whitebread before going home. The only convenient time and place for him were at six in the morning in the cafeteria at Belmont Park, where he had risen to assistant trainer at McClatchy Farms. He needed to be there every day at dawn to supervise workouts. We'd stayed in touch through the years with trans-Atlantic post cards, mostly funny, every three months or so, but the days of long conversations had passed and I missed them. I wanted to know whom he had become. So we caught up over bacon and eggs — we were not all that Jewish — and rolls and strong coffee while trainers and stable boys and jockeys at other tables buzzed about horses over their *Daily Racing Forms*.

Whitebread had become enamored of track life as soon as he was hired as a stable boy. With the affection for horses he had discovered during his vegetable cart years and his innate attraction to gambling that I knew well from my boxing days he longed to become a jockey; the little men walking about the backstretch like elves in their brightly colored silks with mysterious and perhaps magical emblems on their blouses became the people of his dreams. He was much too tall to

be a race rider, as the jockeys were known at the track. But he got
permission to ride morning workouts, when his weight did not matter,
and he quickly showed a talent for it. The horses seemed to like him,
ran easily for him, and he had a natural clock in his head that enabled
him to time workouts precisely as the trainers wanted. He loved what
he was doing, with the passing years was promoted to assistant trainer.
I was happy he was doing so well, had found his niche in life. It would
be more than a decade later, when his eye was caught by a two-year-
old colt named Navigator II, who had perfect configuration and in
Whitebread's eyes the breeding of a champion, that he convinced
Mr. McClatchy to buy him. As the horse broke his maiden first time
out and won most of his early races by huge margins the racing press
began to mention Navigator as possibly a future candidate for the
Triple Crown. In one of those coincidences that psychologists say don't
happen — but which I believed, like FDR, happen all the time — that
same year our own Joshua Farms was blessed with a stunner called
Joshua's Pleasure. The rest would become part of racing history.

So Whitebread was doing well in his professional life. But not so
the personal side, he confessed to me that morning over our second
coffees.

He woke up at dawn as he did seven days a week to get out to the
track. But like the rising sun outside his bedroom window the baby
was crying in hot waves. Ramona did not seem to be comforting him.
He reached beside him but his wife was not in the bed oversleeping,
as she did too often. He went to little Howie and picked him up in
his blanket with the yellow baby horses on it which stopped the
crying immediately, then to the kitchen to yell at her for ignoring the
kid, expecting to find her preparing his bottle. From the corner of
his eyes he noticed something odd: their closet door was open. The
small kitchen was empty, no sign of a bottle warming and no sign of
Ramona.

He settled Howie into his high chair and put up a bottle and then saw
the note on the table. It said in pencil on a brown paper bag: "Can't
stand this life anymore. Kiss the kid. See ya prob'ly never."

His parents had moved to Chicago where his father had a business
opportunity. A small rented apartment near Belmont had became his
bachelor pad. He loved being close enough to the track to smell the
horses. But in time he got lonely and began going to dances in the old
neighborhood, first at the YMHA, then the YMCA. He began dating a
young lady named Ramona Schultz, well-built if not a Rhodes scholar,
and much too soon she became pregnant. They arranged a small

wedding several months before little Howard was born. They loved the child — Whitebread especially liked that the baby had two thin layers of white hair on one side of his head, as if imitating his father, a genetic happenstance. But the small apartment made life difficult. Ramona could not work even if she had wanted to, needing to take care of the baby, and Whitebread's small salary would not support a larger house, even had he not blown part of his weekly wages on sure things at the track that lost. Ramona hated waking as early as they needed to and was lonely and isolated so close to the backstretch, where Whitebread was popular and she, a moody young woman, was not. Her widowed mother told her repeatedly that she had gotten what she deserved for marrying a tightfisted Jew, and refused to help with the "Yid kid."

It was on Howie's second birthday that Ramona had fled the scene. Whitebread admitted he had gone on a drinking binge, almost losing his job, losing the baby to a foster home run by some charity or city agency, I forget which. He visited the boy often the first few years. Then the foster family decided to move to the south somewhere, and after agonizing for weeks Whitebread realized he had nothing to offer his son, and for the boy's sake he gave up legal custody so Howie could have a real family.

Which is worse? To give up a child, as Whitebread had, or never to have had one?

"Did you say something?" Hallie asks. She is brushing her teeth. Delightfully, she has not yet donned her pajama tops.

"Just mumbling to myself."

She rinses her mouth, spits into the sink. "Wisdom for the ages, I assume."

"Of course. If I can remember it in the morning."

## THE DIRECTOR

So, symbolically I killed my father. And did not tell Hallie. It should have been Allen Dulles I killed.
Perhaps I should have informed her about him. Perhaps it was my moral obligation. Before she decided whether to become an agent, she was entitled to all the facts. But I did not want to influence her decision.

Eventually Dulles knocked off a bunch of democratically elected leaders. Ordered coups in places like Iran and Guatamala. Got literally thousands of our spies, both Americans and Oriental recruits, murdered when the enemy was repeatedly tipped off to operations by counterspies within our ranks. Ill-begotten operations he dreamed up without getting permission from Ike.

Dulles and his brother and the CIA ran the country for years, for the benefit of the United Fruit Company. But I'm thinking of long before that. Towards the end of the war Dulles was our top spy in the OSS, based in Switzerland. He sent cables regularly for Roosevelt's eyes only. I used to file them, but I glanced at them when I could. Every week he warned about small Communist cells forming in Europe. He became obsessed, kept warning FDR to keep an eye on them. At the same time, the Nazis were rounding up thousands, tens of thousands, of Jews all across Europe and hauling them to concentrations camps, and then to the ovens. The Dulles cables rarely mentioned them. Six million dead Jews did not seem to bother him; once in a while maybe a footnote. All this, and our dead spies, were kept secret from the public. I was sent a lot of this information and fed it to the President, while Dulles postured his agency as a bunch of shining knights. In truth he had turned it into a secret government. The Eisenhower years are a blur of golf just now, but in 1960 Dulles hated JFK, the handsome new President; too soft on leftists, he believed. Kennedy knew it, and soon fired him. A case can be made that it was Dulles and United Fruit who ordered the assassination. In fact, the case has been made, if not always accepted.

But, going back to his ignoring the Holocaust, should I have told Hallie that before she decided whether to join? I was not sure then. I am not sure now. Eventually, at least, my silence did bring her face to face with Mengele.

## DINNER WITH EINSTEIN

His unruly forest of wild white hair proclaiming his universal identity, Albert Einstein sat at a hand-hewn dining table in the home of David Ben-Gurion. The Prime Minister, his two white ear-tufts offering only modest competition, was across from him. Hallie and I sat along one side; on the other sat Dr. Brian White, research scientist at Mass General and grandson of my housekeepers Margaret and Ben, who, along with Einstein, was in Israel to speak to the Hebrew University graduating class of 1952. Chaim Weitzman, the first President of Israel, had died two weeks earlier, after only four years in office, and the *Knesset* — the Israeli parliament — had voted to offer the presidency to Dr. Einstein. A strong supporter of the new Jewish nation, Einstein told Ben-Gurion that honored as he was, he must turn the down the position. He was getting on in years, he said; he had much of his own work to do.

Hallie looked prim and lovely as always that day but said little; mostly she dined on the man-talk, as if it were part of the roasted chicken that had sat in the middle of the table in New York with a knife in its back. She was not shy, I remembered the time she confronted Sartre in a crowded café. But Einstein, relaxed and affable as he was, could by his mere presence freeze the tongue of most mere humans. She did ask him one question, which, when he answered, made us laugh. She asked if he could explain relativity to her without breaking her brain.

"When a man sits with a pretty girl for an hour," Dr. Einstein said, "it seems like a minute. But let him sit on a hot stove for a minute — and it's longer than any hour. That's relativity."

We all laughed.

Which prompted Ben-Gurion to ask if religion played any part in his mathematics.

"When I am judging a theory," Einstein said, "I ask myself whether, if I were God, I would have arranged the world in such a way."

I wanted to say, You mean you're not God? But I was afraid it might be taken as rude instead of complimentary.

I'm sure we also talked politics, but the words that glow in my memory from that evening are science words: synapse and its half-sister, synaptic gap, from the Greek word *synapsis*, meaning conjunction. Before going to Harvard Law I had toyed with the idea of becoming a doctor. But I knew that what attracted me to medicine was not dispensing prescriptions from behind a desk but the cutting-edge study of the human body, especially the brain. So law school it was, but I never lost my fascination with the brain. I subscribed to the relevant magazines. I loved reading about synapses and their gaps — the connections between brain cells — perhaps because of their word sounds, perhaps because of how they looked on a page. I blush, but they seemed to speak of love.

## WHERE MEMORIES RESIDE, 1960

My favorite story about the hippocampus is the platonic (perhaps bloody) affair between Dr. Brenda Milner, a young neuropsychologist at the Montreal Neurological Institute, and a patient who for years was known only as H. M. to protect his privacy. Following surgery to cure him of epileptic seizures — which worked — H.M., a 29-year-old Connecticut man, was unable to form new memories. Following assorted clues, Dr. Milner worked with him for decade after decade. At first he could not even remember her name, she had to introduce herself anew each time she visited him. Until the early 1950s science had believed that memories could be stored in any part of the brain; if someone lost part of their brain in an accident another part would take up the slack. But working year after year with H.M. — with his permission, of course —Dr. Milner proved that memory exists only in the hippocampus. This finding was critical; it led to the foundation of Neuroscience, which since has uncovered countless secrets about the way the human brain functions. It made Dr. Milner famous around the world.

The full story of her discoveries and her relationship with H.M. could fill several books, and does. Suffice it to say that it's in the hippocampus that neurons bouncing about like pinballs cross synapses to be stored as memories. If the hippocampus is seriously injured, most of the memories disappear forever.

By coincidence, a related role of the hippocampus had been discovered just weeks before my dinner with Albert Einstein. It helped to illuminate an ancient question — why do people need sleep? Dr. Einstein was eager to hear about it from Dr. White.

"A lot of what we learned was through the use of mice," Ben began. "I won't ruin this lovely dinner by detailing the experiments. Just the facts, as Sergeant Friday used to say in the morning reruns.

"Sleep is not just to restore the body with rest, as was long assumed. It is necessary for memory. Short-term memories, unimportant ones, are stored in the hippocampus in what I call 'refrigerator cells.' To be retained for a long time, important memories have to tunnel down to 'freezer cells,' where they can remain as long as the patient is alive."

Einstein interrupted him. "Maybe longer," he said.

We all gave him queer looks.

"The problem," Dr. White continued, "is that every day the hippocampus gets cluttered with enormous amounts of short-term memories — what time we woke up, what color dress or tie we put on, what we ate for lunch, ad infinitum. Gossip of the mind, for which we have little long-term use. But when something important comes along — when Dr. Einstein came up with E equals M C squared, for instance, which changed our entire understanding of the world — it was damn well important that he remember how he got to that equation. If his hippocampus had been jam-packed with minor memories — that he needs to buy shampoo, for instance — his vital discovery might have been blocked from reaching a freezer cell. He might have lost the equation, God forbid.

"What does sleep have to do with this? Well, we recently discovered that during sleep, and only during sleep, the brain sends into the hippocampus a squad of street cleaners to empty the trash, so to speak — to clear the synapses and synaptic gaps of the day's blockages — that awful striped tie you wore, which has acquired a soup stain on it, or the dress that is in truth getting a bit too tight around your waist. Once all that unimportant stuff is cleared out, the freezer cells have room to take in and store the Theory of Relativity, or your wife's birthday, or the fact that you have to pick up Aunt Zelda at the train station at 4:30 and Heaven help you if you forget. It's possible that this function of sleep, this making room for the long-term storage of vital memories, is even more important than the physical rest we get. There's a lot more work to be done, of course."

I was watching Professor Einstein's face throughout Ben's little lecture. He seemed fascinated, smiled at the little jokes, nodded slightly at times, as if somewhere along the way he might have toyed with these ideas himself, without doing the lab work needed to prove them. Perhaps he did not like mice.

What happened next was extraordinary. Einstein's face began to fall apart. His skin fell bit by bit onto the dining table. His skull, the bones of his face visible now, began to crack into pieces, which dropped randomly onto the table, like a jigsaw puzzle. His teeth soon followed. Yet there he sat, still upright, but without a head. I tried to shake myself from this strange and perhaps devastating dream, but I could not. Because I was not sleeping. This entire sequence, the dinner in Tel Aviv and what followed, had not been a dream. It was an illusion, probably created by my overburdened hippocampus.

I sat and pondered. As a memory it of course had been false. It could not have happened. I was fairly certain Dr. White had never been to Israel. I did not think anything in the real world could cause a face to fall apart like that. Most provably, Dr. Einstein had died in 1955, while the linkage of the hippocampus and sleep had been discovered only recently, and had just been published in *Science* magazine.

Such false memories intrigued me. One Friday night, when Margaret invited her grandson to share a boiled-chicken dinner with Ben and Hallie and me, I asked Dr. White about them.

"Thanks to you and Dr. Milner and a bunch of others, we know about memories," I said. "But tell me about false memories. Evolution has let us survive with them. But why? How do they occur? How can we see clearly in our minds images that never passed through our retinas? Where do the neurons in the hippocampus get them? Most puzzling, their being false, what the hell use are they?"

Dr. White, who only recently had taken up a pipe, leaned back in his easy chair and puffed gently. The light white smoke at eye level reminded me of Einstein. "There's no way to determine if rats, or any other laboratory critters, experience them," Dr. White said. "So traditional research has been impossible. False memories, the truth is, are a bitch."

# Part Two

## JFK CALLING

The summons came on Christmas Day. "The President is on the phone," Hallie called from the other room.

A strange Christmas, 92 degrees in Tel Aviv.

"The President? He hasn't called in eight years. Not once. Not the Vice President either, though I would not have expected it from him."

"I'm sorry," Hallie said, approaching me, covering the mouthpiece with her hand, whispering. "I should have said the President-elect."

"Oh. Now that's a different barrel of mistletoe."

I lifted the phone on my desk. "Ambassador Maisel speaking."

"Mr. Ambassador, tell your wife — I assume that was Hallie — that I still need a few weeks of seasoning before I take over. The Republicans would say a few years. I assume I'm not interrupting a Christmas celebration."

"Not here in Tel Aviv."

"That's what I figured."

"But you're working, Sir?"

"It's snowing here in Hyannis. The kids are all out for a pre-breakfast sledding. A good time to fit in some calls. And Israel seemed the safest on Christmas. I have a question. You folks have been in Israel a long time. A riveting place, throbbing with ancient poetry. Jackie and I enjoyed meeting you both on my required three-I tour last summer. Each beautiful in their way. But my question is, are you ready to come home?"

"A curious coincidence, Mr. President. Hallie and I were discussing that very idea last night. Perhaps because a new year is approaching. But we're unsure what we would do back there? Teach, I suppose."

"That's why I'm calling. I would like you to be an Under Secretary of State."

"For the Middle East?"

"That would be your title. But also for Intelligence. We've got the CIA, the FBI, the NSA. But nobody is pulling all their findings together. You would do that, and present it to me. An NSA adviser. Every week. Every day when necessary. As head of the National Intelligence Council. Which, if you have never heard of, I have just invented.

I hesitated, glanced at Hallie, who was half-listening in. "I'm flattered at the offer, Mr. President. But I read in Newsweek that you're looking for the best and the brightest. I doubt I qualify."

"Don't worry, I've done my research. Eleanor says FDR held you in the 'highest esteem.' That's a quote. When I called Harry Truman in Missouri, he went on as if you were his son."

"He was a good person to work for."

"And maybe a great President. The only doubt being whether he should have used the bomb on civilians. Even Einstein was not in favor of that."

I did not know how to reply. My teeth stumbled. "I guess history will decide."

"Yes," JFK said. "It always does."

"Would the Senate have to give its approval?"

"No. Only Bobby."

I smiled, relieved. I hate those hearings.

"But getting back to you, I studied your file. I wish I could find ten more like you. And Hallie, of course — we might find something for her as well."

"May I confer with her?"

"You've got sixty seconds. I've got more people to call."

I pressed the phone to my chest, told Hallie of the offer in half the allotted time. She was nodding her approval before I finished.

"That's wonderful," the President-elect said. "One last thought, which might ease your way. You'll be needing a dwelling here. Senator Birnam is retiring and selling his house. It's not a mansion, but rather nice, enough rooms for guests or live-in help. Magnificent lawns. Does Hallie like to garden?"

"I really don't know. Not here in the desert."

"Well, you might want to call Birnam and reserve a look before he puts it on the market. Use my name. He's a Republican, but with a heart, maybe that's why the house feels cozy." I hear him dropping the phone, picking it up. "Hear that hurricane? That's the troupe coming in for pancakes. I want to phone George Ball before the mob descends. Keep in touch."

He clicked off. I remember imagining life in Washington even before I hung up. Even before Hallie hugged me and kissed my neck.

"What did he want?"

"He wanted to know if you like to garden."

"That's an odd question."

"Do you?"

"I guess we'll find out." She kissed me hard, on the lips, murmured an endearment in German.

Which brought into my vision a young woman named Charlotte Saloman. A painter, also German, whom I never met. I saw one of her exhibitions at a gallery. A brilliant talent who also fled the Nazis. But was arrested two years later in Occupied France. Her work reminded me of Munch. Powerful. She was not at her gallery opening. The Nazis packed her off to Auschwitz and sent her, five months pregnant, to the gas chamber the day she arrived. God forbid she should have one happy moment. Age 26. Much of her work was rescued by friends and published in a large-format book of 769 reproductions, called simply *Charlotte*. Weighing what feels like 20 pounds, though when I put it on a postage scale at the office it was only 5.6. Does that qualify as immortality?

I bought a used copy of the book for $75, shipped it to Rachel in New York without telling Hallie. I was wary of what her reaction would be; some of the paintings were of Nazis in uniform. But Salomon's work is a piece of history that is mostly overlooked, and I wanted to have it. An obvious but rarely thought truth: our immortality is lugged about pressed against the breasts of others.

A related story involves the most difficult question I have ever had to ask Hallie. Five years after statehood Israel built on a mountain outside Jerusalem a place called Yad Vashem. It is a memorial to all those Jews who died in the camps, all those who survived, all those honored Christians who had risked their lives to help Jews escape from the Nazis. The opening of Yad Vashem was a highly publicized international occasion. Invited to attended were heads of state from all over the world. As the U.S. Ambassador to Israel I was naturally invited to attend, with Hallie. I did not know how she would feel about walking among these photographs of the dread barracks, the open pits of hundreds of skeletal bodies tossed haphazardly together, skeletal men and women who were barely alive, every sort of atrocity in progress.

Hallie declined to come. "For me to go there," she said, "would be like traveling to see a copy of a Michelangelo when you have lived with the original."

Kennedy was as good as his word. While I moved in to the State Department, with a phone call or two the President arranged for a teaching position for Hallie at Georgetown, as associate professor of mathematics. After Yale it probably was the busiest campus in the country for CIA recruiting. Whether JFK knew of Hallie's tie with The Company I have no idea. Under Secretary of State for the Middle East! And more amazing, for Intelligence!

"What a comedown," Hallie teased. "From Ambassador to Secretary."

Washington, 1963

The Capital was the perfect place for us. Rachel worked for Mrs. Roosevelt, who despite getting on in years remained the dynamo she had always been, chairing numerous committees and charities that met there monthly. Once a week Rachel accompanied her from New York and instead of spending government or charity money on hotels began to stay in our guest room on such trips. We had never lost touch while I was in Israel, of course, with letters and an occasional phone call traversing the ocean. But with her frequent visits we became close again, as close as we had been as children. We discussed politics, her work with Eleanor, her occasional loneliness when Steven was out of town. Dr. Steven Gold, M.D., had become one of the most prominent cardiologists in the country, chairman of the department at Einstein Medical Center in the Bronx, where they now lived, in the Pelham Bay area, him treating wealthy dowagers or industrialists anywhere in the country, speaking regularly at medical seminars; he even was called to Denver to attend to President Eisenhower, who suffered a heart attack while vacationing with his in-laws there. Ike recovered enough to run for a second term. The twins were away at college so Rachel was never in a hurry to go home to a quiet house. The one thing that shut us up, that came between us, was when she asked every few years if I knew what had happened to Mama. That was a subject I would never discuss. Perhaps the witness at Nuremberg had been mistaken; perhaps my hippocampus had erred. There was no need to plant the terrible image in Rachel's brain.

## Dogs

German Shepherds. More than 50 of them. Most unleashed. Unmuzzled. Racing about freely, barking, growling, leaping masses of flesh, teeth, claws. Often blood. Every camp with its own fearsome K9 patrol. Thousands of dogs, part of the German Army. The daily scene at Auschwitz as Hallie described it: each dog 60 to 80 pounds of hurtling terror as they charged at prisoners for walking out of line, for stopping to rest during work details. Kenneled unchained in wooden cabins at each corner of the camp, left free day and night to discourage attempts to escape over or through the barbed wire and into the forest. Most unusual fact: all fifty dogs were called Rex. If tattooed numbers were good enough for the inmates, a single generic syllable apparently was good enough for all the dogs.

The cherry blossoms at the Tidal Basin were in full throat one lovely Sunday late in March when we had our last fight over the dog (if fight is a proper word for torrents of fears and thoughts left largely unspoken.) Half way between Dunsinane and the Tidal Basin was a park (I've forgotten the name) surrounded by a low iron fence against which on our weekend walks we often leaned to watch children playing. Sometimes we held hands silently; other times we chatted as we sat. Either way our eyes rarely left the dogs to which each child seemed to be attached by leashes of leather or love: small curly dogs, often gray or dirty white and yippie to the ear; medium dogs, black and thin, short-haired and restless, prowling the grass for a snack or a tussle; larger dogs patterned in maps of brown and beige and highlights of white, standing tall and proud beside blankets until their pride wore out and they collapsed on their heaving sides to nap; occasional mammoth, monster dogs, most of these leashed to a human wrist like super heavyweights in training, wondering what they were doing among these silly toddlers, wondering why they were not churning up the mud on a proper hunting trail. Me wondering every week as we watched the bounding or sleeping critters whether Hallie would like to have a dog; deciding most likely she would not but that she was thinking probably I would, to make up for the children we did not, could not, have; this uncertainty of feelings twisting in her gut while she tried not to show it but kept smiling as we took in the sun; me thinking she was thinking I ought to have a dog to race with across the lawns of Dunsinane but that I was afraid to raise the subject, fearful it would ignite again her nightmares of fifty Rexes leaping onto her bed and tearing at her throat. But she would not suggest it for fear I would worry that the purpose of such a dog, whether mine or hers, whether large or small, would be to replace for my benefit, out of her guilt, the invisible kids. Each of us in our mutual love interpreting or misinterpreting the other; each of us in our mutual love too hesitant to speak. Until that sunny Sunday when somehow she found the courage to break the silence of the years.

Perhaps it was the image of the little girl that drew her out. Sitting beside me on a park bench, removing her sunglasses but raising a hand to shade her eyes, Hallie said, "They're so much fun to watch." Leaving it to me to respond to either the laughing children or the playful dogs.

"Look at that girl in pink," I said, pointing. The blond child, perhaps four years old, was kneeling on a pale blue blanket. Beside her the mother sat in gray sweats, barefoot, nursing a recently born child. The girl, imitating Mama, had pulled off her own socks, was attempting to nurse a little brown puppy.

"She's so cute," I said.

"And the puppy is so frustrated."

"That's what dogs are for."

"Really? I thought that's what children are for."

She was veering very close to the forbidden subject.

"Would you like to get a dog to play with?" she asked.

I squeezed her hand. It was one of the first spring days, neither of us was wearing gloves.

"I will answer if you will answer me first."

"About what?"

"Can your question be taken on the surface, or is it still underpinned with guilt? Guilt that somehow you have deprived me of something, you and Mengele. If that is the case my answer is no."

"Exi, I made my peace with that a long time ago. Joan Didion's peace. *Play It As It Lays*. Haven't we discussed that?"

"'Not that I recall."

"Then it's my fault. It must have been while we were still in Israel, when you were off on a trip somewhere. I must have rehearsed the conversation so much that by the time you came home I thought we had already talked. And all this time you waited."

"I didn't wait. I lived. As we are living now."

Her hands dropped mine. She leaned across and kissed me on the lips, at first gently, then passionately.

"What was that for?" I asked, moderately intoxicated by the unexpected passion, or the aroma of the cherry blossoms, or both, as she pulled her face away.

"That was for you being you."

"I'm glad it was not for me being someone else. I've tried that, it doesn't work."

Another kiss. A chocolate cordial. She grabbed my hand.

"Let's go," she said, in a slight hurry.

"Look. The puppy is still trying to nurse."

"Never mind the puppy. Let's go." She pulled me off the bench and along the street outside the park. At the corner we crossed to the other side. A light wind tumbled cherry petals across our path.

"Down here," she said as we turned right at the next corner. The sounds of children laughing, a few crying, dogs barking, a few whimpering, faded behind us.

"Where are you taking me, woman?"

"To make sure you like your new dog."

I stopped walking. Squinted at her. Then slowly followed her to and into a gray cement building marked Animal Shelter.

"What have you done?"

"I ain't done nothin' yet," Hallie said, trying for Mae West, almost reaching it.

A long room. In the front half, wire separations. The strong odor of dog. In the rear half, smaller wire cages piled three high, the strong smell of cat. We did not go back there; neither of us liked cats. In the front a beige puppy, no more than five inches high, skitters to the wire of the enclosure, begins to jump, whimpering. A worker opens the gate. The puppy emerges, sniffs the bottom of Hallie's khaki pants, whimpers, jumps up, cannot reach her knees, jumps again. A small purple bow is tied between its ears. Hallie leans into kennel, lifts the puppy to her chest, puppy washes her face with its darting pink tongue. She cuddles it.

"He likes you," I say. And warily, to the pony-tailed employee in a blue apron — looks like a college girl — "He's so cute, why has he not been adopted already? Is he sick?"

"He's fine. He's only been here three days."

"Hallie, you've been coming here how long?"

She smiles like a mouse caught in a lie. If mice lie. "Three days."

Pony-tail: "The purple ribbon means he's on hold. Several people would have taken him the first day."

"On hold until when?"

"Tomorrow."

"He likes you," I say to Hallie. "He's your dog."

"Hold him," she says. "He'll be your dog, too."

I write a check. Hugs exchanged between Hallie and pony-tail. "Don't forget to get him his shots."

We carry him home; letting him walk the few blocks on a shelter leash would take forever. Sit in the pergola, set him on the ground. On his short legs he hurries to the edge of the poppy field like a puppy with a mission. Mission accomplished, he disappears among the blossoms. Which tower over him like winter wheat. No longer able to see him we follow his eager explorations by the trembling of the petals.

"What kind is he?" I inquired. "A mutt?"

"I didn't ask his religion. Actually, they aren't sure. They think he's part Border Collie. Mixed with a short-legged breed.

"Does he have a name yet?"

"Of course not, that's for us to decide. I've thought of a hundred the past three days and don't like any of them."

"We could wait a bit, until he tells us his name."

"That might be fun."

"On the other hand, there's one perfect name for him."

"What's that?"

"Macbeth."

Hallie smiles, looks out at the wavering blossoms; he's invisible among the reds. "That's a big royal name for a little tyke."

"He'll grow into it soon enough. Be racing around on his little legs like the king of Dunsinane. Until then we can give him a nickname. Like Mac."

"I'm not crazy about Mac. Sounds like a butcher or something. I guess I could call him Beth."

"Mac and Beth? In three months he'll be schizophrenic."

"There's enough schizophrenics in Washington that no one will notice."

"Anybody special you have in mind?"

"Of course. Me. And you."

"You think we're schizophrenic?"

"Of course, Exi. Me teaching math at Georgetown while recruiting for The Company, and pretending you don't know what I'm doing. You lecturing all over while recruiting for the State Department — same thing. Both of us acting like innocents. While taking target practice every other Wednesday. Separately. Secretly. In case we're needed by Ops. Isn't that some kind of crazy?"

"Are you tired of it? You can always quit."

"When Angleton recruited me back in Israel, he was persuasive about how increasingly important good intelligence is to the country. He convinced me. But he didn't talk about the crap they've been up to lately. Guatamala, Cuba, Chile, you tell me where else. What's the fancy new word? Destabilizing. Destabilizing foreign governments. As in assassinating democratically elected Presidents because they're too far left for our taste. Sometimes I feel we work for apples and bananas. The United Fruit Company."

"That's Allen Dulles. He orders murders without even telling Ike. And gets away with it. Hangs out only with corporate millionaires, who are terrified the Communists will nationalize their millions of acres of pineapples, peaches, whatever. Does their every bidding. Acts like he's running the country."

"I heard during the war," Hallie said, "the Dulles brothers were interested only in getting hold of hidden Nazi gold. In exchange they would leave the top Nazi brass alive and in place. Except for Hitler, I guess. To provide a 'stable wall' against Communist Russia. No Nuremburg trials. No real surrender. No punishment for the Holocaust. No homeland for the remaining Jews. Or maybe one — in Africa."

"Seems to be the worst-kept secret in the Company. I've heard on good authority that at least one Supreme Court justice thinks the Dulles boys should be tried and hanged for treason."

"Yet they remain in office," Hallie said. "That could get anyone feeling low."

"And in need of a puppy," I said.

I kissed her. I took her hand. "Well, at least there's hope. Not if Nixon wins, but Kennedy and Allen Dulles hate each other. Kennedy really believes in freedom and self-government for the colonial nations. If he becomes President there's a good chance he'll fire the son of a bitch."

"Does he have the guts?"

"I think he does. Truman fired MacArthur. JFK is prettier than Truman, but I think deep down he's just as tough."

A whimper from deep amid the poppies. We both turn to look.

"Mac!"

"Beth!"

The moving trail bursts open. The puppy runs to us in his bumpy puppy way, struggles onto our shoes, first Halle's then mine. Licks the leather. Lets his little pink tongue hang out.

"Let's go in," Hallie says. "He probably needs a chaser."


## PITTER, PATTER

All this unexpectedly a prelude to learning to enjoy the patter of little feet. Which led a year later to our adopting little William Maisel, whose single mother was battling an addiction of some kind. A generation later Bill and his wife Dorothy begetting David (after Ben-Gurion) and Marcia and Florence and Douglas and . . . I can't remember the names of all the kids, especially those who moved away to California, Chicago, Florida, New Mexico. The expanding universe of Maisel humanity became divided like so many into two almost separate families, the kind that kiss and hug and share homemade dinners every few weeks, and the kind that send Hanukah or Christmas cards for a few years and then send them preprinted from the business office and then dispense even with that, falling victim to the ever-spreading sadness of hippo fatigue. That's my name for the undiagnosed, unspoken misery of our age, in which things take precedence over people, e-mail over phone calls, social media over social interaction, or, to sum it up in a single perhaps exaggerated idiom, computers over stubby pencils. There's too much going on too fast for the hippocampus to contain. Evolution has not yet caught up. Which means much of lived life — the weddings and sweet sixteens and new babies and funerals dissolve into a bland gray rendering we call our past. But do we have pasts if we cannot really remember them, not in any detail? In our family there is only one rich vein of memory— that of William, whom Hallie and I adopted, who with Dorothy begat David, and so forth. Who with Hannah begat Jacob, my dad, who with Merele begat me.

## BELMONT PARK

The phone rings too early in the guest room at Pelham Bay, where we are staying for the big race. I grab it on the second ring hoping it would not wake Hallie. It's Joe McInerny, my trainer, sounding as if he'd just been hit by a car.

"Mr. Maisel? It's Joe. You better get down here real quick. Pleasure has hurt himself."

"What? How?"

"His leg . . ."

"The race is today. How could . . . Never mind, I'm on my way."

Elbows on her pillow, hair disheveled, Hallie is watching me.

"Today is Saturday. The race is today."

She's rubbing her eyes. "I know what day it is." She looks at the bedside alarm clock. "Are you planning to ride him yourself? You won't make the weight, Sweetie."

I put on my blue suit, long socks, dress shoes; should have brought boots in case it rained out there. I do not smile at her jape.

"What happened?"

I find it hard to breathe.

"Joe says he hurt himself."

"Where? How?"

"I don't know. I'm taking the car. Probably can do a hundred before dawn on the morning roads. Cross the Throgs Neck, be there in twenty minutes."

"You be careful."

"No problem. Cops are racing fans. If I'm not back by noon call a cab."

I lean over and kiss her nose and am gone.

The horse's leg feels too warm. Left rear. He's standing gingerly. When he tries to walk it's worse. As if he is showing me. Denial wrings tears. Even the stable boys. Mac tries cold bandages. Seen too many pictures like this. His evening trough is full, he has not eaten. Snuggles his nose into my armpit when I go close. Whimpers when I kneel to touch him. He's acting as if his leg was whacked in the night with a crowbar.

I look about in the sawdust of his stall. Many footprints. Some appear to have been swiped as if to blur them. I refuse to believe that. Who would do such a thing? But I dare not call the track vet, or security; I have to think this through.

I'd hired an armed security guard for the night to protect JP. Name of Milo. I chew him out good, but his story is reasonable. He and

our regular man Maxie were in sync. Small flames at a nearby stable.
Spins of gray smoke rising in the night. Horses whinnying, first a solo,
then a fearful serenade. Shouts of fire, calls for help. A disaster in the
making. Milo and Maxie had run toward the smoke, about fifty yards
from Joshua's Pleasure. Leaving him unguarded. "You can't ignore a
fire at a track," Milo said. "All this wood and straw goes up in a flash. A
dozen horses could be killed. Maybe a hundred. Millions of dollars in
horseflesh burned alive, or choking on smoke. Including yours."

By the time they returned to the barn — it was only a few moments,
they said — JP was already favoring his leg. It was hard to argue they
had not done the right thing.

The fire had started in an empty stall. A good break. A hose had
swept it away. But few people in the backstretch got much sleep after
that.

The vet felt JP's leg, rubbed it gently, brushed it this way and that.
Confirmed my guess. A slight abrasion, miniscule cuts blow the knee.
I called Rachel who came out in a taxi, a raincoat over her sweater and
jeans. Hallie was with her, dressed up a bit, we had brought only good
clothes for the Winner's Circle, how often do you win a Triple Crown?
Rachel knelt before JP and touched his leg; when he pulled away as if
stabbed a pin she began to cry. Is there any way he can run like that?
Bandages? A splint? Not without risking his leg. The vet nodded. We
need to get MRIs, see how to splint him, get the weight off that leg. If
it's just an inflamed fetlock we can handle it. But Missus, there's twenty
separate bones in that leg. If there's a crack in any one of them then
talk to the Lord.

She was holding a colorful Derby Rose handkerchief to her nose.
Saratoga would be a miracle, the vet said. The Breeder's Cup is
possible. But no promises. He may have run his last race. Pray that he's
a stud muffin.

Knots of track workers had gathered around the barn. A white van
pulled up to take him away. Fastened him inside with belts and towels,
like a mummy. We hugged him first, Rachel rubbing her tears on his
face. The morning sun slowly rose across the track as the van eased
away. Owners, trainers, exercise boys drifted off to their own barns,
figuring we would want to be alone. Only Whitebread stayed. He
hugged Rachel and me, shook hands with Hallie. He couldn't speak,
could only shake his head. It's your race now, I said. He nodded glumly
and walked away.

The police could find no clues. No sustainable footprints in the
gravel walks. No fingerprints. Just an old pair of torn canvas gloves

outside the barn door. Who could have done that to our beautiful horse? Rachel kept asking it over and over, as if in a trance.

Do you have any enemies? a detective asked.

None that we know of.

Except every other owner at the track, Rachel said.

Who has the most to gain by your not running?

We both hesitated, did not want to speak. Finally Rachel did.

Whitebread? He's a trainer here. His horse will win now. Win a million bucks instead of half that for second. But he would never do that.

Can you spell that, Ma'am? The detective pulled out a pad.

He's my best friend, I said. He loves horses, he wouldn't do that to this horse and definitely not to us. Most of the winnings will go to the owner, the assistant trainer, the race rider. It won't all go to him.

You never know about people, the cop said.

Besides, the morning line has our horse at 1-to-5, his at 6-to-1. Now Navigator will go off as the heavy favorite. Probably two-to-five. You can't make money that way.

Rachel drew a deep breath, exhaled, trying to relax. She slipped her arm around mine, heartened by my analysis. The June sun moved higher in the sky. The betting windows would be opening soon. I walked to the track office alone to officially scratch Joshua's Pleasure from the Belmont Stakes, which would be run in less than eight hours. The clerks expressed condolences. At the publicity office I broke the news and helped them write a media release. I told them the colt had injured his rear left leg during the night; that we did not yet know how. No point bringing up a possible human attack — the mere thought put me in a rage —until X-rays told us more. Slowly I walked back to the barn, shaking my head. A vast black cloud settled over America.

The Belmont is one and a half miles, the longest Thoroughbred race in America. Can Pleasure go the distance? That's been the question all week. In both previous Triple Crown races he was losing ground at the end, they say. Nonsense. He was just playing with the gray.

Present tense, or is this future tense? Could he have held on? We will never know. Dabbing my eyes with my handkerchief. Trying not to wonder who the fuck fucked with his leg. My body sleep-shortened and overheated, I removed my coat, folded it in half, lay it on the straw as a pillow. Was half asleep when I heard voices outside the stall. Now, 46, 47 years later, unable to fall asleep — that happens too often when you get old — I remember them still, the voices and the scene.

## HANDCUFFS

Flashes of chrome assaulted our eyes like illusions of bayonets as
the sun sank in the West and the dregs of the Cadillacs and Chevys
drained out of the Belmont parking lots. The last air ferry to
Washington did not leave until ten so I had a couple of hours
to get to La Guardia and fly home, ready to try and convince Lyndon
again not to send more troops to Vietnam, it was not our war . . . No,
wait, my brain went into reverse there. This was 1973, Lyndon was
long gone, this was Nixon's war now and he had a plan to end it, he
had told the voters in every speech. I didn't believe him for a minute,
it was a lost cause, but he did not seek my views, he had his Kissinger
to drink with at night and walk the eerily dark White House like a
drunken ghost and lead the cheers for bigger bombs in the morning.
But the gabfest outside the barn, beginning to break up, had been good
therapy, because as soon as they started to leave the weight of the lost
Triple Crown sunk over me again like a leaden veil. Then along came
Whitebread, but he did not exactly lighten my spirits. He was walking
between two cops. One held each of his arms, his wrists in handcuffs
behind him. A trailing cop held two plastic evidence bags.

"Hey, Exit," he said, approaching with the officers. "Am I glad you're
still here!"

"What's going on?"

"These punk cops have the idea I'm the one who whacked your
horse."

"That's crazy."

They did not charge Whitebread. No witnesses. Lack of evidence.
The patrol car sped away, kicking gravel back like a mule. Rachel
pressed her face into my shoulder, Hallie trailing a few steps behind.
Slowly we walked into JP's stall. No place had ever felt so empty.

Except that day when Mama didn't come home.


## THE INAUGURATION, 1961

Hundreds of men in black tie. Hundreds of women in the latest
colorful fashions. Music by Guy Lombardo and his Orchestra. JFK's
Inaugural Ball, in the largest ballroom in Washington's largest hotel
(I don't recall the name.) Mrs. Kennedy stunning in white silk. Hallie
equally stunning in red. The clicking of a hundred press cameras
almost drowning out the orchestra. The dance floor cleared. The lights
dim. The orchestra begins a slow version of Camelot. The President
leads Jackie onto the floor, they begin to dance. They are alone on the

floor, a single spotlight following them. The torch has been passed. Bobby and Ethel join them. Then more Kennedys, the new cabinet members and their spouses. As Undersecretary I am not yet in the cabinet.

The dance floor is as jammed as a Metro car in rush hour. The orchestra swings into a slowed-down version of a rock and roll tune, for the younger folks. As we oldsters wander to our seats at white-clothed round tables that ring the vast room, a tap on my shoulder.

"If you'll excuse us, Hallie, I need a private word with the Ambassador. We won't be long."

"Of course, Mr. President."

Young Ted is leading Ethel back onto the floor. Hallie, alone for less than a moment, is approached by a tall fellow with a large nose.

"I'd be delighted," she says

The man is Jesus James Angleton . . . Or was it James Jesus. I always forget.

I follow JFK to the nearest door, which is opened for us by a fellow dressed for Mardi Gras. I realize it is a Swiss Guard, like those who protect the Vatican. Unless the Secret Service has been bullied into wearing these outfits for the evening. Across the gold-painted hallway a guard holding a lance, similarly dressed, opens another door and we enter a small lounge. Seated on a love seat, holding a beer, is a man I recognize but have never met, the new President's press secretary, Pierre Salinger. JFK introduces us as the door closes behind us.

"Evening Jack . . . er, Mr. President."

"The hardest job in America for the next eight years," JFK says, "will be Salinger's. To get over calling me Jack."

The portly spokesman rises, joins us at a table where a small cooler of beer is waiting. "Don't want to be interrupted by servers," the President explains.

Salinger pops the cap off a fresh beer. "Mr. Ambassador — or do you prefer Mr. Secretary in this time of transition? — what do you think of our Swiss Guard?"

"I was going to ask about that, Sir. Are they real or Memorex?"

"I am Pierre, not Sir, only Jack here is Sir. As for the guards, they are real Secret Service. What do you think?"

"Very colorful. Very surprising. A nice conversation piece. But also risky, don't you think?"

JFK pops two beers, hands me one. "Risky how?"

"Well, Sir, you know half the country is terrified of having a Catholic President. Afraid you would be taking orders from the Pope.

You calmed most of the fear with that speech in Houston, enough to get you elected."

"Thanks to Mayor Daley and his cemetery votes."

"Shhh!" JFK warns. "This man might be a Republican spy."

"I didn't hear a thing," I say. "But about the Swiss guard. It's only Inauguration Day. They guard the Vatican. Isn't that like poking a sleeping dog? Tomorrow the papers might be screaming The Pope Rules! The GOP might be seeking your head."

"I'll tell them it was a joke."

"Jack," Pierre says, "if you have to explain a joke, it's not a very good joke. You know that."

"If the Catholics object, I'll tell them it was an homage to the Vatican. They'll be pleased."

"'And everyone else will scream."

"So what do you suggest at this point?"

"Mr. President," I offer, "what if you tell the country something like this: 'If the Pope demands one more favor, I'll remind him my Navy is bigger.'"

Salinger and JFK almost choke in mid-guzzle.

"I knew I liked this guy," the President says.

He looks at his watch. "But we'd better get down to business. I don't want to leave the ladies waiting. What I want to pick your brain about, Ambassador, is myth-making."

"Sir?"

"The best Presidents become immortal by evolving into myths. Washington did it by refusing to become King."

"And by being unable to tell a lie," Pierre says, raising his beer.

"Quiet, Salinger. You know I have to pass on that one; that's what I hired you for. Now Lincoln, he kept the country together. He also freed the slaves —not that he wanted to, but to solidify his myth. FDR won two wars from a wheelchair. Plus an impossible third term, and an even more unlikely fourth. While he was dying. And he knew it. He died so his myth would live. Maisel, you're a good idea man. That's what this is about. The press has been battering Pierre about my plans for my first full day in office. That's tomorrow. Well, I have no interesting plans. I've polled the staff, got lots of suggestions. Visit the Liberty Bell. Boring. Tour the monuments. Problem with those is, to get me in the picture the photographers would have to back away until I was small as a toad. Not good for the front pages. Pierre suggested Jackie ride her horse down K Street, naked. She was not amused. Besides, that would start her myth, not mine. I need something different to start tongues wagging, to start building a myth on Day One. I'd like to know if you have any thoughts on that."

For a while I was stumped. No sound in the room except the clinking of beer bottles on teeth. Then lightning struck in the dimly lit room.

"This may seem odd . . ." I begin.

"That's okay, we Kennedys like odd."

"Einstein's brain. You could visit Einstein's brain."

They both look at me as if I am mad. Maybe I was.

"You haven't read about that?"

"I haven't read anything in a year beside drafts of Sorenson's speeches."

"Too busy stealing Illinois," Salinger says.

"Pierre! He's joking, Ambassador. Tell me about Einstein's brain."

"I'll make it short. Albert — I met him a few times — died five years ago. Almost six. April of '55. A burst aneurism near his heart. He was 78, I believe. In Europe, earth-bending scientists like him often lie in state for days. Einstein did not want that. Under Jewish law you are supposed to be buried before dark, if possible. He was not very religious in the ritual sense, but he did want that rule followed. A doctor at Princeton, where he died, performed a normal autopsy. But without permission, he secretly opened Einstein's skull with a saw, removed his brain, put it in a preservative solution. For future scientific study, he was thinking; to discover if anything in that brain would reveal why he was such a genius. After awhile he sliced the brain into thin pieces the size of a microscope slide. Sent slices to a few scientists he admired, for their perusal. Nothing very unusual was found, just minor differences you would find in comparing any two brains. As the years passed the slices disappeared like junk in an attic. Except for two. One is on display in England. The second is at the Mutter Museum, right up the road in Philadelphia."

"I never heard of it," JFK says.

"It's small, attached to an old hospital. A museum of medical artifacts."

"Maisel, where are you going with this?"

"The Mutter is the only place in the Western Hemisphere where people can see a piece of the great man's brain. As of next week, that is. Sunday the museum is staging a grand opening of its Einstein exhibit. That's when the public will start lining up. There has been, and will be, plenty of publicity. Saturday night is a private opening by invitation, to raise money for the museum. What I'm thinking is that tomorrow there could be a private Presidential Preview, just you and your wife and anyone else you care to invite."

"And that is my first act as President? Viewing a slice of Einstein's brain? Sounds weird. I never met the man. That's a strange way to shake hands. Might be something there, but with these beers I'm not quite focusing."

"Mr. President, I see it," Salinger says. "In most countries they pass the torch of power with a parade. Show off their tanks, jeeps, aircraft — if they have any — as a show of military might, to impress the world. And to scare the hell out of their own people. In America we don't have to do that. Everyone knows we're the strongest country on earth. But according to several studies we're falling behind intellectually. In math and science our kids aren't cutting it. We're way behind Japan and China. In one survey we came in 19th! Behind a couple of countries that still chant chants and burn idols."

"Too much television?" the President asks.

"Who knows? But teachers and scientists are warning that we need to turn that around before we fall even further behind?"

"I haven't noticed that in our family. Well, maybe with Teddy. But seriously, I am aware of that."

"Well, who better to lead a scholastic Renaissance than the President?" Salinger says. "JFK, Year One — The Year of the Intellect."

"Day One — Visiting Einstein's Brain," I enthuse.

"I like it," the President says. "And my Jewish donors will love it. So will the historians. But tomorrow? Can it be put together that quickly, Pierre?"

"No problem. One phone call to the Museum. Closed to the public while they are setting up. They'll live on the publicity for years. No crush of press, just one pool reporter and the White House photographer. In the afternoon — the Secret Service will want to sweep the museum in the morning."

"But early afternoon," JFK says. "So stories and pictures can go nationwide by the evening news."

"We'll rush press kits out," Salinger says, "embargoed until tomorrow night."

JFK stands, we follow, shake hands. "I'd like you and Hallie to come with us," the President says. "To thank you."

Walking into this room half an hour ago I never imagined causing such excitement.

"Maybe Jackie can play Lady Godiva next year," Salinger says. "Nude except for her hat. She has to wear her hat."

"Pierrre is cruisin' for a brusin' from the Missus. He doesn't know she packs a wallop."

"I'm glad the President liked your idea," Hallie said. "Might even get the Georgetown kids excited about something beside basketball."

## THE MUTTER MUSEUM

The motorcade was short, only three limousines, designed for protection, not ostentation. The President and First Lady (wearing a dark blue suit) sat in the middle limo along with Hallie (in purple), myself, and Salinger. When we rolled to a stop alongside the curb at the Mutter Museum, near Rittenhouse Square in Philly, four Secret Service men leaped from the first limo and dropped into crouches, one near each fender, scanning the street for signs of a threat. They were not dressed as the Swiss Guard. When they waved all-clear, four others leaped from the rear limo and surrounded us. After a quick surveillance one of them pulled open a reinforced side door. As we had been instructed, Salinger and his bulk emerged first, then Hallie, me, Mrs. Kennedy, the President. Wooden barriers painted red, white and blue formed a walkway to the front steps. Behind the barriers knots of spectators stood, drawn by the unusual activity outside the old museum. When they saw the new President, hatless, wearing a light gray raincoat against a cloudy sky, they broke into cheers, applause.

"Glad they're not here to see my brain," JFK murmured, soto voce, perhaps a bit tense at this his first public appearance as leader of the free world.

"Quiet, Mr. President," Jackie whispered.

A bronze sign above the entrance said: Mutter Museum, Founded 1874. A burnished wooden plaque beneath it, marked by old worm holes, said: Home of the Soap Lady. A banner fluttering above the entrance, read: EINSTEIN'S BRAIN: New Permanent Exhibit Opens Sunday, January 23.

The director of the Museum, a Ms. Hayworth, dressed in a brown suit, emerged through the front door and shook the President's hand. Mrs. Kennedy turned to me. "The Soap Lady? Is this a flea circus?"

Salinger interrupted. "It opened in 1858. It's run by The College of Physicians of Philadelphia, which is nearby. It's reputed to be the most impressive museum of medical oddities in the country. I checked."

"Well, I'm still not sure what we're doing here," Mrs. Kennedy said. "What would have been wrong with the Liberty Bell? Oh, there's Bigby.

Pierre, tell him to shoot the President and the brain. No naked side shows or soapy ladies."

"Yes, ma'am."

Hallie was glancing through a tour guide we'd each been given, reading aloud. "Another popular attraction at the Mutter is the liver that linked Chang and Eng together."

"Communists?" Mrs. Kennedy said. "A bad choice for the first day. Let's hope Winchell doesn't get hold of it."

"And history. Part of the thorax of John Wilkes Booth."

"That's gross. Please tell the President I shall be waiting outside."

## THE DISPLAYS

Jars of preserved livers and kidneys. The skeleton of a dwarf 3 feet 6 inches high. A distended ovary larger than a soccer ball. Dried severed hands shiny as laquer. The skeleton of a giant seven and a half feet tall. Spines and leg bones twisted by rickets. The corpse of a two-headed baby. These and more than a hundred thousand other human delicacies awaited our delighted or nauseated inspection. But first things first. It was a slice of the hippocampus of Albert Einstein that we were here to see.

To the right of the door as we entered the main exhibition space was a tall display case of dark wood and glass. A large black and white photo of Einstein. On the lower left were specimens of other brains, for comparison. On the right side — or was it the left?— other brain slides. In the center, a single slide on display under a microscope.

An information sheet tells you surprisingly (it surprised me) that the great man's brain was smaller than most. But slightly different in three ways. One area was larger than in other people. I have forgotten which area. His parietal folds (whatever those are) were unique, one part smooth instead of rippled. And some mechanism that ages the brain was absent. (He was 76 when he died.) Most scientists have agreed, however, that none of these small differences could have been responsible for his outsized intellect.

What, then?

The President moved to the microscope first. He seemed to be favoring his lower back, as if it had stiffened during the two-hour ride. Gingerly he bent over the eyepiece, squinted with his opposite eye, peered at the slide below. I was watching his expression; it did not change much. Not sure what I expected. He studied the slide for a minute, perhaps two, then backed away. He seemed disappointed.

"It's gray," he said. "Aren't all brains gray?"

I nodded as if I knew something.

"Smooth?" I asked. "Textured?"

"A little of both. Even if that's what what all our brains look like, it's amazing what they can do. How they came about. How God invented them, if you ask Mother Rose. There's a darker gray area on the far left, not sure if it means anything, it could be just a fingerprint."

I edged past him to take a look. Einstein's brain was just as the President had described it. Similar to a hundred photographs we've seen in magazines. But the gray on the left seemed a bit more defined than a fingerprint. I looked around for a staff member, saw none, put my fingers on a dial on the side of the scope, turned it slightly, barely touching it. The image edged into sharper focus. As I had suspected, it was not a fingerprint. The image was of a woman. I focused my good eye very slightly to the right. A gray image on that side as well. Also a woman. What the fuck was going on? I strained my eyes for greater clarity. The women were the same size, perhaps an inch and a half high on the slide. Both were dressed in gray. There was no color in the room in which they stood, just a fireplace to the left middle, a mantelpiece above it that held an unlit candelabra, what appeared to be a parrot in a hanging cage to to the right. I breathed deeply, asked the President to take another look. He had been saying something to Jackie. He turned back to the microscope and peered in.

'What's going on?" he asked. "That picture was not there a moment ago. It looks like an old Polaroid. But how could . . ."

"I sharpened the image. But that is not a photograph, Sir. This is a slice of Einstein's hippocampus, according to the plaque. Which means that is, incredibly, a memory."

"A memory? He's been dead for five years, you said."

"Yes. Which could suggest there might be life after death."

"Like the priests say!"

"As many religions maintain."

"Yes."

"Has this sort of thing ever been seen before?"

"Not that I've ever heard of. Of course, the brains of very few people are saved and preserved and sliced apart and put under a microscope. So who knows? And those brains come mostly from people with a serious disease, for scientists looking to find a cause."

I waved Hallie to the display. She peered into the microscope.

"What is this, a hoax?"

"I doubt the Mutter would be a party to that."

"I heard you say it's a memory. Is Evolution experimenting with life after death? Just a little trial?"

"I have no idea."

"But memory fits," Hallie says.

"How do you mean?"

"Don't you recognize the woman? The young one? That is Albert's first wife, Mileva."

I took another, longer look. "By god, you're right. That is her, still in Albert's brain. Five years after he died. About fifty years after they divorced."

"What a discovery!" the President said. "A four-leaf clover. What a story for my first day. If anyone believes it. That is true myth-making, Maisel."

"Mr. President, if I may. You must not publicize this discovery. I beg of you."

"Surely you're kidding."

"No, Sir. We have no idea what this means. What it represents. The world will twist and turn, different theories from scientists and laymen, from priests and rabbis and even the Pope, will flood the intellectual world. I suspect very little work will get done."

"What are you suggesting?"

"That we get a handle on it first. Know a little better what we are talking about."

"How do we do that?"

"First, classify its existence. Top Secret. Which is justified, until we learn what effect, if any, it might have on life on earth. Then scour the country for the best neurosurgeons. Bring them to Washington, swear them to secrecy. With prison waiting if they break security. Show them this slide, tell them to go home and look for another one. Or ten more. Slicing apart every hippocampus they can get access to. A secret, government-financed science project. Is this only Einstein, or is the human brain evolving into eternal life? After a year, or whenever, convene them again, see what they have found. Only then should you decide what to reveal to the public, and when."

As I spoke Jackie looked into the microscope, frowning.

"The Ambassador is right, Jack."

Salinger followed her.

"Pierre," the President said. "Do you think you can sit on that for a year?"

"I suppose I will have to."

We stood about silently, like flies with nothing to buzz about. Until the President spoke again.

"Okay. This is Top Secret. That applies to all of us here, of course. Tell no one."

"The Museum has advertised this exhibit," Salinger said. "How do we keep the public out?"

"I'll speak with Ms. Hayworth. Tell her the Einstein slide is now Top Secret, that we have to confiscate it for scientific study. They must have slides of other brains they can substitute. If we deceive some of our citizens, it's for the public good. It won't be the first time. Or the last. Ambassador, slip that slide into your pocket for safe-keeping."

Hallie, eyebrows raised, moved behind the microscope for another look. Hiding the action with my body, I unclipped the slide, carefully wrapped it in my handkerchief, slipped it into my pocket.

"I also have another idea. Pierre, you've got the news release ready to go out this afternoon, right? About my first full day in office. Explaining the purpose — to draw attention to how as a nation we are falling far behind in science and math. And that I am determined that in a decade we catch up. How on the steps of this museum I have declared this the Year of Learning. Nothing about the slide, of course. Add that in coming weeks I will announce federal scholarships that will go to the best students in every state, every school district, every college. Whatever.

"And something else I have been thinking about. Using our new knowledge, by the end of this decade we shall put a man on the moon.

"All that will dominate tonight's TV news and tomorrow's newspapers. We'll shoot video for them. But this can't be a one-day story. So tomorrow I will make more big news. Announce a cabinet shake-up. I'll create a new cabinet position to take charge of all this. The Secretary of Intelligence."

"Jack, that sounds like a spy operation," Mrs. Kennedy said.

Murmurs of agreement. Other suggestions began to fill the fetid air in the dim museum, like sick butterflies.

"Department of Advanced Study."

"Will you be replacing the Department of Education?"

"No, there's a thousand civil servants in Education. Most of them Democrats. They'll stay where they are. Handle nuts and bolts stuff. The schools, the unions, curricula. Most of that belongs to the states anyway. I want something different, that will catch the country's attention. Cover of *Life,* that sort of thing."

"Creation. The Department of Creation."

"Better. But it suggests the arts. Or religion. Congress won't spend an extra penny on the arts. Also suggests making babies. This is a footnote, but did you know that Chang and Eng, the Siamese Twins over in the corner there, had between them 21 children? People will call it the Department of Catholic Propaganda."

"Siamese twins who had 21 children?" Hallie said. "I think I'll wait for the movie."

Pierre Salinger laughed so hard he had to grab a table to keep from falling.The President covered a smile with a cough. Jackie blushed. My own reaction I don't recall. I probably was angry at Hallie but said nothing. We rarely fought.

"Okay, folks, back to reality," JFK said. "We need something real, and imaginative."

"That's it, Jack. 'The Department of Imagination.'"

A sudden silence as we swished that around like new Beaujolais.

"If I may," Hallie said, "there's a relevant quotation in an Einstein bio I just read. He said, 'Imagination is more important than knowledge. Knowledge is limited. Imagination encircles the world.'"

"Einstein said that? Perfect! That will be the motto of the new Department. Chiseled in marble. Einstein deserves a monument on the Mall, why should it be just for politicians? How does that sound to you, Mr. Secretary?"

I looked around, uncertain.

"Ambassador Maisel, I'm speaking to you. I'd like you to be the first Secretary of Imagination." He paused. "Sorry, I suppose I should have asked you first."

"What about the Middle East, Sir?"

"The Middle East? There's a hundred self-described experts on the Middle East. I'll choose a Republican — that way they can share the blame when nothing works." He grinned. "Pierre, call Sorensen, tell him I want to see him when we get back. Do you think a thousand words will be enough?"

"I'd let him go fifteen hundred," Salinger said. "And we'll need a picture of the Ambassador. Mr. Maisel, would you prefer Secretary of Imagination or Ambassador of Imagination."

"To be honest, neither leaps lightly off the tongue. How about Director?"

"You got it," the President said, and shook my hand. "Director of Imagination."

"Or Director of Imaginative Thinking?"

"We'll discuss it tomorrow. About the Top Secret classification, when we're ready to stir up a fuss we can always spring a leak. Living memories after death? The mere possibility will alter the human psyche."

Director of Imaginative Thinking.

They kept calling me Ambassador anyway.

## Two Women

Macbeth was waiting patiently at the door. He jumped at Hallie's knees, burst outside to empty his bladder. A light snow had begun to fall as we re-entered the District. I watched the little booger scamper across the lawn, leaping and snapping at the larger flakes. Dog as metaphor did not escape me. My new job might amount to nothing more than snatching at snowflakes. In the end there might be nothing to show for it but a large pile of damp. Maybe a small pile.

But you do not say "No" to the President.

An oxymoron: do imaginative thinkers take direction?

Hallie placed a hand on my shoulder and joined me in watching Macbeth. The sun broke through the clouds of my mood as it had been doing at her touch for more than ten years now. The mutt joined us on the veranda, shuddered his little body as if he had a blizzard to dislodge.

"Are you feeling okay? You've been very quiet since we looked at the brain."

"I've just been thinking."

"That can give you a headache."

"No kidding."

We closed the door, sat together on the sofa. I took her hand as we spoke.

"That picture. Or whatever it was on his hippocampus."

"A memory."

"Okay, a memory. Think about it, carefully We missed something. I took a second look, and I know I'm right. There were two women. One was young, about twenty. Not beautiful, but smiling, happy. Is that what you saw?"

"Mileva Marić, Albert's first wife. They must have been deeply in love back then."

"So you did recognize her!"

"Of course. But not the older woman beside her. I thought maybe Madam Curie, they did visit her in Paris. They were all physicists,

they must have had plenty to talk about. Albert with his Nobel
for Relativity, Curie with two Nobels, one in physics, the other in
chemistry. And Mileva an excellent mathematician herself — some
believe she helped Albert in devising his theory, then he took all the
credit. But I was forcing the image. It was not Madam Curie."

"Did you then realize who it was?"

"No. Did you?"

"On the ride home it struck me. The two women were dressed
in black with a big ruffled collar. Exactly alike. They were standing
in the same room: a rocking chair in one corner, a candelabra on
a mantelpiece above a fire. Exactly the same, except on the second
woman wrinkles were beginning to show near her eyes; her face was
thinner, if you looked closely she appeared to have been crying. She
was angry, she may have been in an argument with the person viewing
her. She was not happy, like the younger woman."

"What are you saying?"

"That they are the same woman, Exi. Mileva young and Mileva
older."

A whimper of negative ions scorched my brain.

"It can't be. This was not a photograph that can be combined from
two negatives taken years apart. It's a memory."

"So what can it be? That is what has been breaking my brain."

"I'll buy a good microscope tomorrow. We can study the slide at
leisure."

"You know you will see exactly what I have described."

"I suspect you're right. But if this is one of Einstein's memories . . ."

She squeezed my hand. "His theory that I can't get my brain
arounds . . . that what us mere mortals feel is crazy. Even though a few
of his colleagues agree. Feynman, others."

"Time! His theory of time!"

"Exactly. We humans experience time as linear, moving ahead
straight as an arrow: Past, Present, Future. Then death. But according
to Einstein and a few other geniuses, time does not move forward like
that. Time is sort of circular. It is all happening at once! The way we
experience it is an illusion. I think they arrived at that idea through
mathematics. Normal people like us will never understand it, I don't
think. But the slide might be the first visual evidence that their theory
is correct. In that slide — in Einstein's hippocampus — Mileva is happy
and about 20 years old. And also miserable and about 40 years old. At
the same time!"

"That's not possible," I said.

"Of course not. I agree. But it fits with their personal history. In their early twenties they fell madly in love. Got married. Worked together on physics projects day and night, which thrilled Mileva. It was the first time she'd been taken seriously as a mathematician. As an equal to the men. She went through her early years smiling to her inner core. As in that slide. That's all she wanted from life — to use her intellect side by side with Albert. But gradually, for Albert, life became more and more physics, less and less Mileva. He started hanging out in the cafés at night talking physics with his male buddies, not his wife. He began to order her around: do the shopping, cook the dinner, clean the house. He began having affairs. And Mileva became what she had always vowed she would never be: a housewife, like all the other cows — or *fraus* — on the street. When she objected to this treatment be began to hate her — and she began to hate him. Wretched together, they finally divorced after 18 years, and Einstein married his cousin Elsa. Looked at that way, it's all there in the picture. In their faces. In his memory. In his hippocampus."

"Five years after he died?"

"Give me another explanation. Real time is standing still. Or all time is happening simultaneously, as Albert postulated. If that's true, and was proven, it might change all of philosophy. The entire way we look at life. No more waiting for our deaths, which are not in the future, but are happening now — simultaneously with our being born. I can't accept it either — but what other explanation is there? That slide might be worth a fortune to the Museum. To the world."

"Unless there are others like it."

Macbeth began scratching at the door. We had forgotten him on the veranda.

"Another voice heard from," I said. "Please let him in while I get the aspirin."

Before I did I went upstairs and took the slide from my jacket pocket and put it in a jewelry box and stuck it far in the back on the top shelf in Hallie's closet and stuffed a mess of towels in front of it.

## LOVE, LOVE

Adore. Adored. Adoring. Old words but good words; irreplaceable Medieval words, rarely used nowadays. Too bad. Perhaps heard in a momentary movie scene: *I adore you honey, but I need to run to the store for cigarettes.* I envision Cary Grant spouting at Grace Kelly. Or Bogart to Bacall. *Here's looking at you, kid.* Serious, but not Serious.

Not *The Adoration of the Magi* (Botticcelli) Or *The Adoration of the Magi* (Leonardo) Or *The Adoration of the Magi* (Rubens.) The Magi were wise men. Perhaps that is where the word went; we have few wise men nowadays. And should any turn up, we certainly do not adore them. We Twitter them, Pinterest them, Facebook them, Instagram them, Tumblr, Reddit, Google, Flicker, Vine, Meetup, Linked In or YouTube them. There seem to be more every day. But adore them? Not in this millennium.

Which brings me to my point, You may accept it or not, but Exit Maisel and Hallie Rosen adored one another. Seriously. An adoration which they did not flaunt, but which was Biblical in depth and strength, lodged behind their eyes, unbelievers though they were; adoration that multiplied by ten when sprinkled with poetry; when they were reading aloud to one another in the welcome cool of the evening or the winking eye of the moon. (Mostly it was he reading to her; neither had a problem with that.) Hippocampus can provide a simple image, it occurred so often: of a summer evening, Exit sitting on the wrought iron bench, wearing a T-shirt and tennis shorts (though he was not fond of tennis, his missing eye a decided handicap in returning ferocious serves, which were all they taught at Langley), a small lovely book in his hand. Hallie stretched at right angles on the bench, her hair tied off her neck in a bun nestling in his lap, also wearing a tennis shirt and shorts (she did play when she had the time), one tennis shoe and sock peeled off in the damp grass, the other shoe dangling from her toe unconsciously, as it often did when she was a child. Two glasses of iced tea on the redwood table. She listening to him intently; he reading to her with equal intent, Macbeth nibbling her toe polish.

Hippocampus stores scores of similar memories snapped like photographs on winter nights when there was no wind and the air was chilled but not iced, the two of them in the same positions but with presumably more and heavier clothing invisible beneath a heavy comforter borrowed from the vacant guest bedroom and wrapped around both of them. When they returned to the house, summer or winter, flakes of poetry clung to their hair.

## A COMMITTEE

In a corner of the office stood a normal-sized skeleton. On a corner of the desk sat a normal-sized skull. Scattered across the glass that covered the oak desk were a mess of folders, some blue, some red.

Leaning back comfortably behind the desk, his large hands linked behind his neck, looking fit enough to play point guard in the NBA and young enough to do so at Princeton, sat Dr. Brian White, son of my housekeeper, Margaret, and her handyman husband, Ben. Formerly a brain surgeon at Mass General, Brian had risen quickly to becomes Chair of Brain Research at their Medical School. Best of all from my point of view, when I had phoned him from the White House an hour earlier he had sounded genuinely happy to hear from me. It had been years since we had spoken — only once or twice when his mother was ill and I wanted to check how she was doing. Pneumonia, I think it was. Happily she recovered, and she and Ben came back to work for us.

I suppose I should confess that while I was wearing a standard blue suit for the swearing-in — there is still a photograph of me with the President on my dresser — Brian had on a burgundy shirt and a solid yellow tie below his neatly trimmed goatee. The arms of the shirt were rolled to his elbows, the jacket of his dark brown suit was draped over the back of his executive chair. He must have looked twenty years younger than me, though the difference was not quite that great.

As I read his name and title on the door, Brian —Dr. White — literally leaped from behind his desk, stepped forward and embraced me with those basketball arms of his.

"Congratulations on your promotion," I said, pointing to the gilt lettering.

"I was about to say the same thing to you, Ambassador. A member of the President's cabinet! Have you been sworn in yet?"

"Just before I phoned. Hallie was with me of course, and my sister Rachel came up from New York to witness the induction. I sent them off to lunch together, for which I suspect they will be eternally grateful. My title is Director of Imaginative Thinking! How do you keep up with such minutiae when there are cerebellums to be probed?"

He smiled. "If I miss anything important in the papers, Mother gets me up to speed. And reminds me each time that that's rightfully a job for a wife. When I tell her later that you came by, direct from the White House, she'll jump like a cheerleader, varicose veins or not. Macbeth, of course, will yip for a treat. Come, sit down. Though it's wonderful to see you, I assume this visit, on this special day, is not social."

I sat on a Navy blue couch that hunkered against one wall. Brian sat easily beside me.

"As a matter of fact, there is a hitch to my visit. The trick is to swallow it quickly, like castor oil when you were a kid."

"Mother often reminds me of those days. Mostly if I invite a girl to dinner who is not pretty enough for her. Mom assumes she has veto power over my women." He laughs. "Some day I'll set her straight."

"Actually, it was Ben who told me about the castor oil. He chuckled the entire time."

Dr. White closed his eyes. "Okay, I'm ready. Hit me with it."

"I need you to form a committee."

Eyes open, he shook his head. "Anything but a committee. I've turned down three government offers because they involved committees. Meet meet meet. Talk talk talk. All of it a waste of time. I'd rather be carving cerebella."

"Hear me out, Doctor. You would be the chairman. So only you will schedule meetings. If you want them. Only you can arrange for discussions. If you want them. I'll grant you that in the end it could all be a waste of your time, and that of other surgeons. On the other hand, depending on what you discover, it could re-invent the human race."

"Is that a good idea? On balance I suppose it is. What are the odds of one outcome over the other?"

"The truth, Doctor? I have no idea."

Because of the Top Secret classification, without mentioning names or saying what they would be looking for, I told him the minimum: select the best surgeons available, acquire brains of the deceased, as they do from organ donors, or from the unclaimed heading for Potter's Field. Carefully slice up the hippocampi and record what you see. Photograph anything unusual.

"Define unusual."

"As someone, a judge I think, once said about pornography: You'll know it when you see it."

"Does this committee have a name?"

"I thought we'd call it Project Mileva."

"That tells me nothing."

"That's the idea."

"Half a dozen top surgeons. Slicing away at the hippocampi of the dead. To see if they find anything unexpected? Without telling them, or even me, what they are looking for? This sounds like a snipe hunt in Arkansas. Pop used to tell me about those when I was a kid. But I know you too well for that, Ambassador."

"Which I suppose is why you were my first call, Mr. Chairman. Or should it be Doctor Chairman?"

"See," Brian said. "Already there's something we have to discuss."

"Another reason is that I don't know many brain surgeons. But when you talk to them you can tell them the President has classified the research Top Secret. It ought to make them curious."

When we shook hands, at first I thought from his tepid touch that he already was having regrets. But by the end of the shake his clutch was warm, strong. Even optimistic.

"I can't wait to not tell Mother," he said.

Driving home, with the first study in the Department of Imaginative Thinking set in motion, my brain was flooded with questions about how Memories After Death, if these were found to exist widely, might function. Not the physics of it, I had no deep knowledge in that area. Were they created by extra neurons in the synapses? A new kind of electricity in the brain? That would be up to doctors and specialists from San Francisco to Singapore to St. Petersburg to figure out in coming years, decades, even millennia; Evolution works slower than Preacher Roe. I became intrigued by what we might call the liberal arts aspect of the phenomenon: how was the enduring memory of our Deathtime selected? By ourselves? By some outer power? Could that power be the origin of what we have come to call God? If a beautiful memory filled our hippocampus forever after death, did that lead to the notion of Heaven? If a terrible memory persisted through eternity, was that the origin of Hell (with elaborations added through the years by priests and other con men?) Did our actions in life, for good or ill, really influence our eternal Polaroid? Or was that concept created by spiritual flacks to keep us in line?

Such thoughts were a waste of time, of course. The study might determine, as someone had suggested, that eternal memory was an experiment that Evolution had already discarded. I switched on the car radio to clear my head of this spider web. I listened to Oldies but Goodies, on which was playing "Fly Me to the Moon."

## "I Didn't Do it"

We were able to exchange only two sentences when they shuffled him in handcuffs and an orange jumpsuit and leg irons into Nassau County Court, charged with cruelty to animals and interfering with interstate commerce.

"Exit, I didn't do it," Whitebread said, looking me in the eye as they opened the door to the crowded courtroom.

"Of course you didn't," I replied, looking right back at him.

I was upset already. Three weeks in jail without bail had given his face a pallor that was not normal. Clearly he had not been eating well, either.

Arraignments often take no more than a minute or two, time to establish that there is enough evidence to go to trial, or for the defendant to plead Not Guilty. Whitebread's took longer. His public defender was a sturdy woman named Anna Apple. Since the felony charge, interfering with interstate commerce, was a federal offense, the judge ordered the prosecutor to refile it in federal court. Ms. Apple gathering up folders, snapped her head forward once, businesslike, in agreement. Whitebread, standing beside her, raised his left fist, as if he had just been crowned middleweight champion. I'd hoped we'd get to talk but two prison guards quickly hustled him from the courtroom out through a wooden door behind the judge's bench while another case was called. Justice, if that's what this was to be, had little time to waste.

The federal trial was scheduled for six month later. Whitebread requested that he be permitted to have the same attorney, Ms. Apple, even though she worked for the state of New York, not the federal government. The federal judge who took over the case, Manuel Sosa, said he would allow that as long as the feds would bear no responsibility for her salary. Ms. Apple agreed. I suspected the judge wanted to be sure he would not be overturned on appeal should Whitebread be convicted. But he refused to set bail.

I rode the train down from Washington to visit Whitebread again some time during the first few weeks. I shall always remember his first words as he took a seat behind a barred window and looked at me and spoke into a phone.

"Exit, I did not do it."

"Of course you didn't," I replied.

The words had an eerie, metallic echo, perhaps because of those phones.

## The Unimpressed

Three days after we met in his office, after the weekend, Dr. White sent telegrams to eleven brain surgeons he knew well or had met casually at various conferences. He told them the basics of what they were being asked to do, but not the part that was classified, about what we had found in Einstein's hippocampus. He told the scientists they might rewrite the history of mankind. The results were not encouraging.

Eight of the responses were about the same: the surgeons said they could not make time in their schedules, could not commit to this vague experiment, without knowing more about it – mainly, what they were supposed to be looking for. Three of them did not respond at all. I could hardly blame them. But this left me in a quandary: how else to proceed with the experiment? If I had been the only one who had seen Mileva in the brain slice of the dead Einstein I would have convinced myself it had been a hallucination. But JFK had seen it, and Hallie, and Mrs. Kennedy, and Pierre. This was worthy of Copernicus, of Gallileo, of Newton, of Einstein himself. Not all of us were going crazy. I went upstairs, climbed to the top of Hallie's closest, reached to the back. For a heart-pinching moment I was afraid it would be missing. But reaching further I felt the box, took it down, found the slide and unwrapped it. Breathing heavily, as if in the aftermath of sex, I went downstairs and slipped it into the microscope I had bought for Hallie. Mileva young and Mileva older still were there.

## THE JEWELER

The dog lived lordly and loudly in and out of the guest house behind our place. With sprawling green lawns and two gardeners who kept them looking as neat as Pebble Beach. The near-mansion was owned by Arnold D. Trumpf the billionaire playboy known widely as The Cheeseburger King because he owned franchised burger eateries marked CK in almost every state and made a fortune. He and his third French wife, Cara, a former fashion model, spent their lives boating and skiing and mostly golfing on courses he built among estates in Palm Beach, the Virgin Islands, Brazil, Nice, and Switzerland; they were rumored to be constructing a sixth in Odessa. He also had authored a best-selling book, written by a ghost, called *Onions: The Art of the Peel*. Soon after we bought Birnham Wood and renamed it Dunsinane, they gave us a Welcome Party. Then they left on a world tour.

Late one afternoon a battered gray pickup we had not seen before had rounded jerkily the long gravel drive that passed our place on the left and kept going toward Trumpf Manor, which fronted the next street. Out of thoughtless politeness I waved at the driver, who jammed on his brakes, the pickup skittering on the gravel, and with the engine still running hopped from the vehicle. At first glance he was not the kind of fellow one usually encountered in our spoiled neighborhood. He was wearing brown leather shorts cut to the thigh, a soiled white muscle shirt, loafers without socks. His legs looked as though they were naturally hairy but had been shaved. Most memorably, his head was thick with bright white curly hair you would more likely find on a sheep. Hallie had gone inside, leaving me to finger-wrestle with Macbeth. I stood and went to greet the fellow, see if he were lost, our pint-sized canine nipping at my heels, sniffing the visitor's shoes. Up close the fellow, perhaps 30 years old, looked familiar; his thick white curly hair above a handsome face and aging agate eyes made an impression you do not forget; he suggested to me a fencer got up as a clown.

"Can I help you? I asked. "The name's Maisel. I live in this bungalow."

We had been there four months and I still was not comfortable with the opulence, though it was a shack compared to some of the nearby estates; our entire place in Tel Aviv could have fit in the dining room. Yet Israel had never felt cramped in the twelve years we were there.

The fellow extended his hand. "Fleq," he said, and we shook. I did not know if that was his first name or his last. I realized he might have felt the same about Maisel, but after half a lifetime Exit was still an awkward name to drop on strangers.

"Glad to meet you," he said. "And who is this?"

"Macbeth. The house — we bought it in December — is called Dunsinane, so my wife and I thought . . ."

"I understand. I love Shakespeare. Did some acting at Bard. 'Avon in His Time.' I played Lady Macbeth. Delicious. I'm in the midst of moving into my aunt's guest house over there — the Trumpfs are tired of Washington, they travel most of the time."

"That's some place they've got."

"Yep. Arnold Trumpf is quite a story. The Cheeseburger King."

"When we moved here Mrs. Trumpf was kind enough to throw us a party. Welcome to the Neighborhood. That's the only time we've been in there. We didn't seem to hit it off."

"Let me guess. Uncle Arnold had three bourbons and began spouting politics."

"Something like that. He seems to have a strange Lincoln fetish. I guess you know. He kept saying that before he dies he wants to pass Abe Lincoln as the most admired man in America."

"Yeah, I've heard that fairy tale. He's hinted at running for President some day."

"Is he qualified?"

"Aside from making money — by breaking the law, mostly — he's not qualified for third grade."

"You sound serious."

"I am serious. He wants to bring back slavery, return America to the 'good old days.' The meaning of life, in his view, is personal publicity. My aunt is not like that, I don't know how she puts up with it. Because of the endless pennies, I guess. Uncle Arnold must have swallowed one as a child pretending it was a sacred wafer. I would never stay in their guest house if they were in town. But it's fully furnished, a maid comes in every day to straighten up — everything but my studio, nobody touches that. Only thing I need is a dog. I used to have cats — Tiny Tim, Peter Pan, Garfield — but they didn't do much to keep people away. After passing the name Dunsinane on your place a few times and hearing, I guess it was your wife, call Macbeth, I thought, my dog should be Banquo's Ghost. With your permission, of course; we don't want the neighbors to think we're creating a Disneyland version of the Globe Theatre in their precious neighborhood. They might burn a mouse on our lawn. Instead, Unc has turned the entire country into Disneyland."

Immediately I liked the guy.

"Washington has been Disneyland for years," I said. "And you surely don't need our permission for what you name your dog. Perhaps the pooches will become friends. What kind of dog are you thinking of?"

"A guy in Arlington is moving to Tibet and he's giving me one of his. It's a German Shepherd, which is perfect, they make great guard dogs, easily trained. I need a guard dog."

"Why is that?"

"I'm a jeweler. Keep a fair amount of gold and silver around. Occasionally, precious stones — diamonds, sapphires. Unfinished rings. Small safes are too portable. Nothing keeps the rabble away better than a large dog with fangs."

"A jeweler? Wait, you're not Anton Fleq?"

"Sometimes I wish I wasn't. Unc certainly wishes that. A gay jeweler. His so-called 'base' does not approve. So I humor him and keep it quiet, go just by Fleq. One name has been where it's at for years anyway. Madonna, Beyoncé, Adele."

"Congratulations. I see your name and work all over the place. Spreads in every magazine I flip through at the dentist. You do nice stuff."

"It passes the time."

"Do you know of Perle Mesta? A real socialite, big party-giver. Most sought-after invitation in town. Senators, cabinet members, industrialists, even the President might be there. She must be in her 70s by now and still going. Personally I hate cocktail parties. Embassy receptions in Israel were bad enough, unless there was a hot political rumor around. Mrs. Mesta is known everywhere as 'The Hostess With the Mostest.' Because of her bubbly personality, and whom she knows, I guess. Didn't I see an ad for your work recently based on that phrase? 'The Hostess With the Mostest Wears Fleq — On Her Fingers, Her Wrists, Her Neck.'"

"Yeah, we hit half a dozen books with that. Did you like it?"

"I did. Did you write it?"

"Sort of. Perle actually has bought some of my pieces. So. What were you doing in Israel?"

"Ambassador." I hesitated without knowing why. "For eleven years."

"Jeez, I'm sorry. I should have recognized you."

"Not really. Nobody else does. Except David Ben-Gurion. And a few angry Arabs."

The sun was beginning to set. The poppies were beginning to curl for the night. Fleq looked at his watch.

"I got to be going. Check the fence around the guest house before it gets dark. Make sure it will hold my dog."

"Banquo's Ghost?"

"Banquo or Ghost. One name only."

The fellow drove off in his pick-up, leaving behind a spray of gravel and the pungent smell of pot. Macbeth scooted after me to the veranda. From upstairs I heard the shower running. Hallie would not appreciate a German shepherd living one fence away. I didn't tell her just then.

## CHARLOTTE IN DEATH

One day when I came home from class Hallie was already there, sprawled on our bed, reading, or at least looking at, a huge book. I was horrified. The book was *Charlotte,* the life's work of that German artist who had been put in the oven by the Nazis when she was 26 and pregnant. I had never showed Hallie that book. For years it had been semi-hidden high and far back on the top shelf of the bookcase on my side of the bed. Among the mysteries. I feared the images hippocampus might bring back to her.

"Where did you get that?" I asked.

She looked up at me, puzzled. "Where I always get it. Off your top shelf. Is that okay?"

"Where you always get it? I didn't know you knew we had it. When did you find it?"

"Years ago. When I'm feeling low I look at it and feel blessed that I was not born a few years later, when the Nazis were already in power. When I'm feeling high about how blessed we are I look at it to remember what might have been. To bring me down a peg."

"You never told me."

"What was the need? I was afraid you might get upset. You never showed me the book."

"What was the need? I assumed you have enough bad memories."

"I do. But we can't deny memories. We can only try to bleach them a bit."

"How?"

"With kisses."

With difficulty I moved the heavy book aside.

"Lots of kisses."

## WHERE HAVE ALL THE NAZIS GONE?

Jesus James Angleton. . . James Jesus?. . . wearing tennis whites, bends to his right, picks a tennis ball out of a wire basket, straightens up, stares across the net, tosses the ball above his head, swings his racket hard, grunts as he smashes the ball to the far court. The ball does not come flying back. There is no opponent on the far side of the net. Angleton is brushing up his serve before a Company tournament at Langley the next weekend.

When he whacks the last ball in the basket he takes a white towel that is draped over the green net and towels sweat from his face, his arms. They leave their car to meet him but as if he still is not aware of them he walks to the far end of the court and begins to gather up the balls that are lying all over. Both wonder if they should offer to help. Neither does. With both arms laden he circles the net and places the balls back in the basket. Two balls fall out and roll across the service area.

They sit on the nearby wood and stone bench just outside the fence. The counter-intelligence chief, holding his racket, seems finally to notice them, approaches and sits on the seat at right angles to theirs.

"Good morning," he says. "I haven't seen you two in a while. How are things at Georgetown, Ms. Rosen?"

"Not very promising right now."

"Well, it usually gets better as summer approaches and the seniors don't know what to do with their lives. And you, Maisel? Any developments?"

"Nothing worth mentioning."

"Nothing and nothing. You both seem nervous. Is something wrong."

Husband and wife glance quickly at one another, then back at their boss.

"It's just that we didn't know you knew both of us are Company," Hallie says.

"Extreme secrecy and all that," Exit adds.

"Children, children," James Angleton says. "We are human, you know. We assume even our best agents are going to tell their spouses. That's a given. So long as you don't discuss projects at home."

"We never . . ."

Hallie is interrupted. "I know."

Exit's face flares hot. What the fuck does that mean? Were their bedrooms bugged in Tel Aviv? Here in Washington? He breathes deep. Angleton, he realizes, is putting them on.

"All right, folks, down to business. FYI, this bench and the nearby trees have not been bugged, we check almost hourly. First the background, which you probably know, but I like to be orderly. After the war many Nazis, high and low, escaped capture. Disappeared into the forests, lost themselves in the liberated cities. The Red Army rounded up some, but many fled to South America – with one or more fake passports, we assume. Mostly to Argentina and Brazil. Mossad flooded those countries and brought plenty of Nazis back to Israel to stand trial. But about a dozen they know of remain free. Early on they asked us to form a joint anti-Nazi squad with them, and we agreed. Got some good results — camp guards and such. Last week they pulled off their biggest coup yet. Mossad jumped a man on a street in Buenos Aires, shoved him into a car and took off. They're debriefing him in a safe house, will fly him to Israel when they see fit. To face Israeli justice. Which means he'll get a public trial before they hang him."

"Eichmann?" Hallie guessed. "They got Adolf Eichmann?"

"Bingo!" Angleton said. "The architect of the Final Solution. The shit who made the death trains run on time. He was skinny, wearing a false mustache, a bow tie, carrying a briefcase. Playing an accountant, we're told."

"Damn, Mossad is good."

"Next best after us," Jesus said, laying his patriotism on the table like a tray of chocolate cake. "He was Number One on their Hit Parade for a couple of years. Now he's off the table, so Number Two moves up to Number One. And they want our help."

"Why? When they're riding high."

"They get lots of sightings, some real, some fake. A few pay off, most don't. They chase down every one. But this turd has been a special challenge. Moves around a lot. Every time they believe they're closing in he disappears, weeks later turns up in another city, with a new job, under a new name. Gets lost in the urban crowd. And Mossad goes home with its tail between its legs."

Angleton seems to have run out of steam. Maybe it was the tennis. For moments we sit quietly. He looks at Hallie. "Want to take another guess?"

She shakes her head no.

"I thought you might figure this one. Josef Mengele."

Hallie's right hand flies to her throat like a dazed bird. The blood drains from her face; suddenly she's almost as white as Angleton's shirt.

"Mengele is dead," I say. "Drowned while swimming in Brazil. Had a stroke or a kidney problem or something."

"That was the last of his three reported deaths. Six months ago. But Mossad could not find a body. In the newspapers they let it stand. Figured maybe that would make him careless about surveillance. Then last week they got a tip they believe. Including a grainy telephoto of a man walking in a street. Looks pretty much like him.

"Mossad operates in quantity. Get a sighting, send in a dozen assets, infiltrate the area, close in. No way for him to escape. Except so far he has. They believe most of the tips were real, just late. He bounced around from Brazil to Paraguay to Argentina and back. One job he was a traveling salesman of pharmaceuticals. Perfect cover for moving around every day, sleeping in a different town every night. Another time he worked on a farm for six months before Mossad heard about it. By then he was gone. Some ex-Nazi must be supplying him with false IDs whenever he needs them. He's eluded the West Germans, the Israelis, the French, Simon Wiesenthal's group. Now it's our turn. But I've got a different idea of how to do it. I think a smaller search team might work better. Less chance of being spotted. You two are it."

A chipmunk perched invisibly half way up a tree came scampering down the bark, stopped on the grass a few feet away, head cocked as if to listen. We all glanced at him.

"It's okay," Angleton said. "He's one of ours."

We smiled. But our smiles were tight. We were anxious to hear details of the operation.

"You leave in three weeks," the spymaster said.

"Three weeks? Why not tomorrow, or Friday? Before he moves on."

"This was a tip, not a sighting. Recent word is that he attends Carnival in Brazil every year. Dresses in outrageous costumes. Drinks and dances in the street all night and picks up young boys. We're hoping he sticks to that pattern. But Carnival doesn't start for three weeks. Housekeeping will arrange for your flight, your passports, a suitable hotel. Buy your own bathing suits and sunscreen. And costumes."

"According to the magazines, Carnival is all about bikinis," Hallie said. "Where will I carry my gun?"

"A fair question. You've got twenty days to figure that out."

He reached behind himself into a dark hole in a tree and withdrew a folder. It was a copy of his Mengele file, which he had stashed there during his workout.

"Mossad has a Crackerjack asset there now, but they want to pull him before Mengele sees him," Angleton said. "Here's what we know. He's been using the name Werner Garmisch for almost a year, so apparently he feels safe with that. Last year he spent Carnival at Ipanema, which is rated the best beach in Brazil. That's out of hundreds. But he stayed at some dinky hotel. This year, mode of transportation unknown, the asset, an amateur psychologist, believes he will stay at the Hotel Rio, in São Paulo. It's rated the best hotel in Brazil. Which is the biggest country in the Hemisphere. So you've got your work cut out for you, as the Director would say. No real beach there, the city is about 20 miles inland, but there is a large river that runs through it. Lots of museums, galleries, restaurants.

"For Mengele, best beach one year, best hotel the next? It's guesswork. But apparently this asset has used such deductions before with some success. And Mossad is getting frustrated. The asset's guess is that Mengele sees himself as both God and the Devil, worshipping and punishing himself at the same time. Who knows? But he's evaded capture for thirteen years, so Mossad is ready to try anything. The asset checked costume shops. Werner Garmisch has rented two costumes for the four days of Carnival de São Paulo — one

of the Devil, the other of the Pope. If he has a reservation at a hotel—
probably the Hotel Rio — it's under a different name."

"His costume choices back up the psychology," Hallie said.

"Sounds to me like it came off a ouija board," Angleton said. "But
Mossad will pick up all expenses, win or lose, so I got approval. We
cooperate with the Israelis a lot, want to keep it that way."

## The Hostess With the Mostest

Perle Mesta was throwing a party the week before we were to go
to Brazil. A costume party. I had slumped into a funk the day the
invitation arrived. By contrast, Hallie's step became more sprightly.
Making a costume would help take her mind off confronting Mengele.
The thought of catching Mengele might take my mind off the dread
party

"I read somewhere that there are about nine trillion things on
earth," I said to her as she rinsed the breakfast dishes and I dried. "That
includes seven billion people, three trillion insects and other animal
species, an estimated five trillion inanimate objects. Out of all those
things I figure there is only one that we disagree on."

"And what is that?"

"Costume parties."

"Damn!" Hallie said, turning off the faucet. "Do you think the
marriage will last?"

"I don't know. I've been wondering. Given that tomorrow is our
eleventh anniversary . . ."

Hallie interrupted. "Twelfth."

"Better still. Given that tomorrow is our twelfth anniversary, I will
try to be optimistic."

She took the last dish I was drying, and the cloth, set them on the
formica counter, slipped her arms around my waist. "Exi Maisel, you
are so silly."

"That's what makes me lovable."

"Well, I wouldn't go that far."

"That and my dazzling eye patch. For bravery under hurdles."

"Since it's winter break I have time to make my costume. I've
decided to go as a nun. That way I can take the same outfit to São
Paulo, fit right in with the Pope or the Devil. And plenty of room to
conceal my weapon."

"Shucks. I thought you meant a nun in a bikini."

"Well, that would take less fabric. And you?"

"Disraeli."

"You were Disraeli last year. Mrs. Mesta was upset with you."

"She had no reason to be."

"Just because every time someone approached you to talk small talk you pulled out your notebook and quoted Disraeli?"

"Disraeli made better small talk than me. Perle just wanted political gossip to liven up the party. But her guests crowded around me to throw questions at the dead guy. They loved it. I actually enjoyed it too, if you recall. Perle did scream at me, half drunk, that we would never be invited again. Yet here we are. And the costume still fits."

"Once is funny, Exi. Twice is boring."

"Then the Hostess With the Mostest needs to rotate her guest list. Why does she need us anyway?"

"Because we give the party class."

"Because of my Moshe Dayan pizzazz?"

"That's one way of looking at it."

I rescued my tattered journal from the den, where I had been getting reacquainted with it before breakfast, and read a few to her.

Q. You and your wife love to travel. Will returning to the cabinet inhibit this?

D: Like all great travelers, I have seen more than I remember, and remember more than I have seen.

Q. They say you sometimes try to alter things from your previous term.

D: I never deny. I never contradict. I sometimes forget.

Q. Is it true you are a Jew? (This from a member of the House of Lords.)

D: Yes, I am a Jew, and when the ancestors of the right honorable gentleman were brutal savages in an unknown island, mine were priests in the temple of Solomon.

Hallie, watering plants as she listened, put down her watering can.

"Some of those are clever," she conceded.

"They were that night. Until JFK stole the spotlight."

No one who was there will forget it. Perle, suddenly sober, ringing a little bell that normally would have summoned the waiters to bring the next course. Her voice seeming to tremble as the party-goers quieted to listen.

"We have just received a telegram from the White House," she said. Sudden silence. "The President expresses his regret that he will not be able to join the party." A few uncertain gasps among the women, who apparently were thinking the worst. The terrible thought circled the ballroom like a virus. Mrs. Mesta pulled a small lavender handkerchief from her wrist and dabbed at her nose. I had never seen her do that before. She continued reading from a yellow telegram: "American intelligence has confirmed with the highest degree of confidence that the fleet of Soviet ships moving toward Cuba is carrying intercontinental ballistic missiles. The President regrets that he will be busy tonight."

"One more thing," Perle added, raising a fleshy arm for quiet. "If this applies to anyone here, the President has called a cabinet meeting for eleven ayem tomorrow."

She dropped the telegram onto a table, seemed to be turning white, grabbed about for a seat, some Senator rose and helped her into his chair before she grew faint. "War!" she murmured.

A wet handkerchief was being applied to her face as we filed out.

## MISSILES, 1962

Bleary eyes in the Situation Room. I didn't sleep that night. I doubt the President did either.

His shirtsleeves were rolled. Bobby was wearing a suit he may have slept in, but no tie. General Curtis LeMay I see most vividly, his broad chest thrust forward, covered with enough ribbons to float a World's Fair. He seemed the only one glad to be there, enjoyed his coffee as if it were laced with gin. Orange juice at every place-setting untouched.

Hippocampus has saved for me only part of the talk.

General LeMay: Gentlemen, I don't see what the fuss is about. Had to cancel an important golf date for this. The solution is simple. I'll just blow every one of their ships out of the water. Take two hours at most. End of so-called crisis.

President: What if the Soviets are not pleased with this response?

General LeMay: Fuck 'em. I mean, screw 'em.

President: What if they are upset enough to nuke Washington? New York? Oak Ridge? Los Alamos?

Ambassador Maisel (sotto voce): He'll push back his tee time.

President (glaring at Ambassador): What will happen then, General?

General LeMay: To put it politely, we'd respond in kind. Flatten Moscow. St. Petersburg. Whatever we feel like. Hell, we could flatten Siberia if we like.

President: In other words, we'd have a war. Most likely a nuclear war.

General LeMay: Exactly. I don't know why everyone is so afraid of those words. What do we have an Army for? Excuse me Admiral, and a Navy. And Fat Man. And Little Boy. If we're never gonna use them?

President: General, do you like the odds of gas masks against the winds of Hiroshima? That's how I think of the Soviet nukes.

General LeMay: Have you lost your faith in American ingenuity, Sir? I think of their bombs as Little Orphan Annies.

President: Let's move on. Other suggestions?

Ambassador Maisel: How long will it take the Soviet fleet to reach Cuba?

President: The Navy estimates three days.

Ambassador Maisel: And we could be there in two? Maybe a day and a half?

President: Easily. We've got two destroyers off Florida right now.

Ambassador Maisel: What if we line up a fleet at the edge of international waters. A blockade.

President: That is an act of war.

Ambassador Maisel: Not until a shot is fired, I think. Call Khrushchev on that nice red phone. Tell him to turn his ships around, because we're blockading Cuba. If they do not turn around we will board them and remove the missiles.

President: And what if they do not turn around?

General LeMay: Then we blow them the hell out of the water.

President: LeMay, quiet please. Ambassador, you get my point? Then we will be right back on Square One. War. Maybe nuclear war. What I don't understand is why K is doing this. How many of you think he really wants war?

There are thirteen people in the room: twelve men and one well-upholstered, serving coffee. Only General LeMay raises his hand.

President: So what is this all about, then?

Robert Kennedy, attorney general: He's testing you.

President: Testing me how?

Robert Kennedy: We all know the Bay of Pigs was a disaster. Not your fault, Jack, a stupid plan left behind by Ike, but still a disaster. No air support, no dice. Khrushchev wants to find out if he can bully you, or if you will stand up to him. With this plan Nikita can find out with no risk.

President: How do you mean, no risk?

Robert Kennedy: He doesn't want war any more than we do. The Reds are still recovering from the last war. If our ships stand tall, fire across their bow if necessary, all he has to do is execute a slow turn for

Kiev. The whole world will cheer his sanity. We win, no casualties, K tells himself who gives a shit, it was just a game. If we're scared, and let his ships pass and plant his missiles in Cuba, we lose. He knows he has your number, can do whatever he wants.

President: You know that's not an option. That's why we're meeting now. But what if neither of us blinks? He doesn't turn his ships around, we start shooting. He starts shooting back.

Robert Kennedy: They say Saturn is lovely this time of year.

President: So I've heard. Okay, that's it for now. I'm going to speak to the nation tonight. Tell them honestly the situation. Tell them of my decision. They have a right to know.

General LeMay: Tell them to pack their bathing suits.

The President stands, the others follow, leave the Situation Room. He smiles with a boyish smile, asks the well-upholstered to stay behind for a moment.

They have a Situation.

## A RESTING PLACE

My friend Whitebread died in prison. The federal prison at Allenwood, Pensylvania.

The jury convicted him of interfering with interstate commerce, even though the only evidence against him was an old wooden shovel containing a few horse hairs, which could easily have been created to frame him. When I called his attorney in New York and asked how that could happen, she had a rueful take on the case.

"I was hopeful that if they convicted, with a judge seeming to want real evidence, Stark at worst might get off with probation," Ms. Apple said. "But it was not to be. Despite the modest charges, he threw the book at Mr. Stark—the maximum five years in Allenwood federal prison in Pennsylvania, another maximum two years on the interstate charge, suspended. I appealed of course, but the appellate court showed no interest in reducing the sentence."

"Jesus, they treated him like a serial killer!"

"I'm sorry, Mr. Ambassador."

"They're destroying an innocent man."

"There's half a chance you're right."

When she called me a few months later to notify me that he had died, I wept over all the years of our friendship. And heard her crying, too.

"What's done is done, Ms. Apple," I told her. "No point chewing yourself to pieces. Whitebread hated that prison. Each time I visited him he told me he didn't hurt my horse. I believe him. Maybe God is defending you by paroling Whitebread after less than two years."

"I thank you for that, Ambassador."

I did not tell her I don't believe in God.

I heard her sniffling into a tissue or handkerchief.

"There is a technical matter we have to deal with," she said. "When Whitebread checked into the prison he apparently did not list any next of kin. The only contact name they have is his attorney — me. If his remains are not claimed within seven days he will be buried in a potter's field near Philadelphia. I have to tell them what to do."

The thought of Whitebread buried for all eternity in a place he never knew, near nobody he ever knew, turned my blood to ice. Frantic, I thought of the old neighborhood on the Lower East Side, where we used to shoot baskets, where he taught me to box, where he delivered fruit and vegetables and fell in love with the horses that pulled the carts and then with Thoroughbreds. Some of the old people who still lived in the neighborhood might visit his grave from time to time, put a flower on it, if he were buried there, and discuss the price of cucumbers. Some of the old gang who came in from Brooklyn or Jersey of a Sunday afternoon to visit their parents, dead or alive, might ask him what he thought of Little Loaf in the third at Aqueduct. I asked Ms. Apple if I could call her back in a few minutes, that I would make arrangements at a nearby cemetery.

Beit something! What the hell was that Temple called? Beit Israel? Not quite. The short memory section of my hippocampus was fading week by week, I could tell. Beit Jerusalem, that's what it was. I called the operator for the number. The old temple still was there.

My call was answered by a Mrs. Dora Schwartzkoff, whose name I recalled vaguely, who remembered my father. She told me in a thin, dry voice that she was sorry for my loss, but that unfortunately the cemetery was full; they were referring callers to a new cemetery in Queens, alongside the Long Island Expressway. Instant depression. That was an impossible trek, particularly for old folks who did not drive. Until I asked her if a donation to the temple building fund of $5,000 might induce the grave diggers to look again for a space where Wilbur Stark might fit; I would send a check at once. She could not guarantee anything, she said, but since she was the temple treasurer, as soon as she received the money she would see what she could do. D-o-r-a S-c-h-w-a-r-t-z-k-o-f-f. She spelled her name carefully.

I thanked her for her understanding. I told her that for this mitzvah she would surely go to Heaven.

## RIDING IN THE BRAIN

Elevator. Elevator. Why am I thinking of an elevator? I can think of no reason. Do I mean escalator? No. The rings of Saturn are closer to the earth than an escalator is to an elevator. I am thinking elevator. But don't give up, the books say, if short memory for a moment or a minute is faulty. Don't say, the hell with it. Think of things related to the word that is escaping you. Shopping. Macy's. Macy's on 34th Street in New York. Our first escalator ride. Me and Rachel holding Cecile's hands as we rode up. The floors passing beneath us filled with all kinds of brightly lit things we had never seen in Wien. Goodies. Hallie. Hallie is a goodie. The best thing in my life. Elevators have something to do with Hallie. She came up with a notion. Yes! How elevators might be related to Einstein's brain. Yes! Short-term memory still works. Just be patient. Exercise it.

It was after dinner, some time ago. But not too long. I can't recall what we ate. No matter. Hallie is reading a fashion magazine, *Vogue*, I think. I'm trying to read *War and Peace*, which I had never read through. I'm on page 740. I check the back of the book. Another 750 pages to go. Frankly, I'm getting bored, masterpiece or not. Hallie — her legs are crossed — lays the magazine on her thigh.

"Exi, I have an idea."

Pleased at the interruption, I slip a bookmark into *War and . . .*, set it aside on the table beside me. Macbeth, who'd been lying on the rug at my feet — at my moccasins, which I wear after work — glanced up at me as if he had not yet finished reading the page I had. Rubbed his nose in the rug and lay his head down again. Among the classics I prefer *Jane Eyre*. Hallie's favorite — we often discuss books — is *Wuthering Heights*. I dare not project for the dog.

"Okay, what's your idea?"

"It's about Einstein's brain. The hippocampus."

"From *Vogue*?"

"Listen to me. In a way it is about *Vogue*. I've been sitting here looking at this page. A full page black-and-white shot of a model. Very pretty."

"She look like you?"

"I wish. Anyway, I realized I haven't turned the page in ten minutes."

"I've been doing the same with Tolstoy."

'Shhh. Don't interrupt, I don't want to forget this."

"Okay, no interruptions."

"So then I realize it's not the model I've been staring at. Well, maybe I was that pretty fifteen years ago, before I started to wrinkle and sag . . ."

"You don't wrinkle and sag."

"And you need new glasses. Now quiet. The photo was taken in a fancy lobby somewhere. Probably New York, it reeks of New York."

"New York does not reek."

"One more word and I'm gonna throw the magazine at you. It's pretty thick."

"You could throw the model instead."

She did throw the magazine. Caught me on the cheek. Macbeth jumped and snapped as if it were a mammoth wasp.

"How many bourbons have you had tonight?"

She sat silent and uncrossed her legs and crossed them in the other direction and smoothed her forest green skirt and folded her arms in front of her white silk blouse. I knew if I were to hear another word from her that night I would have to beg for it.

But I was wrong.

"Do you want to hear my idea or not?"

I thought of saying "Maybe, after I read this article," but I did not dare. Instead I said, "I'm all ears." Which was my standard surrender.

"Okay. Where was I? The elevator. The idea I had was that the hippocampus might work like an elevator."

I wanted to say "How so?" but I bit my lips.

"Say you're in the lobby of a building. You want to go to the thirteenth floor."

I am about to say that many buildings do not have thirteenth floors. A stupid superstition. Which she might know of. I behaved myself.

"So you push the button marked UP, the doors open and close, and whoosh, they open again to let you out at 13. When you are done there you push Ground Floor and the elevator goes down. You with me so far?"

I nodded, did not dare say a word.

"Now imagine the elevator is in your hippocampus. It wants to send you the memory from 13. Or you want to call up that memory. You push the Down button. But nothing happens. The hippocampus elevator is broken. The doors remain open, but you can't leave the elevator; you can't change the memory you are looking at. You are stuck looking at the model on 13. Or Mileva Marić. Through eternity.

The so-called door — whatever or wherever it turns out to be — can't close, no matter how hard you try. As if you are hypnotized. So that part of you cannot die with the rest of you, as it normally would. Presto! Albert's brain. And maybe many others.

"I know there are a million questions. Do we choose which memory we want to see, or relive, at a certain time? Why that one? In other words, which floor button do we choose to push? Or does the hippocampus decide what memory it wants to send us at a given time, and push its own button? Does the memory we see last as long as the real event did? Probably not, that's just a guess. But what percentage of real time do we see in memory time? Is that the same with every memory? For instance, if we recall making love with someone, then recall strangling someone, do the memories take the same percentage of real time? And is the percentage the same with every person? If Brian's committee gets bored they have a lot to look into."

She stopped suddenly, like a car suffering a blowout. I realized I was holding tight to the side of my chair. She was awaiting my reaction to her elevator. Looking at her I saw in her chair the same attractive young WAC I had taken to lunch my first day in Berlin. Looking fresh and clean, her auburn hair cut short under Army rules, no makeup and none needed, not even lipstick, an unassuming but pretty typist on the glossy cover of a patriotic business magazine. Buy War Bonds! The way she always looked to me, no hint that her brain was filled with invisible math, the square root of her life; no hint either that if if she stripped herself for the shower, or if I stripped her, her firm abdomen would be criss-crossed with small scars, the personal graffiti of Mengele. Would one or both of those memories remain in my brain after I died, like Einstein's Mileva? But who am I kidding? And what was Hallie's most singular image of me? I had never asked her that, perhaps because I don't know my image of myself. Dry brown hair that refuses to stay in place, reasonable good looks kept from being handsome by a slight resemblance to the actor Jack Lemmon, a smile that pays homage to an often cynical humor, a faintly dark Jewish visage that did battle with my eye patch and my crisp Captain's cap in the days when I wore a Captain's cap instead of an Ambassador's wisdom or an aging professor's vacant gaze. (I should have described what I look like at the beginning, I focused on my ears too much, exaggerating them, but what does it matter? And like Hallie's barely visible scars, no hint that I was a cancer survivor in my early 70s — how I hated that word — not cancer, but survivor — as if it labeled a different species which I did not wish to join. In my medical records

at Johns Hopkins I surely was thus certified, but not in my own head.
A once bloody throat was healed with radiation five days a week for
seven weeks and chemotherapy once a week, also for seven weeks. The
recovery, because of various pills, required two years of grogginess and
therefore no driving; Hallie became my at-home nurse. I choose not to
believe that I had C in my throat, never having smoked at all or drank
more than wine. My hippocampus mostly accepted that choice until
this moment, when the memory swooped across my forehead like a
bat at twilight.

An oddity — there were thousands of bats at Auschwitz, as
there are most everyplace on Earth not covered with ice, and Hallie
befriended many of them when they flew out of their caves in the
night looking for insects to eat. By day when she was not on Mengele's
table she trapped as many bugs as she could and that night fed them
to the bats. I read later that a single bat could eat 25,000 bugs in a
single night. At liberation, when she was not as skeletal as most of the
other women, she swore she had been eating neither insects nor bats.
I don't know what her substitute diet was, probably the beef and pork
Mengele fed her to keep her healthy for his experiments. The truth is,
I liked her elevator metaphor. It added clarity to Einstein's post-death
memory. She beams like the North Star rising. She is right, there are a
slew of fascinating questions. Which it might take us years to answer.

## MAIL FROM AUSTRIA

A letter arrived one morning, postmarked Vienna. Must be a mistake,
I thought, I don't know anyone in Vienna. But my fingers began to
tremble as I peeled it open. Is it possible? Not possible, I thought. But
my whole body began to get jittery. It was from her.

I had not seen nor spoken to her since the day Papa was buried.
Perhaps a consolation card after Hallie was killed, I don't remember.
We had just lost touch, the way people stupidly do even if they like one
another.

It was a brief note accompanying two photographs:

*Dear Exit,*

*After all these years I have been wondering about you. I hope you are well.*

*After Joshua passed and then Jacob I felt lonely for the Old Country. I took a trip
back here and was amazed to discover that Wien had survived the war. Even the old pillow
factory still stood, though shuttered. The aroma of chickens and feathers filled my nostrils
anew, and my blood. I knew I wanted to live here again. With the money Joshua so kindly
left to me I was able to buy the building and the barn. I decided that since people still have to*

*sleep — and many may hate modern pillows stuffed with plastic filler as much as I do — I would restart the business and see how it goes. I named it Maisel's Feather Pillows, after Jacob and Joshua and of course, you. So far we are doing well.*

*Without Nazis, Wien is once again a lovely place to live. I still recall fondly our time together. To keep you abreast I am enclosing two recent photos.*

*Love, Cecile.*

The first photo showed her — the blonde version, older but hardly seeming so —standing alone in front of her shop, wearing a white apron over her dress, as if she were taking a quick break from stuffing pillows. In the second photo she is kneeling beside a stern-looking fellow about her age, her hand mussing the hair of a boy in short pants. She had written at the bottom: Me and my men.

## SARAMAGO AND MACBETH

The name of the book I brought on the plane was *Manual of Painting and Calligraphy.* Despite the title, it was not a textbook but a novel — the first novel written by the Portuguese writer José Saramago. When first published it received little attention and less praise. Years later, of course, Saramago would be awarded the Nobel Prize in Literature. Not long ago I came across a copy in English in a used book store. He's always been one of my most challenging writers (see *Blindness.*) This would be perfect reading for our trip to Brazil; sophisticated passersby in the aisle might assume I was brushing up on my Portuguese for Avenue Paulista (the truth being that I know only four words in Portuguese, have forgotten three of them and at the moment cannot recall the fourth. I am confident, hippocampus willing, that it will come back to me.) Saramago's dense prose was effective, however, in intimidating Georgetown's writing students. As Flannery O'Connor famously said, "Many a best seller could have been prevented by a good teacher."

Hallie had been planning to reread one of her Sartres, but I made an additional suggestion. Sitting in the window seat beside me she perused with excitement only partially feigned the latest *Fodor's Travel Guide to Rio de Janeiro & São Paulo*. Periodically she interrupted my reading, loud enough for nearby passengers to hear. This was my fault, I had suggested she do that, to create for the other passengers a portrait of an American middle class couple whom you would not want to become friendly with. As I focused on the Saramago her interruptions, invited or not, did not prevent my anger from rising to a slow burn, painful as a nap without sunscreen. I think it worked, no one said a word to us. We could have been suffering from a forest virus the way the other passengers kept away.

I set down the book, asked the flight attendant for pen and paper, decided to reply to Celine's letter right away.

Dear Celine,

It is wonderful to hear from you. One of my fondest hopes the past few years, since we lost touch, has been before I die to see you set up with a good man in a good place to live, and perhaps starting a family. Your note and the photos show that this has come true. I never imagined you would wind up going back to Wien, but you make it sound like Paradise nowadays. which makes me very happy. I'm on an airplane now, will write you more another time.

Love,

Exit h.

At baggage claim, matching green suitcases, a small brown dog in a worn carrier hitched to a worn leash. Bringing the dog had been Hallie's idea. What better way, she reasoned, for Richard and Nancy Holliman, a high school teacher and a school nurse from Ohio, to be totally convincing than by going on vacation with their mutt. At first I was reluctant, he might cause problems — get lost near the river, cause one of us to stumble at a crucial moment — but it was such a perfect visual, like a *Saturday Evening Post* cover, that I was easily convinced. We did not tell Angleton. During an Operation it was always best to have as little contact as possible with the home office.

At the main exit from Guarelhos International Airport a gray-haired cab driver hoisted our suitcases into the trunk. Hallie leashed Macbeth and let him walk around for a few minutes and pee, then held him on her lap as I told the driver to take us to the Rio Motel. He looked over his shoulder and rattled off a language that sounded like twigs of English scattered among logs of Portuguese. After several valiant tries I managed to convince him with the aid of a *Portuguese Made Simple* pamphlet that we did indeed want him to take us to the Rio Motel. Shrugging, as if to say What Can You Do With These Crazy Americans? he gave us one more queer look, shifted the rattletrap once-white cab into gear and sped belching smoke onto the new road from the airport into rush hour traffic, hurtling bumper to bumper at 50 miles per hour. A slightly torn identity card taped to the dashboard said his name, or nickname, was Pelé. Since I knew that was the name of Brazil's brilliant soccer idol — some said he was the best the world had ever seen — I took a chance at starting a conversation about soccer — football to him — during the twenty minute ride, tossing in every so often a Maradona, the brilliant star of the Argentina team. Miraculously we completed the ride with a nonstop conversation about "football" in which neither of us understood a word the other was saying. I knew soccer from Vienna and from college, Columbia having been a national powerhouse at Baker Field during my years there, thanks to the rafts of immigrants still pouring into New York ahead of Hitler. During our conversation both Hallie and Macbeth on her lap stared at me open-mouthed with an expression suggesting I had just arrived on the last plane from Krypton.

## THE WISDOM OF PELÉ

The first clue I had that Pelé might know something I didn't was when the newly planted trees in the medians of the clean suburban roads near the airport began to be replaced by older, thicker, darker trees, then by broken down shrubs, then not by fading greenery but by piles of rusting cans that once been filled with refried beans. We were not headed toward the luxury section of the city. As I looked wonderingly at Hallie and she at me, Pelé swung off the road in front of a rundown motel that had been designed years ago perhaps by the same person who designed the bean can. Macbeth was getting visibly excited, no doubt by the aroma of sun-baked beans and rust. On the motel portal a sign that once had been daisy yellow — you could tell by the edges — but now was urine yellow, said: Rio Motel. This was the place. But the Number One Hotel in the hemisphere? The second bit of doubt stumbled into my brain like a drunken ant. Housekeeping did not make such mistakes.

Standing beside the motel door were two young ladies —perhaps they were still teenagers — dressed identically in red boots, white leather short shorts — what used to be called "hot pants"— pink brasiers as tops, silver necklaces, cheap silver rings on every finger. Both wore their black hair pulled into pigtails tied with ribbons. Their features also seemed identical, small dark eyes, noses and chins slightly broad. The only way to tell them apart was by the ribbons in their hair — one's ribbons were yellow, the other's blue — and the fact that yellow was smoking a cigarillo and blue was not. The first notion that came to mind was that they were twins — real or fake — possibly a special attraction of the Rio Motel, aimed at men, local or visiting, whose guilt-ridden fantasies involved fucking identical sisters.

I said to Hallie. "You stay in the cab, I'll see what's going on."

"Angleton is not a practical joker, is he?"

"Not during a special op, that's for sure."

"I did have one other thought," Hallie said. She glanced at the back of Pelé's head. He was leaning out the driver's window, squinting at a folded newspaper, apparently trying to read the "futebol" scores in the failing light.

"It's true," she said, "that 'our former friend' was insane for twins" — she looked at Pelé again —"not for taking them to bed but for . . ." She stopped talking and made a sawing motion with her hand in front of her abdomen. "He tried all sorts of experiments to see how they would react, to different amputations, different toxic mixes. Whatever came to his sick mind. I think maybe in his eyes this made him a real scientist, using control groups. In most cases one of the twins died. Frustrated, he then killed the other. And scoured the nursery for more twins."

"Housekeeping could not have known about this."

"Anyone who ever read a word about him knows about it."

"I mean those two girls. Even supposing his twins fetish still burns within him like an eternal flame, how could housekeeping know about these two girls? In Brazil! And what, guess that he hangs out here?"

"I agree it doesn't seem possible."

"Stay in the cab," I said. "I'm gonna find out what's going on."

I climbed out and walked to the entrance of the motel. The girl who was smoking ignored me, her eyes seemed focused on a distant shimmering sea of a liquid not found in Nature. The other smiled and said something in Portuguese that I hoped meant "Welcome to Brazil." It sounded more like "suckie-fuckie?" I pulled open a broken screen door and entered a small office hung with strands of sticky fly paper I remembered from my youth. Behind a dirty formica counter a very short man was bent over a soccer newspaper peering at the scores like a person who needs reading glasses but had broken his last pair. He ignored Richard Holliman for a long minute while finishing reading. When he spoke he grew no taller, his back did not unbend. I could not tell if the man had a hump or a spine condition perhaps endemic to Brazilian and Argentinian soccer fans.

"I believe I have a reservation — Richard Holliman" — not really believing I was saying that in this place.

The man pulled in front of him a salt-and-pepper composition book with a torn cover and a piece of dry chewing gum stuck on it. He turned pages filled with pencil markings and fingerprints and wrapped his normal-sized hand around the stub of a pencil. He spoke in heavily accented English. "You want two hour or four?" he asked.

"My reservation is for four days," I said.

The man's widening brown eyes seemed to look at me with new respect. "Hey Clara," he called out. A door behind the counter opened half way and a woman naked except for purple bikini panties peered out.

"Zis fella say he want four day," the man said.

Clara tried to stifle a smile. "Four day?" she asked, and raised her arms to fiddle with a large pink plastic beret in her hair, giving me a clearer view of the largest areoles I had ever seen. She turned her head into a back room. "Girls, come!" she said. "Come see Superman, who want four day!" The heads of two other women, both with long blond tresses that did not look real, pushed into the doorway and looked at me. They jabbered in Portuguese.

"Hey, Pancho," Clara said to the bent man. "You be sure give Superman last day free. Four day!" she said again, and ducked behind the door.

Still confused, I pulled a small spiral pad from my breast pocket, showed the bent man the penciled scrawl on the first page. It said: Hotel Rio.

"Ah, here mistake," the man said. "Hotel, motel, big difference. Word for hotel in Portuguese mean hotel, same as English. Here, word for motel be different. Here motel mean place to . . . how I say nicely? . . . place to suckie-fuckie."

"Is there also a Hotel Rio?"

"Downtown. Very nice. Very cost."

"Jesus, I'm sorry I wasted your . . ."

"S'all right. Happen alla time."

"So why didn't you . . . ? Never mind, do you have a phone?"

"Si, Señor."

"Could you call that hotel, ask if they have a reservation for Mr. and Mrs. Holliman?"

The bent man nodded, pulled a black rotary phone closer to him, dialed a number. He did not have to look it up. After a brief conversation in Portuguese he hung up.

"You be fine, Holy Man," he said. "They got reservation."

I thanked him and turned to go.

"Four day!" he said, and shook his head and smiled.

## Paging Werner Garmisch

Kings, queens, angels, gauchos, bathing beauties, firemen, nurses, princesses, football players, bathing beauties, jockeys, swimmers, policemen, cooks, dragons, shepherds, musicians, bathing beauties, ballerinas, princes, tap dancers, strippers, priests, singers, bikers, snake charmers, cardinals, superheroes, drunks (fake), zebras, drunks (real), food vendors, drink vendors, banner vendors, balloon vendors, button vendors. The downtown streets of São Paulo were jammed curb to curb with revelers on this first evening of Carnival, packed so tightly that Pelé, waving and shouting, had to lean on the raucous horn of his taxi the entire last three blocks before he could maneuver to the entrance of the dazzling Hotel Rio. But the Hollimans of Columbus, Ohjo, enchanted as a little boy on his first visit to a zoo, or as emotionally confused as a teenage girl on her first dripping climax in a motel, saw no God. No Devil. No Josef Mengele.

The spotless lobby had a white marble floor, gold statues of people they had not heard of, presumably Brazilian heroes, and a large gold chandelier in the center bearing soft bulbs in the shape of candle flames. Pelé carried their suitcases in, I tipped him well without knowing how much the fistful of paper money amounted to. The taxi driver tried out an English sentence. "How I know you no want motel? You own wife too pretty, no?" I tipped him again.

At the registration desk, Hallie holding Macbeth, we showed their passports to a stunning, dark-haired Brazilian woman — everything about the Hotel Rio was stunning — and checked in as Nancy and Richard Holliman, were assigned room 1601, given two keys. When a bellhop, a handsome kid about 18 years old in a white uniform with gold braids, took our suitcases, I told him they needed to go out for a few minutes. The kid said that would be fine, he would leave the luggage in their room with the door locked. The dog could stay in the hotel nursery. I told the registration clerk we would be meeting a friend — it was a birthday surprise, so please don't say anything — and asked if Mr. Werner Garmisch had a reservation. The woman, who said her name was Sophie, ran a long red fingernail down her ledger and said yes, Mr. Garmisch had a reservation for one.

"Too bad he'll be alone on his birthday," Sophie said, and I responded, "Yes, that's why we're here. A surprise."

"Your friend will like that. I love surprises."

Hallie, who had been roaming the large lobby with wandering eyes, interjected. "But he has not checked in yet?"

"No, ma'am."

I nodded. "Where did you learn your perfect English?"

"Brooklyn," Sophie said. "Brooklyn College. I studied — majored, I should say — in Hotel Management. I hope some day to have a desk upstairs."

"I'm sure you will. Listen, we're famished — starved, hungry —"

"Yes, I know famished."

"But before we eat we have to pick up a package. It's nearby. Will the restaurant still be serving dinner?"

"The restaurant is not even open yet. We eat later here than in Flatbush. During Carnival dinner is served until midnight. The café serves drinks and light snacks until 3 A.M."

"That's great."

"If your room has a problem, just dial me. 500. You two have a wonderful Carnival." She smiled, revealing perfect teeth in her tawny face. "That package you're getting, I bet it is a birthday surprise for your friend. A souvenir of Brazil. He will love it."

"We hope so," Hallie said. "But remember, don't say anything."

"Not to worry." Sophie locked her lips with a thumb and forefinger. "Numb's the word."

## São Paulo Chic

Samba, samba, samba, bossa nova, bossa nova, samba, samba, jazz, soul, pop, samba, sertaneja, samba, rock, samba, blues, tango, samba, bossa nova, merengue, mambo, samba, forro, gafieira, pagode, samba, bossa nova, samba, samba. Since Mengele had not yet checked in to the hotel, Hallie and I paid little attention to the costumes of the revelers, who filled the streets even more densely than before. We instead lost ourselves in the music, which covered the streets like a canvas of joy all three blocks from the Hotel Rio to the Bleecker store, and no doubt well beyond, the street lamps rifling sharp shafts of golden light off trumpets, trombones, saxophones, black and silver clarinets, homemade kazoos — if you could name it it was making music on Paulista Avenue, except of course for pianos. And if you weren't swaying to the swaying tunes you were on duty, like the very occasional uniformed policemen watching from far apart so as not to inhibit the fun. Hallie and I — the vacationing Mr. and Mrs. Holliman from Columbus, Ohio — danced a few steps in every block lest anyone was watching, Hallie with far more natural rhythm, me trying hard not to step on her toes.

Tall and tan and young and lovely . . .

Bossa Nova or samba? They were not sure. Sambas outnumbered the other rhythms by three to one, except this one. Recently released, it had circumnavigated the globe in three months. I loved it, Hallie preferred Mozart. But just now they could walk an entire block without missing a single lyric of "The Girl From Ipanema." This was, of course, Hallie reminded herself, the heart of the tourist section, as the prices in *Fodor's* had warned her. Their hotel room alone would cost Angleton — well, Mossad — more than $750 a night. One of the lesser reasons why she wanted so badly to succeed.

Shops and food stands on the street were open and appeared to be doing good business, so I was a bit surprised that in the Bleecker shoe store most of the lights were out except for a single naked bulb just inside the entrance. The two wrapped shoe boxes they picked up in the name of the Hollimans were handed to us, after an exchange of coded sentences, by a Mossad asset whose shop was nicely situated to receive packages right in the busy heart of the city. We did not open the packages until we were back in our hotel room with the door locked. As expected, the boxes each contained a carefully packed Beretta semi-automatic 9mm pistol with matching bullets. We showered and changed clothes and descended to the restaurant and ordered drinks. Technically we were on duty but this was Carnival and we were supposedly on vacation, so it was acceptable, even necessary, procedure to get into the boozy spirit, within reason, not stand out among the other diners like spinsters at a wedding. We ordered a second drink each and entrées of shrimp and seafood with Brazilian spices that was superb. The hour was late, the restaurant was clearing out. We passed on desert and coffee but the waiter bringing the bill in a folded leather wallet also brought them each another drink, courtesy of the hotel, a Carnival welcome for all guests. We wondered jokingly if they would be treated so well at the Motel Rio. I wrote a generous tip and signed the bill to room 1601. I wanted to pass by registration and ask if our man had checked in yet but seeing that Sophie was no longer was there,I did not want to ask her night replacement; too many people inquiring might alert our prey.

I checked the chambers to make sure neither gun was loaded. Two magazines of 16 bullets each were still sealed.

"Shit!" Hallie said.

"What?"

"Macbeth. Where's Macbeth? I never picked him up from the kennel! I sure hope they keep overnights."

"They must, especially at Carnival."

She rolled onto her side, reached for the telephone on a night table. Numbers were listed on a pulldown directory. She dialed 22.

"Yes. This is Mrs. Holliman in 1601. I left my dog there earlier, and got detained . . . A small brown mutt, Macbeth. . . Do you keep them overnight? . . .Oh, thank God. . . .So you can keep him tonight. Yes, put it on the room bill. Fifty dollars? That's fine. On top of the $35. Yes, I understand . . . I feel so bad, he must feel abandoned . . . Oh, that's good. So he's not alone . . . A Rottweiler? . . . Are you sure that's safe? . . . What is your name? . . . Okay, Enrico, I'll take your word for it. But keep your eye on him. . .Yes, Happy Carnival to you, too."

## BERETTA ROULETTE

She hung up. "He's fine. But he's playing with a Rotweiler. That makes me nervous. Maybe I should go down and get him."

"They probably sleep in separate pens." I pointed the pistol at her and squeezed the trigger. "Besides, you can't get him now. You've just been shot." I tossed the other gun onto the bed, beside her.

"What do you mean?"

"I got you in the chest. Take off your blouse, we're playing Beretta roulette."

I squeezed the trigger again. "Just blasted your knee all to hell. Off comes the dress. Aren't you going to shoot back?"

"Is this your second childhood, Exi?"

"No, but it's my first Carnival."

I ducked down and lay on the rug beside the bed. She grabbed her gun, made sure the chamber was empty, leaned over, aimed at my face. I dove behind a dresser. She shot me in a mirror, tried to hide in the closet. I pulled it open, protecting my groin with my hand. After ten minutes we were winded, perhaps from the alcohol. When we quit playing I had on only my shorts. Hallie was wearing nothing at all.

Hours later I was awakened by the shaking of the bed. My eyelids, stuck together by sleep nodes, slowly pulled apart. I breathed quietly, let my eyes roam the room. Neon signs outside, even on the 16th floor, provided just enough light to bathe the place. No one was there. The bed shook again. I realized it was Hallie, shuddering in her sleep. Under the bedsheet, both of us naked, I moved closer to her, cuddled against her. The shuddering softened.

"Hallie, what is it? Can I help?"

She turned to face me, struggled to grip a sweaty arm around my shoulders.

"If we don't find him, it will be terrible," she said. I nodded, found her hand, raised her fingers to my lips. "If we do find him," I said, "it will be worse."

## BIKINI TALK

In the morning we showered together, threw on some clothes, fetched Macbeth from the kennel, walked him and showered love on him in a dog playground out back. We drank two espressos each to revive us from a mostly sleepless night, returned him to the kennel. The sun was shining, high dark clouds blocking it at times. Back in 1601 we changed for the beach that wasn't there; changing for the river sounds odd, but it was damned hot.

Hallie looked stunning in her white bikini; her figure blinded gazing males in the lobby to her scars. The truism of those years thanks to Brigitte Bardot and Roger Vadim was that God Created Woman. Hallie in her bikini made you rethink the absence of God. She never wore it outside of Brazil, where it was de rigeur for women of her shape. She had been right, however, about there being no place in it to hide her Beretta. Not even close. Before we left Washington she had purchased a dog sweater for Macbeth and sewn a pocket on the underside, with a button flap, hoping he could be her gun bearer. The poor thing stumbled about like a canine drunk. Scratch that idea. In the end she settled for a white terrycloth robe that ended above her knees, with a pocket that was plenty large. That way the gun would always be at hand except when she was in the water. My Beretta fit nicely in the small of my back, held tight by the elastic top of my burgundy swim suit, concealed easily by a loose Brazilian shirt.

At the registration desk lovely Sophie was back at work. A perfect candidate for a bikini herself, she was wearing her work clothes — gold shirt and Navy blue slacks. She asked if we were enjoying Carnival. We said we were, but had not met up with our friend yet. Asked her if Mr. Garmisch had checked in last night. She said yes, with his son. Which surprised me. I forgot he had a son, I said. Well, a boy about 17, she said, with a shaved head, like those Neo-Europeans. I just assumed it was his son, here on his dad's birthday. No matter I said, but I don't want to miss him, how long is their reservation, for four days? Only three, Sophie said. I nodded, said something I should have only thought, knew it would cause trouble even as I began saying it but said it anyway, as maybe every few months I stupidly do. "Don't you ever get to wear a bikini?" Sophie grinned as if I was mother's milk and she was thirsty. We walked to the river two blocks away, Hallie carrying Macbeth and me carrying a blanket, not holding hands or speaking. Not a good way to start the day. Especially after our inventive game of Strip Beretta the night before.

## A Pink Flamingo

An inch of tape — an inch and a quarter at most — is an odd item to alter history. But it did so that first morning. Walking to the river among other sleepy people, passing stores selling T-shirts lettered in English and Portuguese, bathing suits for kids, rubber rafts, flippers, peaked caps in every color, sunscreen, sunglasses, sweatshirts, souvenir towels, cheap cameras, film, binoculars (for voyeurs?,) cans of coffee in several sizes (coffee is what made São Paulo famous,) playing cards, Carnival posters and pennants, rubber lizards, maps of the city and the country, even skateboards, we finally reached a grassy area and could hear lazy water rolling along carefree, as if it too had spent the night playing Strip Beretta. We had not said a word to one another since leaving the hotel. Crossing onto the grass we looked about for a place to make camp, as it were. We knew the "beach" was not nearly as wide as the more famous ones further up the coast, nor the sand as fine. No matter.

The water was a dark blue, the sky a light blue, the breeze salty, Washington a life away. It was still early, the river walk was half empty, the close-in water alive with squirming, splashing, shouting children. As we looked for a quiet spot my good eye was set to focus like a camera on any blanket on which sat or sprawled a middle-aged man with dark (or maybe dyed) hair and a teenaged boy. I saw no such combination, but easily could have missed them among the arriving throng.

"How about here?" I said to Hallie, finally breaking our stupid silence as we approached a bald spot. When she nodded I tried to spread out the hotel blanket I was carrying. She set down a beach bag marked "Miami Florida", grabbed two corners of the blanket to let it settle to earth in the breeze that was being gusty at times. Looking at the river she said, "I'm going for a swim," unshrugged herself from her terrycloth robe, dropped it on the blanket and took off, navigating slowly among people and blankets at first then sprinting as she saw a clear path to the water. Suddenly she stopped, began hopping on one leg. What the fuck? I was about to go see what was wrong when folding one leg over the opposite knee she reached down and pulled something from her toe, resembling in her pink bikini a flamingo. Gingerly she returned the injured leg to the sand, looked carefully at whatever she had stepped on — a sharp piece of clam shell, or part of a tin can. She reached back like a baseball pitcher and threw it into a patch of shrubs among shallow rocks, turned and waved to indicate she was fine, I waved back, she walked slowly into the water. My tight chest cleared. We were friends again. Hallie began swimming the sidestroke, gliding as smoothly as a shark, further out than the children. Everyone nearby was watching her. When she emerged from the water— I half expected to hear applause, as if she were Esther Williams — and toweled herself off and shrugged on her robe, I slipped her Beretta from my elastic waist band under my Redskins shirt and dropped it into her pocket. The sky began to cloud over, the breeze became cooler, a few light drops of rain fell. We decided to go back to the hotel. Since most of the sunbathers did not stir our eyes roamed over them as we slowly crossed the broken clamshells and grass. Hallie stopped short and took hold of my wrist.

"Look" she said softly. "Over there. About 30 yards. On the blue blanket. The man and the boy."

I wiped my forehead with a towel, staring behind it. "What about them?" The boy seemed to be sleeping. The man was reading a paperback.

"Let's go a few steps closer. Look around as if you're looking for a friend. Then look at the man's face."

"What about it?"

"Look at his nose."

"Are you saying that's him?"

"I'm not saying anything. Just look."

"He might be wearing a toupee."

"Anything else?"

"There's something odd about his nose. There's a bandage under his nose. Above his lips. Sideways."

"Try squinting. It's not a bandage."

"Your eyes are better than mine. Especially with two of them. If it's not a bandage, what is it?"

"I think it's a piece of tape."

"If he cut himself shaving, why not a bandage?"

"I think he's hiding something."

"By his nose? Like what?"

"Like a small dark mustache."

"He's too smart for that. He's been free for 15 years. Why would he do that now?"

"I don't know."

"Does he look like the doctor?"

"He's about the same size. M's hair was darker, which is easy to change. But . . ."

I closed my straining eye to let it rest. "Honey, are you getting impatient already?"

"No, I'm not getting impatient already! There's just something about him. The way he turns the pages of his book. With delicate fingers, I don't know."

"So you're not saying it's him."

"No."

The boy beside the man rolled over, as if he'd had enough sun on his back and wanted to tint his chest, despite the thin clouds. He looked old enough to have body hair but his chest and his underarms were hairless.

"Did the doctor like boys?"

"Exi, I don't know. I was locked in the camp for two years. The Monster could come and go."

The boy stretched and settled onto his side. The man ignored him, remained engrossed in his book. Hallie was looking out to the river. A barge was moving slowly downstream. A loose black dog came sniffing among the blankets, as if looking for its master.

"Hallie, look at them now."

She turned. "What?"

"The kid moved. They've got a beach bag with them."

"So?"

"Look what it says."

"'Welcome to Bariloche.'"

"The asset said he loves it there. That he's likely to visit there."

"That's what I mean. They could have been there yesterday."

## INSTANT JEP

Dunsinane is a house of books. An image as delicious as a chocolate sundae with two cherries on top. Our den is lined floor to ceiling with bookshelves, there are more in my office, the bedroom, the living room, cookbooks in the kitchen. Many are scholarly works — there's hardly a book written about the Middle East, from Biblical times to the present, not standing tall in hardback glory, many marked nonetheless with paragraphs underlined in ink — that is not on those shelves, some signed by the authors. I read most of them during my ambassadorial years — not that they contributed visibly to peace. Hallie has at least a dozen about gardening, several devoted only to the care and breeding of poppies. On my side of the bed are row upon row of paperback mysteries and thrillers, my favorite relaxation of a quiet afternoon or a rainy evening. Dozens by my favorite casual writers: James Lee Burke, Michael Connelly, John le Carré, Robert Littell. Reams and reams of others. In high school I learned to read English with those tawdry dramas. *A Stone for Danny Fischer. I, the Jury.* In that one there was a line the whole school, girls as well as boys, could quote in a week. A devilishly beautiful female has stripped naked, she's walking towards the hero, a pistol pointed at him, and he informs us: *"She was a natural blonde."* We thought that was the coolest line ever written; made Mickey Spillane famous. How old am I, hippocampus? Pushing 100? But that line I remember word for word. My supreme failure however stands smack in the middle of the first shelf, a clothbound, signed first edition of *Ulysses*, given to me by Uncle Joshua when he was dying. It has a fading Mazel Frames card stuck as a bookmark at page 99. Three times during the years I have attempted to read it, the first in paperback for a lit course at Columbia, the second in Israel, the third at Dunsinane. I've never reached page 100 before skipping to Molly's soliloquy.

> Yes because he never did a thing like that before as ask to get his breakfast in bed with a couple of eggs since the City Arms hotel where he used to be pretending to be laid up with a sick voice doing his highness to make himself interesting to that old faggot Mrs Riordan that he thought he had a great leg of . . .

Recently I've begun again. I hope to finish the book before I die, whether I understand it or not. If I could have eased into writing at some point — not classics, but at least entertainments, as Graham Greene called some of his novels — perhaps at a redwood picnic table on the veranda, an iced drink at hand and a dog at my feet, Hallie engrossed in Chekov, I would have said goodbye to The Company with no regrets. The problem is that while I can scrawl a passable position paper I can't create fiction worth a damn. I tried, learned the rules, but never could get the words in the proper order. In good fiction there are not any rules, the leader of the workshop said.

Take jep. Short for jeopardy. In mysteries and thrillers, in books and movies, the hero or heroine must toward the end be caught up in a gripping situation — in life-threatening jeopardy — before using their brains and/or muscles to escape to freedom, to struggle wearily into the next episode. (When heroes die, writers go hungry.)

All this brought to mind by the bag marked Bariloche.

The tape and the bag did not prove the man with the boy on the blanket was Josef Mengele. Not even close. Before snatching someone you'd better be damn certain whom he or she is, or you can find yourself in legal jep yourself. But they were the only leads we had. What to do next? We stopped in the hotel restaurant for expresso, claimed Macbeth from the kennel, took him for a short walk, punched 16. In the empty elevator the thought jumped me like a shadow that we would find someone else in the room, someone who meant us no good, but it passed quickly. We rode up and tossed our stuff on the sofa, sprawled side by side on the bed, tried for a time to get Mengele out of our minds. We did not succeed.

If this were fiction, now would be a good time to inject some jep.

In a brightly lighted room, a woman's hand, nail polish deep red, dials a phone on a desk. In a different, darkened room, a sturdy hand lifts the receiver, puts it to his ear. Says nothing. The woman speaks: "It's time." The man hangs up. From a table he picks up a Glock pistol, cracks it open to make sure there is a bullet in the chamber, closes it, shoves it into a leather holster beneath his left shoulder, zips up his jacket so that the gun does not show. He opens a rear door, looks out into darkness — a light rain has begun to fall, drops illuminated by street lamps. "Let's go," he says. Pauses. "I can't see shit out here. Cop clothes over your costumes? Nightsticks? Okay. I'll be right behind you. Wait outside the door until I get there. Room 1601."

Inside the hotel room, Exit and Hallie are changing into costume for Carnival. Exit is all in black, tight pants and jacket, a large collar. Disraeli clothes. He runs his fingers inside the neck of his black blouse, opens the top button, murmurs, "A bit tighter than last year. No more pizza for awhile." He moves toward a dresser, lifts one of two Beretta 9 pistols, lays it down when Hallie says, "Exi, will you help me with these?" He steps behind her, fiddles with a row of large black buttons. "If I were a real nun," she says, "You know what I would pray for? Wider buttonholes."

In the lobby of the hotel the man, carrying a manila envelope, and two young women wearing police raincoats move to the elevators. They do not stop to register. Behind the registration desk an attractive woman is making a phone call. The polish on her fingernails is deep red. The man in the elevator pushes the button for 16.

In the hotel room Mr. and Mrs. Holliman hear a knock on the door.

"Who's there?"

"Fed Ex for Holliman."

"We're not expecting another package. Must be the wrong floor."

"Hey, it's me. Braga from Bleeckers. I've got a picture from Sônia. She signed it."

"Really?"

Exit hurries to the door, pulls it open. Standing there is Braga, holding the envelope. Below it his other hand is wrapped around an automatic pistol, one finger on the trigger. He motions Exit to step back.

"What the fuck is this?"

"Who is it, dear?" Hallie calls from the bedroom.

"I don't believe this!" Exit says. "You some kind of double agent?"

"I'm a contract asset with both CIA and Mossad. Except when someone is closing in on Uncle Josef."

"That's crazy."

"You call it double agent. We call it family." He motions behind his back. "Come on in, close the door."

The two fake cops enter, take off their coats. They are the two pretend prostitutes from outside the

Rio motel. Exit lunges for one of the Berettas on the dresser. A guy named Braga points the gun.

"Drop it," he says. Exit lays the gun on the dresser.

Hallie enters the bedroom. "What's going on?" she says.

"Grab her," Braga says to the girls. "Tape her mouth shut tight." He ties her to the bed.

Exit moves toward the bed to help her. Braga presses the pistol against the back of his head. Hallie is struggling to fight off the girls.

"Take it easy, lady," Braga says. "Two whores beat one nun every time."

The girls press tape over Hallie's mouth; the tape is the same kind we saw on the man's face on the beach. They subdue her, tape one arm above her head to the headboard, which is made of ornamental wrought-iron bars; tape both ankles to the bars at the foot of the bed. The gun is still pressed against Exit's head. A knock on the door. It opens to a short man standing, his back bent forward. He is holding a metal object. A drill.

"Everything under control?" the bent man asks.

"Loosey-goosey, Boss," Braga says.

"Where's my stuff?"

"In a sec," Braga says. "Listen to me, Holliman, or whatever your real name is. We don't want no trouble. Nobody gets hurt if you play it cool. You just have to relax until morning. That's when Dr. Mengele, under a different name, will be on a plane to another city. In another country. Where that is you don't need to know. The girls will even bring you food. As long as you don't make trouble. If you do, Bent here will work with his drill. Your woman will be carried out with a few more holes in her brain than she has now. Or maybe my Glock will take out your other eye. We'll see."

Exit looks around for a way to escape. Sees none. Reluctantly settles into an armchair.

Braga hands his manila envelope to Bent, who tears it open, shakes it, allows a number of 8 by 10 photos of naked women to fall to the rug. From where he is sitting Exit can't tell if the photos are of Sônia Braga nude in her younger days or of Sophie from the registration desk modeling a bikini. Bent reaches deep into the envelope and pulls out a bag of white powder . . .

Okay, enough of that. Jep. Junk jep, which even I can write. But this is a true story, real memories. There was nothing we could do on the beach without being sure.

Stately, plump Buck Mulligan.


## Jewels for Nuns

Hallie is seated at the dressing table in the hotel, looking in the mirror. "Nuns should wear jewelry," she said.

"When we get home I'll call the Pope. Why should nuns wear jewelry?"

"Look at this black expanse of habit. Like a night sky without stars. But imagine a great hunk of uncut diamond here in the center. Or a spill of platinum beads across the breasts."

"Is that allowed for nuns?"

"What, platinum?"

"No, breasts."

"Or even here on the white apron. It's so plain. So virginal. As if God couldn't think of what to do with it. Maybe one of Fleq's huge pieces."

Dressed as Disraeli, I sat beside her on the bench. One hand slipped into the folds of her habit. My fingers gentled between her legs, fondling a rush of heat. Hallie, her thighs loosening, moaned.

"But He came up with a good solution," I said. "Don't you think?"

Moaning again, Hallie worked open the tight buttons at my crotch. "I think you need some air," she said.

It was over quickly, but powerfully. As we gasped for breadth, I said, "Disraeli and the nun. Let's take these costumes home with us."

"I could live with that," Hallie said, scrunching to straighten her habit.

"You have a big wooden cross to put on," I said. "What would diamonds and pearls say to the faithful? Here in Brazil, for instance."

"That the church is too fucking rich. That the church should be tithing them."

"I'll call the Pope when we get home."

"Unless we run into him in the street."

"God just signaled that we might. Don't forget to load your Beretta."

## SPOTTING THE POPE

The street, crowded with sweaty costumed Carnival-goers and sweaty rock music nonetheless smelled of food; every other shop on Paulita was a cafe or bar or restaurant. Most were serving aromatic Brazilian dishes — I don't remember the names — and most seemed to be doing well; some had lines out the door. Exhausted by our pre-dinner workout, we decided on something simple: pizza.

Those ugly Americans, you say, chained to the comforts of home. Have you tried the Brazilian favorite: pizza dough covered not with tomato sauce but with chocolate? With toppings of cheese and ketchup? Don't knock it until you've tried it.

In films, chocolate syrup, not ketchup, is sometimes used to represent blood. Bosco Entertainment Presents . . . Notably in Hitchcock's latest, *Psycho*, in the shower scene everyone is talking about. (We have not been tempted to see it.) We walk outside into a light mist that does not seem to be inhibiting the costumed revelers. A moment later a sudden downpour floods the street; people duck into the entrances of shops or try to cover their heads. But it lasts perhaps a minute, passing like a gust of wet wind, slows to mist for a moment, then a gust again. Keeps alternating that way, as if God can't decide. (Go with Bardot and the bikini!) Can't decide if we should try for Mengele tonight. Just as we can't decide on tactics, on which will give us the best coverage, the most likely chance: walking up the crowded noisy street of clashing rhythms. one on each side, or both of us in the center weaving midstream to the annoyance of the counterflowing revelers. They did not teach us strategy at Catching Mengele School.

"Shit, look," I said. Half way up the next block were a group of nuns — four or five at least, some in black habits, some in white — standing together. "Now what?" I said.

"What what?"

"They could be high school girls in costumes. But they could be real nuns, right-thinking women enjoying Carnival."

"What's it matter? We're not looking for nuns, we're looking for the Pope or the Devil."

A gust of wet blew through the streets again, soaked my neck, squiggled down my back. Across the way I thought I saw Braga from the Bleecker shoe store. A momentary break in the crowd closed and he was gone. Hallie was right, of course, what with each blaring piece of music beating up on the tunes flanking it and happily drinking people calling greetings to friends and the stench of wet bodies replacing breathing, my brain was in remission. The monster Mengele was who we needed to spot, not another sexy nun or two; him, and proof that it was him.

How long we paraded through the Carnival that misty evening, that soggy night, I can't recall. This was long ago, 1961 or 1962, JFK still was President; my hippocampus did not wear a watch. But when we came to the nuns again, fourth or fifth time, they were standing around a folding card table together, laughing. The rain had stopped and on the damp and rickety table a man stood, smiling. He was dressed like the Pope, in a white robe and white yarmulke and white slippers grayed by the damp. In alcoholic Portuguese into which an occasional German phrase crawled he was regaling the nuns with jokes. We moved closer. Behind the table as if guarding the Pope's rear a young man stood, dressed as a pirate. He was about the size of the boy on the blanket that morning. Covering his right eye was a black eye patch, like Long John Silver's. Like mine. At the same time we noticed there was no tape beneath the man's nose. But quickly agreed that the bursts of heavy downpour could have loosened it and washed it away. Was the Devil trying to deceive us by tampering with the evidence? Or had the man been hiding a half-grown Hitler mustache that he had since shaved?

"It has to be him," Hallie whispered. "The bastard used to recite German poetry while cutting into us. And then laugh."

I shook my head with rage, but said, "That's still not proof."

Beside the table was an empty orange crate, empty as our case against this Pope. He used it as a step to get onto and off of the table. "Wait here," Hallie said. She moved to the crate and when between jokes he was sipping from a glass of water or beer she asked, "Father, may I ask you a question?"

"Of course, my dear," he replied, "come on up here with me."

Hallie lifted the bottom of her habit off the damp street, stepped onto the crate and hoisted herself onto the table.

"What is troubling you, my sweet? the Pope asked. "You have already found the correct answer by turning to God. But perhaps I can also help."

She stepped closer to him. I hoped she knew what she was doing. The pirate bodyguard, who had been surveying the passing throng, turned to focus on her.

"I have this problem," Hallie said. "Can you tell me what it is?"

She began to roll up the wide, sash-like black sleeve of her left arm. Only then did I understand. She inched closer, pulled the sleeve to her shoulder, pushed the inside of her arm, just below her elbow, closer to his face.

"That bothers me. It hurts."

The Pope pulled rimless glasses from a pocket of his skirt, slipped them onto his nose, leaned closer. The ring of nuns seemed to lean closer as well, eager for his heavenly diagnosis. "That's nothing," the Pope said. "That's just . . ."

He broke off. Perhaps something in his brain snapped. His face paled. The rain thickened. "Who the hell are you?" he asked. "What do you want from me?"

The nuns gasped at his language.

"You don't know who I am? You don't remember me? I am 34912. I remember you."

His pale face flushed. "Names! I don't know names. I never knew names. Names didn't matter."

The watching nuns or girls in costume were breathing quickly, gulping air. The Pope looked about wildly, frantically, seeking salvation or escape. I reached for my Beretta but knew I could not draw safely in the crowd. Neither could Hallie. Lunging forward, the Pope surprised us by shoving Hallie's chest. She staggered backwards to the edge of the table, wavered, began to fall before two of the nuns stabilized her. The Pope jumped off the other side without the help of the orange crate, landed heavily on his slippered ankles, fell forward to his knees, stood and began to push his way through the clowns, dragons, strippers, clarinets. Seeing a small break in the crowd he dove through it, cut across the street, putting the Carnival between him and us, kept running. The pirate-bodyguard, slow to react, perhaps from smoking something, followed. Also taken by surprise at his sudden flight, Hallie took off after him. I followed. The flow of revelers halted, not knowing what they were watching, spectators at a Punch and Judy show.

## DASH FOR FREEDOM

The Pope was well ahead us. Then, perhaps shocked by Hallie's sudden accusation ripped from the past, he made what was perhaps the

biggest mistake of his years of misbegotten freedom in the forests of
Germany, Argentina, Paraguay, Brazil, Mossad aways on his tail but
always a sniff behind. Perhaps he had grown complacent, perhaps
he had with the aid of his hippocampus successfully forgotten his
despicable sins, washed them away like scum. But that is difficult to
accept, him having been the primary judge as innocent Jews — men,
women, children — were pushed or pulled from airless cattle cars at
the Auschwitz train station. Some he assigned to walk to the left, to
be stripped and gassed at once at the adjacent Birkenau camp; others
he chose for his own sadistic pleasure to let live for a few more weeks,
months, perhaps a year or two, while he played on them his torturous
experiments like obscene jazz before sending them to the ovens. I
don't know how one could forget doing that unless their hippocampus
was dead. Perhaps that is the solution, short of hanging, for serial
killers such as him and a hundred thousand other Nazis: surgical
removal of their memories.

His error was to leave the Carnival and cross to the dark river,
moaning like a Greek chorus by a moaning wind, lit only by a quarter
moon instead of holiday lights. Hampered in his damp slippers by
the slippery grass, he howled like a trapped coyote as he neared the
sighing water and ran alongside it, listening for a kind word from God,
hearing only the susurration of the mild river waves. Hallie could run
as well as she could swim and caught an occasional glimpse of his
white robe while closing on him. But she stopped and began hopping
about as she had in the morning, her cut apparently forced open by
the stony grass. Still trailing, cursing my lazy civil war with exercise,
I glimpsed a shard of moonlight moving above the ground. It was
the pirate. Having pulled a shining sword from the scabbard at his
waist he was racing toward Hallie with no good intent. That was his
mistake. With any training he would have run to Mengele, to protect
his patron — his lover — his sickening saint. Instead he was rushing at
Hallie. My lungs were straining as I tried to get to her first but I knew
it was impossible. I stopped, pulled the Beretta from its holster. Was
about 12 feet from her in the mostly dark when he raised his sword
and screamed like a rabid lion. Hallie could not free her gun from her
twisted pocket. I would have only one shot. One of them would die.

In which direction would he spin? He leaned right, wanted to sever
her head. A body shot would not halt his momentum. He leaped,
sword and head held high. I fired, leading him by a fraction of an inch,
a fraction of a second before his blade fell, before his skull exploded.
Blood and brains flew like garbage in the night. A philosophical query

tore through me like an electric charge: if God had made guns before he made people, would he have made man different?

## LADY MACBETH

The pirate lay on the thorny grass, motionless. Hallie, fallen, shivered beside him. I knelt, took her hand. "Are you alright?"

"Fine. The breath of his hair and his brains caressed my cheek. The breeze felt wonderful."

I wiped her forehead with my fingers.

"Where is Macbeth?" she asked. "I am Lady Macbeth."

Pain stabbed my lower back. What had I done to her?

"You are not Lady Macbeth," I said, lifting her into my arms.

She sounded more like Ophelia.

Ground-shaking footsteps, a large man approaching in the moonlight at a run, large Glock held with both hands, pointed at me. Something about the shape . . .

"Is that Braga?"

"You the Company man? I saw a flash, heard a shot, thought it might be you. But I doubt the half-headed pirate is Mengele."

"What the hell are you doing here, Braga?"

"James Jesus asked me to keep you in sight, in case you find trouble. Without interfering. A long leash, he said, you prefer to write your own script."

"He's not as blind as I thought. You've been tracking us all evening? You're good."

He slipped his gun beneath his jacket.

"That's what I tell myself in the shoe store every afternoon. Some day somebody will notice."

"You saw me shoot. It was self defense."

"Of course it was. With my testimony and Company dough the cops will make the kid disappear. They don't like the putz anyway. Mengele might be harder. They do honor Mengele."

I couldn't think what to say.

"They know?"

"Lots of local bastards know."

Hallie sat up suddenly, twisted her gun free.

"I have to get him."

"Relax, sweetie. He's not going anywhere. There's a hundred yards of rushing water behind him. Besides, I think I heard his leg snap while we were running."

Her habit shined with splotches of blood.

"I'm going to get him," she said, and began limping at the edge of the water.

"Put the gun away," I said. "Mossad wants him alive."

"I know," she muttered. "Maybe I don't."

I was frightened. What was that psychic stumble into Lady Macbeth? A momentary shock that could happen to anyone when a bloody, shatter-skulled 16-year-old pirate falls from the sky like a dead raven inches from flattening you? Or a precursor of something worse, of future dementia? Rueful Ophelia, who for one moment had sounded like Lady Macbeth, who for one moment had become Lady Macbeth.

I hurried after her, Braga behind me. We found them at water's edge, Mengele supine, holding one leg pressed to his chest, his boney knee poking out like a pygmy skull. Hallie standing beside him, her Beretta dangling like an Angel of Death.

"Who the hell are you?" our prisoner asked. "Mossad? CIA? Wiesenthal?"

"Does it matter?"

"Not really. You gonna kill me, or torture me first?"

"I vote for torture," Hallie said.

Braga said nothing. I contradicted her.

"Knowing Mossad, they would debrief him for weeks, fly him back to Israel for a public trial, with graphic testimony from a hundred or a thousand of his victims, then hang him high in a public square while desert birds eat his eyes. Won't that be torment enough?"

"No," Hallie said.

Scarcely moving, she hesitated for perhaps ten seconds. Then she shot him in the groin. Mengele screamed, moaned, rolled over, hands flying from the naked bone of his knee to protect himself. I was horrified.

She looked up at the quarter moon, at the absent stars.

"Hallie! Enough!"

"Sshhhh, I'm listening."

"Listening for what?"

"Six million voices want me to do it again."

"Don't!"

She fired. Mengele screamed.

"Hallie!" I yelled, grabbed the Beretta, hurled gun and magazine as far as I could into the river. Mengele was twisting like a smashed cockroach. To end his pain I pulled out my own gun, placed the tip of the barrel against the base of his neck, fired. The Monster of Auschwitz grew still.

"What do we do now?" Braga asked.

## No Answer

Impish hippocampus, sober despite Carnival, asked a question he had found in my library and memorized before we came to Brazil. As I recall it was in a book by someone named Matthiessen or something, called *In Paradise*. Quotation hippo memorized had stabbed my innards for years.

What is so hateful about Jews that others need to demonize and kill us? Bulldoze piles of our naked bodies into pits like so much offal? . . . What did we do?

I waited for Mengele to answer. He did not speak.

What did we do? What me and Braga did was predictable. Each grabbed one of Mengele's legs, dragged him across a few feet of sand into the water. The wide white cloak of the Pope billowed like an open parachute. Further out it folded as if by a papal chamber maid. We let go and the current carried the body further, waging battle with three embedded bullets.

Two days later a body rode up on the shore downriver. It carried no identification. The coroner removed three bullets from the body and dropped them ping ping ping into a tin pail in the morgue. He ruled the cause of death a stroke while swimming. Because of the costume of the unknown corpse a desk man at the largest local newspaper wrote a small headline over a small story: CARNIVAL TRAGEDY. In the ensuing days the news made the rounds of every newspaper in Brazil, Argentina, Chile, Paraguay. The most repeated headline read: THIS POPE IS DEAD. Many citizens felt sad, others wondered what the Pontiff had been doing swimming so late at night. In Rome, the Vatican, not amused, filed a black and white photo to publications around the world, a photo of the real Pope, captioned, The Pope Is Alive, and Their Pope Is Not THE Pope.

After a week an elderly couple from Ipanema entered the rear door of the Rio de Janeiro main police station and admitted that for a year they had fed and clothed a homeless man on their family farm, and that the man whose picture was in the paper was the same man. He was very spiritual but had mental problems, they said, and he liked to dress as the Pope. They gave police the name he'd been using. Happy to be rid of the corpse, four workers from the morgue

escorted the still-damp body up a mountainous dirt road north of Rio
and voluntarily dug a grave into which the body was dumped without
ceremony. Atop the grave the couple placed a hand-carved cross
that bore the name the man had been using. They knew he was Josef
Mengele, but did not place that name on his grave, for fear his many
admirers in the region, who came on Sundays to pay their respects,
would by their numbers destroy the dirt road and upset the cows.

## A Biopsy

Impish hippocampus is being especially impish these days.
He is causing a ringing, a buzzing, in my ears. Such is not the
accomplishment for which he set out, but a byproduct of some other
project upon which he is working. The buzzing does not seem to
bother him, he gives no indication of caring that it bothers me. I visit
an Ear, Nose and Throat doctor to learn the cause of this annoying
noise. The doctor is a fetching young woman with a name out of a
comic book: Leah Lang. She is the same size as the actress Sônia
Braga.
There is a lot of that going around these days, Dr. Lang says. What is
it? I ask. It is called tinnitus, Dr. Lang says. But what causes it, I ask,
how do I make it stop? You are getting ahead of yourself. Or ourselves.
We doctors have to work carefully, taking our time. When something
new like this comes along, there are three things that have to be done.
The first is to give it a name. If we didn't, how would one doc know
what another is talking about? The second thing is to find the cause,
the third is to devise a cure. Unfortunately, with tinnitus, which was
first heard in the opera district of Milan about the year 1500, we have
not yet reached steps two and three. By the way, I notice you have a
lump in your throat. It looks suspicious. I think we should do a biopsy.

Thus innocently did that unimagined phase of my life begin. Which
I shall not discuss in detail. In my life's unlived, unconscious plan I had
no idea how I would die, but it would not be of cancer; I never gave
cancer a thought. Because it would be too pedestrian? I had no idea.
But thanks to radiation and chemotherapy when we got home, it is
long gone.

The more attention I paid to the buzzing in my ears the more it
sounded not like pointless noise but like words strung together very
quickly and bumpily, a railway train in motion. Since the hippocampi
sit inside the brain not far from where the ears penetrate the skull,
I began to pay closer heed. I realized that hippocampus was still

absorbing the same book from which he last memorized a sentence. Either he is a slow reader or it is a slow book. I confess I have no idea how he reads: through my eye(s) or with some device of his own. Perhaps I should suggest examining this mystery to a committee. In case you have forgotten, the book is called *The Shadow on the Wind*. The buzzing, I eventually discerned, was the hippocampus reciting one insightful sentence over and over: *There are few reasons for telling the truth, but for lying the number is infinite.*

Impish hippo was smiling mischievously, like that Carroll cat who stupidly leaves a smile dangling in the air for no good reason. As anyone with half a brain knows, a smile is a terrible thing to waste.

A rumor persisted in pockets of South America that Josef Mengele was still alive. As late as 1985 departments of the Israeli government were receiving inquiries about his fate. In the intervening years much progress had been made in identifying human remains by comparing DNA, which determined "to a high degree of certainty" whether two sets of bones or specks of blood had been, in life, related. The State of Israel petitioned Brazil to extradite the body in his grave to the Holy Land to make certain he was a wanted criminal. Brazil refused. But it did give permission to Israel to exhume the body and perform scientific tests in Rio. Mossad put together a crack committee to make the determination. The committee ruled that it was him. The body, placed this time in a mahogany coffin donated by the German Sisterhood of Argentina, was returned to the same grave in Brazil and covered with earth. Again, nowhere near the site did the name Mengele appear.

The doctors returned to New York, Oklahoma City, Manchester, Paris, Tel Aviv. Some carried in sterilized cases bits of the evidence to show to their grandchildren, or to preserve should their findings be challenged. Israel published the study, quietly relieved. The Ambassador and Hallie opened a bottle of Pinot Noir, invited James Jesus Angleton to their home to toast the validation of their achievement. In remote parts of South America some people, not trusting the word of Israel, continued to believe — perhaps wish — that the Monster of Auschwitz were still alive. Monuments to the dead doctor, some including a bust of Hitler, were found hidden behind secret doors in many raided homes.

## DEBRIEFING IN WASHINGTON

"Why did you shoot Mengele?" Angleton asked. "You knew your instructions were to deposit him near a Mossad safe house and leave the rest to them."

"As I told you on the phone, sir, they were about to behead my wife. In about half a second. I figured six million Jews was a nice round number. Six million and one would have been overkill."

After two days of relaxing in Brazil after the capture and killing, they were back home, being debriefed in Angleton's office in Langley. Allen Dulles, the Director, had chosen to sit in.

"That was the bodyguard you took out, am I correct?"

"Yes, sir."

"Where was Mengele at this time?"

"About twenty yards up the river. Sprawled. Moaning. Bleeding."

"Why was he sprawled, etcetera?"

"Because I had just shot him, twice," Hallie said.

"You knew your mission was to take him alive," Dulles said. "Why did you shoot him?"

"I wanted to show him he was not as tough as he thought."

"You wanted to show him?"

"I needed to show him."

"There is a difference?"

"A big difference. With due respect to Mossad, the Jewish people needed him to be shot. In the balls. Twice."

"How did you determine this?"

"I was looking at the moon. A quarter moon. Mengele was moaning for me to show mercy. But his begging was blotted out."

"By what?" Angleton asked.

"By six million voices. As I stood holding my Beretta, I realized I need not take orders from Mossad."

"Who told you that?" Dulles asked.

"I told myself that."

Hallie uncrossed her legs under her khaki skirt, recrossed them the other way.

"There was also the matter of the Pope. Mengele was dressed as Pius XII, who after the war aided hundreds maybe thousands of brutal Nazis to escape. I hesitated before shooting him. I am not sure why."

"What happened?"

"I grabbed her gun from her," Exit interrupted. "I flung it as far as I could into the sea. To leave no trace for the police. I placed the barrel of mine against the back of Mengele's head, to end his moaning."

"Did you squeeze the trigger?"

"Yes, sir."

"And?"

"It worked."

"Berettas usually do."

"I am telling you gentlemen this to make clear that Ms. Rosen did not kill Mengele. Much as she might have wanted to. It was I alone who killed him, who put the bullet in his brain, destroyed his skull. In case you are planning disciplinary action against the perpetrator."

Silence filled the office, broken by Angleton.

"How was Agent Braga?"

"Excellent in every way. Afterward he told us to disappear while he and a barrel of Mossad shekels took care of the cops. He even arranged a celebration for us."

"A celebration?"

"Braga said he knew a good Jewish restaurant not far away. The four of us met there for dinner the next night. We drank toasts to the State of Israel. To the Company. To Mossad."

"You said four of you," Angleton said. "Who was the fourth?"

"Braga brought along his cousin, Sônia. Sônia Braga, the actress. She is five-feet-two, a delicate joy, but sexy as hell. Nearly drank us under the table. I asked for her autograph. She drew a picture of herself on a napkin, wild hair flying all over, and signed it underneath. My South American souvenir. She was only sixteen at the time, but already a star."

"Sônia Braga," Angleton said. "Sônia Braga. Should I know that name?"


## APOCALYPSE 1, WASHINGTON, 2007

A bit of advice. If you are asked to write or record your memoirs, do not put it off. One reason is obvious. Like all parts of the body, the hippocampus tends to wear down with age. While old memories usually remain, they tend to become confused. They are there but not always accurate. This is what the doctors call long-term memory. In the course of normal life this is not a major problem, but you can see where it might sabotage other memories. Another reason is very different. It has to do with death. The older you are when you begin summing up, the more death you must deal with, often the death of loved ones. If you reach 100, as I have, you have outlived most everyone who was important in your life. Hopefully this does not

include children or grandchildren, so I will let that pass. But death is
not pleasant to write about or to read about, so there is a tendency
to give it short shrift in memory. For instance, some pages back I
mentioned briefly that Hallie, my beloved, died of breast cancer not
long after I survived the disease in my throat. The part about Hallie is
not true. I did not have the strength back then to write the truth. But
increasingly I have been feeling guilty about that. How we die is not
important — unless perhaps we die in combat while saving the lives
of our brothers in arms. How we live on this tiny, unimportant planet,
adrift in the vast, unending universe, may not be important either.
Nonetheless, I have a need to set the record straight. Later. First I need
to discuss a subject that was filled with jeopardy, only we did not know
it. Politics. A presidential election was coming up. But there was no
suspense, nothing really to talk about, 17 Republicans were running
for the nomination to oppose Julia for a second term. Not much to say,
Julia would defeat any one of them easily. So we went about our lives,
outer and inner, holding hands at the beach, unaware of the apocalypse
that lay ahead. If the hippocampus stored the future instead of the past
we might have been able to take preventive action. But it did not.

Actually, there was more than one apocalypse. The first struck
after I had completed the seven weeks of radiation and chemotherapy,
Hallie driving me to the lab five days a week. We did not realize it
at the time, but stressing about me was causing a weakening of her
circulation.

I was lucky with the nurses who administered my treatments, fitting
over my face for the radiation a plastic mask like those worn by hockey
goalies, carefully inserting into a plug put into my chest by a surgeon
the tubes for the chemo. I am grateful especially to Christa, Lissa
and Corinna for their tender caring; there were many others. Neither
treatment was painful, but they tired me for some time each day. It was
a lovely lady doctor who after a biopsy of the lump in my throat told
me I had cancer. I was not frightened. I knew I did not have cancer.
Cancer was not part off my life story, as I have mentioned earlier. We
all have such stories, such predetermined endings, whether we are
aware of them or not. But on the way to recovery I became a prisoner
of naps. It was during one of those naps that the first apocalypse
occurred.

A lovely day at Dunsinane. As I dozed upstairs, Hallie was on her
hands and knees outside, working among the poppies, which were in
full bloom a hundred yards from the house. Macbeth — it may have

been Macbeth the Second by then — was helping her, or pretending to, as he always did.

A scream pierced my sleep. Or a second scream, before I became groggily awake. What the hell was that? I listened carefully. Another scream, curdling, a bit weaker. Was the voice Hallie's? My secretary's? The housekeeper's? It seemed to come from outside. It seemed to be Hallie. I heard the housekeeper yelling my name. Carefully I got out of bed, found my bedside cane, walked slowly down the stairs. Housekeeper and secretary were at the bottom, giving me imploring looks, like frightened puppies.

"What is it?"

"Hallie needs help! But we can't get to her."

"Why not?"

"The dog won't let us. He'll tear us apart."

"Macbeth?"

'No, the big one next door."

As in a movie I heard a police siren in the distance, coming closer. I pulled open the drawer of an end table near the veranda door and gripped my old Beretta; I had kept it there for years as a precaution, cleaning and oiling it every few months. In this ultra-violent new world we have made Hallie kept hers under her pillow, especially when I was out of town. The veranda door was open — it was a warm day. Luckily the screen door was closed and latched. But Ghost, 120 pounds of dripping venom, was snarling and leaping against the screen, trying to break through, tying to break down the door to get at the ladies. He had never before escaped his fenced yard. I moved closer to the screen. He began to bark louder, to jump higher, hurling himself through the air. The ladies were huddling behind me. As the dog leaped at the screen again I aimed and fired. The bullet tore through the screen and ripped into his throat. He stumbled, fell still for a moment on his legs, as if wondering what had happened. I fired again, into his chest. That seemed to weaken him quickly. He fell to his side and lay that way, breathing heavily, bleeding heavily. His brown and black fur was wet with blood, as were his fangs, more blood than my two bullets would have spilled. I waited to make sure his fight was gone, aware every second that Hallie was out there somewhere in need of help. I heard the police car turn into our gravel drive. I pushed the screen door open, eyes trained on the dog. When he did not stir I fired directly into his skull to make sure he was dead, as I had done with Mengele.

The ladies burst outside and ran toward the poppy field. Grabbing my cane I walked quickly as I could in that direction, across the gravel and into the grass, terrified of what I would find. Two police officers were in the middle of the poppies, the white ones, one standing, the other kneeling. The ladies got there before I did, stood stunned, hugged ferociously.

"What is it?" I yelled.

The cop who was standing walked towards me through the poppies. It was Lt. Lou Barton, a veteran of the village force. He threw me a salute, though all I was wearing were plaid boxers and an undershirt, not even a robe. As I continued to walk — I was trembling by then — he placed his hand lightly on my chest.

"Mr. Ambassador, I wouldn't go any closer just now."

"It's my wife, I have to help her!"

"She's in bad shape, sir. A lot of spilled blood. You don't want to remember her like that."

"Remember her? What are you talking about?"

I tried to push past him but he would not let me.

"An ambulance is on the way," he said. "But it may be too late. I'll be straight with you, Sir. Helen can't find a pulse."

"That fucking dog! I'll kill him." I grabbed tight to my cane against a moment of dizziness. "I just did kill him."

The ambulance pulled into the drive and flattened poppies to where Hallie lay, hidden by the tall stalks. The ladies, both weeping, told me Helen had covered all but her face with a blanket. Two ambulance attendants in white leaped down. The rest is beginning to fade. I suppose they looked for a pulse, for blood pressure. I think they were shaking their heads. They loaded her onto a stretcher and slipped her into the rear of the ambulance.

"I want to ride with her to the hospital."

"You can if you insist." Lou Barton said.

He walked me to the ambulance, helped me climb in beside her. She was not conscious. An IV unit was already running fluid into her arm. I took her hand. It was cold. I touched her cheek. It was almost as cold.

"Where Is the dog, sir?"

"On the veranda."

"I'm going to tell your people not to touch anything. We'll need pictures of the scene. Of the dog. See if the gate next door is open. We'll of course be talking to the owner. Fleq? Whatever his name is. I've never seen a Shepherd do anything like this. Unless he was being beaten or starved."

Officer Helen came to us from the direction of the house.

"It's not a pure German Shepherd," she said. "It's a wolf dog."

"It's illegal to harbor those in the district," Lt. Barton said.

The engine of the ambulance turned over.

"Up to five years in prison for mans . . . if your wife does not recover."

The two officers stepped back and closed the rear doors of the ambulance and it rolled over the poppies to the road and picked up speed as they switched the siren on. I pressed Hallie's cold hand to my face and cried. In the ensuing days I cried a lot.

Most of the rest doesn't matter. I heard later that Fleq's defense was that a drunken buddy staying at his house had left the gate open in the middle of the night, which Fleq did not notice, and that Rex— who it turned out had never been named either Banquo or Ghost, because of his fearsome looks — Rex found the open gate and pushed through. Fleq said he had not known it was a wolf dog. (I wondered, because of the name switch.) The judge was not sympathetic. He sentenced the artist to the maximum five years for manslaughter, though he suspended two of them. The day Fleq was supposed to begin serving his sentence he did not show in court. Rumor had it that he had fled the country, probably to Mexico. As far as I know he has not been heard from since. Although his chunky and expensive jewelry — new pieces — continue to appear in classy shops around the world.

The only mildly calming news came from another doctor after the autopsy. He said Hallie had not died from the dog bites, but from shock. Seeing the half wolf leaping at her as she crouched amid the poppies probably had transported her instantly back to Auschwitz, the doctor said; her heart had stopped, she had swooned into shock and died unconscious. Which meant only, he granted, that the vicious rippings of the dog's fangs across her flesh might have been less painful than they appear. We can only hope, he said.

I remember our last conversation before my nap that day. Oddly, it had been about the Universe. One of Albert's pet theories, agreed to by many other brains, is that the Universe is constantly expanding. (Don't ask me why.) But no matter how I try to accept that, it ties me in knots. For example, imagine the Universe as a vast balloon. It's filled with . . . well, everything. We can use helium as a simple example. As more gas enters a balloon, the rubber expands, for good and sufficient reason. The balloon grows larger. Fine, I'll give Albert that. My problem is, what does the Universe expand into? Space? But isn't that space already part of the Universe? If not, what is it part of? But if it is part of accepted space, the Universe, poking a new finger or a new ocean into it, is not really expanding. It's just getting an erection.

Anything not to think of Hallie. It did not work.

## Sweet Sixteen (Plus One Dunce)

What did I do then, alone? After a week of mourning I continued to teach. I don't recall for how many years, I have no memories from that period. Just images of classrooms filled with unidentifiable faces, like so many bats. My hippocampus for those years is blank. Perhaps it, too, went into shock.

After I retired I met with Obama a number of times — a lovely family they were — and then with Julia. And of course rooted for her to win a second term. Which was hardly in doubt. Opposing her for the nomination were 16 worn politicians of varying acuity and a clown with no acuity at all: no governing experience no military experience, no policies to work toward, no goals in life beyond stuffing his pockets and bank accounts with whales of money and stuffing the vaginas of nubile young women with sperm. Their silence on such activities purchased with secret packs of substantial sovereigns and secret photos of the women nude on the covers of tabloid journals. While Julia put together lengthy complex depositions for the future: advances in education, technology, cleaner air and water, immigration and so forth, which were largely ignored by the tired masses, the Clown, whose brain worked three seconds of every hour, exposed himself as a moron or an idiot — choose your favorite — enjoyed himself between putts on his 666 golf courts thinking up and tweeting disparaging nicknames for his opponents: Little Mario, Crooked Cruz, Low-Energy Jeb, and displayed only three qualifications of his own for the Presidency: a) he was a moron; b) he was an idiot; c) his elder daughter had large and (possibly) shapely breasts, which she flaunted in shapely bras. But while the elites, as Piggy Trumpf called them, bathed in the sure prospect of another intelligent term for Julia, a whopping percentage of her opponents discovered a strange affinity for morons, idiots and (possibly) shapely breasts, with a much help from their Russian friends. This phenomenon went largely unnoticed by the Elites as they worked on their Suduko scores.

## A NEWSPAPER PHOTO

Atop the front page of *The New York Times* today is a photograph of an elderly woman. At first I felt deeply saddened. The woman's name was Brenda Milner. Her age was 98. I assumed it was an obituary.

But it was not. It was a lively feature about how Dr. Milner, the founder of neuroscience, the first scientist to discover, back in the 1950s, that human memories are created and stored in the brain by the hippocampus, was still at work at her lab in Canada.

Almost my age. My sadness morphed into a feel-good smile.

In the photo she is seated in what looks like a small, crowded office, stuffed bookshelves on three sides. On the desk in front of her are piles of old folders. She is wearing, the caption says, a black satin dress and a gold floral pin. The question in the story appears to be, why is she still working at her age? Her quoted response: "People think because I'm 98 years old I must be emerita. Well, not at all, I'm still nosy, you know, curious."

She works where she has always worked, the story says, at McGill University in Montreal and the related Montreal Neurological Institute. Neither has asked her to resign. In 2014, the story says, she received three prominent achievement awards that came with money for research. Her current project is a study of how the healthy brain's intellectual left hemisphere coordinates with the more aesthetic right one in thinking and memory.

In her one bow to age, she works only three days a week instead of five.

I stare at the photo, mesmerized. For many minutes. Hippocampus, unasked, is running memories through my brain. Jack Kennedy. Mrs. Kennedy. Hallie. Pierre Salinger. What do these people have in common? What is hippo trying to tell me? I feel exhausted, I have not eaten since tea and toast for breakfast. A headache is brewing behind my good eye. That usually occurs only when I have been especially stupid. Was I supposed to meet someone for lunch? Was I supposed to phone someone? I hope I have not forgotten a funeral. No, it was yesterday we buried Brian White.

I think of Einstein. Of the slice of his hippocampus depicting his Maleve, young and older. How no surgeons had joined the secret study project. I am not a scientist, I had not known how else to approach it besides slicing more samples from the dead. Then JFK was shot, President Johnson got busy with civil rights bills, voting rights bills. Desperately important work. I could not even get an audience with Johnson. The image in my mind faded. But now, Brenda Milner! All these years I had assumed she was dead. The discoverer, in effect, of the hippocampus. She would have been desperately interested in the living memory. She would have had ideas. She would have known how to formulate a study. Perhaps assigned her graduate students to the work. They would have lined up outside her door. Funding would have been unlimited. Living memories in dead people! We might have had answers by now. And a hundred new questions. What a fierce debate would have ensued. How could I not have thought of her?

Now she is 98 — and still working. Could it be possible? My forehead was wet with sweat. My body was wrought iron in my chair. Forcing myself to stand by leaning on the desk, I used my cane and balanced myself in small steps to the phone. Sat slowly. Fingers trembling, I dialed information for Montreal. Was put through to the university. Fought to remain calm.

"Professor Milner, please."

I introduced myself, told her the story of the image in the dead hippocampus. In a sliver of a brain. Einstein's brain.

"This is not a joke, Ambassador? I am too old for jokes."

"Alas, so am I."

She was, of course, fascinated. Her voice sounded much younger then her age, as most women's do. She said she would draw up a research plan with her post-graduates, work with them as long as her health permitted. "But it will last," she said, "surely God will allow me at least a glimpse of such a post-mortem memory."

"I'm sure He will. Or She."

For a scientist she seemed very much involved with God.

"A last question, then I must ring off. How is science faring in the States these days? No, don't tell me. Condolences on your President, Mr. Ambassador. Isn't it time he was put to sleep?"

"To sleep?"

"Like a rabid dog. Here in Canada he would not have lasted a week. Make Quebec Great Again. Indeed!"


## THE PEOPLE VOTE

It was early November. Light snow was falling on the embassies of Washington. The next day being Election Day, many in the city were nervous, or even frightened (though they tried to hide it) as they pulled on their boots against the snow. Julia had been a good President, was a huge favorite to win. But polls showed the Clown closing the gap quickly. He had a mesmerizing down-home speaking voice honed by years of telling lies, the more outrageous the better, which seemed to cancel his lack of brainpower. He sounded like a good-ole country boy who struck it rich by falling on his head in an outhouse. He had never read a book and was proud of it. He denigrated women at every turn and was proud of that, too. Since falling into the outhouse he had suckled on any available nourishing tit, especially the cheers of crowds, to prove he was, well, worthier than shit. He could never be President, he had no sense of reality or anti-matter, of truth and half-truth and no truth at all, of exaggeration and hyperbole. He created a world within his brain in which only one person dwelled: himself. Most people believed his candidacy was a cosmic joke, but God, or whatever passes for God, had never before shown a sense of humor. One glorious day, the moron used to say, a word in purple neon stars had blazed across the sky. Everyone knew, he liked to say, that purple words were the voice of God. Suddenly he knew what to do with his life besides eating cheeseburgers: Politics. Though he had never bothered to vote, he had learned from his father, and from filthy-rich friends, that elections were won not by the sweat of your brow or the flabbiness of your belly but were bought and paid for by the rising price of stocks and by cash donations from men and women and scurrilous corporations. So he decided to run for President; a man needed some way to keep busy when his grown daughter grew too old to kiss. He acquired demonstrable wisdom, for instance that immigrants to America whose skin was black or brown or yellow were criminals and rapists and drug dealers who were destroying a once-pristine country; that government handouts to the poor and the elderly merely took away their incentive to work; he knew — cynics said it was all he knew — that God had created white men to rule the earth and pretty women to serve and service them. Promising to respect these natural laws, at rallies where he preached to like-minded people from coast to coast, he drew cheers at every stop from ten thousand people who looked human, then twenty thousand, then thirty. He stressed in a sing-song voice his own beliefs: that most man-made rules had been created by his opponent to keep the poor in their place; that the world needed more nuclear weapons to survive. "I have only one philosophy," he told scurrilous (in his eyes) newsmen and women, "truth doesn't matter. Only victory matters." Across the country supporters of President Julia rolled their eyes and shook their heads and wondered by how many votes she would win.

But she lost.

The Clown won.

Impossible. Im-fucking-possible!
Our country is not that stupid.
Or is it?

## THE NEW PRESIDENT

It can't happen here, Sinclair Lewis wrote long ago. But can it? Has
it? Not here! Not in America, to which people have been sailing
across swirling seas for hundreds of years at the risk of their lives.
The American dream turned nightmare, threatening. Headaches and
nausea washed brows and throats with hopelessness. People clucked
like roosters, wanted to cry like babies. Waited to wake from a stupor
from which there was no awakening. Knew for certain, finally, that
there is no God. Assaulted psychiatrists, psychologists, to drool out
their depression. Longed to punch these wise men and women. Some
did. Television anchors jumped through newsroom windows. Which
do not open. A vast black shadow fell upon the land. Broke into
millions of smaller shadows, began to choke the land and the people,
falling from the sky like black confetti. It was not rain but alternative
rain; the drops were not wet, just tiny shadows falling from gray skies,
sticking in people's hair, hurting people's eyes like sties. Weathermen
and weather women paled when they read the same forecasts day after
day: cloudy, with intermittent shadows. The people no longer needed
a weatherman. For three weeks they crossed the streets to avoid
speaking to friends. What was there to say? After three more weeks
they began crossing the streets to speak with their friends. They had to
talk to someone.
The elite called it a Beckett world; they were waiting for God to return.
Children cried, dogs howled, cats died. When the shadows touched
earth they did not float gracefully along curbs like ice cream sticks but
piled up in the sewers of the cities until the sewers overflowed and the
shadows tumbled like tiny rivers. At night they suggested scurvy rats,
which is how many people began to think of them. They drifted over
the curbs and onto the pavements. Drivers trying to park automobiles
inadvertently killed hundreds, thousands, whose bodies lay twisted
and broken in the streets, no one having the will to gather them. What
was the point? What was the point of anything? People felt miserable
walking on shadows day and night; the only grace was that they did
not squish. Shadows of trash trucks silently emptied shadow cans of
trash. On every street corner a shadow cop stood, keeping the rivers
moving. Day after day, night after night, the weather forecast was the

same: cloudy with intermittent shadows. All outdoor events were canceled except for professional football games. Historians, rarely at a loss for words, named this sickening period The Time of Fake Confetti.

Then the skies grew darker. All this was very depressing.

That was in the bigger cities. In the countrysides, on the brightly seeded-farms, in the sun-paneled mountains, washboard bands played lively jigs. Real Americans, wearing overalls made in China, laughed and perspired and whirled. And danced. And sang. While a lone fat Clown, eighty feet tall and weighing ten thousand pounds (not including his tie) smiled and sat on everyone's head, alternately a liar, a cheat, a con man, a thief, a racist, a sexist, a brute.

By executive order, without opposition, he moved up his Inauguration to the morning after the election. The rate of suicide vaulted Heavenward.

## A LETTER

Dear Celine—

Thank you for your recent note. A baby girl after the two boys! I hope that is what you wanted.

I do not know if the German newspapers keep up with the news from America, so I will catch you up. The deportation of all undocumented residents has been completed (the scenes on television of families being ripped apart have been heart-breaking.) Yesterday the nation celebrated (that is the word the government used) the completion of the 100th Negro Internment Shelter (use of the words 'concentration camp' are not legal except when applied to Mexicans.) Next they will start the Muslims digging. I believe that will be in Utah. The last of the Great Lakes has been closed because of deadly bacteria. The dynamiting of the mall monuments to past Presidents is underway, the huge chunks of stone will be used to create a 'magnificent' monument to the current Prez. The First Daughter has become engaged to the Prince of Kushner. Distant cousins of the First Family have been installed as the editors of every remaining newspaper, of which there are not many. (The outgoing editors have been tossed into the Atlantic or Pacific, depending to which coast their papers had been closer.) The Prez acquired with 5 billion of taxpayer money a building at 666 Fifth Avenue – the address of the devil, people say in New York – for which his son had paid $3.2 billion – and traded it for a cup of Qatar. This is top secret: the President is courting his sixth wife. (The religious appear to have no problem with this, *as long as their monthly paychecks arrive on time.) Have to end now, the censors will be arriving soon to collect the mail. – Love, Exi.*

Occasionally a ray of stray light would zig through the falling shadows and touch the Ambassador's forehead or his unpatched eye. He would remember what it had felt like to be happy. Happy as with Hallie and little Bobby. Then the news would come on the television and there would be the Prez — the Ambassador no longer granted the creature a real title — and the Prez would say and perform whatever obscene evil he had coughed up that day. Usually it involved industrial waste or another country's blood — and Exit would plummet from a rare moment of temporary acceptance into a coal mine of depression. He would want to rise from his easy chair and lunge at the knobs of the TV set and turn it off, fiercely. But found himself paralyzed; he could not move his arms or legs until the Prez had vanished from the screen. I must indulge myself in a new remote, he told himself every night, having smashed the old one to pieces against the right-hand wall at some particularly unconscionable lie. But that had been months ago and he never changed the channel from Fox News to something digestible; he still had no remote; he endured the same torture every evening, ending up in the same grim coal mine. What was it someone wise had said, which everyone now knew? "Getting old is not for sissies."

One night he could not sleep for hours, perhaps from the sound or feel of fuzzy shadows. Or from smiling at having conversed with Brenda Milner. Or thinking of rabid dogs, of putting them to sleep. Millions of people not only in America but around the world must have had that thought; why had no one acted? Perhaps because of the enhanced Secret Service protection around Him. (All references to Him, under a new presidential order, must now be capitalized.) Saudi bodyguards with curved swords patrolled every mean street; police with automatic rifles faced in every direction on the shadow-strewn White House lawn; snipers peered from every rooftop holding razor-sharp boomerangs. Most of these defenses did not exist in 1963, it's true. But all Lee Oswald needed was an open window. Have we become so mesmerized by this impossible turn of events that we dare not try?

Einstein reappeared in his brain. The post-mortem slice of his hippocampus, his women still there. inspired a frightful plan.

## LET US ALL . . .

Let us all praise evil men. My heart is pumping too quickly as I lie in bed. Lies, damn lies and fucking lies. That is what He is made of. As when He says repeatedly that there had been a million and a half people at his inauguration, when photographs prove that there had been only eleven. More lies, dirty lies, fucking lies, a lie in every sentence, three lies in every paragraph, hundreds of lies in a month, thousands in a year. True facts dug up by newspaper and cable television reporters. he called Fake News, and the phrase caught on in the countryside. He revealed himself to be a dumb narcissistic two-fisted four-flusher, repeating lies as if they were Gospel (though He would not know what that meant), lying not only without conscience but without sanity; capitalized untruths, contradicting Himself the next day the next speech the next paragraph, denying He did what He had done, denying He'd said what He had said, denying what was clear on video, denying reality. He was a molesting harassing bastard, greedy, money-grubbing con man lecher adulterer whiner complainer crybaby fraud, gathering into His government — OUR government, Jefferson's government, Lincoln's, Roosevelt's, Obama's, Julia's — every sleazy mob-connected crook and two-timer he knew: hypocrites, felons, blowhards, peckerwoods, assholes, charlatans, worms, scoundrels, crybabies, mealy-mouths, bastards, wimps, dick-heads, yellow-bellied cowards, the piss-licking and the perverted, the loathsome and the grotesque, leeches, convicts, swamp dwellers, their obscenities all acceptable to "the base," an appropriate word. OK, Julia, I'll say it: a basket of deplorables; surrounded by scum and know-nothings; the most evil man in America, saying immigrants were not human but animals; the first Prez who is a traitor; the first Prez who should be hanged. Someone has to do it, someone has to stop it, three wars and another on the way — the nuclear one — Exit twisting, turning under a worn blanket from Brazil. I have to stop this. I have to sleep. One hundred years old — a modern Methusalah, I have to sleep; I can't stay in bed a moment longer, carefully pad to my desk by the small blue light of a Night-Bulb, pick up a book by one of my favorite authors, E. L. Doctorow, a short novel called *Andrew's Brain*. He wrote one novel for each decade of American life, sort of. His most popular is *Ragtime,* but his best I think is *The Book of Daniel,* about the sons of the Rosenbergs. Anyway I was stunned again how prescient Doctorow was. In the book the narrator called Andrew tells President George W. Bush: "You are only the worst so far, there is far worse to come." He died in 2015. How did he know that two years later we all

or most of us would feel sick like this? I dozed off while reading, and
when I woke lining the shades was the usual gloomy morning light, the
confetti shadows falling, then on the TV larger shadows in the shape
of elephants. They are playing games that are destroying the country,
games with Syria, Russia, China, North Korea, Mexico, Saudi Arabia,
Iraq, Iran, Canada, Gaza, *The Washington Post, The New York Times,
The Wall Street Journal, Buzzfeed, Politico, The Daily Beast; all enemies
of the people.* Filling His pockets with scams, schemes, emoluments,
no one seeming to care, making no attempt to intervene. I needed to
rid my mind of His trash, stop this trembling, erase this heartsickness.
Where have you gone, Joe DiMaggio?
A bullet in my brain might do it. Could Bobby do it? Would he?

## From Wikipedia

He adored cheeseburgers, this Prez, ate little else. As with everything
he assayed in life his creation or performance or gold-plated turd
was always the best in the world, just as the burgers he personally
grilled were the best. His father, on arriving from Germany — not
Switzerland, as he told the neighbors and later the press — had
opened a small burger joint on a small street in Dallas not far from a
University, and did very well with it, and opened four more, each one
near a different Texas college, after papa served a sentence in jail for
fraud, and they all flourished. The future President began working in
the joints after high school, discovered he had a knack for grilling,
moved from place to place to hone his greasy skills. In the joints he
began to take specific orders: very rare to rare to medium rare to
medium well to well to burn it. As if blessed by the Heifer God, he
rarely missed. Word spread through the city, he was photographed
and written up by the newspapers, filmed for cable. Decided he would
rather open more burger joints than go to college — a fact rarely
mentioned in the stories, because he wrote them himself to break
his father's heart. His reputation as a chopped-meat *maven* crossed
the country as he opened Cheeseburger Joints in every state, training
young men — no women or immigrants—to grill almost as well as he
did. (Should any young chef prove too good, he was fired.) Some of the
joints he expanded to Cheeseburger Emporiums, and he grew wealthy.
He was also a master of publicity. With his first ten million dollars he
endowed with great fanfare Cheeseburger University, on the site of
his late father's first establishment. Moving money through several
banks and LLCs for secrecy, he endowed across town Nothingburger

Community College. Each fall, in the biggest football game in the state of Texas, Cheeseburger U. played Nothingburger CC— and won each of the first ten games, before the future President became more interested in women and politics, and signed the burger joints over to his fourth wife. But despite becoming a billionaire — or so he claimed — he somehow remained close to the people, who adored him for having no college degree, for being scarcely literate despite his wealth. They somehow saw him as one of their own, they loved being able to vote for him, being able to deny a second term to Julia, who had outraged them by becoming the first woman President. Insulting judges. Exalting tits. The pundits and the pollsters had been decimated on Election Day. The new Prez then began to decimate the country while the blacks and the browns and the Mexicans and the Moslems and the Jews watched helplessly.

## LINES THE AMBASSADOR CAN'T GET OUT OF HIS HEAD.

. . . While some rough beast,
it's hour come round at last,
slouches toward Bethlehem to be born.

## ENEMIES OF THE PEOPLE

The dark confetti grew thicker. Alternate Facts, people soon realized, meant he was against everything the former two presidents had been for, and for anything they had been against. By following these rules He never had to think; He might indeed have been incapable of thought. A dodo. A dumbbell. He could divide his time between playing golf and screwing pretty models while his lawyer paid them off with enormous bribes to keep their mouths shut. All this became known to the public. No one did anything. America lost its moral standing in the world.
The dark shadowed confetti piled up in the streets. Only Congress could remove Him from office, and Congress was afraid; His friends in the mob might kill them; He'd be honored with presidential medals for His service to the country. The moron Prez presided single-handedly over not only the country but much of the world. Most of the cabinet — his own people — resigned in what was called the "Moron Rebellion." The Prez tweeted — his favorite pastime after adultery — that he was doing a great job, the best of any Pres in history; said his reputation had been tarnished by the press, which he declared was

an Enemy of the People. He was thinking of taking away, en masse, its collective citizenship. His greatest achievement, he often boasted, was the banning of the teaching of science from high schools and colleges, which convinced the nation that all science is junk and fake, leaving no one of authority to belittle his marvelous gut feelings. A rumor surfaced that he planned to cancel the 2020 elections on the grounds of National Security and install as his successor his son-in-law. The rumor was undercut, however, when he discovered that Jared was a Jew. At the same time his daughter Ivanka, Jared's wife, a Fake Jew, the chief of the National Police, charged her husband with collaborating with Russia to get their father elected; she announced that when the time came it would be she who would take over the throne. Meanwhile she sentenced Jared to twenty years in Siberia. With no clean shirts.

## BOBBY

Turning slowly beneath a summer sheet in his bedroom on the second floor of Dunsinane, the Ambassador wished he were young enough to do the required deed. But he knew he was not, especially with increasing muscular interference by the Parkinson's. The question was, would Bobby be willing. He would become a national hero. Three hundred million Americans had done no more. But Sergeant Robert Maisel, as if following Exit's own DNA, was always seeking action, seeking an Existential reason for being, which most of the country had lost. Hallie would have liked that.

In the morning the Ambassador phoned Bobby, who came over for coffee prepared by Exit's live-in housekeeper, Margaret's daughter-in-law (or was Becky her granddaughter?) The boy — no longer a boy, he must be 25 by now — grew tense and excited. The notion seemed to set his face on fire. He remembered the words carved into the former JFK Memorial on the Mall for generations of Americans to read and be inspired by, until the current Prez in an explosion of jealousy razed all the marble monuments. *Ask not what your country can do for you, ask what you can do for your country.* JFK or Sorenson, it hardly mattered. Bobby Maisel was restless, Exit knew, he needed to "do something." In charge of the White House Marine Mess, his principal task was to oversee the grilling to perfection by another Marine of the Prez's cheeseburgers. The Ambassador thought the most symbolic site for the deed would be in the House of Whacks, which was having its grand opening the following week, where the Prez would be speaking; the first time in his life he would be entering a museum, doing so because he thought it was the House of WACs. But the Ambassador said never mind symbolism, the museum will be crowded, we can carry it out with fewer casualties after he speaks — perhaps in the White House itself.

## AMONG TRUMPF-O-PHILES

In the predawn gray the Ambassador heard and then visualized the revving of the engines — a shiny red Ford widebody (it reminded him of the Prez's next wife), behind it on the New Mexico hillside where they met every week —where the widow O'Keeffe has painted the canyons pink — a primered black Chevy, behind that the Dijon yellow Chrysler, two beer-plump men wearing jeans and checkered red and black flannel shirts and worn hunting boots and red baseball caps carrying with bent backs and setting in the bed of the Ford (the inventor had cozied up to Hitler, they knew) a paint-peeling trunk once white now noisy with the settling of hunting rifles and M-16s and Glocks and Berettas, which trunk they would square off and shove against the side of the flatbed and return to the cabin and carry out another gun-filled trunk and set it beside the first hoping the stocks or the barrels wouldn't rattle as they bumped down the rutted mountain road onto the county blacktop where they would meet the others before drifting toward the state highway and later into the hostile cities, occasionally tugging at the sweat-stained caps they wore like uniforms with pride in the lettering stenciled on them, each cap stenciled the same. To the officer who stopped them — no particular officer — we ain't going nowhere in particular and the officer, who will later on be going the same place in particular, letting them pass for there is nothing to charge them with if they got permits for them guns; the younger man who has been watching without helping slips behind the wheel of the Ford Model A Fuehrer slamming the door and as the others sidle into the older trucks leans out the driver's side window and waving his left arm forward as if to denote "Charge" on horseback like in a John Ford black-and-white movie which they own but don't watch much because like most honest working stiffs they don't get good reception out where they live, shouts. "Onward!"

I hear them now, Hallie says in my mind (I know you think she is dead, but not in my heart.) They must be practicing their aim at night and acquiring like-minded fellows along the way, but whom do they propose to shoot? Blacks and browns and immigrants, we supposed. Muslims. Jews.

Next night the trucks are louder and coming from every direction, the West of course but also the South and part of the North, them still maybe five hundred miles away and already we smell them, them not being particular about changing clothes, which could not make the prostitutes or whores if you like feel good as they pick them up and lean them against the wooden crates. In memory of the wives in flannel gowns left at home in the doorways of trailers when they took off to fight they said for the good and the right. While me and Hallie lie on the grass or under the grass and wait to see how things turn out and try not to remember Mengele while my hippocampus tinkers with the past or is it the future, with the living or is it the dead, while Dr. Brenda Milner confers with Evolution and invents a new kind of synapse.

## D-Day

Tonight is the night, Bobby informs me. As she is every Friday, First Lady Stormy Muffins has been sent to Florida, to the Prez's favorite hotel, The Malomar, with its famous Cheeseburger Lounge; he will join her later, after his usual Friday night Thinking Time. "Without my Thinking Time, America would collapse," the Prez says at least once a week. *The New York Times* and the *Washington Post* both have reported that the Prez is considering expanding his Thinking Time to seven nights a week, for the good of the country. This would match his Television Time, which uses up four hours every morning and is much the same thing. The grounds have been cleared of the Secret Service, the Prez has assured Major Breitbart that there is no danger, He likes his Friday night privacy, the only outsiders left are the Marine Kitchen Contingent, First Sergeant Robert E. Maisel, commander (an F.D.R. coincidence?) The Playgirl of the Week is escorted into the White House through a rear door, led up the stairs to the second floor and shown to the Prez's dressing room, where she undresses and slips into a robe, the unseen cameras rolling. Film on Fox News at eleven.

In truth the grounds have not been completely cleared of the Secret Service. There are never fewer than thirty on duty. But on Friday nights they know to keep out of sight; this night they probably were wearing black raincoats, like His, lest the shadow clouds open up again. Standing behind the trunks of trees, because the Prez likes the illusion of being alone during trysts when at climax, feeble or not, he bellows like a hippo in heat. The Prez of course insists that none of this happens, that it is all Fake News, despite the pirated 3D videos shown on MSNBC every night and available by mail for only $19.95, payable to Occupant, the White House, or Kershner Enterprises in Sing Sing, N.Y.

## Martha and George

I just thought of something funny, Martha.
    What is that, George?
    What if I had been like this asshole?
    George! God forbid.
    Then my historic motto would have been, "I cannot tell the truth."
    And you would have been king!
    I wonder what that would have been like.
    You've got some turf on your teeth, dear.

## With Onions

While the good-hearted people tried to not worry, the others even more openly carried guns and grenades beneath bunting banners batting and balloons hung suspended in every village and town, to be released upon the millions of spectators on both sides of the argument and the recently formed Society for the Preservation of the Uncensored Past. Amid wild applause and obscene cheers the trucks already rolling by night were proof to everyone that America soon would be Great Again. Everyone on earth could feel finally that the earth was spinning beneath their soles.

    In the White House kitchen First Sergeant Maisel is checking for neatness the uniforms of the Marine chefs. Each is standing at attention beside his or her designated oven. As he does every Friday, the Prez has ordered a grand dinner-in-bed for himself and his rotating guest. (Don't think it is easy to rotate while being fucked.) The ingredients are lined up neatly beside each stove, near a gleaming White House frying pan: the ground hamburger, fresh and bloody from grazing on the White House lawn; stacks of square American cheese piled high, each slice in its own plastic wrapper; huge bowls of condiments — ketchup, mustard, relish, Rocket Man soy sauce, salt, pepper, garlic, each with a silver spoon beside it. Potatoes already sliced for frying piled on dollies marked Go America; most cherished of all, the special onions housed on other dollies, these marked Made In America, though the onions actually were grown in the rich brown fields of Odessa and flown to a small Marine Airfield in Georgetown, in converted bombers marked "Contents Top Secret — Leaks Punishable by Death." Not even His best-selling, ghost-written book, *My Onions: The Art of the Peel*, disclosed the Russian-onion secret. At the far end of the kitchen near the rear exit Sergeant Maisel slipped unnoticed into the Russian Knife Room, closed the door, ran his thumb carefully along every historic blade, seeking the smoothest and the sharpest.

The iconic image of the past decade, Bobby has told me, has been The Cloud, although that is the wrong word because The Cloud is invisible, it has no solid part no bottom no top no sides, yet physicists use it to store things; hidden in The Cloud they say is Artificial Intelligence and whatever shall be derived from it. The storage vault of the future they call it; whether it will find a new way to split atoms or rearrange the human genome or even the solar system or glimpse how to defeat disease with a procedure not yet ready; what should be done with these? Tossing them into a tool box is fraught with danger; most obviously the work likely would be lost after you die but store it in The Cloud and eventually someone will find a practical application and make the world a better place, it's like storing a homemade object in the garage instead of in a garbage bag, someone at a yard sale might see it which is dangerous because The Cloud contains materials of the unknown future. It is the largest space yet created by man.

## MR. LINCOLN

The Greatest President. What does He mean by that? I see it all over I read it all over but what is the fat man talking about, when was America so great that He would make it so again; guess what Mrs Lincoln I have been wondering the same myself I wish I could say it were our time but with the war and the slaves and the beatings and the lynchings and all those who killed or were killed in blue and in gray, that can hardly be when he means. But Mr Lincoln if they say you were the Greatest President don't that mean America was great right then? If you get my meaning. Which I do Mary Todd but they was fools back then or better to say they are damn fools now to think it were great back then, especially with the slavery, why can't they so much as read a book about what it were like before the country was torn apart, brother making war upon brother. Great, they portray me. If I was so great why did I walk about disturbed and depressed never at peace never feeling a smile cross my beard or my lips. Booth did not believe I was very great. But Mary go and get your dress before the emporium closes you would not be happy in a dress that is not appropriately great.

## MR. ROOSEVELT

Franklin it would be easier to sleep at night if I say a prayer of thanks every day for the Prosecutor who brought in so many charges Obstruction of Justice Collusion With the Russians Fraud Treason Money Laundering Prevarication Perjury Despoiling Voting Machines Bigotry AntiSemitism Obesity Condoning the Altright and all the others. I wish he had included Gross Stupidity but of course what he and his Blessed investigators found was more than enough to make it easy for the House even with its Republican majority to vote Impeachment they could hardly not do it the same with the Senate sitting as the jury today. If Life had gone better Eleanor this all would be over and Julia properly ensconced as President again as she should be having won 15 million more legitimate votes cast including through the Electoral College and the Court ruling every action of His taken since Inauguration Day nullified and reversed because he had not been a lawful President having obtained the Oval Office by fraud and chicanery and spitting; been meaning to ask, Franklin, did you know that nice old Ambassador it seemed as if you did, well I did a long time ago he was just a kid my Military Attaché sharp as a whip, the last few months Harry kept him on and treated him well, I was glad of that, Exit was his odd name Exit Maisel. I thought so his sister Rachel eventually became my chief of staff what a bright family did you tease him as you often do with the newbies well I did expound some on my Theory of Coincidences you didnt well I did, the battles between the hundred coincidence folks and the fifty coincidence folks a bit like we have in the streets today. I think he was confounded not knowing if I was serious or pulling his leg but it did not seem to mess up his head he went on to work on the Berlin Airlift for Truman and was our first Ambassador to Israel and an adviser to Kennedy during the Cuban Missile Crisis, which was the closest we've come to nuclear war until fatso-moron and the s-hole from North Korea began to whine at one another and compare the size of their buttons. Our President would rather get credit for destroying the Earth than look weak in the history books, if there are any books left by then; when they began throwing threats at one another and scared the hell out of the right-thinking people, which was when the idea began to mushroom (get it, Eleanor?) insisting that He be removed from office, either through Impeachment or Article 5 or some other way, before nuclear dust covers the planet and God has to start over somewhere else.

## The 88th Airborne

Hey Loot kin I ask you a question, what is it Corporal, them folks packed in the streets out there wearin jeans an rifles an carryin signs of that fat dumb Prexy with the foxy wife an foxy daughter who they wants to make into a saint like he dont hate niggers an Mexicans an Arabs an immigrants an refugees an Jews an prob'ly women once he be done with em, all of which he prob'ly learnt on his knees from his white-robed white-hooded KKK-struttin' daddy, 'cause he sure never learnt nothin by hisself, learnin bein' gainst his religion, cept learnin how to cheat his fellow man. Is that why they fly us alla way up here from Carolina, the Crack 88th Airborne, best unit in this mans Army, to defend the guvmint gainst these nothinburgers these fake rebels these alternative soldiers I mean two Harlem cops an one cruise missile could end this thing in a minute. They didnt fly us up here to make war but to keep the peace, they say. Ony way them car vans can make trouble is by shootin at us in which case we be shootin back which doan soun' like peace to me but self defense. Well as I hear it orders is to ring the White House and the Capitol and the Supreme Court and hope the protesters got better sense than to charge into the face of the 88th Airborne. Another thing that be funny Loot be the Commander-in-Chief soon be a Woman agin whats her name President Julia thats right Julia so how come we gots two Presidents. We dont, they'll kick the fat one out today or knife him in his bed —I heard that too it is hard to tell which News is real and which is Fate some want him to stay in power Him they voted for, an other folks would rather Him shot, which I would not mind doing myself with one of them cruise missiles shoot him right in the face and call him Crooked Arnold, him who tried to take over the country for white folks only and his zillionaire friends who never fought for it or done nothin cept steal an get away with it. Hey Loot I got a idea, stead of shootin all these folks who I guess is not too bright why doan we just Off Him an get some KFC an go home?

## The House of Whacks

The wax museum where I had been asked to speak at the dedication went by the official name The Presidential House of Whacks. Some private joke of the Prez. The museum was packed for the opening, a platoon of Marines in full dress lining the front to provide security, Bobby at their head. A fixed spotlight illuminated a curtain that presumably covered a wax image of the Prez in his parakeet yellow hair. I imagined his pudgy face dripping on the floor, his dark blue suit white shirt Malomar flag lapel pin and solid red tie that reached almost to his shoes except where a chunk was missing, eaten by rats or mice. The holes in the tie contributed to the overall feel of the place — impending disaster, the same worrisome feel that bathed much of America in sweat and psychosis. Mr. Mar Lago, director of the Museum, was trembling because the place with its $400 admission had not been completed in time for the Opening. The names of honored guests were stenciled on director's chairs in the front: Putin and the other leaders whose names the Prez can never remember, stupid names from shithole countries, he says, East Korea and West Korea and China and Turkey and Goose and Lie-beria and Cereal. And all of Afrika of course.

The lights dimmed, large photographs twelve feet square slowly developed on the walls like giant Polaroids: Emmett Till I recognized, Schwerner Chaney and Goodman, Evers, the Scottsboro Boys, all the black-life heroes of the past I guess they were meant to be. Off to the right was an even larger color hologram of Billie Holliday singing "Strange Fruit".

I mounted the stage but Hallie grabbed my sleeve — yes, I am aware that she is dead in other people's eyes, but not in my heart — and pleaded "don't speak, Exi" which surprised me. Why not? I asked and she replied that surely in this Overall crowd are guns hidden in this room. I kissed her hand and said don't fret Hallie I survived Boot Camp and OTS and Israel and Mengele, I am in no danger here. Leaning on my Kentucky Derby 1973 cane I climbed to the lectern and began:

"We all know the Constitution guarantees Freedom of Speech but as most of you must remember from school, if you went to school, this is not an absolute freedom, the most common exception being Yelling Fire in a Crowded Theater, which is not protected speech because it likely would put folks in danger. Similarly Freedom of the Press has its restraints the best example (not in the Constitution) having been stated by H L Mencken (or was it A J Liebling, or maybe Groucho Marx) who wrote that Freedom of the Press Exists in This Country for Every Man Who Owns One." On and on I went, growing hoarse. When I finished a Boy Scout pulled a rope and a maroon velvet cloth that covered a wax figure dropped to the floor. The dignitaries up front and the farmers filling the back applauded in unison and shouted "Bravo" but then as if the Earth were holding its breath the bravos choked into silence. His head was missing from His neck. It lay scattered on the floor like a dozen pieces of shadow music.

Some kind of prophecy?

What! How? Mr. Mar Lago was yelling as he stepped to the front waving his arms and trying to hide the decapitated Prez like a naked woman trying to hide her breasts and pussy from an intruder and not succeeding. Everyone else in the hall was not moving, stunned into silence, and I along with them. Action was needed. I moved to the velvet rope that circled the statue and reached up and with the curled handle of my Kentucky Derby 1973 cane managed to snare the rope that had held the curtain. The nearest Marine guard grabbed the rope and pulled it up to the bar from which it hung. The broken Prez was hidden again.

Some of the guests remained in stunned silence, others began to whisper among themselves. The honored guests —Putin, etc.— were hiding their mouths with their hands to conceal their whispers and their laughter and the foreign words in which they were hooting. Mar Lago, wiping his brow with a handkerchief, fighting to regain his composure, swept shards from in front of the curtain. The largest chunk resembled a shiny piece of jewelry by Fleq. My friends, Mar Lago announced, I cannot imagine how this happened. Under the circumstances I think we must postpone the official opening of the Museum for a week. I am sorry for the inconvenience. I also am postponing the gala dinner we had planned for tonight. As you have seen, all four streets fronting the museum are sparkling with brand new Cheeseburger Emporiums. The dinner passes you have will be honored at all of these Emporiums, from now through the weekend. Loud whimpering was heard from behind another curtain. It sounded like the Prez, crying. After several loud snorts he showed himself, moved to the front of the stage, almost tripping over his red and yellow hammer-and-sickle tie, stood beside the covered headless statue and addressed the crowd.

"I want to thank you all for coming out to love me, you are such Great People I love you all I really do. Great People; and also the Great People of Michigan and Wisconsin and Pennsylvania and I forget where else, and the coal miners I love coal miners I love you all. I hope to see you all again next week. I have to leave now for my daily golf game Air Force Seven is already parked on the runway out back.

I hope next time there will be more WACS here this is after all the House of WACS. Right Rudy? That's why I'm here."

## Dry Tears

That day it rained in the city. No wind or thunder or lightning. Nothing got wet, not the grass or the trees, not the streets or the roads or the cars or the men and women walking through the streets and on the pavements in the same black raincoats and rain hats and boots of plastic or leather they had been wearing for more than a year in the silent gloom of the dry rain, waiting or rather hoping the rain would turn wet again. It was not raining water but nubbins of shadow, all day and all night, a steady shadow rain the size and shape of locusts. which began in the pre-dawn dark and continued through the post-dark night, shadows that piled up on the White House lawn and on the steps of the foreign Embassies, on the rubble of the monuments and the caps of the cops directing traffic in Dupont and the other Circles, on the plows trying to clear the streets and curbs. They floated on the Tidal Basin until piles of shadows pushed other shadows under, they swirled down the Potomac where police were busy rescuing people who foolishly tried to walk across. It had been raining shadows, sometimes pouring that way for so long people were getting annoyed, then depressed. then despondent. Wet rain would have been wonderful for the parks and lawns and Hallie's Poppy Field — still I called it that — but this shadow rain covered the city and most of the country every day. The foreign press began to refer to the United States as Shadowland. Fox News commentators charged that it was all a Russian plot, others that it was a Democrat plot. Every day the weathermen on the radio and the networks and the cable stations and what few newspapers remained said there was a slight chance of showers, but wet showers never fell; only shadows. People became not only dehydrated but also nauseated. They could be seen in the streets trying vomit up the shadows that clogged their throats, soon gave up because talking only made it worse. For days I had been sickened on top of the common nausea by guilt over the assignment to which I had lured Bobby — my own flesh and blood (a few times removed if you must.) The guilt mingled with a slight sad trembling from the Parkinson's, which unlike cancer does not kill you but patiently, like the shadow rain that never provides water but never stops falling, waits for you to die from something else. But the day for action had come. Bobby and I were in sync. It would be dark in an hour, dinner

time. Uncertain whether to be amused or saddened by the Prez's
missing head I forced myself to dress — tight buttons are the hardest
— pulled black rubbers over my shoes, donned a beige rain hat and
tugged the side peaks down all around to keep the absent water out
of my eyes, just in case. For some reason I struggled into a formal
black suit, which I had not done for my speech at the museum that
afternoon. Will history really care?
I rang up the local taxi company whose number I knew by heart and
which also was written on the wall beside the veranda door in case
I forgot. This being a Friday evening, Mac himself was working and
answered the phone. When I told him I needed a cab he said oh you
do, do you, don't you know it has been pouring all day and is raining
shadows still, we are plumb out of cabs, I might have one in an hour
but not before. Then he hesitated as if he had recognized my voice,
which had been growing a bit hoarse, which the Parkinson's will do.
To whom am I speaking he inquired, with perhaps more dignity than
necessary. This is Ambassador Maisel, I said, how are you on this nasty
night, Maximilian? "Fine, fine, just a bit winded from the shadows.
Wait a minute, a cab just returned," (I could tell he was making that
up), "how far will you be going tonight?" Not very far I said, maybe
four minutes, six in the swirling air. (He did not need to know, I
wanted to protect him in case he were questioned later by the police or
the FBI.) He's a good fellow, I call the company probably twice a week,
sometimes more, never a single accident in all the years. "I think it was
Jerry who came in, how soon do you need him?" Well, I'm about ready
to go, how about fifteen minutes, give Jerry time for a snack? "That's
thoughtful of you, Sir, fifteen minutes it is." I hung up and walked
carefully down the stairs from the bedroom, holding on to the banister,
and from the drawer of the end table beside the veranda door — was
glad to see my hand was not shaking much — I pulled the Beretta out,
made sure it was loaded and shoved it into my right-hand rainpocket.
It was cold to the touch, heavy; I had not practiced with it for years.
But it was too late to think of that now. In my other rainpocket I
shoved the laminated lifetime White House entry pass that Julia had
secured for me to use when I came by to discuss various crises with
her or to play croquet. Not that the pass would be necessary to identify
me, my wrinkled eye-patched face and Joshua's Pleasure cane had been
gaining me admission with just a nod since before the Marines at the
gate had been born.
    I waited on the veranda, watching the evening shadows on the
ground swirling like gribenes in a frying pan. Which made me

remember that day long ago in Wien, Papa slamming his face into the heavy skillet. I could still feel the pain. Max himself arrived in only five minutes. Parking close to the back door he left the engine running and slipped from behind the wheel and opened his large black umbrella and held it over my head in the shadow dryness. I imagined to a spectator we would have looked like a New Yorker cover by Saul Steinberg. The falling shadows had slowed to a drizzle but fog remained low over the city. "What calls you out on a night like this Mr. Ambassador?" he asked as he noisily slipped into gear and the vehicle grunted to the top of the gravel drive. The country's business, I replied; I mean, what was I to say? We're going to the White House? Only when you get back to the garage I would appreciate it if you told them you took me somewhere else. Be better for both of us. Actually, I did say something like that. "Sure thing, Sir, how about the Whacks Museum opening? It's just about the same distance, be about seven bucks on the meter." That's perfect, Max. "I didn't know they was still calling you over there, with President Julia in disrespect. I know she leaned on you a lot. Did not know this Prez did too. Tell you the truth I'm surprised to hear it." This is the first time, I confessed. I dare say it will be the last.

The shadow collectors on the windshield slowed to a rhythmic crawl as he stopped the cab at a light. Several pedestrians crossed in front. "All them cable commentators say he won't take advice from anyone, is that right?" I don't think he's got anyone left to take advice from. What I hear is he prowls the grounds alone at night thinking up things to Tweet at first light.

"But not tonight? Oh, right, Friday is his thinking night." He grinned slyly, I could see it in the rear-view mirror.

We started up again. Max swerved the taxi to the left, pulled up at the guardhouse gate at the entrance to the White House grounds, and stopped, as was the procedure. A Secret Service agent in a blue shadowcoat stepped out into the shadow drizzle and looked at the pass Max showed her, then she — Natalya — peered into the back to see who the passenger was. Because of my hat she had trouble recognizing me. I turned up the brim. "Oh, it's you, Ambassador. I couldn't tell. Haven't seen you for a while. Well, have a good dinner, if that's what you're here for." Yes, I will, I said, my voice growing ever thinner. Thank you.

As we entered the grounds the White House in the fog resembled a photograph from the coast of Maine; Hallie and I spent two summers there long ago. I wondered if she was watching me now from above, if there is an above. Old yellow leaves the color of the Prez's bright toupee littered the roadway. "Where to, Sir?" Max asked. Drop me around the back, at the kitchen entrance, I told him.

Falling shadows were blowing from the White House gutters. As I circled my fingers around my cane Max opened my door and held the umbrella over my head against stray flecks. The fee on the meter read $7.00, just as he had predicted. The cab rolled to a stop at the delivery entrance. Max asked if I would like him to wait there with the taxi until my business was done. I knew I would not need a cab after this mission, but I hesitated, asked Max to return in half an hour, figuring that if a Secret Service man overheard me dismissing the taxi he might wonder how this limping, cane-wielding, one-eyed old man planned to get home that night.

I waited outside the screen door until Max was out of sight. Although no lights were visible in the hallway there was still a torrent of shadows. I remembered this passage as twenty feet long; now it looked like five hundred feet: the disease playing tricks. I dreaded the day when I could no longer read. Closing my good eye I counted to ten. The blackened hall returned to normal size. Through a closed door on the left at the far end I could hear kitchen sounds: meat sizzling on a grill, oil bubbling, a knife rhythmically hitting a cutting board (probably the Prez's onions flown in from Odessa being sliced — perhaps it was the smells not the sounds I was identifying, as dogs do,) pickles, which took me on a magic carpet back to Prince Street, to Whitebread, to Cecile and I rolling naked on my bed, to Rachel skipping down a dirt lane in Wein, to the factory of floating feathers, the harsh sea washing over the deck, the customs man disbursing new names. And to Hallie, my first sight of her, at the table in the Berlin Embassy, her poring over arial photos of the bombed-out city, hunched over her desk making calculations of potatoes and diapers and beer, hair blowing in the separate winds of the propellers at Templehof. A kaleidoscope of memories, my hippocampus overflowing. I smiled, kicked myself in the ass without falling (picture it) to stop stalling. Leaning lightly on my cane so as not to broadcast my arrival I paused at the edge of the kitchen entry, cracked the door, peered inside. No one was looking my way, they were busy grilling, deep-frying, slicing. I checked my watch. The Prez's Friday night feasts were always served at 6:30 — my watch read 6:27. The menu was the same each week, Bobby had told me. For the Prez, two greasy cheeseburgers on a large plate surrounded by half a pound of fries, a pool of Heinz ketchup, a rasher of Odessa onions. Also on the tray a clear plastic glass of water — tap water ferried up daily from New York City. The Prez drank nothing but water— Borough of Queens tap water. (Some said that was his problem.) He didn't care about the bitter taste, He owned the trademark on Borough of Queens Tapwater, made a fortune selling it around the country. (The first scandal of his administration had been the revelation by the *New York Daily News* that the water actually was drawn from the Potomac near its Maryland dumping site. The Prez denied this, the editor of the *News* disappeared, the allegation was never heard again.

The tray of food for the Prez's date contained half of a nothingburger ("we have to keep you girls slim," he explained to them each week) and a pint of Stoli in case in they needed to be revived after fainting at the sight of His fleshy body.

6:28. Sergeant First Class Maisel turned toward the kitchen exit door and pulled it open with one hand, carrying the tray bearing the Prez's dinner in the other. Hidden in the large folded white cloth napkin embossed WH was a 12-inch butcher knife, the sharpest he had found. He stopped short when he saw his great great grandfather in the passageway, left hand leaning on his Kentucky Derby cane, right hand deep in his raincoat pocket. "Poppy, what the hell are you doing here?" he asked.

I came to stop you, I said. It was a bad idea.

"Are you kidding? It was a great idea. The whole world will celebrate. I bet millions of people had the same idea, just none had the guts to do it."

Not that part, the idea that you might do it. If they catch you they'll torture you. Then hang you. Then butcher you. Then make you go on Oprah.

"What are you saying? The knife is in the napkin. In five minutes it will be done."

No. You have a long life ahead of you. Live it! It was wrong for me to risk taking that from you. Unforgivable. Give me the knife.

Robert set the tray on a white-clothed table beside the closed French doors. Slowly he unfolded the knife from the napkin. The handle was wood, the blade fine Ivanka steel.

"Poppy, there's no way you could handle this knife against the 250-pound slimeball. He'll grab it and kill you instead."

He may still have bone spurs. Give it to me.

"Get out of my way, Poppy. Before someone hears us."

Exit Maisel dug his right hand into the pocket of his shadowcoat. He pulled out the Beretta, pointed it at Bobby.

Put down the knife!

"What? You would kill me to stop me from killing Him? The most hated man alive? I dare you."

Don't dare me, Sergeant, of course I would not kill you. Not intentionally. But my hands are shaky. If the guards catch me there is nothing they could do to me. My life is over. A hundred years is enough. All they could do is reunite me with my Hallie. For which I of course I have no greater desire.

The Marine looked at his great great grandfather. He did not want to give up the knife. The time that passed was only seconds but to Exit it seemed like hours. A voice shouted from behind the bedroom doors: "Hey, is that my dinner? Let's get a move on, I have things to do. Six wars to think about. A 15 year old to fuck."

The hated voice struck the room like an electric charge. Robert Maisel nodded toward his great great grandfather, reached toward the double doors, pulled them open. Ambassador Exit Maisel, cane in his left hand, Beretta in his right, stepped through them.

I hesitate to write down the rest. But I have always believed that when you start something you finish it, whether it is eating a pickle or writing a memoir or life itself, a hurdle race in OCS with one eye hanging loose or a search for the Monster of Auschwitz. To the squeamish I offer my apology, my knees are beginning to weaken, I will not be able to stand much longer. The Prez was sitting up in a Queen's Ass bed. A sheet covered Him to His waist, His hairless chest was bare. "You're four minutes late," He growled, though He was not wearing a watch. My Beretta was pointed at his chest. He had not yet noticed.

Beside him under the sheet was his date for the evening, lying flat — not very flat — beside him, her head on the pillow. When He barked at me she sat up quickly, her half of the sheet falling to her waist. She did not bother to raise it. Her breasts were lovely. I waived her to the side of the bed, wanting her out of harm's way. She hesitated. then seemed to understand, rolled away from the Prez, fell to the plush white carpeting. When I waived the gun He finally noticed it.

"Who are you," He growled, "what do you want from me?"

Only your life, Mr. President.

"Oh yeah? There are a thousand guards on the lawns. Where the fuck are my cheeseburgers?"

My knees were sinking. My hand holding the gun was trembling. He had just sealed his fate, His last word on earth would be Cheeseburgers. But I was wrong.

"I'll pay you $130,000 not to shoot," He said.

I squeezed the trigger of the Beretta. A red Poppy bloomed in the center of his chest. But the other fellow was a split second ahead of me. Blood spurted in four directions. Food scattered in disarray on the rug. Always shoot for the chest first, they had taught us in Basic, it's the widest part of the body. On the other side of the bed the frightened girl extricated herself from the twisted sheet. As I mentioned earlier, Mickey Spillane had said it best, back when I was in high school on the Lower East side. That's what hippocampus sent me now: She was a natural blonde.

He still had the girl. But no edible cheeseburgers. No Russian onions. The Prez lost control. He bellowed like Tarzan and dove at me. Shakily, holding the grip with both hands, I squeezed the trigger again. For a moment I was back on the shooting range. Something round leaped from his face. An eye. It landed on the sheet, trailed by a thin line of blood. He did not move. I finally had done Spillane one better: The Naked and the Dead.

## AN EXAMINED LIFE

My arms go dead. My legs go dead. I collapse at the foot of the bed. I have not taken my pills today. Carbidopa levadopa. Now at 25 mils by 250. I will not be able to rise from the rug. I try pulling at the edge of the mattress. No use, I cannot move. There is nothing to do but relax, breathe. Wait for someone to come for me. For us.

I am fading quickly. I think of Socrates. The unexamined life is not worth living. I have always known these words. I never understood them. Unexamined by whom? Unexamined for what? I have no idea if I passed muster, if my life was worth living.

## THE SOUNDS OF WAR

Cannons and muskets echo over the Capitol like random thunder. Julia, ruled by the Supreme Court to have been the lawful winner of the election, is sworn in anew as President. Alas, the Second American Civil War begins.

## A PHONE CALL NOT ANSWERED

In the large house in Washington called Dunsinane the telephone is ringing. Again. Again. No one answered, Dusinane was empty. After the fourth ring the phone, an old land line, switched to voice mail. The female voice spoke again.

I have had one other thought, Ambassador, which I am hesitant to voice on the telephone. But I will plunge ahead. It occurs to me that memories after death would serve no useful purpose that I can see. But what if this experiment has little to do with the hippocampus at all? What if hippo was just a convenient testing ground for a much more ambitious attempt — an attempt to discover if human life is possible after death? We must not even breathe that notion. Imagine the Pandora's box it would open in the sciences, the philosophies, the psychologies, the religions. I can't even think about it.

I see it is past my bedtime, Ambassador. I hope you are well. Call me when you can discuss this. Brenda.

The voice mail clicked off.

## BENEATH THE GRASS

Hallie rests beside me, quiet, serene, holding my hand, gentle beneath the gentle Earth. The shadows on the grass have darkened, absorbing moisture from remembered rain. I resume reading to her: Eliot, Cummings (of whom, growing up in Hamburg, she had never heard), Yeats, Dickinson, Masters, the Sonnets of course. Lately, Joyce. I hope she can hear me. Mostly, I hope she can see me.

"Will you visit me tonight in the pergola?" I ask.

"Lord willin' an' the Creek don't rise," Hallie says.

I chuckle. I am about to utter my usual sly response when I am distracted by two puffs of white drifting toward me. I squint for a better look. Impossible,.What would he be doing here? I holds my breath. A face seems to form beneath the puffs. It is definitely him. No one since photography came to be ever has had hair as distinguishable as that.

"Dr. Einstein, is that really you? What are you doing here? Is that a pistol you are holding?"

"I'm sorry if the blood upsets you, Ambassador Maisel. But he has gone too far. Somebody had to stop him."

"Why you?"

"Why not me?"

"Why not, indeed? What did *Time* magazine call you? The Man of the Century."

"Perhaps I will be the first to be honored twice."

◆◆　　◆◆　　◆◆

# Alternative Facts

This is a work of fiction, not history. Scenes in which real people appear under their real names — including several presidents, and Albert Einstein — emerged solely from the imagination of the author. For purposes of the plot I have taken the most liberty with the fate of Josef Mengele, the brutal doctor from the Auschwitz concentration camp. Mengele never was apprehended by Mossad, the Central Intelligence Agency or any of numerous organizations that spent decades after World War II hunting for him. Mengele fled Auschwitz shortly before Soviet troops liberated the camp, and spent two or three years hiding in Europe. Using a fake passport, he sailed to South America, and lived the rest of his life there, mostly in Argentina and Brazil, holding various jobs under assumed names with help from German friends, many of whom considered him a hero. He died of natural causes in 1979 at the age of 67 while swimming in Brazil, and was buried under a false name. To put rumors to rest, scientists from five countries examined his remains in 1985 and agreed that the body was Mengele's.